Sue Dyson is half-Manx and was brought up on Merseyside, later moving to the Isle of Man. After studying modern languages at university she trained as a secretary and went on to win the 'Secretary of the Year' award. She is an experienced author of business and self-help books, including BLUFF YOUR WAY AS A TOP SECRETARY, COPING SUCCESSFULLY WITH MIGRAINE and A WEIGHT OFF YOUR MIND.

Sue Dyson now lives in Bedfordshire, and makes frequent visits to the Isle of Man.

Across the Water

Sue Dyson

First published in 1995
by HEADLINE BOOK PUBLISHING PLC

First published in paperback in 1995
by HEADLINE BOOK PUBLISHING PLC

This edition published 2003 by
Knight an imprint of Caxton Publishing Group

10 9 8 7 6 5 4 3 2 1

ISBN 1 86019 6810

Typeset by Keyboard Services, Luton, Beds

Printed and bound in Great Britain by
Mackays of Chatham PLC, Chatham, Kent

Caxton Publishing Group
20 Bloomsbury Street
London
WC1B 3JH

Across the Water

Prologue

May 1939

It was so good to feel the sun on your back.

At last winter had given way to spring, and far below, the sea sparkled, sunlit and flecked with foam. Stretching out its broad wings, the herring gull hovered for a few blissful seconds, buoyant on a cushion of warmth.

Then it cut through the air again, a grey-white arrow shot between sea and sky, following in the wake of the fishing boats, and the passenger ferry that ploughed a broad white furrow between the mainland and the Isle of Man.

On sped the gull, and the island rose up before it, a roughly cut green jewel set in a blue-green sea. Away to the north lay the noise and bustle of Douglas, backed by the soft, smudged greens and browns of the rolling Manx hills. But the gull banked and swooped south, towards Santon Head and Cass-ny-Hawin, finding at last a deep green valley that followed the river a mile or so inland to the tiny village of Ballakeeill.

Past kirk and farmhouse and croft flew the gull; past banks of yellow gorse and fuchsia; past lazy, silent cattle chewing reflectively, their breath misting the morning air.

To the right, a shady slope lay under a dusty shimmer of bluebells, and all around, the white flowers of wild garlic radiated a pungent aroma in the May sunshine.

The gull swooped low over the village, in search of food and warmth, surveying this new terrain. Ballakeeill schoolhouse stood a little apart from the other buildings, a solid structure of good grey Manx stone with a slate roof that shone like a mirror after rain. With a chattering of pleasure, the gull set down on the warm chimneypot, fanning out its tail feathers as it enjoyed this stroke of good fortune.

Today there were no children playing in the school yard, or on the rough, grassy meadow which backed on to an orchard, though snatches of conversation floated out occasionally through an open window, no louder or more meaningful than the buzzing of insects. There was nothing to disturb the tranquillity of this perfect spring day.

The girl in the green dress strolled slowly and thoughtfully across the grass, enjoying the feeling of the moist, springy blades brushing against her silk-stockinged ankles. Her long blaze of wavy red hair, past shoulder length, hung in glossy tendrils, too unruly to be teased into smooth and fashionable compliance.

She was slender as willow, this girl of twenty summers; tall and a little gauche in her home-sewn cotton dress. She was not beautiful; and yet there was something striking and memorable about that mane of red hair, those eyes of emerald green.

'Creena!'

A woman's voice broke the silence, and the girl stopped in her tracks and turned round.

'Creena, do hurry up! Lunch is ready.'

She sighed, and a pink-petalled daisy fluttered from her fingers, to be lost among the long grass stems.

'Coming, Mother,' she called, and began walking back towards the schoolhouse.

Chapter 1

'Mona, are you all right?'

Creena Quilliam set down the tea tray and walked quickly across the kitchen. Supporting herself on the edge of the sink, Mona forced herself to ignore the pain and turned to smile at her cousin.

'Me? Oh, I'm fine. Just one of my headaches.' She straightened up and started busying herself with the dishes. 'Nothing to worry yourself about.'

Another headache caused by that brute of a husband Duggie Mylchreest, thought Creena grimly as she picked up a tea towel and set about drying the dishes Mona had just washed. Cousin Mona's was one marriage which definitely hadn't lived up to its fairy-tale beginnings – and that was a mistake which Creena was determined not to make.

'I was wondering,' Creena began awkwardly, not quite sure how to word her concern for Mona.

'Wondering what?'

'It's just . . . well, I couldn't help noticing those bruises on your arm . . .'

'I had a silly accident,' said Mona simply, wishing heartily that Creena would drop the subject.

'What sort of accident?'

'I fell.'

'But . . .'

'I told you, I fell.'

Mona threw her a look that said 'no more', and Creena's words dried in her throat.

'Anyway,' said Mona brightly, 'I don't know what we're discussing me for. You're the birthday girl!' She nodded her blonde head in the direction of the dining room. 'You should be in there with the rest of the family, not doing the washing-up with me.'

Creena gave a groan and tossed back her long mane of red hair.

'Believe me, I'd rather do the washing-up,' she smiled. 'Anything for a little peace.'

'Your dad laying down the law again, is he?' Mona laid a soapy cup and saucer on the draining board.

'He says there won't be a war, Robert says there will, and Mother keeps going on about what a nice boy the vicar's son is.'

Mona chuckled.

'Still trying to marry you off then?'

'You know Mother. She thinks that because I'm the village schoolmaster's daughter, I ought to move in "respectable" circles. And Father won't be happy till I'm married off to some dreary old solicitor.'

'I expect they mean well,' observed Mona. 'Parents usually do.' She recalled her own late mother, who had been so keen for her to marry rich young farmer Duggie Mylchreest. 'It's just that they aren't always as clever as they think they are.'

'No,' agreed Creena wholeheartedly, 'they aren't. And there's such a lot of things I want to do before I let anyone tie me down.'

'Good for you,' said Mona, looking straight ahead of her as she scrubbed stubborn grease from the bottom of a roasting tin. 'What matters is what *you* want to do, not what they want you to do.'

'If only it was that simple,' Creena grimaced.

Creena dried another bone-china cup and set it on its saucer on the scrubbed oak kitchen table. She glanced around the old schoolhouse kitchen, with its low ceiling and blackened range, its solid flooring of Manx stone and its rows of gleaming copper pans. This place had been her home since she was eight years old and now, at twenty, she knew that she had outgrown it. Not just the schoolhouse, or the tiny village of Ballakeeill; but the Isle of Man in its entirety.

She wanted to get on with her parents, of course she did; but it wasn't easy when you had two brothers who were practically geniuses and a younger sister who, at eleven years old, was already turning into the perfect housewife. Well, that certainly wasn't for her.

And as if that wasn't difficult enough, half the village seemed to have married her off to Frank Kinrade. It wasn't that she didn't like him – hadn't they been inseparable friends since they were eight years old? – but she did wish people wouldn't keep assuming she was 'Frankie's girl'.

It was no use trying to be what other people wanted her to be. She was different – why, with her red hair and green eyes, she even *looked* the odd one out. It was hardly surprising that she should want different things. Like a caterpillar itching to shed its final skin, she felt the desperate need for a whole new life.

'Penny for 'em,' said Mona.

'Oh. Oh, sorry, I was daydreaming.'

'Wishing you were somewhere else?'

'It was good of Mother to put on a birthday lunch for me.' Creena felt churlish in her ingratitude. 'But really . . .'

'Really you'd rather be spending your special day with Frank? Bet I'm right.'

'And Máire and Padraig,' she said pointedly. She was getting rather tired of these unsubtle hints. 'I do wish Father wasn't so set against them. He never seems to like any of my friends.'

'Oh, Padraig! Now there's a young man I could really enjoy spending time with,' commented Mona as she indulged in romantic thoughts about Máire O'Keefe's dark, rugged brother. 'I wouldn't mind getting a good deal better acquainted with *him*, I can tell you.'

'Mona!' giggled Creena, amused but also faintly shocked. At thirty-two, Cousin Mona might still have the blonde, blue-eyed charms which had attracted all the lads to her when she was eighteen – but now she was a married woman with two small children and an ailing farm to look after.

'You have to admit he's a dreamboat, Creena!' Mona was laughing so hard that she no longer felt the ache from her bruised body. She looked like a young girl again, thought Creena. 'He's so strong and dark, and, oh! those velvety-brown eyes of his. Couldn't you just *melt* when you look into them?'

8

'Oh, Mona! Whatever would Duggie say?'

At Creena's tactless words Mona seemed to freeze, as if all the joy had suddenly gone out of her, like a balloon deflated with a pin. Creena could have kicked herself.

'Ah well, I may as well make some more tea whilst I'm here,' said Mona, all at once businesslike and brittle. 'Get the tray ready while I boil the kettle, would you?'

There was a long, uncomfortable silence, punctuated by the nervous tinkling of china as Creena filled the milk jug and set it down on the tray. Then Mona spoke again, her voice softer now.

'Why don't you fetch my bag out from under the table? There's something in it for you.'

'For me?'

'No need to be so surprised, Cree. It *is* your birthday.'

Creena pulled out the large, soft leather holdall, loosened the drawstring and felt inside. There was a crinkly paper parcel and she took it out. Mona hauled the immense copper kettle from the sink on to the hob and swung round.

'Well, open it then.'

Gingerly, not wanting to spoil the paper, Creena unfastened the knotted string and withdrew the present. It was the prettiest white clutch bag she'd ever seen, and she loved it instantly.

'I thought it would go with your new white shoes,' Mona explained. 'You don't have half enough nice things. And you've got to look pretty for your boy Frankie, now, haven't you?'

'I keep telling you, Mona,' Creena objected. 'He's not my boy.'

'Never mind that.' Mona waved away Creena's protests. 'What do you think of the bag? Is it all right?'

'It's lovely. It's really lovely. Thank you!' Creena gave Mona an enthusiastic hug which erased all the tension that had been between them.

But as she smoothed her fingers lightly over the soft white leather of the new clutch bag, Creena couldn't help thinking that the atmosphere in the dining room might soon be a good deal more tense.

Cousin Mona had surprised her with this gift; but Creena had her own surprise to spring on the family before the day was over – and she wasn't looking forward to it one little bit.

'Where on earth has that girl got to? I thought she'd only gone into the kitchen to make a cup of tea.'

Faintly irritated by her elder daughter's prolonged absence, Ida Quilliam brushed invisible crumbs off the snow-white tablecloth.

'Let her alone, Ma – I expect she's chinwagging with Mona,' cut in Creena's elder brother Robert, at twenty-five a fully qualified advocate and his parents' pride and joy. 'You know what those two are like when they get together.'

'Girls will be girls,' grunted George Quilliam, for once in a good mood. He had eaten well, he had had a lively argument with his elder son, and now he was going to enjoy a pleasant afternoon in the bosom of his family.

'Top-notch apple pie, Ma,' grinned Robert, leaning back in his chair and unfastening the bottom button of his waistcoat. 'You've filled me fit to bust!'

'It was a lovely meal,' agreed Aunt Bessie, and Ida

glowed with pleasure. Praise from her elder sister, an accomplished cook herself, was praise indeed. 'Perfect for a special occasion.'

Today's meal *was* a special one – a family lunch to celebrate the twentieth birthday of George and Ida's second eldest child. Most of the family were there: thirteen-year-old Tom and eleven-year-old Amy, the babies of the Quilliam family; Ida's sister Bessie; Cousin Mona and her two children; and George's three elderly spinster aunts from Laxey – all gathered together at Ballakeeill schoolhouse, which had been home to Creena ever since her father had become schoolmaster, some dozen years ago.

Life in the tiny Manx village of Ballakeeill, almost equidistant from the towns of Douglas and Castletown, revolved around the church and the school, and George Quilliam was one of the most important people for miles around. Sometimes Creena wished he wasn't; that she could have a father who was less unbending and more affectionate.

Not that his first-born son had ever lacked for affection. Even as a young boy Robert had got away with everything under the sun – scrumping apples, getting bicycle oil on his Sunday-best trousers, letting the ram get in with Farmer Duggan's ewe lambs – and with only the mildest of beatings to show for it.

It had been different with Creena. Creena didn't shine in exams, and certainly didn't share her younger sister's enthusiasm for baking and sewing. Her patience, perseverance and gentleness were less tangible accomplishments which drew little praise from her parents, even when

she had sat up for long nights on end, helping her mother
nurse young Tom through a bad bout of scarlet fever. It
wasn't that her parents meant to be unkind to her, they'd
just never been able to understand.

Nobody had – except Frankie Kinrade.

As if in tune with her thoughts, young Tom piped up:
'Where's Frankie? I wanted to show him the model
engine I made in metalwork.'

'This is a family occasion, Tom. Frank Kinrade isn't
family.' Ida Quilliam folded up the tablecloth and put it
away in a drawer in the sideboard.

'Nor will he be, if I have anything to do with it,' muttered
George, toying with the stem of his glass.

'But Frank is such a nice boy,' said Aunt Bessie
soothingly. 'I can't for the life of me see what anyone could
object to . . .'

George opened his mouth as though to say something
very unkind, caught his wife's mortified gaze, and closed it
again. He grunted as he refilled his glass from the jug of
home-made cordial.

It wasn't that he particularly objected to Frankie himself.
There was nothing fundamentally wrong with the lad, and
now that he had joined the Isle of Man Constabulary he was
very nearly respectable. No, it wasn't Frank he really
objected to – it was his family. George had taught all the
Kinrade children in his time – scraggy little urchins the lot
of them, left to their father to bring up when their Italian
mother had succumbed to tuberculosis. It was a wonder
they'd survived at all, scraping a living out of the few acres
they'd got, and everyone knew Don Kinrade was practically an alcoholic.

If there was one thing George Quilliam couldn't abide, it was strong drink. He'd never touched a drop in his life, and – no matter what Frank's merits might or might not be – Don Kinrade certainly wasn't the sort of man he'd want for an in-law.

Ida had to agree. Socially, Frankie Kinrade simply wouldn't do. Someone far more suitable would have to be found for Creena. The Bishop's son, Gerald, for example, or that well-bred junior partner in Robert's office. Creena might be inclined to stubbornness, but once she'd been introduced to some eligible bachelors, she'd soon see sense.

In the kitchen, Creena filled the huge brown teapot and lifted it on to the tray.

'When do you think I should tell them?' she asked.

'You'll have to tell them soon,' Mona pointed out.

'But now – on my birthday? Maybe I should leave it . . .'

'You can't put it off for ever.' Mona arranged home-made biscuits on a patterned plate. 'That is . . . if you really mean to do it at all.'

Mona's searching gaze jolted Creena. Her cousin was right. There was no time like the present, and she'd put this off for too long already.

'Wish me luck,' she said.

You'll need it, thought Mona, but she said nothing. Creena would have to fight her own battles.

She watched as Creena crossed the passageway to the dining room, pushed open the door and announced in an uncertain voice:

'Mother, Father, there's something ... something important I have to tell you.'

George blinked back at his daughter in complete astonishment; his wife and Bessie were caught open-mouthed in mid-sentence by Creena's sudden reappearance.

'Good heavens, dear,' smiled Aunt Bessie. 'What on earth is the matter?'

'I'm going to London,' said Creena, her voice sounding deafeningly loud in the silent room. 'I want to be a nurse.'

For a few seconds, nothing moved and no one said a word. In the end it was Robert who broke the silence.

'By Jove, Cree! I'd never have thought it . . .'

George Quilliam's eyes travelled around the room, compelling attention from everyone at the table. Then he fixed his clear and unforgiving gaze on his daughter.

'What sort of nonsense is this?' he demanded.

'It's not nonsense,' Creena insisted, her mouth dry and her legs wobbly. It was more dreadful than she'd anticipated, feeling all those pairs of eyes staring at her. But it was much too late to get cold feet now. 'I've applied to train as a nurse at the Royal Lambeth Hospital.'

'Well, well!' exclaimed Aunt Bessie. 'The Royal Lambeth. *Such* a good hospital, or so they say. One of the best in London. Mureal Gelling was a sister there, you know . . .'

She caught George's eye and, realising that her brother-in-law did not entirely share her enthusiasm, fell silent.

'Have you quite taken leave of your senses, child?' demanded George. 'Have you the faintest idea . . . ?'

'I'm not a child, Father,' said Creena, surprising herself with her own determination. 'And nursing is what I want to do, more than anything else in the world.'

14

'It is quite out of the question,' cut in Ida with a firmness which made Creena quake. 'No daughter of mine is going to London, and that is that. Sit down, Creena, and cut your Aunt Bessie a slice of birthday cake.'

Chapter 2

A grubby grey sparrow fluttered across the back yard of number 12 Bishop Street, a small piece of bacon rind hanging, worm-like, from its beak. Triumphant, it settled on top of the yard wall to devour its prize. Rich pickings were rare in Lambeth Marsh, but Bishop Street was an oasis of prosperity compared with the poorer streets around it. People had pride here; cleaning till their front steps gleamed, and always saving what they had, saving against the bad times.

It was Monday morning again, and a washing line extended from one end of the yard to the other, stretched between the gatepost and a rusty iron spike, driven into the masonry. Two much-mended sheets and several large pairs of bloomers fluttered in the breeze, their dazzling whiteness a testimony to Mo Doyle's high standards.

'That's the last of the wash hung out, Auntie Mo,' called Dillie Bayliss, wiping the dampness from her hands and bringing the peg bag indoors.

'Thanks, Dillie, you're a good girl.'

Dillie regarded her aunt with a practised eye.

'Back still giving you gyp, is it?'

Mo Doyle straightened up rather stiffly, tucking a wisp of iron-grey hair behind her ear. At fifty-five, her face was lined but still handsome, her body hard with muscle.

'It's not so bad, Dillie. Fancy a cup of char?'

Without waiting for Dillie's reply, Mo put the kettle back on the stove. The kettle was almost permanently on the boil at 12 Bishop Street – what with her grown-up son Jack and her niece Dillie still living at home, and an ever-changing population of lodgers on the top floor.

'I had a letter from Eddie this morning,' she said as she warmed the pot and spooned in tea from the caddy. 'He's got his hands full with Micky and Kitty.'

Dillie settled herself in the battered chair that had been her late Uncle Paddy's favourite. Brown curls danced around a friendly face more accustomed to laughter than to frowning.

'What have they been up to now?' She liked her Uncle Eddie Bates, Mo's younger brother, but seldom saw him and his two children, because they lived over the other side of London.

'Oh, the usual – Micky got nabbed tryin' to sneak into the picture palace without paying. And now Eddie's talkin' about joinin' up again.' Mo shook her grey head slowly as she poured boiling water on to the tea leaves. 'He really ought to send them kids to me, they need a mother. If he's not careful Micky'll turn out as bad as Jack,' she added as an afterthought.

'You don't mean that, Auntie Mo,' said Dillie. She knew how much Mo loved her only surviving son. 'Gentleman trader' Jack Doyle's activities might not all be strictly legal, but everyone knew his heart was in the right place.

18

'No, you're right.' Mo put the lid back on the teapot and plonked a knitted cosy on top. 'Jack's not a bad lad, but . . .' She fixed her gaze on her niece. 'He's not steady like you, Dillie.'

Dillie crossed her legs nervously.

'Auntie Mo . . . There's something I wanted to talk to you about.'

'What's that then?'

'You know I've been at the Royal Lambeth for ages now,' Dillie began.

Mo sat down in a chair opposite her, faintly concerned.

'Oh, Dillie. You're not thinkin' of giving your job up? I thought you loved workin' at the hospital.'

'Yes, I do, it's not that.'

It was over two years since Dillie Bayliss had started working as a nursing assistant at the Royal Lambeth Hospital. Hospital work was all she'd ever wanted to do since the day Mo took her in as a scrawny orphan, but now she felt she needed a new challenge.

'Do you think I'm good at my job, Auntie Mo?'

'I know you are,' Mo laughed.

'But am I good enough to be a *real* nurse – a registered nurse?'

Mo stared back at her, mouth slightly open. She felt hot and cold with disbelief and excitement.

'You want to do your training?'

Dillie nodded.

'At the Royal Lambeth?'

'If they'll have me.'

'But . . . but it's a whole four years there, ain't it?'

'I don't mind. I've thought about it, and it's what I want.'

Dillie stared down at her shoes, her pulse racing. Perhaps she should have kept it to herself for the time being – she hadn't even made a formal application yet, and Matron was bound to turn her down. Everyone knew how difficult it was to get accepted by the Royal Lambeth Hospital. And perhaps she was wrong to think that Mo would be pleased – her aunt might even think she was giving herself airs and graces.

Uncharacteristically stunned into silence, Mo marvelled at Dillie's transformation from timid little girl to level-headed young woman. It was a good fourteen years now since Dillie Bayliss had turned up at the door of 12 Bishop Street with nothing to her name but a change of underwear wrapped in a brown paper parcel. Who would have thought that Paddy's poor dead sister's orphan kid would turn out such a credit to them all?

'A registered nurse!' Mo was giddy with astonishment.

'Are you pleased?' asked Dillie, still doubtful.

'Pleased! Oh, Dillie . . .'

'I haven't got my School Certificate,' Dillie pointed out hastily. 'They most probably won't have me.'

'Oh yes they will,' said Mo firmly, drawing Dillie to her feet and giving her an immense hug. She hoped Dillie couldn't see the tears of pride welling up at the corners of her eyes. 'They'll snap you up, and if they don't they'll have Mo Doyle to reckon with!' She gave her eyes a quick wipe with her apron. 'Now, we'll have that cuppa, shall we?'

Late spring sunlight poured through the windows of Gelling and Craine, the advocates' office where Creena had worked as a typist for the past two years. She knew she had been fortunate to get a job with one of the island's most prestigious legal firms, and was grateful to Robert for his efforts on her behalf. But that didn't make the work any less boring.

Outside in Athol Street, the island's business community was bustling with activity at the beginning of another working week. Voices in animated conversation floated up through the open first-floor window, and Creena – already unsettled – found it almost impossible to concentrate.

In contrast to the crisp May morning outside, the atmosphere inside the office was somnolent and stuffy, enlivened only by the click-clack of typewriter keys and the light, musical voice of Máire O'Keefe:

'Fifty pounds they'll be giving him! Isn't that just wonderful, now?'

Creena stopped typing and wriggled her aching shoulders. Cleaning out the henhouse was never such hard and unrewarding work as this.

'It is,' she agreed, trying to share her friend's enthusiasm. 'And Padraig got all that just for one job?'

'Well, no – he's got the contract to shoe all the tramhorses. Not that I'm surprised. Everyone knows he's the best farrier on the island!'

The Irish girl's dark eyes sparkled as she spoke of her gentle giant of a brother. It was four years now since they'd come to the island, and they'd always supported each other through thick and thin. Now, at long last, things seemed to be coming right for Máire and Padraig O'Keefe.

'Brilliant *and* good-looking?' Creena teased her. 'It's a wonder all the girls on the island haven't set their caps at him.'

'Oh they have! But all Padraig cares about are his horses.'

'Robert's no better,' admitted Creena. 'All work and no play. I can't remember the last time he brought a girl home to tea. Perhaps we should dress both of them up and send them out on the town together!'

'Is your Robert still talking about joining up?'

'If there's a war,' replied Creena, rubbing frantically with her typing eraser at another mistake – so hard that a tiny hole appeared in the paper. 'What about you and Padraig? What would you do if there was a war?'

Máire shrugged.

'I shouldn't think there will be. It's all talk, like last year. And even if there was, we're settled here; I can't see us ever going back to Ireland.'

'So you're still looking for a better place, then?'

'Now that we've got the money. It'll be wonderful to get away from those poky lodgings – maybe we could even rent somewhere with a bit of land, so's Padraig could keep a horse or two.'

'That'd be nice,' agreed Creena. 'It must be lovely for you and Padraig, being able to do what you want.'

Máire's flying fingers hesitated over the keys of her machine, and she leant forward over the desk.

'Is something the matter? You look a bit down in the mouth.'

'I *feel* it.'

'Didn't your birthday go well, then? I thought you were having a big family get-together.'

Creena passed her hand across her brow. It was slightly damp with sweat, and she could feel strands of her wild auburn hair escaping from its imprisoning clips.

'I told them.'

Máire's eyes opened wide.

'You never did!'

'I had to. I couldn't leave it any longer, could I? The next intake is in September, and I didn't want to let Mrs Gelling down. She's been so kind, offering to give the hospital a character reference.'

'Well!' Máire sat back in her chair, an admiring smile at the corners of her mouth. 'And how did they take it?'

Creena grimaced.

'Can't you guess? Father threw a fit, and you know what Mother's like. She simply said I couldn't, and that was that. And when I told them I wanted to go across the water, well . . .'

'Your mam raised the roof? Said she wouldn't have any daughter of hers living in the fleshpots of the great metropolis?'

'Something like that.'

'There's always next year,' pointed out Máire. 'You'll be twenty-one then, they can't stop you.'

'I know, but I'd have to buy all my PTS uniforms, my equipment. I don't think I could afford it without help.'

'Well . . . what if you trained a bit nearer home?'

Creena shook her head.

'The thing is, they hate the whole idea. Father says nursing's "not respectable". And the hospitals are crying out for nurses, too.' She threw down her typing eraser and it bounced on the desktop before falling into the wastepaper bin. 'It's so unfair!'

'Maybe if you waited a little while? Let things calm down?' Máire longed to tell her to stand up to her bullying parents, but she knew how difficult that could be. She patted Creena's hand. 'Cheer up – at least you've got Frank. You're a lucky girl.'

Creena bit her lip. She *was* lucky to have Frank, Máire was right. And it would be the easiest thing in the world just to sit back and let things happen the way everyone seemed to want them to. Was it so very wrong to want more?

'How's about you and Frank and me and Padraig going to the pictures next Saturday? There's a matinée on at the Palace.'

'All right then. I'll ask Frank.'

Just then the outer door of the office opened and in bustled a tall woman in a chic suit and small feathery hat. Hastily, Creena wound a fresh sheet of paper into her typewriter. Best to look busy.

'Good morning, girls! Working hard, I see.'

'Good morning, Mrs Gelling,' they chorused respectfully. It wouldn't do to get on the wrong side of Mureal Gelling. Her husband was one of the most important men in the island's legislature.

She paused by Creena's desk and laid a gloved hand on her shoulder.

'How are you getting on, my dear? Told your parents yet?'

'Yes, Mrs Gelling. I'm afraid they didn't take it very well.'

Mureal Gelling made a small tutting noise in her throat.

'Not to worry, Creena. My parents were horrified when I first told them I wanted to nurse. But once they realised how determined I was, they soon came round to my way of thinking. Yours will come round too – just you wait and see.'

'Someone to see you, Davey. Keep it quick, mind. The guv'nor wants this one ready for the two-thirty practice.'

Carefully gathering up the pieces of the carburettor he had been cleaning, Davey Cashin placed them on the bench, then wiped his hands on an oily rag and stood up. Every muscle and bone in his body creaked in protest after hours squatting down beside the racing machine.

In the last couple of weeks, Taggart's Garage had been transformed from a sleepy backwater into the frantic hub of pre-race activity in the build-up to the 1939 TT fortnight. Over the last couple of years, Davey had acquired more and more expertise in maintaining and fine-tuning race bikes, and he had high hopes for the future.

Davey loved the grease and the grime, the deafening roar as the throttle was squeezed back and a thoroughbred machine hit the open road. He had spent many a happy hour riding the mountain circuit and hoped one day to make it as a rider. But for now he was happy enough to be a mechanic – in fact, one of the island's most sought-after mechanics, a craftsman with an instinctive feel for the smooth blending of man and machine.

He strode through the workshop, breathing in the heady aroma of two-stroke and warm leather. This was his world, his kingdom – and soon he would be the king. 'Local boy makes good': that was what the *Isle of Man Examiner* would say. He could hardly wait.

She was waiting for him in the tiny glass box of an office which had been crammed into a far corner of the vast service area. He could see her collar-length blonde hair shining through the obscured glass, and the peacock blue of her dress – the dress that she always wore because she knew it was his favourite. Instantly he felt slightly uneasy. She didn't normally come to see him here – this filthy, noisy garage was no place for a woman. What was more, the guv'nor actively discouraged his mechanics from forming 'attachments'. Didn't want any distractions, that was how he put it.

Giving his hands a second wipe on his overalls, Davey pushed open the door.

She turned to greet him, her generous mouth curving into a crimson peony of a smile. Really she overdid the lipstick; it didn't look quite, well, decent. But she was pretty all the same, and it made Davey's young heart ache in spite of his resolve.

'Pleased to see me, Davey?' She put her arms round his middle and nuzzled into his neck, but he drew slightly away, his embarrassed fingers trying to prise her hands from his body.

'Yes, of course I am, but look, Mona . . . we can't. Not here, not that sort of thing. I mean, my pals are all out there and they might see. What if your husband got to hear about it, what then?'

Mona Mylchreest cocked her head on one side and looked her lover up and down with a quizzical eye. He wasn't normally so jumpy. But then again, she didn't normally come to see him at the garage. Perhaps she should do it more often. He looked very young and absolutely irresistible in his tight-fitting overalls and leather knee-boots, his curly black hair falling over his face and a little smudge of oil on his left cheek. She had a tremendous urge to kiss it away with her crimson-painted lips.

'If I gave a damn about what Duggie thought, I wouldn't be carrying on with you, Davey Cashin, now would I? Besides, he's too drunk to notice what's going on under his own nose.'

'All the same.' Davey pulled out Taggart's battered old chair and gave it a cursory brush down with his grubby handkerchief. 'Why don't you sit down, eh? Don't want to get your pretty dress all dirty from my overalls.'

Mona accepted the proffered chair and sat, crossing her thighs so that the thin crêpe of her blue dress moulded itself to her shapely legs. She took pride in the fact that, even after ten interminable years of marriage to Duggie Mylchreest, her figure was every bit as good as it had been on her wedding day. It pleased her to see how Davey's eyes travelled down over her slim but womanly curves, taking in every detail of the confection she had created just for him.

'So . . . er . . . why did you come to see me here then?' Davey was grateful for the sound of revving engines in the workshop outside; it lessened the chance of anyone over-hearing their conversation.

'I've been thinking, Davey. You and I . . . we get along together pretty well, don't we?'

'I . . . well, yeah. Course we do.'

'Me and Duggie, we don't get on. I made a big mistake

27

marrying him, but he was the local hero, wasn't he? And then there was that great big farm. I thought I was getting myself a real catch there.' She laughed drily. 'I thought he cared.' Her blue eyes flicked up to meet Davey's. 'But you care about me, don't you?'

Davey opened his mouth then closed it again. He didn't know what to say. Mona went on talking without waiting for his reply.

'I think it's time to make a fresh start – somewhere else, where no one knows us. On the mainland, we could be together – you, me and the children – and no one would ever know...'

Davey's mouth was as dry as dust.

'We have to get off this island,' she went on. 'It's suffocating us. We need freedom. And there's something I have to tell you...'

'Actually, Mona, I've been meaning to talk to you,' butted in Davey. If he didn't say it now, perhaps he never would. 'I've had an offer. The Norton manager came to see me the other day and he asked me to join the team – as chief mechanic.'

'But – that's wonderful! Why didn't you tell me before?'

'It ... it means a move over to the mainland. The team's based in the Midlands. And then there's the travelling overseas...'

'Then we can be together!' Mona got to her feet and stretched out her arms to her lover. 'At last we can get away!'

Davey took a step backwards.

'No, Mona.'

'I don't understand. No what?'

'You can't come with me, Mona. I . . . I don't want you to.'

The colour drained from Mona's face. She was shaking all over, her lips barely framing her words, her legs barely strong enough to hold her. She clutched the desk as though it were the only solid, reliable thing left in the whole universe.

'You don't want . . .'

'It's over, Mona. No hard feelings. I'm fond of you – you know that. But we always knew it had to end sometime. Didn't we always say so? You're married, and I'm too young to settle down . . .'

Mona's trembling fingers clutched at her handbag and curled convulsively around it as she drew herself up, trying to look proud and indifferent, trying to hold back the tears of pain and anger that were welling up, clouding her sky-blue eyes.

'I'd better go then. It doesn't look as if there's anything more to say, does it?'

She turned to leave and Davey put his hand on her arm.

'But you said you wanted to tell me something.'

Very slowly and deliberately, she prised his fingers away.

'I did. And then I realised it had nothing to do with you.'

She opened the door and stepped out into the dirt and cacophony of the garage workshop. A few pairs of eyes watched her stiff, uncertain progress towards the road outside, but she was oblivious to the unwanted attention.

It's just you and me now, she told herself as her hand strayed to her stomach and she thought of the new life just beginning inside her. Just you and me, and a big secret that won't keep.

Chapter 3

Beyond Ballakeeill rose the distant hills, their green slopes climbing towards bare brown crests like the bald pates of very old, very wise men. Higher than the rest loomed the dark, brooding mass of South Barrule, the cornflower-blue blanket of heaven resting on its cloud-flecked dome.

It was Sunday afternoon, and Creena was walking to Ballakeeill Kirk, carrying an armful of spring flowers. From the end of the lane which led to the schoolhouse, she could just make out the distant blue line of the sea, its own shade of blue just a fraction darker than the clear, sunlit hue of the sky above it.

She crossed the road and walked through the tiny village. It was little more than a cluster of cottages strung out along the main road, a pub, Mrs Shimmin's post-office-cum-general-stores and, of course, the village school.

About a quarter of a mile further on stood the kirk: a squat, whitewashed church with an open tower in which swung a single bell. The typically Manx simplicity of the kirk had always appealed to Creena, and as she entered the

31

churchyard, she could not but be affected by the over-whelming peace and tranquillity of the place.

When Creena's beloved Uncle John had at last come home, it had been to Ballakeeill churchyard. It was ten years now since that terrible night when George Quilliam had received the news of his brother's death, and yet that night remained fresh as yesterday in Creena's mind.

It had been the week before Mona's marriage to Duggie Mylchreest, and the whole village had been involved in the wedding preparations. The banns had been read and Duggie – the hero of the island after rescuing a girl and her baby in a cottage fire – was fairly beaming with triumph at finally winning his bride.

They made a fine couple: the handsome son of a rich farmer, and the pretty, blue-eyed blonde. And yet for a while it had looked as if the marriage would not take place at all. Mona had fallen in with some boy over for the TT races, and when he left she'd taken herself off to Liverpool, getting a job as a chambermaid at the Adelphi Hotel. But Duggie had followed her, and set about courting her all over again – until at last she had succumbed to his charm and agreed to be his wife.

That week, George Quilliam had received a letter with a foreign postmark. His brother John was coming home for the wedding. Creena was thrilled. John Quilliam was a merchant seaman, travelling to places Creena could only dream about. George might be ashamed of his brother, looking down on him for his globetrotting and his lack of education. But Creena adored him, for they understood each other perfectly.

Uncle John never made fun of her dreams. In fact, John

and George Quilliam could hardly have been more different. Where George advocated practicalities and self-denial, John believed in following his heart.

'Stick to your dreams, Creena-gel,' he would tell her as she sat at his feet, listening to tales of wild adventure. 'Don't let anyone take them away from you.'

Remembering her uncle's words, Creena knelt down before the little white headstone and brushed away some of the fallen petals from the grave.

Uncle John had not been at Mona and Duggie's wedding. Two nights before – a terrible, dark night with fat, silvery clouds that rolled across a bloodshot moon and lightning that ripped across the sky like a jagged blade – his ship was wrecked off Maughold. That night John Quilliam had drowned – not hundreds of miles away, in some foreign ocean, but in the treacherous, untameable Irish Sea which he knew and loved so well.

Creena took the wilted flowers out of the little china vase, and replenished the water.

'I've brought you goldencups and wood anemone, Uncle John,' she told him as she arranged the flowers. 'Sumark and the last of the bluebells, all your favourite wild flowers. And some from Mother's garden.'

She cleared away a few straggly blades of couch grass and sat back on her haunches.

'Well, I did it, Uncle John,' she whispered. 'I told them. I've never seen Father so angry. Whatever am I going to do now?'

The grass underfoot felt soft as a bed, the sun gently warm and comforting. She breathed deeply and savoured the blend of scents that filled the air: sweet, sun-warmed gorse from the hillsides, piny forest smells from the woodland behind the kirk, fresh-scythed grass, and the slight tang of salt that floated in from the sea. So peaceful.

It seemed barely possible that across the Irish Sea, the British Government was preparing for a war which nobody wanted; even more bizarre that Manx landladies could be advertising their establishments as safe havens from German air raids.

War. The mainland. London. The train of thought brought Creena back to her dilemma. She questioned the empty air:

'Did I do the wrong thing? Should I be content with what I've got?'

Creena received no reply to her question, but the quiet squeak of the wicket gate made her turn her head. Her face broke into a smile as she saw who the newcomer was.

'Frankie!'

'Thought I'd find you here.'

She got to her feet slowly and dusted a few stalks of grass off her tweedy Sunday skirt as she stretched her stiff back.

'Aren't you supposed to be on duty?'

'I thought you might fancy a bit of a stroll. They won't miss me for half an hour.' He leaned his bicycle up against the fence and took off his helmet. 'The only thing that's happened so far is that someone found a piglet wandering about on the Castletown road, and took it in to Ballasalla police station. Sergeant Maddrell's got it locked up in the cells!'

He laughed, and Creena couldn't help laughing with

him. If you set aside his shock of wavy blue-black hair, Police Constable Frank Kinrade was not remarkably handsome, not remarkably tall, not remarkably anything. But he and Creena had been firm friends since the first day they met, despite George Quilliam's oft-voiced disapproval.

Young Frankie had not had an auspicious start in life. With his father over-partial to a 'lil cooish' and a tot of the hard stuff, and his mother chronically ill, life's responsibilities had weighed hard on Frank's shoulders and after his mother's death he had had to be father and mother to his two young sisters, Ailish and Gwen. From necessity, he had spent more time poaching rabbits and trout than he had at Ballakeeill village school. When he left to work as a farm labourer, George Quilliam had confidently predicted a bad end; but even George Quilliam could be mistaken. Within two years Frank had got himself a police cadetship, and he was now a fully fledged constable at Ballasalla police station, south of Ballakeeill.

Creena accepted a kiss on the cheek and they linked arms. It was impossible not to be proud of Frank. He too had had dreams, and in spite of everything he'd made them come true. She could remember him as a small boy, thin almost to the point of emaciation, his legs brown and skinny in his father's cast-off moleskin trousers, and there was no doubt about it: against all the odds, Frankie Kinrade had made good.

'It's been a fair while since I saw you,' said Frank. 'I heard about the big bust-up, though. You know – you and your ma and pa.'

Creena sighed. The family disagreement must be all over Ballakeeill by now. It was a small place – and it could be small-minded too. Maybe that was why part of her ached to leave it far behind.

'Father doesn't think nursing's decent,' she replied. 'Can you imagine that? Mureal Gelling was a ward sister before she married, and her father was Second Deemster. Honestly, Father's such a . . . a Victorian!'

Frank squeezed her hand. In all honesty he didn't want Creena to go off to London, any more than her father did. He wanted her to stay here with him, on the island; even cherished unspoken hopes that in time they might settle down together and get married. But he loved Creena too much to try and impose his views on her. By his simple reckoning, she had enough of that to put up with from her parents.

'It'll come right,' he reassured her. They strolled past the church, arm in arm. It felt better like that; closer, more permanent. 'What you need is cheering up.'

'It's easy being cheerful with you,' she replied with a laugh. 'Now, if you could only do something to cheer *Father* up . . .'

Frank chuckled.

'I'm not a miracle-worker. Look, I've got some time off coming up. What if we took a picnic down to Grenaugh, like we used to?'

Creena gazed up at the blue sky-dome above her, and suddenly it seemed dauntingly vast, unfathomable as the swirling sea which had taken poor Uncle John, all those years ago. Perhaps adventure wasn't everything. Europe's troubles seemed to be creeping a little closer to the island with every day that passed. Maybe there was something to be said for security – even if security sometimes felt more like a cage.

She looked up into Frank's honest, open face and smiled. 'Yes. Yes, why not?'

Miss Dorothea Milton-Payne, Matron of the Royal Lambeth Hospital, was working hard to keep up with the avalanche of paperwork. With the increasing threat of war, it seemed that every day brought another form to fill in, another pile of letters to answer.

'Another batch of applications for training, Matron.' Sister Duvergier placed half a dozen sheets of paper on Miss Milton-Payne's desk. That desk and its owner had a good deal in common, mused Sister Duvergier irreverently: solidly built, resilient and capable of dominating any room with their presence.

Matron gave an irritable sigh.

'I trust these are better than the last batch, Sister. Such a shortage of suitable applicants; I cannot imagine what will become of this hospital if hostilities do commence.'

'No outstanding candidates, I am afraid.' Sister Duvergier was only too aware of the crisis in nurse training. And the Royal Lambeth, as one of London's oldest and most respected training hospitals, was having more difficulty than most in adjusting to a different type of applicant. 'But one or two whom we might consider admitting.'

Matron leafed through the pile of papers, passing judgement with her usual devastating finality.

'No. Mm, yes, possibly. Oh no, definitely *not*. Quite unsuitable.'

Sue Dyson

'What about this one, Matron?' Sister Duvergier drew a
sheet out of the pile and directed the Matron's attention to
it.

'Oh, I really don't know, Sister. One must insist upon
the correct qualifications. Many of our students have
Matriculation, as you know . . .'

'But, Matron, we do make exceptions, and she comes
highly recommended.' Sister Duvergier flicked over
the page to a second sheet. 'Mureal Gelling – Mureal
Kennaugh as was, do you remember?'

'Ah yes! Sister Kennaugh. A real treasure on the
children's ward. Such a loss to nursing when she decided to
marry.' Matron's bird-bright eyes scanned the page. 'High
recommendation indeed. What did you say the girl's name
was?'

'Quilliam. Creena Quilliam.'

'Hmm . . . yes, Sister, this *is* a splendid character
reference. I think it might perhaps be within our powers to
offer the girl a probationary place.'

A knock on the door interrupted the deliberations.

'Come.'

The door opened a fraction, and Matron's secretary
popped her head round the door.

'If you please, Matron.'

'Please be brief, Miss Pately. We are busy, as you can
see.'

'It's one of the nursing assistants, Matron. A girl called
Bayliss.'

'What of her?'

'She'd like to see you, Matron. Apparently she wishes to
apply to do her nurse training at the Royal Lambeth.'

* * *

Lungs fit to burst, Creena pedalled energetically to the top of the hill and then coasted down, her mop of flaming red hair streaming out behind her. A few yards ahead was Frank, his body bent over the handlebars of his bicycle as he savoured the feel of the wind in his face.

Before them lay a good part of the south of the island, spread out like a patchwork bedspread dotted with the fluffy white and brown cotton balls that became sheep when you got closer to them. Today was one of those rare clear days when you might take the electric railway to the summit of Snaefell and see five kingdoms spread out before you.

On the island the weather could change in a matter of moments from bright sunshine to thick sea mist, or a lashing rain-soaked wind that stung your skin. But today the immense sky which stretched from horizon to horizon was an almost cloudless blue, and the sun shone golden and warm, tempered by the bite of a cool breeze which never quite left the island.

At the bottom of the hill Creena caught up with Frank, who braked gently so that they could ride abreast along the country lanes towards Ballakeeill and the sea. This morning they had taken a cup of tea at Máire and Padraig's new cottage outside Onchan, and now they were cycling south again, towards the little cove of Port Grenaugh.

They sped along narrow lanes lined with tall hawthorn hedges, and into Ballakeeill village; the grey slate roof of the schoolhouse just visible beyond the high banks of wild fuchsia. Past Mrs Shimmin's village store and post office, its whitewashed walls almost obscured by enamelled advertisements for Bile Beans and Rowntree's Cocoa; past the old Methodist chapel and the Cummal Beg Inn beside the field where the great Ballakeeill Fair used to be held.

In moments the village was behind them and they dismounted. Side by side, they pushed their bicycles along the quiet, sun-dappled lane which led gently down to Port Grenaugh, following the meanderings of a clear trout stream. Sometimes, if you stood very still and made no noise or shadow, you could see the small brown trout leaping and playing in the river, their mottled skins unexpectedly beautiful as they wriggled and slid through the water. As children, Creena had watched Frank poach trout by catching them with his bare hands – a feat of unimaginable skill which had earned him no small measure of respect among his fellow pupils.

On one side were cottages and open fields, on the other a steep-sided bank rising up from the stream to a distant ruined cottage, standing silhouetted against the clear blue sky. The entire slope was so thickly covered with the broad-bladed leaves of wild garlic that when the wind blew across it, it looked like the green, rippling pelt of some huge slumbering animal.

It was warmer in this sheltered spot, and Frank took off his jacket, slinging it over his shoulder. He looked happy, relaxed. This was a happy day altogether. Creena was glad she had dressed up in her new print frock and the pretty lacy cardigan with the glass buttons.

They walked close together, almost but never quite touching.

'Did you sort out that trouble with Sergeant Maddrell?'

enquired Creena as they walked towards the sound of the sea tumbling lazily on to the rocks at Grenaugh.

Frank shrugged and looked down at his boots, his smile momentarily clouded.

'Oh, it's something and nothing,' he replied. 'You don't want to go worrying yourself about things like that.'

'But, Frank . . . it's not very fair, is it? I mean, it's not your fault about . . . you know, your mother and father.'

'Life's not fair, Cree,' Frank pointed out with an unaccustomed touch of bitterness. 'If life was fair, Ma would still be alive and you'd be doin' your nursing.'

At this, Creena fell silent. Frank was right; she was being immature. They walked on for a few moments, deep in their own thoughts.

'Sorry, Frankie. I didn't mean . . .'

'I'm sorry too.' He put his arm round her shoulders and gave her a brotherly hug. It felt nice. 'Anyway, you're right, Creena, it isn't fair. I know Dad likes his drop of jough, but he's a good man; and as for poor Ma – well, it wasn't her fault she was born Italian, now was it? But still old Maddrell goes on and on about it, and everyone knows his grandmother was German! I'm fair sick of it, I can tell you.'

'Surely you can do something,' Creena said. 'Complain to Inspector Kneen . . .'

Frank shrugged again.

'It'd do no good,' he assured her. 'I'd just be branded a troublemaker and then Maddrell really would have it in for me. In any case,' he peered through the trees at the sparkling greens and greys of the sea, 'if things go on like this, maybe this time next year I shan't be a copper any more. Maybe we'll all be soldiers.'

'You really think there'll be a war, then?'

Frank's grip on her shoulder tightened. It was as though he didn't want to let her go, as though he was frightened that if he did, the moment would end and never return.

'All this training we're getting for air-raid precautions and blackouts, and the Government leaflets ... well, it makes you think.'

'Yes.' Creena cast her mind back to the smelly gas mask in its brown cardboard case. That had made her think, too.

The road curved to the right and suddenly they were there, the sea breeze buffeting their faces and the little cove spread out before them. Its small shingly beach was guarded by ancient rocky headlands where prehistoric people had built hillforts to protect themselves against attack. And now the island's story had come full circle, what with all this talk of invasions and civil defence.

'Still, no point in worrying, is there?' Frank leant the bicycles up against a rocky outcrop and strolled down on to the beach, hands in his trouser pockets. Creena joined him, struggling to keep the long tendrils of red hair from blowing across her face.

'Remember that day you taught me how to skim stones?'

Frank chortled at the remembrance.

'You almost brained that old man,' he recalled.

'I did not!' protested Creena indignantly. 'I only knocked his cap off. Anyway, I got the hang of it in the end, didn't I?'

'Bet you can't remember how to do it now.'

Creena's green eyes narrowed in defiance. She loved a challenge.

'Bet I can.'

'Go on then.'

'All right, I will.'

She stooped to select exactly the right size and shape of stone. Not too large, smooth and flat, nicely balanced. This one would do very well. Walking almost to the margin of the sea, she crouched, drew back her arm and watched the stone fly through the air, hovering for a tantalising moment before disappearing beneath the waves with a disappointing plop.

'Don't you say a word, Frankie Kinrade,' she warned him.

He grinned.

'Would I do that?'

Selecting a second stone and a third, she took aim again. This time memory guided her arm, and the stone skipped twice, three times before dipping into the water.

'Well done.'

'I can do better.' She threw again, but this time the stone shot straight under the water with a splash.

Frankie placed a stone in her hand, then guided her arm backwards.

'Like this,' he said. 'Remember? Now throw it – not too quickly.'

She threw. And the stone described five perfect arcs, each slightly smaller than the last, before disappearing from view.

'Teamwork,' Frank told her as she turned to face him, laughing. 'Didn't I always say we make a fine team?'

His dark brown eyes were looking straight into hers. The intensity of his longing was too much for her, and she turned away, walking over to the bicycles to take the food out of the saddlebags.

'Hungry?'

'Ravenous. You know me – Dad says I've got hollow legs.'

'I brought two sorts of sandwiches – cheese and tomato, and egg. The egg's from Mother's hens. Oh, and there's a bit of seedcake that Amy made.'

Frank spread out his raincoat for Creena to sit on, then flung himself down on the pebbly sand, in the lee of the headland. He selected a sandwich, bit into it and chewed appreciatively.

'Remember that hen you had when you were a kid? The one with the funny leg?'

'Polly? Oh yes, poor little Polly. Father was so sure a fox had got her.'

Polly had been Creena's special pet when she was a child – a hen born with a crippled leg and which had been destined for an early death until soft-hearted Creena stepped in and offered to look after it. From that moment on, Polly and Creena had been inseparable. But then, one day, little Amy had left the henhouse door open and half the chickens had escaped. It had taken ages to recapture them all, and when they finally managed it, they'd realised that Polly was missing.

'I found her for you in the end, though, didn't I?'

Creena laughed and nodded.

'You did. She was up a tree near Ballacregga, and you brought her back to the schoolhouse wrapped up in your pullover. You've always been good to me, Frankie Kinrade.'

This time, as she found herself looking right into Frank's soft brown eyes, a little warm shiver ran through her. There was an opened greaseproof-paper packet of sandwiches on her lap, but they lay there quite forgotten as Frank reached out and stroked the tangles from her hair with his strong brown hand. He didn't speak, but she could feel a great pulsing heat in him, so strong that it was almost frightening.

'I'll always do my best for you, Creena. You know I will.'

He caught her hand as she pushed the hair back from her face, and for a moment their fingers met and entwined.

Creena closed her eyes and felt his touch, his fingers tight and warm and strong about hers, protecting and safe. Sea birds called to each other across the vast sky, and the waves kept on surging towards the beach, singing their own passionate song.

She knew. And she hardly understood if she was pleased or afraid.

Chapter 4

Time passed quickly as late spring melted into summer; and the dark clouds of fear spread across Europe as swiftly as the sun climbed to its zenith, chasing away the shadows.

Creena had never known a July like it. The weather was unusually good, and the holiday town of Douglas was bustling. There were perhaps not so many visitors as usual, but those who had come seemed determined to enjoy themselves as never before. After all, it might be their last holiday for a long, long time.

Everywhere the talk was about war – shortages, and conscription, and air-raid shelters. Consequently Ida Quilliam's pantry was fairly groaning under the weight of sacks of sugar and Kilner jars of preserved fruit.

Beside the meat safe and underneath the marble slab where Ida kept her butter and cheeses stood an immense earthenware crock. This contained dozens and dozens of eggs, preserved in isinglass so that the family would continue to have a ready supply even if Herr Hitler had the temerity to send the hens off lay. Britain might not be quite ready for war but, as usual, Ida Quilliam was ready for anything.

Fourteen-year-old Tommy was in a permanent state of excitement, continually asking questions about bombs and poison gas, and being told to shut up and stop frightening his sister. For his part, Robert was a good deal more thoughtful than his younger brother, and that rather worried Creena. It wasn't like Robert to be so un-communicative.

Still, she thought as she got off the bus from Douglas, none of it might ever happen. There was still time for Hitler to see reason, and as Máire's pacifist brother Padraig was fond of saying, what did any of it have to do with a tiny island in the middle of the Irish Sea?

Other problems – Creena's own problems – inevitably felt closer to home. She slipped her hand into her raincoat pocket and felt for the crumpled brown envelope. Even now, after three days, the touch felt electric.

Excitement coursed through her as she curled her fingers around the letter, reassuring herself that it was still there, still real. The Royal Lambeth Hospital had offered her a training place. The Royal Lambeth! It still hadn't quite sunk in. Yet the letter had been perfectly clear. At the end of September she was to present herself at one of London's most prestigious hospitals, where she would spend the next four years of her life. It was true. She really was going to be a nurse!

She must find some way of breaking the news to her parents – and soon. It was three days since the letter had arrived, and she still hadn't told them. But she wasn't going to let this opportunity slip away. The thought of spending the rest of her life typing affidavits at Gelling and Craine filled her with even more horror than the thought of

48

confronting Ida and George. She would just have to be brave and get it over with.

It was a perfect summer's evening and she strolled slowly past the Cummal Beg Inn and Mrs Shimmin's ever-open stores, then turned down the lane which led to the schoolhouse. There it stood beyond the hedgerow, warm and welcoming in the mellow evening sunlight: a long, squat grey building with a pitched slate roof. Home.

In the yard stood Ida Quilliam's henhouse, and long before Creena reached the house she could hear Orry the cockerel crowing his head off – which he did indiscriminately at all hours of the day and night. As Robert liked to point out, it was almost as though Orry had been put on earth expressly to annoy George, who was Douglas-born and had never quite come to terms with the noise and sheer untidiness of the countryside.

Behind the schoolhouse and next to Farmer Duggan's orchard lay a couple of acres of rough meadow, part of which was used as a school playground. The rest had been dug up on George Quilliam's instructions, to provide each child with a plot in which to grow vegetables. Despite his town origins, George had believed in self-sufficiency long before the present emergencies. Each year the school held a produce show and – notwithstanding a few instances of cheating and sabotage – he considered the project to be another triumph in the long line of his many educational achievements.

As Creena emerged from the tall hedge of hawthorn patched with wild fuchsia, she saw her eleven-year-old sister Amy sitting on a wall outside the schoolhouse, her straight dark-blonde hair tied into a neat plait secured with pink ribbon. But Amy was not her usual good-natured self. She looked crestfallen, swinging her heels disconsolately against the stone wall and twisting the end of her long plait between her slim fingers.

She looked up as Creena closed the gate behind her. Her eyes were watery.

'Oh, it's you.'

'Whatever's the matter, Amy?' Creena tried to touch Amy's hand but she pulled it away. 'You've been crying – have you hurt yourself?'

Amy sniffed dramatically and wiped her eyes on the sleeve of her cardigan. Not normally given to histrionics, she didn't see why she shouldn't draw attention to her plight just this once. After all, it *was* all Creena's fault.

'No.'

Creena frowned. Amy was usually so sunny, so even-tempered.

'What is it then?'

'What's it to you?'

'Oh, Amy. Won't you tell me?'

Amy's bottom lip jutted sulkily as she replied:

'Mother and Father are angry. *Really* angry.'

As if to emphasise the truth of Amy's words, the sound of raised voices made Creena look towards the kitchen. Inside, she could see her father's tall, bony figure silhouetted against the window.

'If we had only put a stop to this nonsense sooner, instead of letting her fill her head with silly notions...'

Her mother's voice cut in, quiet but oddly clipped:

'I have told you, George, Creena is not going to London, letter or no letter.'

Letter? Creena stiffened, and a black tide of anger rose up inside her. That letter had been in her pocket ever since it arrived. She hadn't shown it to anyone, not even Frankie or Máire. The only way they could know about it was if her mother had been through her coat pockets . . . How dare she!

'You see?' Amy's plaintive voice broke through Creena's resentment. 'Father shouted at me and Tommy, but it's *you* he's angry with.'

Creena took a deep breath.

'Don't worry. I'll sort it out.'

She hesitated on the doorstep for a moment. Could she sort it out? She would jolly well have to, for everyone's sake.

Summoning up all her reserves of determination, she pushed open the front door and walked along the stone-flagged passageway to the kitchen.

'Hello, Mother, Father.'

Caught in the middle of their recriminations, Ida and George Quilliam froze, their eyes fixed accusingly on their elder daughter. Creena seized the opportunity to take the offensive.

'It wasn't right,' she said quietly, 'going through my pockets like that.'

'And is it right for a daughter to conceal things from her parents?' demanded George.

'I'm sorry,' said Creena. 'Truly I am. I wanted to tell you . . .'

'How could you, Creena?' Ida's voice was tinged with bitterness and Creena noticed for the first time how tired her mother looked, her eyes rimmed with red. 'How could you go behind our backs?'

Creena could feel her heart thumping in her chest. This was the first time in her life that she had really defied her parents, stood up for what she wanted to do.

'I'm sorry,' she repeated, 'but you were so angry when I told you I wanted to be a nurse. And it's what I want to do, it really is.'

'I have told you, Creena. Nursing is not a suitable occupation . . .' began George, but Creena astonished him by cutting him short.

'Nursing is what I want to do,' she said firmly. 'Please try to understand. I so want you to be happy for me, but I'm not going to give up now. With or without your approval, I'm going to be a nurse.'

'Well! I never thought one o'clock would come,' commented Máire as she and Creena walked down the front steps of Gelling and Craine's Athol Street offices. 'I don't know about you, but I don't want to take any more shorthand dictation, not ever!'

'That Mr Craine!' chuckled Creena, pulling on her crocheted summer gloves. 'He's such a nice man, but he will dictate with his head out of the window, and he doesn't understand when you can't read it all back.'

They strolled down through the town, heading for the seafront. On this mid-July day Douglas was thronged with tourists and day-trippers. Most would never venture outside Douglas, mused Creena, watching a small group of rowdy Lancastrians jostling and laughing outside a public house. They would never know anything of the rural world that lay beyond the gaily painted boarding houses and the amiable vulgarity of Strand Street's penny bazaars.

'Still, there's a lot worse things than being a shorthand-typist,' observed Máire, thinking back to her former life in Ireland: the life which no one on the island but she and Padraig really knew about. 'Speaking of which, what about your application? Have you had an answer from the hospital yet?'

'They've offered me a place. For September.'

'Well, isn't that marvellous!' Máire's dark eyes sparkled with genuine pleasure. 'Not that I won't miss you terribly, though.'

'I'm beginning to wonder if I ought not to go,' replied Creena.

'Not go! Of course you're going. You *must*, now they've offered you a place. It's such a wonderful opportunity for you.'

'Yes, I suppose you're right.' There was a hint of doubt in Creena's voice. 'It's just that it's causing so much trouble at home. I had a dreadful row with Mother and Father last night. They're so certain they know what's best for me.'

'Parents,' sighed Máire sympathetically.

Creena turned to her friend.

'What about you? Do you think I'm doing the right thing?'

Máire smiled.

'If you're sure it's what you want, then it's the right thing.' She patted Creena on the shoulder. 'And what's more, you'll make a fine nurse.'

'You really think so?'

'I'm positive. You just wait and see how proud your mam and dad are when you qualify!'

53

They strolled together down Victoria Street, past the Jubilee Clock and on to the Loch Promenade. A horse tram clip-clopped lazily past, filled with chattering holiday-makers. It was the sort of July day which would have been oppressive anywhere but on the island. A light breeze was rippling in off the Irish Sea, and the faintest haze of mist hung over the horizon, blurring the thin blue line between sea and sky. The water looked like textured glass, its surface oily and placid.

The two girls walked into the sunken gardens and settled themselves down to enjoy their packed lunches. Creena sat back on the bench and let the sun soothe her with its gentle fingers. Slowly she scanned the scene around her. To her left, Douglas Bay curved round to form Onchan Head, a tall headland dotted with hotels and skirted by the electric railway, whose Victorian carriages began their long journey at Derby Castle and carried their passengers north along the coast to Laxey, Ramsey and the summit of Snaefell.

Behind her ran the long sweep of promenade with its horse trams and hotels; and directly in front, a short distance offshore on Conister Rock, the curious little Tower of Refuge rose up out of the sea; a miniature castle built in the previous century to shelter shipwrecked sailors.

Gazing out to her right, beyond the crowded beach, Creena could see one of the Steam Packet ferries and a cargo ship loading kippers at the quayside. As she watched, a fishing boat glided towards the inner harbour, and casting her eyes upwards, she made out the Grand Union Camera Obscura on Douglas Head, and a painted sign advertising 'Feldman's Songsters'.

Creena could remember one or two golden afternoons in her childhood, when the family had come to Douglas in a charabanc to see the pierrots and the concert parties on Douglas Head. In those days, before the motor buses came to the island, a trip into Douglas from Ballakeeill had been a very special treat indeed.

Nowadays, of course, Creena had to travel into Douglas practically every day and it had rather lost its novelty. And much as she loved the island, *her* island, she longed for a change of scene; a chance to find out what was happening in the rest of the world, and to live in a place where her face wasn't instantly recognised wherever she went.

'I saw Mona Mylchreest the other day,' remarked Máire, biting into a sandwich. 'She looked . . . well, you know . . .'

Creena looked at Máire quizzically.

'How do you mean?'

Máire leaned a little closer.

'You mean you haven't noticed?'

'Noticed what?'

'Her skirts are looking awful tight these days. If you ask me, she's expecting again. Hasn't she said anything to you?'

'No. No, nothing.'

'I expect she'll be pleased. And Duggie too, of course.'

Creena was unconvinced. In fact, she felt downright uneasy at the thought that Mona might be expecting. Mona and Duggie didn't seem to be getting on at all well lately, and what with all the drinking he'd been doing, she wasn't sure that Duggie was capable of being pleased about anything.

'Yes, I expect so,' she said, hoping Máire couldn't hear the note of doubt in her voice.

'So there you are! Sure an' I thought I'd never catch up with you.'

The familiar rich, mellow voice made Creena and Máire look up. Sure enough it was Padraig, his chunky, muscular body half blotting out the sunlight as he stood before them, hands on hips.

He was a good-looking man, there was no doubt about that, mused Creena. With his dark hair, deeply tanned skin and velvety-brown eyes, his craggy features gave just the faintest hint of the gypsy. His collarless linen work-shirt was open at the neck, the sleeves rolled up to the elbow to reveal powerful forearms marked here and there with the small scars of burns from the forge where he worked. He seemed a little out of breath as though he had been running.

'Padraig!' exclaimed Máire. 'I thought you were working up at the tram stables.'

'An' I was, to be sure. But then I came lookin' for you.'

'Why don't you sit down?' suggested Creena, shuffling along the bench a little to make room for him. But Padraig shook his head, wiping his bare forearm over his perspiring forehead.

'Thanks all the same, but I can't stop. I just wanted a word with Máire, then I must be off back to my work. One of the tram-horses has been taken awful sick, and I said I'd stay late to look after it.'

'Ah, you always did have a way with the horses,' smiled Máire. 'Isn't that right, Creena?'

But Creena wasn't listening. She was gazing dreamily across the bay at the Steam Packet ferry, readying itself for the afternoon sailing.

The ferry that would carry her across the water to a whole new life.

At Maynrys, the Mylchreest farm over Kewaigue way, Mona waited for the clock to tick past midnight and usher in another miserable, insupportable day.

Sitting in the kitchen with her hands around a cold cup of tea, she listened to the sounds of the night; the screech of an owl, the little scratching sounds the rats made in the coal cellar. The Manx had a special dread of rats, insisting that they must be referred to as 'Long Tails' or 'Big Fellers', and paying a bounty of twopence per tail to the local rat-catchers. But at this moment Mona couldn't understand why the rats were so hated. They were better company, by far, than Duggie Mylchreest.

How could she have been so stupid as to marry him? She should have known he was a bad lot from the first, with his free-spending ways and his fondness for the bottle. But she'd been stupid at twenty-two and now she was stupid at thirty-two. What other explanation could there be for her disastrous affair with Davey Cashin?

It still stung, the memory of Davey's rejection. But anger had long since taken the place of the passive hurt, and Mona was up and fighting – fighting for herself and for her children, present and unborn.

She glanced down at the table and a great black wave of

depression and resentment washed over her. How could Duggie do this to her? She had trusted him, and what had he done with his inheritance? Frittered it away on drink and other women, that's what. Maynrys Farm was one of the largest in the district; it ought to be prospering, not heading towards ruin. But Duggie had sacked his farm manager, and now he seemed bent on a headlong rush towards bankruptcy. The scattering of unpaid bills and threatening letters from the Isle of Man Bank filled her with despair and rage. She wasn't going to let him get away with this.

At last she heard the latch click and the outer door opened. A moment later Duggie lurched through into the hall, his breath hoarse and rasping as it always was when he had drunk too much. He wouldn't be falling-over drunk, of course; just far enough gone to make her life a misery.

He punched open the door of the kitchen but Mona was on her feet and ready for him. She wasn't going to cower any more.

'What time do you call this?' she demanded icily.

Duggie stared at her blearily for a few seconds, then his veiny, blotched-red face cracked into a leer and he burst out laughing.

'Waitin' up for me, are ye? That makes a change. Not lockin' me out of your bedroom tonight, then?'

He stretched out a lascivious hand but Mona took a step backwards, pulling her cardigan more tightly around her as though it had the power to protect her. Her voice was quavering but she forced herself to act out the bravery she did not feel. She knew what those sausage-fingered hands could do to her. It was lucky he was drunk.

'It's almost one o'clock in the morning, Duggie. Where have you been?'

With a drunk's volatility, Duggie's predatory leer turned to an angry scowl.

'It's none of your business where I've been. I'm the head of this household, you're just the skivvy. Now get me my supper. Where's my supper?'

'If you're the head of the household, why don't you act like one? Why don't you face up to your responsibilities? You'll get nothing more from me until you do.'

'Shut your mouth, woman!'

Duggie swung a haymaker of a punch at her, but she dodged his fist and he lurched against the York range, crying out in rage and pain as his bare skin touched the hot metal of the hob.

'Bitch,' he gasped, clutching his wounded arm.

'I suppose you've been out with one of your women, have you? Which one was it this time? That fat barmaid, or her mother? You don't give a damn, do you? You're just a pathetic drunk.'

'My God, woman, look at yourself. Look at the shrew I married! At least when I go out I get my bit of fun . . .'

'Fun! Is that what you call it? Well, like it or not you're a married man, Duggie Mylchreest. A married man and a father. And it's time to face up to that fact.'

'Oh, an' you're goin' to make me, are you?'

'Not me, Duggie. But maybe the new baby will.'

'Baby! What the . . . ?'

Mona drew her hand across her swelling stomach. It was four months, going on five now. Incredible that it should have gone on so long without Duggie noticing. But these days Duggie only noticed her if he wanted to give her a good hiding. Well, not any longer. For the child's sake she was going to stand up for herself.

'Yes, Duggie. A baby. I'm expecting again.'

She waited for his reaction. If she was lucky, maybe . . . But Duggie wasn't that drunk. She could see the cogwheels grinding in his brain, the changes in his expression as he put two and two together. She anticipated the storm and, sure enough, it came.

'So you're expectin'. What's it got to do with me if you're up the stick?'

'You're my husband, Duggie.'

'Oh aye, but I'm not its father, am I?' Duggie leant over the table, his beery face inches from hers; but Mona did not flinch. For some reason she had ceased to fear this bully of a man. 'How many months is it since you let me? Tell me that. How many months is it since we even shared the same bed?'

It was true. Mona could remember the last night she'd capitulated to Duggie's physical demands, and the experience had left her so scarred – mentally and physically – that she had taken to locking him out of the bedroom. It hadn't been difficult – he was usually too drunk to notice, and fell asleep slumped over the kitchen table.

'You're a filthy whore, Mona. A filthy, poxy whore.'

'Oh, and what does that make you, Duggie Mylchreest? You and your fancy women?'

His hand shot out and grabbed her by the arm, his fingers gripping so tightly that they made marks in the skin. She winced, but he wouldn't let go. Now, for the first time, she began to feel the fear again.

'Whose is it?'

Mona kept silent.

'I said, whose is it?' He squeezed tighter and then, with the other hand, suddenly grabbed a handful of Mona's curly blonde hair, twisting and wrenching it with such ferocity that she let out an involuntary sob of distress. But she stood firm. 'It's none of your damn business.'

Exasperated, he pushed her away, with such force that she stumbled and almost lost her balance. Leaning against the mantelpiece, she curled her fingers surreptitiously around the heaviest, sharpest thing she could find; a brass figurine of an elephant that Duggie's great-uncle had brought back from India. Family heirloom or not, she wouldn't hesitate to hit him with it if he tried to lay another finger on her.

But she didn't need to defend herself. Drink was channelling Duggie's aggressions into a new direction. An expression of malevolent satisfaction was spreading over his once handsome, now drink-bloated face.

'I know whose it is, you little whore. It's no good trying to defend him.'

Mona's heart beat faster. This was the one thing she feared – Duggie finding out the identity of her secret lover. Davey Cashin may have rejected her, but she didn't want him harmed. Nor did she want her indiscretions trumpeted all over the island.

'You don't know. You're just guessing.'

'Oh no.' Duggie's voice became suddenly quiet and menacingly calm. 'I know who it is all right. It's that bloody farm manager I sacked back in May, isn't it?'

'No, Duggie . . .'

'It's no good denying it. It's him all right. You thought I didn't notice, but I saw the way he looked at you. Well, you needn't think the two of you are getting away with it. Betraying me behind my back . . .'

'Look, Duggie. Just stop and listen . . .'

But it was no use. Duggie was already picking up the thick iron poker from the hearth and tucking it under his coat. She dashed forward to stop him, her mind whirling, but he pushed her aside and she went down like a rag doll, her arms curled over her stomach to protect the child within her. Whatever else he did to her, he wasn't going to harm her innocent baby.

And in any case it wasn't Mona he intended to harm – or at least not yet. First he had other fish to fry. First, he had to find the bastard who'd put his wife in the family way, and teach him a lesson he'd never forget.

Ida Quilliam stooped to place a plate of thickly sliced fruit bonnag on the small table beside Mona's chair, and the young woman looked up and gave her a smile, the mellow August sunshine turning her blonde hair into a halo of light about her pretty but haggard face.

It wasn't a broad, carefree smile like when Mona was a girl, thought Ida sadly. All the ebullience that had bèen so characteristic of Mona seemed to have evaporated over the last few years, culminating in the scandal last week when Duggie Mylchreest had been up before the bench in Castletown, accused of beating up his former farm manager so severely that the poor lad was still in Noble's Hospital.

'Eat it up,' said Ida, nudging Mona's hand towards the

plate of bonnag, the fruited bun made to an age-old Manx recipe. It was still warm from the oven, a thick smearing of butter melting around its crisp edges. 'You need all your strength now, what with the two little ones and another baby on the way.'

'I ... I'm not really very hungry,' protested Mona weakly, her blue eyes sore from the sleepless nights and the crying. But Ida wasn't about to take no for an answer.

'Let the girl be,' grunted George Quilliam from behind his copy of *The Isle of Man Times*.

'She needs her nourishment,' replied Ida tartly.

'If she doesn't want to eat, it's no good making her.'

'Nonsense,' replied Ida. 'She hardly ate enough dinner for a sparrow. Just try one slice, Mona love. It's fresh out of the oven.' She cast her elder daughter a steely glance. 'Creena – pour Mona some more tea; her cup is empty.'

Creena got up from her chair and refilled Mona's cup, then Amy's. Robert was lounging by the window, reading some legal papers, and Tommy was having his hated piano lesson in the parlour with Mrs Gorry. The most horrible noises were drifting through the schoolhouse, as though a three-legged cat had fallen on to the open piano keyboard and was chasing a mouse up and down it.

Creena sometimes thought that Tommy's execrable piano-playing was revenge for being made to have lessons in the first place. Someone – Ida probably – had had the idea that Tommy was going to be musical and that had been the end of the argument. Well, there was one argument her mother wasn't going to win, thought Creena grimly.

She perched herself on her mother's prized sofa with the

tasselled velvet cushions, watching as Mona started eating and Ida's stern expression relaxed a little. It was all very odd, this business with Duggie and the farm manager. Some of the details had come out at the trial, of course, but Creena still had the distinct feeling that something remained unsaid.

It seemed that Duggie – in a drunken rage – had lurched off into the night after Kieran Grant, the Scottish farm manager he had dismissed a few weeks before after a huge public row. Duggie, according to his testimony in court, had been convinced that Grant had embezzled money from the farm accounts, and blamed him for the general decline of Maynrys Farm – although the whole island knew perfectly well by now that the real reason for that was Duggie's fondness for drink and women.

Kieran Grant had seemed quite baffled by the attack, and there was no doubt that he was innocent of any blame. But Creena kept looking at Mona and thinking that her cousin must be hiding something – perhaps she was misguidedly trying to protect Duggie by concealing some information about him which would ruin his once-heroic reputation for good. Perhaps she just didn't want everyone knowing that Kieran Grant hadn't been the only victim of Duggie's violent temper.

At any rate, Duggie had been lucky in the circumstances. There was still some respect on the island for the good, hard-working man he had once been, before drink took its hold on him. The court had given him a choice. He could go to prison, or he could make himself useful, redeem himself – and keep the scandalous story out of the Manx newspapers.

The nation needed brave men in this time of impending war, and Manxmen must be prepared to do their bit as they had done so many times before. In short, Duggie could go to jail or he could enlist in the Manx Regiment. It couldn't have been a difficult choice for him to make – and he had seemed quite eager to get away from the island and the responsibilities he had been so unfit to handle.

Ida sat herself down in her favourite armchair, next to George, and took a sip of tea from a good bone-china cup – one of the ones she kept for special occasions. A visit from Mona wouldn't normally be considered sufficiently important, but in view of the tragic circumstances, getting out the good china seemed the least that Ida could do. They would all have to rally round the girl now that she was alone on that farm with two children and another on the way.

'So how are you feeling?' Ida enquired. 'Now that you have had a little time to get over the shock.'

Mona took a sip of Ida's robust tea.

'Oh, you know . . . not so bad.' She patted her stomach and gave a wry smile. 'I must keep going for Jessie and Voirrey – and this new little one. It will be difficult to keep the farm going, of course. Now that Duggie's gone away . . .'

She hadn't seen Duggie since the day of the trial, and he hadn't even glanced at her as he was led away to the cells. Any day now, he would be on his way to the mainland, to start his basic training. Good riddance, thought Mona. It'll be difficult but I'll manage somehow. If I can just keep the secret safe for all our sakes . . .

There was a rustling noise as George Quilliam lowered

his newspaper and peered at Mona over the top of his round, tortoiseshell-rimmed glasses.

'That scoundrel should have had twelve good strokes of the birch and a year in Douglas Gaol. That would have cooled his temper. It is unforgivable that a man like that – a man who has jeopardised the future of his own wife and children and dragged an honourable family name through the mire – that such a man should be permitted to escape his just punishment.'

Creena noticed that Mona's cheeks went quite red when George talked about honour and punishment.

'No, no,' protested Mona. 'Really, I think it's best the way things are. The way things have worked out.'

'I'm sure you're right,' agreed Creena, feeling a sisterly solidarity with Mona. Why must her father be so bombastic?

'Steady on, Dad,' butted in Robert, raising his normally placid blond head from his papers. 'What good would it do Mona if they put Duggie in prison? At least if he's a soldier she'll get an allowance. What is it – seventeen bob a week and another seven deducted from his wages?'

'Violence is the only thing a man like that can understand,' George insisted grimly.

Ida laid her hand on George's arm.

'Perhaps the Manx Regiment will make a man of him,' she said. 'Duggie has made his choice and we must all have hope for the future.'

Ida surveyed Mona's swelling stomach and wondered about the future of the child within – the child who might be the son Duggie had always longed for. A child who might well be born into the middle of a terrible war.

That set her to thinking about Creena, the silly head-strong girl, insisting on taking herself off to London of all places, and now of all times.

As if in answer to her thoughts, Mona enquired innocently:

'So when are you off to London, Cree?'

Creena caught her mother's disapproving eye. Obviously Ida was regretting her grudging acceptance of the inevitable.

'Soon. The end of September.'

'*If* she goes,' grunted George. 'She'll probably change her mind.'

'Father, I'm going. I've told the hospital I'll be there. I've made the arrangements.'

'Arrangements can be unmade,' George pointed out.

'And what if war breaks out?' demanded Ida. 'What then?'

'Then I'll be needed even more.'

Ida stiffened.

'If war breaks out you will be much more use here. I cannot imagine who gave you the idea that you would make a good professional nurse. And think of the danger . . .' Now there was a note of slight desperation in Ida's voice.

'Mother, I'll be all right, really . . .'

George folded his newspaper with a disgruntled sigh and laid it on the table, placing his spectacles carefully on top. There would be no peace for him tonight.

'There will be no war,' he announced, his eyes sweeping the room as though challenging anyone to disagree.

'That's not what the papers say,' observed Robert

calmly. 'And Chamberlain hasn't a clue – Hitler's just playing games with him.'

Sitting in the sun by the window, Robert thought back to another August, five years before, when he had travelled through Spain before the outbreak of the Civil War. Hitler's bombers had made a terrible mess of that beautiful country – and Robert saw no reason why the same shouldn't happen to Poland, France, even Britain.

Yes, war was coming all right. It was just a question of when.

Chapter 5

It was Sunday, 3 September 1939. A fine, clear Sunday at the tail end of summer, in that glorious time when the August heat had mellowed but the frosts had not yet begun. In Farmer Duggan's orchard, apples and pears swelled and weighed down the branches on which they hung, drawing their sweetness from the scented country air.

Normally at this time on a fine Sunday morning, the main road which ran through the village would be dotted with vehicles – the odd horse and cart, maybe a bicycle or two or a Happy Days motor coach; but on this particular Sunday morning there were few signs of life.

Even old Billy Callister, wizened landlord of the Cummal Beg Inn, was absent from his usual post. Come sun or drizzle, you would find Billy leaning on his front gate with his braces hanging down and his white beard – yellow in patches from the evil smoke of his briar pipe – reaching below the waistband of his ancient and very shiny trousers.

But there was no sign of Billy today – no, nor of Nancy Shimmin. The front door of the General Stores was firmly locked and bolted, and only a hand-written poster advertising the harvest Mhelliah remained as a reminder that life must and would go on.

Behind closed doors, the inhabitants of Ballakeeill waited beside their wireless sets for the announcement they knew would come. Hadn't the British Government given Herr Hitler an ultimatum? The threat of war had been in the air for over a year now, but through all those long months it had somehow dulled and become unreal – like a music-hall joke worn stale. Even the pamphlets about gas attacks and rationing had seemed to belong to some other world.

The funny thing was that the Isle of Man had never got round to signing a peace treaty with Germany in 1918 – so technically they were still at war anyway. Oh yes, it was funny all right. But no one was laughing. Now, with a horrible suddenness, the idea of war had become all too real and all too imminent.

The autumn term would soon be under way at Ballakeeill School, but George Quilliam's thoughts could not have been further from inkwells and chalk. As he sat in the parlour with his family, clustered together around the wireless, his mind drifted back to 1914, when he had joined up as an idealistic young father.

He had had it easy, with hindsight he knew that. Many of his friends had died in the stinking mud of Passchendaele and the Somme whilst he had been working behind the lines as a supply orderly – passed unfit for front-line service because of the diphtheria he'd suffered as a child. But at the time it had seemed like hell on earth, unimaginably more horrible than the tales of scarlet-coated gallantry his grandfather had told him. It was only now, at twenty years' distance, that middle-aged men could look back on what they had done and put a gloss of nostalgia upon it.

George Quilliam was a proud man. He was not accustomed to the sensation of fear, and still less to admitting to it. But in the dark secrecy of the night he thought of his brave son, who was so eager to fight, and his stubborn daughter, who still refused to be dissuaded from her foolishness. This coming war, which he had tried so hard to deny, was already reaching out cold fingers to touch them all.

Ida sat very close beside him on the sofa, their shoulders touching – the only token of intimacy they allowed themselves in the presence of their children. In any case, Ida felt curiously isolated and alone today. Around her sat her family, yet she felt as though a glass barrier were slowly solidifying between and around them, so that in a few moments, maybe less, she would no longer be able to reach out and touch them.

Emotions surged and tumbled inside her, like a turbulent sea that threatened to engulf her. But she wouldn't let anyone see her fears – as usual she would disguise them as anger, and she would be praised for being brave and fierce and capable.

She glanced nervously at the heavy blackout curtains, freshly hung at every window, and the neatly crisscrossed strips of sticky paper, designed to limit the amount of flying glass should a bomb blast shatter the panes. No, no, no – she wouldn't allow this to happen. She couldn't allow anything to happen if it threatened to split up her family and take them away from her.

It seemed to her that if she only thought hard enough, believed hard enough, the announcement might never happen and there would be no war, just like George said there wouldn't. But in unguarded moments her thoughts returned to Mona, alone in the empty farmhouse at Kewaigue. Would she soon be alone, too?

The whole of Robert's athletic body was on the alert. Like a sprinter crouching in the starting blocks, he sat forward on his chair, elbows on his knees and chin resting in his cupped hands. On the other side of the room Tommy was frightening his young sister Amy with his 'bang-bang you're dead' routine, but George seemed oblivious to the scene and Robert didn't have the heart to tell Tommy to shut up.

Robert's thoughts were strangely mixed. In the beginning it had all been so easy, so cut and dried. If war broke out he would volunteer straight away, as his father had done in the Great War. He loved the island and yet really, truly, there was nothing holding him here, no special person, no reason for him to hold off and wait for conscription to make up his mind for him. Now, though, with war just a hair's-breadth away, he was beginning to wonder if he'd been right telling everyone that he was going to join up. There was a trace of hesitancy inside him. Was it fear? Common sense? Or was it just that he knew things would never be quite the same again?

Robert's eyes flicked across to Creena and she smiled at him, the smile a little anxious, but the eyes warm. There was at least the beginning of an understanding between them – an understanding that George and Ida Quilliam could not share. Creena knew how it was to feel different, special. He would miss his kid sister when he went away. But it wouldn't change anything. The day after war was declared, Robert Quilliam would take himself to the recruiting office in Douglas.

Creena shifted uneasily in her chair. She didn't know quite how to feel. Here she was, about to take the biggest and most exciting step of her entire life, and suddenly the world was going mad. All at once her great adventure was assuming new and frightening proportions and yet she couldn't – *wouldn't* – give it up.

She glanced across at Amy. She and her even-tempered, perfectly behaved sister couldn't be more different. Whilst all Amy dreamed of was a cottage and a regiment of little Manx children, Creena longed for escape. And besides: if Robert could do his bit, so could she.

George Quilliam consulted his watch. Five to eleven. With a rock-steady hand, he reached out and switched the wireless on to warm up. A few minutes later, the Prime Minister informed the nation that Britain was at war with Germany.

A few days later, Robert collected Creena from her office and took her to lunch at a café near the Villa Marina.

'You haven't changed your mind then?'

Creena smiled.

'No.'

'So you're really going?'

'I'm going.'

Robert gave a low whistle of admiration and laid his knife and fork across his half-empty plate.

'I've got to hand it to you, sis, you're a plucky one. I never thought you'd do it.'

Creena took a sip of water.

'I *have* to do it. You understand that, don't you?'

Robert gave her hand a small squeeze.

'Dad treats you like a kid, and Ma . . . well, I know what she's like when she doesn't get her own way. They've been beastly to you. I'm not surprised you want to get away from them.'

'It's not just Mother and Father.' Creena speared a piece of lettuce with her fork. 'I need to get away from the island, too.'

'And what about Frank?' Robert's eyes never left Creena's. He sensed that she wanted to talk. 'Do you need to get away from him?'

A shadow crept across Creena's face.

'I . . . it's not that I don't care about him, you know.'

'Will you miss him?'

'Of course I will, and I don't want to lose him. But I can't . . .' She put down her fork. 'I can't be what he wants me to be – what everyone in the village seems to want me to be. At least not yet.'

'It's all right, Cree, I understand.' Better than you realise, thought Robert. 'It's hard when people want you to be something you're not. They end up disappointed and you end up feeling guilty.'

'Mother says I should settle down, but I can't. Sometimes I feel as if I don't exist except in other people's dreams, but I have dreams, too. I need a chance to be myself before I can be somebody's wife.' She stopped abruptly, as though

74

surprised at her own determination. 'Does that make sense?'

'Perfect sense. Have you tried explaining it to Frank?'

'Oh, I've tried. He changes the subject.'

'Sometimes it's simpler to avoid talking about things.' Robert pushed his plate away. 'It stops you being afraid.'

'Are you afraid? About joining up?'

Robert looked her squarely in the eye.

'I'd be a fool if I wasn't.'

'But you haven't had any second thoughts?'

For her sake, he lied.

'None at all. And neither should you, Creena. We're both just doing what we have to do.'

These last, late September evenings were so precious, thought Creena as she walked with Máire, Padraig and Frank towards Ballakeeill church hall. The air was balmy and still, not yet tinged by the bite of the autumn frosts which would soon bring a familiar chill to the Manx weather.

'What will you do?' Frank asked Padraig. 'Now that they're selling off the tram-horses?'

'Oh, there'll be other work,' replied Padraig. 'Though 'twould be easier to find, no doubt, if I was a Manxman.'

Frank gave a sympathetic nod. As a police constable, he knew that there was anti-Irish feeling in some quarters. Hadn't that Juan Kerruish been spreading rumours about spies on the Irish cattle boats?

'It's a damn shame,' he commented. He thought of his own problems with Sergeant Maddrell. 'Some people haven't the sense they were born with.'

'Ah, but there are plenty of good-hearted Manx folk who'll judge a man on the quality of his work.'

'Of course they will.' Máire slid her arm through Padraig's. 'You're the finest farrier on the island.'

Old Billy Callister was standing outside the door of the church hall, taking a last puff on his old briar pipe before going inside.

'Good weather they had for the harvest,' observed Padraig.

''Twas all brought in safe,' nodded old Billy. 'And we shall be needin' it all and more if this war goes on long. Starve us out, Hitler will, given half a chance.'

Frank patted him on the shoulder.

'I don't think it'll come to that, Billy.'

'Yes, I'm sure it'll all be over soon,' agreed Creena.

'Ach, that's what they said about the first lot,' replied Billy, spitting on the ground reflectively. 'Said that one'd be over by Christmas, an' all.'

'Let's go in,' Máire suggested, uneasy at the direction the conversation was taking.

'Yes, let's.' Creena nudged Frank forward and they entered the church hall. 'The Mhelliah will be starting soon.'

Every year Ballakeeill held a harvest celebration, or Mhelliah – an ancient custom which had recently been revived and which offered the whole village a splendid opportunity for a party.

The centre of the village hall had been cleared, except for a single large wooden chair. Around the edges of the hall were trestle tables and benches, and one enormous table groaning with food and drink.

'Sit down, sit down,' Nancy Shimmin urged them. 'If you're not quick you won't get a seat.'

Dutifully the four friends squeezed on to the end of one of the benches.

To begin the festivities, two villagers held a rope taut across the open doorway. An old man threw a fistful of coins over the rope and into the hall, with a shout of 'Cur argid son y Mhelliah!'

'What's happening?' Máire whispered to Creena.

'He's ransoming the harvest,' Creena explained.

'Who are those people?'

'The young girl in the pretty dress and the wreath of flowers is the harvest queen – the Ben-Rein ny Mhelliah – and that young man is carrying the last sheaf of the harvest.'

'And that thing there,' Frank indicated a bundle swathed in a white sheet, 'that's a sort of corn dolly – the Babban ny Mhelliah. It'll be kept safe until the next harvest.'

As they watched, the harvest queen was led to her throne – the old wooden chair – and the Babban ny Mhelliah was placed in her arms. Then dancers formed a circle about her and the little village band struck up a jig as the villagers clapped their hands in time to the music.

As the familiar events unrolled before her eyes, it suddenly occurred to Creena that she might never see this scene again. How many of the young people gathered in this village hall would still be on the island in six months' time, in a year? How many would return to Ballakeeill when it was all over – and would she be among them?

She stole a glance at Frank, unable to get this afternoon out of her mind.

It had been an ordinary enough visit to the Kinrades'

croft, a mile or so outside Ballakeeill. She had made many such visits before but always, in the past, there had been the promise that she would return. This time, there could be no promises.

After tea, as Frank was walking back to the schoolhouse with her, he stopped and took hold of her hands.

'Creena, you will miss me, won't you?'

It had taken her a long time, too long, to reply. She knew that he wanted her to say something, anything, that would give him a chance to pour out his heart to her. Oh, she wanted to make him happy, but the words just stuck in her throat. Give me time, she wanted to say, just give me time to do everything I long to do, and I'll come back to you, really I will. But instead she'd just smiled, and replied:

'I'll miss you all.'

How could she have been so cruel?

'Up the Mhelliah!' cried the villagers, and at last it was time for supper and the dancing that would go on far into the night.

Creena reached out and slipped her arm through Frankie's, all at once glad of the warmth that radiated out from him, a single reassuring certainty in a world full of change.

It was the last week of September already, and very soon Creena Quilliam the schoolmaster's daughter would be Probationer Nurse Quilliam, of the Royal Lambeth Hospital.

Creena wished heartily that these last hours at home would not drag so slowly. She hadn't slept well; lying awake for hours listening to the cracking and groaning of the roof timbers, contracting as they cooled in the night air. At last she had got up and walked over to the window of her attic room, to look out on to the peaceful, moonlit hills.

Unable to get back to sleep, she re-read the cards and letters she had received wishing her well in her new life. There was a funny, jolly one from Robert, who was going to be a navigator and was now at an RAF training camp in England; a slightly emotional one from Máire; cards from Mrs Shimmin and Billy Callister, and one on which some of the schoolchildren had scrawled their childish good wishes.

The letter and fob watch from Mureal Gelling meant a lot to her. Mureal had been through it all before her; she too had overcome her parents' disapproval to do what she felt was right for her. And now, whilst Ida and George Quilliam remained distinctly unimpressed by their daughter's ambitions, Mureal was telling her to be true to herself – just as Uncle John would have done, if only he had lived to see this day.

Frank was on duty, and wouldn't be able to come to Douglas to see her off. He had given her a card, a lucky silver charm and an embroidered lace handkerchief that his father had brought back from Ypres. At first, Creena had felt terribly sad. But the more she thought about it, the more she concluded that it was perhaps a good thing for him not to come. She might weaken, turn tail and come home.

The morning dragged abominably. Creena had to check and recheck her packing again and again under the watchful eye of her mother, who ticked off each item against a never-ending list.

'Five pairs of drawers,' she intoned.

'Yes, Mother,' sighed Creena, who had packed and unpacked her suitcase so many times that she knew the list off by heart.

She had wanted five pairs of those rather nice lace-trimmed knickers in artificial silk which Máire had bought at Marks and Spencer in Strand Street – or at least a couple for best. But Ida had insisted on coming shopping with her, so Creena had ended up with the most hideous collection of liberty bodices, sensible slips and woollen drawers imaginable. The drawers were almost as bad as the khaki horrors the Reverend Cullen's daughter had to wear in the ATS.

'Stockings – six pairs,' continued Ida Quilliam.

Creena dutifully counted them out. Six pairs of thick black stockings in cotton lisle, plus a needle and plenty of thread to darn them. Student nurses, unlike servicewomen, were responsible for buying their own uniform shoes and stockings, so regular repairs were essential – though Ida despaired of her daughter's amateurish attempts. How ever would she manage on her own in London? Ida could only hope that George was right and that Creena would be back home within six months.

'Four uniform dresses in grey cambric.'

'Yes.'

'Two pairs of black lace-up shoes.'

'Yes, Mother,' replied Creena, hardly paying attention to Ida's chatter and bustle. In the schoolroom next door, the infant class were learning 'Ellan Vannin', pausing every few bars to repeat the piece until at last they got it right.

Creena dearly wished that they would sing something else. Even when the children went out to play, she could hear their shrill voices chanting the familiar words in her head: 'My own dear Ellan Vannin, with its green hills by the sea . . . its green hills by the sea . . .'

At long last it was time to leave for Douglas to catch the afternoon sailing to Liverpool. George was reluctantly taking a half-day's leave of absence, and leaving the school in the capable hands of his deputy, Miss McGregor. The Quilliams had no car, so Farmer Duggan had agreed to drive Creena and her parents to the harbour. This in itself had not improved George's frame of mind. He had never much liked John Duggan, and he particularly disliked having to be indebted to him.

They duly piled into the farmer's mud-spattered car and Creena said her farewells to her younger brother and sister.

'You will still come home sometimes, won't you?'

'Of course I will!' Creena embraced her tearful younger sister, stroking her long dark-blonde hair with an affectionate hand. She hoped Amy wouldn't notice that her hand was shaking. Saying goodbye was harder than she had expected. 'I'll be home on leave in no time at all, just you wait and see.'

'Write and tell me what it's like on the train to London,' Tommy butted in. 'And the Underground . . .' Tommy had never been off the island, and longed for adventures of his own.

All of a sudden, things started happening very quickly – events jumbling up together in a heap, as though time were an express train which had accelerated with a sudden jolt. Ballakeeill schoolhouse, the fuchsia-lined lane, the grey slate roofs of Cummal Beg and the village store, the distant tower of the little white church ... all these things were slipping far, far behind and the car was speeding towards Douglas with a breathtaking inevitability.

George Quilliam sat in the front seat, next to John Duggan, and kept looking very straight ahead of him. He said nothing, though inside he felt hurt and betrayed. Some things were private, best left unsaid – especially in front of strangers.

By contrast, Ida chattered nonstop from Ballakeeill to Douglas, her incessant bluster concealing the very real anxieties she felt for her elder daughter. How on earth did Creena get these foolish fancies? The silly girl had no sense at all. Wasn't it bad enough that Robert, her precious first-born, had gone off to join the RAF? Why couldn't Creena be more like Amy, and understand that she had duties and responsibilities at home?

'You will write regularly. At least once a week.'

'Yes, Mother.'

'You will go to bed at a reasonable hour.'

'Mother ... !'

'You will not partake of strong drink.'

Creena felt her colour rising. John Duggan was sneaking sidelong glances of frank bewilderment, scratching his balding head.

'And you will *not* associate with bad company.'

'I hardly think I'll have time, Mother!'

Creena was caught between laughter and indignation. She couldn't help thinking that, no matter what company she kept, it would be unlikely to please her parents. George and Ida Quilliam seemed convinced that Creena's friends were in some way responsible for their daughter's determination to go to London.

As far as she could tell, Frank was to blame because of his Italian mother and bibulous father, and Máire and Padraig because they were Irish. No doubt if George and Ida had realised just how much encouragement Cousin Mona had given her, Mona would have suffered too. It was all quite preposterous and unreasonable.

The car dipped down into Douglas. It was a cloudy, drizzly day, in keeping with the general mood in the car, and Creena felt butterflies fluttering in her stomach at the sight of the old steamer *Snaefell* making ready to sail. There was the usual bustle of people and suitcases clogging up its gangplank, and a long line of departing visitors, waving to their relatives and friends from one of the upper decks.

The tail end of summer had given way to the first days of autumn. The first days of war. There was a perceptible chill in the air as John Duggan parked the car and opened the door for Creena and her mother to get out. You could smell autumn, feel that the dark chill of winter was just over the horizon, waiting to close in. Creena pulled her smart new jacket more closely around her, picked up her overnight case and tried to shake herself free of these dark thoughts.

John Duggan unloaded the larger of Creena's suitcases from the back of the car and bent to pick it up, but George Quilliam got there first, twitching his moustache as he curled his bony fingers around the handle. He avoided Creena's eyes. This was the only gesture of support she would receive from her father, and he did not wish to seem to be condoning her actions.

'We had better make haste,' he announced, consulting his watch. 'The ship sails in half an hour.' And he strode off towards the *Snaefell*, with Creena and Ida panting in his wake.

Two policemen halted the group on the quayside.

'Identity cards, if you please.'

George gave an exasperated grunt and plonked down Creena's suitcase, rummaging in the top pocket of his coat for the folded piece of beige card and handing it over with bad grace. Ida and Creena followed suit, Creena feeling peculiarly grown-up and independent as the police constable inspected her identity card and her boat ticket. The ticket had cost the enormous sum of one pound ten shillings and sixpence – all of it money that she had saved up herself. For the first time in her life she felt like an adult – not an outgrowth of her parents but a complete person, an individual in her own right.

'Well, I think that's all in order, thank you, sir, madam.' The policeman handed back the cards with a smile. 'Now if the young lady would just like to put her case up here and open it up for me.' He indicated a low wooden table.

'Why?' enquired Creena.

'Just regulations, miss. We do have to be careful. One or two people have been caught smuggling food off the island, and then there's the Irish republicans . . .'

'How dare you suggest such things about my daughter!' George's frayed temper finally snapped. 'I am the schoolmaster at Ballakeeill and she is my daughter, surely that is all you need to know . . .'

'I'm sorry, sir. Rules are rules.'

'This is preposterous!'

'It's all right, Father, I don't mind.' Creena opened the lid of the larger case and the police constable gave it a cursory search.

'That's fine, miss. If I could just ask your reason for travelling?'

Creena felt herself grow visibly as she replied:

'I'm travelling to London to train as a nurse – at the Royal Lambeth Hospital.'

The constable's face registered instant respect as he handed her back her suitcase.

'All the best I'm sure, miss. I hope you have a safe journey.'

He stood back and the little procession continued on its way towards the gangplank, where a young mother was urging her three recalcitrant children to 'Get a move on, or it'll sail without you, you see if it doesn't.'

This was the moment of truth. The old *Snaefell* waited at its moorings, but it would not wait much longer. As though emphasising that time was running out, the ship's siren blew once, twice, the sound so powerful that it vibrated the whole of the quayside on which they stood. Two men with bowler hats and briefcases hurried past and up the gangplank on to the ship.

'I . . . I have to go now.' The words dried in Creena's throat as unexpected emotion swept over her. She fought back the tears that were welling up behind dry eyes, determined not to cry – or at least not to be seen crying. 'The ship will be sailing in a few minutes.'

'I told you we should have set out earlier,' Ida scolded her husband. She turned to Creena and produced a small brown-paper packet from her handbag. 'This is a little something for your Aunt Alexa in Liverpool. Now, you know her address, don't you – in case she's not there to meet you when you get to Pier Head?'

'Forty-two Crocus Lane,' replied Creena. 'Don't worry.'

'She'll look after you overnight, and then she'll put you on the train to . . . to . . .' Ida's mask of brusque efficiency cracked at last, and her words ended in a sob which was drowned out by the ship's siren. 'Creena – you will be careful in London, won't you?'

'I'll be careful. But I have to go . . .'

Creena gave her mother a brief hug. There was some small warmth there, but as ever Ida Quilliam found it impossible to express the affection she felt for this elder daughter who so infuriated her; perhaps because she was so like Ida had been at her age.

George Quilliam said nothing as he accepted a peck on the cheek from his daughter, and Creena did not linger. If she did, her father's seeming coldness would only upset her, make her long still more for one of Frank's firm, warm hugs.

She picked up her suitcase and stepped on to the gangplank.

'Take care of yourself, Creena-gel.' John Duggan touched
his cap respectfully.

'Thank you, I will.'

She hurried up the gangplank and stumbled on to the boat, grateful for a chance to hide her face. She didn't really mind her fellow passengers seeing the stray tear that escaped and rolled down her cheek – they were all caught up in their own little dramas and tragedies – but in her parents' presence she wanted to be brave and resolute.

Although it was a cloudy afternoon, most of the passengers were lined up on deck, hanging over the rails, shouting and waving to their loved ones on the quayside below. Creena joined them as the ropes were cast off, and she felt the shudder as the engines growled and grated into reverse. Little by little, the *Snaefell* began to draw away from the quayside into Douglas Bay.

The boat glided past the end of the breakwater; past the Tower of Refuge; past the Camera Obscura on Douglas Head. Creena craned her neck to make out the fading landmarks of her childhood – the Villa Marina where the bands played on sunny days, the Palace ballroom where thousands of couples could dance in dazzling splendour, Derby Castle and the Douglas Bay Hotel on Onchan Head. And now Ida and George Quilliam were just lonely white specks on the quayside, with George standing a little way away from the other people, as he always did. War or no war, George Quilliam was not one to mix with 'the common herd'.

Creena stood on deck for a long time, watching first the town and then the whole island receding into the distance, getting steadily smaller and more insignificant until at last it seemed no more than a papier mâché model on a sea of textured glass.

When she could no longer make out the island at all, she turned away from the rail. There was nothing to see now; nothing to draw her back to the life she had left behind. The link had been broken. She dipped into the pocket of her coat and felt for the little silver good-luck charm she had been given.

It looked as if she was going to need it.

Chapter 6

It was evening when the *Snaefell* reached Pier Head. Stretched out under a blanket in the Ladies' Saloon, Creena had drifted into a deep slumber; and it was only when one of the other passengers shook her by the shoulder that she jolted awake.

'We're coming in to dock, luv,' announced her companion, a generously built middle-aged woman with a strong Liverpool accent and no front teeth. 'Best get yerself sorted out, like.'

Creena gathered herself together and tugged a comb through her tangled mane. It was so many years since she'd seen Alexa Powell that she could hardly remember her, but it certainly wouldn't do to greet her looking like an unmade bed.

Her hair temporarily tamed, she joined the seething mass of people heading up the companionway to the baggage rooms. There was an immense queue. Creena was beginning to wish she hadn't put her suitcases in the baggage room after all, and had simply sat on them like some of the other passengers.

Dusk was falling and it was difficult to see anything much

in the blackout. Above the chatter of the passengers, Creena could hear the sailors calling to each other, cursing as they failed again and again to catch and secure the mooring ropes in the half-light. It hadn't occurred to her how difficult it must be to manoeuvre a boat this size into its berth in the blackout.

A sudden bump made the whole ship shudder, and Creena stumbled and fell against the passenger in front of her.

'Ow! Watch whose corns yer treadin' on, will yer?' An indignant Cockney woman glared at her and extracted her foot from under Creena's.

'I'm sorry. I fell.'

'Yeah. Well, watch yer step.'

'Yes. Yes, I will.' I hope all Londoners aren't as unfriendly as that one, thought Creena to herself.

'Next.' A burly sailor called her forward to collect her cases.

'What number?'

'Forty-six.'

The sailor swung out her two battered suitcases, a chalked '46' on the top. He grimaced.

'Glory! What you got in 'em – bricks?'

Creena bent to pick them up and wondered if he mightn't be right. She wished she hadn't allowed her mother to persuade her to take that extra pair of shoes and the home-knitted bed jackets – which in any case she'd probably never get a chance to wear.

The gangplank was in place now, and Creena followed the bad-tempered Londoner and her husband out into the fresh, crisp evening. The port smelt very different from

Douglas – here, there seemed to be a whole symphony of scents: not the familiar seaweed and salt, but tar and oil and fruit and fish and smoke. It had been years since she had been off the island, and she had quite forgotten the exhilaration of that smell. A new excitement filled her and she took deep breaths, filling her lungs with this heady cocktail.

In front of her, everything was half-light and confusion, with a few policemen and port officials doing their best to stop people from falling into the Mersey or tripping over the ropes and chains which were strewn all over the dockside.

'Bleedin' Jerries,' grumbled the Cockney woman. 'All this creepin' about in the dark ain't natural.'

'For Gawd's sake belt up, woman,' replied her husband wearily. 'It's better'n gettin' bombed, ain't it?'

'Yeah, but we *ain't* gettin' bombed, are we? We're just creepin' about in the dark . . .'

Creena's mouth curved into a slight smile. The couple's bickering reminded her of the arguments that old Billy Callister and his wife used to get into over Billy's false teeth. The whole village knew that Billy had a sparkling set of brand-new teeth but he drove his wife to distraction by refusing to wear them except 'for best'. Unlike the general run of humanity, Billy Callister always took his teeth *out* at mealtimes.

At the bottom of the gangplank she stopped, put down her suitcases and wondered what to do next. The crowd surged past her, rushing into the waiting arms of friends and relatives, or off towards the bus and tram stops. It was like being a small pebble in the middle of an immense and fast-flowing river.

The question was, where was Aunt Alexa? Creena strained her eyes in the deepening blue of the dusk, trying to conjure up her own vague recollections of Aunt Alexa, and her mother's unflattering description: 'Sort of tall and thinnish, I suppose, but not what you could call elegant; mousy hair and a smile you could cut yourself on.'

Could that be her? No, no, she was much too old. Alexa could only be – what? – thirty-six or thirty-seven at most. The only people left on the landing stage now were a few families, one or two old people, half a dozen assorted soldiers, two WAAFs and a Wren. Perhaps she would have to make the journey to Alexa's house on her own. She fumbled in her pocket for the address. There it was: 42 Crocus Lane. Now she needed to find a bus or a tram.

Then she felt a hand on her shoulder.

'Well, if it isn't little Creena Quilliam! You were hardly more than a baby when I last saw you, but I'd know you anywhere with that mop of red hair!'

A woman in her mid-thirties, neatly dressed in a fawn coat and matching hat, was smiling delightedly at her. Wisps of light-brown hair were escaping from underneath the brim of the hat, framing her thin, sharp-featured face. Creena did not recognise her, though she certainly had a faint look of George Quilliam in her hazel eyes, that same look of steely determination. But her voice was musical and warm, her accent a lilting mixture of Scouse and Manx.

'Aunt Alexa?'

The woman smiled.

'The very same. Sorry I'm a bit late – I didn't get off shift until after six, and there was Albie and Kenny's tea to get . . .'

'You shouldn't have rushed,' Creena assured her. 'I'd have managed.' But she was glad she wouldn't have to. Everything looked immense and confusing in the gathering darkness.

'Nonsense, couldn't have you wandering about in the dark, could we? Now then – are these yours?' Alexa bent to pick up one of the suitcases and pulled a face. 'What have you got in here, then?'

'Oh, you know . . .'

Alexa smiled more broadly and gave a knowing wink.

'Oh, I know your mother all right. If there's one thing Ida *doesn't* believe in, it's travelling light. Anyhow, how's the rest of the clan – what about that clever brother of yours?'

'Robert? He's joined up. He's training to be a navigator.'

Alexa shook her head as they walked towards the waiting bus, its headlamps masked to narrow slits and its windows crisscrossed with paper strips.

'Well, if that isn't a waste of an education, I don't know what is,' Alexa declared. 'Still, this war'll do worse than turn lawyers into navigators, you see if it doesn't.' She half turned to look at Creena as they boarded the bus and hauled the suitcases on to the luggage rack at the front. 'And now it's turning you into a nurse!'

'If I'm good enough,' replied Creena thoughtfully as she squeezed into the seat next to her aunt.

'Good enough! You're a Manxwoman, girl! It stands to reason you're good enough.'

Number 42 Crocus Lane was the friendliest house Creena had ever been in.

It was shabby in a genteel kind of way, for there had not been much money in the Powell household since Albert Powell's death. Albert had been gassed on the Somme and had never really recovered, so his young wife had long been accustomed to being the family's breadwinner. Now she was looking after her sons – fourteen-year-old Albie and nine-year-old Kenny – all on her own. Creena felt an instant respect for this resourceful woman.

'Come on, love, I'll show you to your room.'

Alexa led her upstairs to a tiny boxroom with a single bed and a lopsided embroidered sampler hanging on the wall. 'Peace and Plenty' it read, in shaky cross-stitch letters, above a picture of a crinolined lady picking apples off a tree.

'Here it is, Creena love. Our Kenny's sharing with Albie. Get yourself settled in, and when you come down I'll make you a bite to eat. You must be half-starved.'

Creena suppressed an immense yawn.

'Actually, Aunt Alexa, I'm not very hungry.'

Alexa blinked at her in surprise. Accustomed to Albie and Kenny's bottomless stomachs, this was a new concept to her.

'Not hungry? You're not sickening for something?'

Creena laughed.

'No, no, really. I'm just so tired.'

This time the yawn would not be stifled, and she

clapped her hand over her gaping mouth, flushed with embarrassment.

'Oh Aunt Alexa, you must think I'm ever so rude!'

Alexa laughed, and her face lost all its worry lines. It was a very striking face, thought Creena, and it certainly bore little resemblance to Ida's description.

'Don't you be silly now, girl. It's obvious you're half-dead on your feet. You go straight to bed and I'll bring you a nice cup of Ovaltine.'

'Well, that would be lovely. If you're sure you don't mind . . .'

'Of course not. You'll need all your strength for tomorrow.' She turned to go. 'Now, you know Albie's taking you to Lime Street station, don't you? I'd take you myself, only I have to be at work.'

'Yes, Aunt Alexa.'

'Don't you let him forget, will you? That boy's got a mind like a sieve.'

'I'm sure everything will be fine.'

'Well, you make yourself at home. I'll be back in a mo.'

Alexa disappeared and Creena began to undress. Tiredness was descending over her like a fluffy grey cloud. Each yawn was bigger than the last, and for the first time in as long as she could remember she couldn't have cared less about cleaning her teeth or brushing her hair. All she wanted to do was fall into bed.

She pulled back the corner of the candlewick bedspread, sliding her bare legs luxuriously between the sheets. It was a hot, rather sticky night, but she relished the comforting weight of the blankets.

She did mean to stay awake and wait for Aunt Alexa,

really she did. But when Alexa returned a few minutes later, she found the bedside light still on and Creena sprawled across the pillows, fast asleep.

'For goodness' sake get a move on, Albie. You don't want her to miss this train as well, do you?'

'I'm sorry, Ma, really I am.'

'Yes, well, sorry's not much good, is it?'

'I didn't mean to oversleep, honest I didn't.'

Creena prayed inwardly that Albie would hurry up, and stop dropping her luggage at regular intervals as they struggled across the forecourt of Lime Street station. Already she had come to the conclusion that Albie Powell's kind-hearted attempts to help generally caused more trouble than they saved.

'I'm doing my best,' panted Albie, sweat trickling down his face. 'We'll get there. There's still five minutes, and you know it won't go on time.'

'Well, get a move on. The poor girl's in enough trouble already.'

Trouble! You could say that, thought Creena. She should have been in London the previous day, but she and Albie had both overslept and Alexa had had to telephone the hospital to explain that – owing to unforeseen circumstances – Creena Quilliam was going to be a day late.

A whole day late! Whatever would Matron say when she arrived there at last? At least Alexa had persuaded the station manager to let her have a new train ticket. It was inside her glove, pressed flat against the palm of her hand so that she could keep reassuring herself that it was still there.

Still striding along the crowded platform, Alexa turned to Creena with an expression of abject apology.

'I'm really sorry, love. About what happened yesterday...'

'It's all right, I understand,' replied Creena, determinedly not turning back to look at the huge station clock with its hands ticking inexorably round to the hour.

'If you want me to try telephoning the hospital again...'

'No, no, everything will be all right. I'm sure they'll understand. Look – this is the London train, isn't it? Platform five...'

Creena was in such a wild panic that she had hardly had time to marvel at the sheer scale of things in Liverpool – the huge buildings, the noise of the traffic, the grime that caught in your lungs. At any other time she would have spent ages just gazing at the enormous iron and glass canopy of Lime Street station, the milling throng of soldiers, sailors, servicewomen and civilians – some laughing, some shouting, some very silent and in tears. And just look at the size of the trains! They made the pretty steam engines which ran between Port Erin and Douglas look like toys in a child's train set.

The carriages were surrounded by a chattering, shouting, teeming crowd of well-wishers, all here to give their loved ones a send-off; and even when Creena managed to get to the door of one of the compartments and wrench it open, she realised that finding a seat was by no means a foregone conclusion. Every available space seemed to be taken up by bodies or luggage, and even the corridor was jam-packed with travellers.

'I could try further down the train,' suggested Creena.

But Alexa had seen the guard unfurl his flag and put the whistle to his lips.

'No time, love. Hurry up with that case, Albie.'

Albie wrestled the bigger of the cases into the compartment, bruising a variety of shins and knees in the process.

'Oi – watch where you're shoving that!' grunted a thickset squaddie; and the pretty girl on his lap rubbed her ankle resentfully.

'These are my best silk stockings, you know!'

'Sorry,' gasped Creena, squeezing herself with difficulty into the compartment so that Alexa could slam the door behind her. The window was down and she stuck out her head, almost shouting to make herself heard over the cacophony of voices and hissing steam and the shrill blast of the guard's whistle.

'I'll write and thank your mother for the handkerchiefs. Now take care of yourself, won't you?'

'I will, I promise.'

A swift peck on the cheek and the train jolted into sudden life, steam billowing about the engine in great clouds that would be sure to leave smuts on Creena's freshly washed face and tailored suit.

''Bye now – and don't forget to write...'

A few moments later, the train was snaking its way out of Lime Street station and on to the main line which would carry Creena all the way to Euston. All the way to a brand-new beginning.

A harassed mother hauled a snotty-nosed, grizzling child on to her lap and Creena squeezed gratefully into a tiny gap at the end of the long bench seat, her overnight case and handbag clutched on her lap and the bigger of the two suitcases tucked under her legs.

'Off to London?' The pretty girl on the squaddie's lap tossed her glossy brown locks and observed Creena with interest.

'I'm training to be a nurse.'

The girl wrinkled her nose.

'Gawd! Rather you than me, sweetheart. Mopping up sick an' all that. Nah, it'll be the Wrens or a nice cushy office job for me. Sick people make me feel . . . you know . . . funny.'

'Well, I think it's wonderful to have a vocation,' butted in the young mother, one arm nursing her baby whilst the other fought to control the acrobatic toddler, who seemed intent on getting out into the corridor. 'But she ain't from London, are you, kid? What are you – Irish is it?'

'I'm Manx,' replied Creena.

'Manx, what's that?' enquired the squaddie.

'You know, silly.' His girl nudged him in the ribs. 'From the Isle of Man.'

'I went there once,' piped up a girl with a broad Lancashire accent. 'We all went together from the mill. Stayed in this lovely boarding house.'

'Well, I reckon she must be half-barmy,' declared the pretty girl, checking her perfectly powdered nose in a small hand-mirror. 'Hitler can bomb us any time he likes – and where will he drop his bombs? Right smack on London, it stands to reason. If you ask me, the silly girl should have stayed at home.'

Creena was dreaming. After several hours of being shunted

into sidings to let troop trains pass, exhaustion finally took hold of her and she had drifted off to sleep, her head resting on the young woman's shoulder and the snotty two-year-old at last curled up and slumbering on her mother's lap.

In her dream she was ten years old again, sitting in the schoolroom at Ballakeeill. It wasn't easy, being the schoolmaster's daughter, for George Quilliam took his position very seriously and had made it quite clear that his own daughter could expect no favouritism.

Favouritism! Creena would have settled for being treated the same as her classmates. Whenever anything went wrong, whenever there was any blame to be apportioned, it seemed that George felt compelled to make an example of his daughter.

It was a cold and windy day, and George was already in a bad mood, for several of the children – Frankie included – were absent, helping with the peat-cutting on Snaefell.

Spiteful little Maudie Maddrell, the policeman's daughter, was sitting behind Creena, pulling her long red plaits. Tug, tug, tug. It hurt so much that her eyes watered, but Creena was trying hard to concentrate on what her father was saying. She wouldn't let Maudie provoke her.

Tug, tug. Twist.

'Ouch!'

She swung round and Maudie was sniggering at her.

'Stop it, stop it!' hissed Creena.

A gruff voice made her heart sink.

'Creena Quilliam!'

She got slowly to her feet.

'Yes, sir?' It felt strange, calling her own father 'sir'.

'What were you doing?'

She bit her lip. She wasn't a telltale.

'What were you doing?' Her father's voice was darker, more insistent.

'Please, sir...'

George Quilliam leant over his desk. He looked like a big black crow.

'You were talking in class. Not paying attention.'

She swallowed hard.

'Please, sir, I wasn't. I was only...'

'Be silent!'

She looked up at him and suddenly he was standing over her, the swishing leather strap in his hand. And Ida was beside him, shaking her head as much in sorrow as in anger.

'Disobedient child. You're a very disobedient child.'

She held out her hand for her punishment and suddenly her mother and father had their hands on her shoulders, shaking and shaking and shaking...

'Wake up!'

She jolted into wakefulness so suddenly that for a few seconds dream and reality seemed blended together. The young mother was standing over her, but for a moment she couldn't take anything in. The dream had seemed more vivid than reality.

'What ... I ...'

'We're almost there. Best stir your stumps or the train'll be off back to Liverpool with you still on it.'

Creena shook the sleepiness out of her eyes.

'Thank you. How long have I been asleep?'

'Oh, couple of hours, maybe three. I dozed off myself for a while. All this shunting backwards and forwards fair wears you out.'

Turning her head, Creena saw that the soldier had got up from his seat and was standing with his head and shoulders out of the open window, through which gusts of cool, smoke-filled air were pouring. The train was slowing down now, sliding between tall, grim-faced buildings which made the ones in Liverpool seem like dolls' houses. Accustomed to vast Manx skies which extended, unbroken, from horizon to horizon, Creena blinked uncomprehendingly up at the patches of steel-grey which were just visible above and between the clustered buildings.

So this was Euston station! Creena wondered just how much bigger things could get. She'd seen pictures of London before, of course – the Houses of Parliament and Horse Guards Parade – but somehow she hadn't quite grasped the sheer vastness of the city.

The train pulled in and there was a mad rush for the platform, passengers stretching limbs which ached from crouching in the corridors, sharing seats, even stretching out on the overhead luggage racks. Others were doing their best to smooth the creases out of crushed suits and dresses, pinning hats on straight and slipping on gloves. Even in wartime, you had to make an effort to look your best.

Creena tucked her handbag under her arm, picking up the overnight bag and smaller suitcase in one hand and the big suitcase in the other. Already she felt as though her arms were being pulled out of their sockets, and she thought wistfully of Frankie and Robert, who had always been on hand to help. From now on, she mused, she would be doing every bit of fetching and carrying herself.

'Excuse me.' Lost in the endless stream of people, awed

by the hugeness of the station, she hailed a uniformed back. Slowly the railway employee turned round.

'What?'

'Please – can you help me? I'm looking for a porter.'

The man guffawed and wiped his hand over his untidy grey moustache.

'You and a few thousand others, little lady. Ain't no porters to be had for love nor money. Most of 'em's joined up, see. You'll have to manage on your own. There's a war on, you know.'

That was the first – but by no means the last – time that Creena would hear that hated phrase. It was to become the universal excuse for everything, from late trains and queues to powdered egg and the unavailability of knicker elastic.

Teeth gritted, she hauled her cases the length of the platform and stood for a few minutes in the central booking hall, partly to get her breath back and partly to marvel at the splendid Victorian architecture. What should she do now? She glanced at her watch: three o'clock already! And she still hadn't managed to get to the hospital.

'Hello, miss. You look a bit lost, if you don't mind my saying so.'

Creena looked round to see a policeman, helmet tipped back on his head. He was quite young, and for a fleeting moment she almost thought she saw Frank standing there.

'Miss?'

'Oh, sorry, I was miles away.'

'Bit lost, are you?'

'I'm trying to get to the Royal Lambeth Hospital – do you know it?'

The policeman laughed at this, as though it were the funniest thing he'd ever heard.

'Know it? Why, every Londoner knows it. It's one of the best hospitals in the whole country. And you're going there, are you? Going to be a nurse?'

'I hope so, yes.'

'Well, we can't have you getting yourself lost.' He picked up Creena's two suitcases as though they were light as a feather, and carried them across the booking hall to a flight of stairs. 'See that?'

Creena nodded.

'Go down that subway and take the Underground to Waterloo – you can get the tram from there. You'll be all right on your own now?'

'Yes, thank you,' replied Creena, peering doubtfully down into the depths of the Underground. Would she be all right? Yes, of course she would. She was a Quilliam, wasn't she? Chin up, shoulders back, she picked up her suitcases and started off down the stairs.

The Royal Lambeth Hospital, reputed to be the second oldest in the whole of London, stood on the south side of the Thames, on the edge of Lambeth Marsh.

Situated near Waterloo Station, Lambeth Palace and the river, the hospital seemed to form a natural bridge between rich and poor, between the haves and the have-nots. As the tram rattled through the city streets, Creena soon came to realise that she had come to a place of contrasts: on the one hand the elegant opulence of the Royal Lambeth Hospital and the Archbishop's Palace, on the other, row upon row of crumbling back-to-backs where thin-legged children played with not a tree or a blade of grass in sight. It was a quite astonishing contrast to Ballakeeill, and Creena had the curious feeling of being transported to a different world.

Stiff from so much sitting down, she got off the tram and lugged her suitcases across the road to the front entrance of the hospital.

So far, she felt she had managed quite well. But now that she was actually faced with the towering Victorian building where she had been accepted for training, Creena could feel her legs turning to jelly.

Everything seemed very quiet and completely baffling as she wandered about, trying to find someone she could ask for directions. The letter of acceptance was neatly folded in the pocket of her grey suit, and she thought that she should perhaps find Matron, explain to her the reasons for being so unforgivably late. If only she could find someone to ask . . .

As she stood in the echoing corridor, a dark-haired girl in a plain grey uniform dress bustled past.

'Excuse me . . .' began Creena.

The girl turned round. Short, curly brown hair framed a pleasant, open face, with the most mischievous eyes Creena had ever seen.

'Hello – you look like a lost soul! Can I help you?'

Creena was surprised and pleased to hear the South London twang in the girl's bright, friendly voice – she had been led to believe that the school of nursing at the Royal Lambeth was rather snooty.

'I'm sorry to bother you, but I'm new. And I'm horribly late. I was looking for Matron's office.' Creena fetched out the letter and handed it to the girl, who smiled broadly.

'Well, well, another new chick for the nest! A bit late, but better late than never, eh?' She held out her hand and Creena took it. The grip was reassuring and firm. 'My name's Bayliss, by the way – Dillie Bayliss. I used to be a nursing assistant here, but I've just started my nurse training. Looks like we're going to be in the same set.'

After making her apologies to Matron, Creena was taken by a fourth-year probationer to find her accommodation in the nurses' home.

'You'll be sharing a room, of course,' remarked Nurse Doreen Waverley as they walked down endless identical corridors. Creena wondered how she would ever manage to find her way round such a rabbit warren. 'Four to a room, that's the rule in the first two years.'

'Four!' Back in Ballakeeill, Creena had hardly ever had to share a room, except on the odd occasions when someone came to stay. The idea of sharing with not one, but three other people came as quite a shock.

'You'll get used to it. In fact,' Waverley turned to her with a smile as they crossed the courtyard to the nurses' home, 'you'll probably find that the set you share with now are the friends you stick with right through your training – and afterwards too.'

Pushing through the front door, they climbed a flight of stairs and turned into a corridor lined with identical brown doors. A girl with mousy blonde hair and a jolly, pink-cheeked face stuck her head out of one of the doors as they passed, and drew the tip of her finger across her throat with gruesome relish.

'Another inmate for the Royal Lambeth jail,' she observed merrily, and disappeared back into her room with a cheery grin.

'Don't take any notice of her,' said Waverley in answer to Creena's blank stare. 'That's just Eleanor Howells – she's always like that. She was new here herself, a few months back. Honestly, she ought to know better than to go frightening brand-new probationers.'

As Creena's expression still didn't lighten, the older girl patted her on the shoulder.

'Look here, Quilliam, if it was that bad, would I still be here, almost at the end of my fourth year? Anyhow, here we are – this is your new home. Supper's at six o'clock in the juniors' dining room, so you've just got time to get changed into your uniform. Whatever you do, don't be late or you'll go hungry – they're like vultures in this place.'

Abandoned in the corridor before a blank brown door, Creena hesitated for a moment then knocked and turned the handle. Too late to go back now!

'Well, don't just stand there,' said the brown-haired girl on the bed by the window. She hardly even bothered looking up from her book. 'Come in and shut the door. Were you born in a barn?'

Creena stepped inside and closed the door behind her. The girl on the bed was stretched out in her underwear, one hand behind her head and the other turning the pages of the novel balanced on her left knee. Her hair was cut and permed in a fashionably short style, and it was clear from her sleek, oyster satin slip that she was accustomed to the very best of everything.

'Don't take any notice of Hester,' said a stockily built girl who was washing her face at the small corner sink. Her voice was plummy and well bred, but had a warmth to it which Creena found encouraging. 'It's just her way.' She patted her face dry with a towel and turned round. She wore her chestnut-brown hair rolled up at the back and sides, with a few frizzy curls at the front. 'My name's Marian Clarke-Herbert and that lady of leisure is Hester Frankenberg. You must be the mysterious missing probationer the home sister's been fussing about since yesterday afternoon.'

Grateful for a little friendliness, Creena extended her hand and Marian took it.

'My name's Creena – Creena Quilliam.'

'Good grief, what sort of name is that?' demanded Hester, lowering her book for a moment to turn her exquisite almond eyes on the newcomer.

'It's a Manx name,' replied Creena, with some pride. She almost countered by asking what sort of a name Hester Frankenberg was, but good manners prevented her.

Hester shrugged and went on reading.

'Just don't expect me to remember it, that's all.'

Creena sank on to her allocated bed and opened the larger suitcase, taking out one of the scratchy uniform dresses her mother had had made up for her. The shapeless grey cambric tent she could live with – and she would have to for the first twelve weeks of her training, until she had finished Preliminary Training School. No, what bothered her were the starched white collars, stiff cuffs and snowy aprons – not to mention the impossible caps, which would have to be re-folded and pinned every time they came back from the hospital laundry.

'Don't worry, chicken. I'll help you with your cap,' Marian reassured her. 'Frankenberg still hasn't got hers right, but that's just because she's bone idle, isn't it, Hester?'

Hester glared back at her and went on reading. At that moment the door opened and a fourth face peered in.

'Hello there. Room for a little one?'

Marian left off folding Creena's cap and gave a brief nod of acknowledgement.

'That there is the fourth member of our happy band,' she explained. 'Her name's Dillie – Dillie Bayliss.'

'Yes, I know,' replied Creena brightly, returning Dillie's amiable grin. 'Funnily enough, we've already met.'

Chapter 7

'And make sure you get into all the corners, Nurse Quilliam.'

'Yes, Sister.'

Creena contemplated the mop and bucket with a sort of fatalistic detachment. She'd been at the Royal Lambeth for two weeks; it felt more like two years.

To date, most of her time had been spent in the classroom or the PTS practical room, learning the basic skills she was going to need when she was allocated to her first ward: skills like blanket bathing, 'hot dusting', giving out bedpans and the fiddly business of invalid cookery. In these two short weeks, Creena had made and remade so many beds that she had begun to dream about hospital corners.

On one or two days per week, each probationer was seconded from the training school to a ward, where these basic skills could be put into practice under the watchful eyes of Sister and Sister Tutor. At first Creena's set had been excited at the thought of getting on to a ward – an opportunity to do some real nursing at last, or so they'd thought.

As it turned out, it was actually an opportunity to get used to doing the most menial jobs: cleaning, scrubbing, dusting, mopping – Creena suspected that over the last couple of weeks she had learned more about cleaning than her mother had learned in thirty years.

She had also learned a great deal about the hospital hierarchy – that surgeons were always 'Mister' and physicians 'Doctor', that nurses must address each other by their surnames, that Sister *never* made mistakes (especially fierce Sister Meredith on Female Surgical), and that junior probationers were seldom, if ever, right.

Hester Frankenberg did not think too much of this arrangement. The daughter of one of the hospital's senior consultant surgeons, she was accustomed to a comfortable existence, and the realities of life as a very junior probationer had come as an immense shock to her. On one memorable occasion she even challenged Sister Meredith:

'Sister, when will we begin learning some *proper* nursing duties?'

Sister Meredith's not inconsiderable bulk fairly quivered with fury.

'*Proper* nursing duties, Nurse Frankenberg?'

'You know, Sister – giving injections, doing dressings, that sort of thing. The sort of thing we're supposed to be training for.'

'Nurse Frankenberg,' thundered Sister Meredith. 'You are training to provide a safe, comfortable and hygienic environment in which your patients may regain their health and strength. Did Miss Nightingale not teach us that the most valuable thing a hospital could do was not to do the patient any harm?'

'Well, yes, Sister, but . . .'

'No buts, Nurse Frankenberg. You will mop and polish this ward floor until it gleams, and when you have finished, you will go into the sluice and polish every single bedpan until I can see my face in it.'

Frankenberg bit her exquisitely shaped lip.

'Yes, Sister.'

Hester had been a little less direct in her criticisms of authority since then, mused Creena. But that didn't stop her being thoroughly unpleasant about Dillie.

It wasn't that Dillie Bayliss wasn't capable of standing up for herself, but people like Hester would insist on whispering about her behind her back. This made Creena hopping mad. What did it matter that Dillie was an orphan who'd been brought up by her aunt in Lambeth Marsh? What did it matter that her accent wasn't 'refined'? Already Dillie Bayliss was twice the nurse Hester Frankenberg would ever be.

On this particular Monday morning, Creena and Dillie had been sent up to Female Surgical to take care of the routine jobs whilst trained staff looked after the most poorly patients.

'It's not quite what I'd expected,' Creena confessed as she mopped around the door of the sluice where Dillie was busily scrubbing bedpans with her usual efficient bustle.

'Bit hard on the feet at first,' agreed Dillie, 'but you get used to it. D'you know, the soles of my feet are like leather now! Plenty of spirit and dry soap, that's the secret.'

'It's not just that,' replied Creena. 'It's . . . well, it's not very exciting, is it?'

Dillie stifled a giggle – peals of girlish laughter would be certain to bring Sister Meredith out of her office, bristling with righteous indignation. Whatever else her probationers might get up to when her back was turned, they certainly weren't going to enjoy themselves.

'What on earth did you expect, Quilliam? I mean, looking after sick people – it's not exactly glamorous, is it?'

'It's not as if we actually get to look after any sick people,' pointed out Creena. 'And the hospital is so dreary, with its windows all taped up and sandbags all over the place.'

'Just you wait till Christmas,' said Dillie with a wink as she squeezed past and disappeared into the treatment room, in search of the back trolley. 'There'll be a carol concert, and a dinner dance, and doctors dressed up as nurses – and even Matron lets her hair down a bit!'

'What's this, girls – a mothers' meeting?'

Harry the orderly limped out of the main body of the ward with a bundle of soiled linen, and stuffed it into the sack outside the ward door. Harry was a popular member of the hospital staff. Many of the orderlies were conchies, but not Harry – he'd been turned down for military service because of his club foot, but as soon as war had broken out he'd volunteered for the dirtiest, nastiest job he could think of. Every time he smiled he made Creena feel guilty for daring to complain.

'Best not hang around,' he whispered. 'Staff's in a paddy because one of the patients wants to discharge herself against doctor's orders. She's bound to be looking for a sacrificial lamb or two.'

114

'Ah well, must get on!' said Dillie briskly and disappeared into the ward with her back trolley, intent on massaging rosy health into all her patients' bottoms and heels. There would be no pressure sores on Female Surgical if Dillie Bayliss had anything to do with it.

'Cheer up – it may never happen,' said Harry, filling a bucket with disinfectant. He winked. 'Missing your intended, are you?'

Creena found herself thinking about Frank for the first time in ages. She really *must* reply to that long letter he'd written, tell him he was silly to think of leaving the police and joining up. But her new life in London was so busy, so far removed from everything and everyone in Ballakeeill.

'I haven't got an intended,' she retorted. 'But if I had, I wouldn't want him to see me up to my elbows in disinfectant! It's hardly a recipe for romance...'

At that moment the door of Sister Meredith's office opened and the Sister herself peered out.

'Haven't you finished that floor yet, Nurse?' she boomed.

'I ... yes, nearly, Sister,' replied Creena, plunging the mop into the bucket with such force that half the water slopped over the sides.

'If you have not finished in five minutes' time I shall know the reason why, Nurse. After you have cleaned the floor, you and Nurse Bayliss will check that all the beds are neat and tidy. I want this ward absolutely immaculate for the consultant's round, do you understand?'

'Yes, Sister.'

Sister Meredith came out of her office and regarded Creena with fiercely folded arms. She was a woman of middle years, with steel-grey hair and a bulky, mannish frame.

'Have you brushed your hair this morning, Nurse Quilliam?'

'Yes, Sister. Of course, Sister.' Creena put up her hand and to her dismay discovered several wisps of hair sticking out defiantly from underneath her cap. 'Oh, sorry, Sister. It's difficult, with there being so much of it.'

'I am not interested in excuses, Nurse Quilliam. Directly you have finished mopping the floor, you will neaten your hair. This hospital has high standards, and I expect them to be maintained. If you cannot control your hair, then you must cut it. Is that quite clear?'

'Perfectly, Sister.' Creena's heart sank. If there was one thing she definitely didn't want to do, it was to cut her long and luxuriant red hair. And whatever would the family say if she went home with an Eton crop or a shingle cut?

Ten minutes later, with the floor outside Sister's office shining and her hair pulled firmly back into a tight knot, Creena was back on the ward with Dillie.

'Fifty-two beds to do,' sighed Dillie. 'Still, it's easier with two.'

The first patient greeted them like long-lost friends.

'Mornin', girls. 'Ow are you this fine morning?'

'Very well thank you, Mrs Ellis. And how are you today?'

Doris Ellis was a round-faced, round-bodied woman of around sixty who had never had a day's illness in her life until her appendix burst and almost killed her. Now she was making the most of her enforced stay in bed, and was keeping her huge extended family busy round the clock, bringing her little comforts.

'Oh, mustn't grumble, girls. Have a grape. Our Billy brought them in last visitin'. Go on – they're all right; got 'em down Lower Marsh Market, he did.'

Creena refused Mrs Ellis's offer politely but firmly. One of the worst crimes a nurse could commit was to be caught by Sister Meredith eating on duty. No matter how loudly your stomach rumbled, no matter how faint from hunger you were, you would have to wait until your meal break for relief. If you actually got your meal break, for the juniors sometimes had to work through, especially at busy times.

'Sorry, Mrs E. They look lovely, but Sister would be furious.'

'Gawd, you don't want to take no notice of 'er, the frigid awld bitch,' laughed Kate Flanagan, from the adjoining bed. She was a stringy Irish woman of indeterminate years and dubious reputation who would keep trying to persuade Harry to bring her in a bottle of cheap sherry, even though the doctors had told her time and again that it was the sherry that had made her ill in the first place. 'Tell her to go to hell.'

'Now, Miss Flanagan, you mustn't talk like that,' Creena scolded.

'Sure an' I'll talk how I like,' shouted the combative Miss Flanagan. 'An' where's my sherry? I need a drink.'

'Do please be quiet,' Creena pleaded. 'The consultant will be round soon ...'

'The consultant can go to hell an' all,' replied Miss Flanagan with relish. She was enjoying having such an attentive audience.

'Then please have a thought for the other patients,' broke in Dillie with practised firmness. 'That lady in the end bed is very poorly, she needs her rest.'

Miss Flanagan's only reply was a grunt, but at least after that she piped down. Creena tweaked the sheet into a kick pleat and tucked it in. She was already learning that not all patients were model patients, despite what the nursing textbooks might say. Inevitably there were one or two who did nothing but complain from the moment they were admitted to the day they were discharged. Sister Tutor hadn't given her students any advice about how to deal with people like Miss Flanagan.

Leaving Miss Flanagan to her *sotto voce* grumblings, they worked through the rest of the patients with a smooth efficiency which would have placated even stone-faced Sister Meredith. At last they came to a bed near the ward desk.

Dillie checked the chart at the end of the bed.

'Good morning, Mrs Perkins.'

The woman in the bed smiled, and the smile lit up her thin face. Her skin was as yellow as parchment, almost translucent, thought Creena. She looked old – and yet she couldn't have been more than thirty-five, maybe quite a lot less. Her long black hair had lost most of its sheen, but must once have been her pride and joy. On the top of her locker lay a tattered studio photograph of two children, a boy and a girl. Creena picked it up.

'Your children?' she enquired.

'That's right, ducks.' Her voice was stronger than Creena had expected, but it had a curious hoarse rasp to it. 'Cath an' Jimmy. Goin' to be evacuated, ain't they? I thought it

118

best, what with my Billy gone an' me not there to look after them.' Her eyes were very bright, as though they were filled with the beginnings of tears, and Creena sensed that what May Perkins wanted most was reassurance that she had made the right decision.

'I'm sure it's for the best,' she said, and squeezed May's hand. 'They'll be safest out of London.'

Dillie drew back the bed covers and Creena hoped that her shock was not reflected on her face. Poor May Perkins was bone-thin, lost in the voluminous folds of her wincey-ette nightdress.

'It's me lungs, Nurse,' said May, unselfconscious about her illness. 'At least, that's what the doctors think. They're goin' to operate an' have a look when I'm a bit stronger – feedin' me up, they are. I've never seen so much food in me life!'

Dillie rolled Mrs Perkins gently towards Creena, who held her frail body firmly whilst Dillie slipped out the old drawsheet and slid a fresh one underneath.

'How long you bin 'ere, dear?' Mrs Perkins asked her. 'That's one of them probationers' uniforms, ain't it?'

'Not long – just a couple of weeks.'

'Not from round 'ere, are you?'

Creena shook her head.

'The Isle of Man.'

May nodded reflectively.

'They say it's nice there. I ain't bin there, mind. Ain't never had no holidays – couldn't afford it, what with the kids, and my Billy bein' out of work. Maybe I'll go there one day, eh?'

'I'm sure you'd like it,' observed Dillie with a twinkle in

her eye. 'It must be nice – Nurse Quilliam is always going on about it!'

May clasped Creena's hand tightly as she was rolled gently down on to her back. Creena felt her thin fingers tighten, and then May relaxed on to the soft white pillows.

'Why don't you tell me about it? The Isle of Man.'

Creena thought of Sister Meredith, counting the seconds to the ward round. But she liked May Perkins, and hadn't she been told it was important to make the patient feel happy and comfortable?

'Nurse! Nurse!' a voice called from the other end of the ward. 'I need a bedpan.'

'Me too, Nurse, when you've got a mo.'

'Nurse!'

Creena sighed. It was chaos again, and there were fifty-one other patients to care for, not just May Perkins.

'I'm sorry, I have to go. But I promise I'll come back later.'

'Are you sure it will be all right?'

'Of course it will! Auntie Mo loves having visitors. And besides, if she's talking to you, she can't be running around after those kids, getting herself into a state!'

'Kids?'

'You know, Micky and Kitty – Uncle Eddie's two. He's overseas with the army now, so Auntie Mo said she'd take them in. She's got her work cut out too. That Micky would only wash his face once a year if it was left up to him. Proper little scruff he is.'

'Speaking of which,' Creena looked down at her old brown coat, 'do I look all right? Will I do?'

'You look . . . ravishing!'

Laughing, the two girls turned out of the hospital gates and headed towards Lower Marsh and The Cut. It was a chilly but bright November morning and one of Creena and Dillie's precious Saturdays off. Ever since she'd arrived at the Royal Lambeth and they'd palled up together, Dillie had been on at Creena to come and meet her family; but Creena was a little worried that Dillie's Auntie Mo might not be as pleased to see her as Dillie kept making out.

'You're sure she knows I'm coming?'

'Of course she does. She'll be delighted that I've got myself a respectable friend at last. Uncle Paddy was a policeman, you know, so Auntie Mo has standards to keep up!'

As they walked, side by side, along the Embankment, they observed some of the changes which had come over London in the past couple of months. The chilly blue sky was filled with the iridescence of barrage balloons, hanging like fat silver bombs over the river. And in the river itself lurked mines, silent, invisible death traps parachuted in by the Germans.

'How's that poor man in Male Surgical?' enquired Creena.

'The one who got blown up by a mine? They transferred him to the EMS hospital in Surrey, once they'd got him stabilised. He lost a leg, though.'

Creena shivered. This was what she was being trained for, of course, but she couldn't help wondering how she would cope, should the expected bombardment of London materialise. How many thousands of casualties were expected each day – twenty, thirty, more? Had she been mad to imagine that she had what it took to make a good nurse? Stuck-up Hester Frankenberg simply irritated her; Dillie and Marian, with their natural efficiency, made her feel all fingers and thumbs sometimes.

As they turned left into Lower Marsh, Creena was astounded by the noise and bustle around her. This area was very different from the elegance of the Royal Lambeth Hospital and the Archbishop's Palace. The narrow street was almost completely filled by two colourful rows of market stalls selling everything from second-hand suits to donkey stones, and the small thoroughfare which was left was choked with passers-by and hawkers selling out of suitcases.

'Whelks! Get your whelks 'ere, ladies. Only sixpence a pint . . .'

'Broken biscuits . . .'

'Pots an' pans. Good pots an' pans . . .'

The street market was a lively, jostling, many-scented place crammed between two lines of irregularly shaped and sized buildings. Around and between the stalls played small children, some with grubby faces and matted hair; others clean as a whistle but clearly wearing their parents' cut-down clothing.

Creena had never seen anything like it in her life.

'Best hang on to your handbag,' Dillie advised her. 'You can't be too careful. Right little urchins, some of 'em.' She glared meaningfully at a small boy in a holey sleeveless pullover and tatty shorts, who was standing innocently beside a costermonger's barrow. 'And it's no good looking at me like that, Billy Wiggins. I know you're up to no good.'

Billy retaliated by sticking his tongue out and making a run for it, in the process dropping one of the oranges he had just pinched from the barrow.

'Little monsters,' snorted Dillie, not without humour. 'Still, you can't blame 'em, can you? They don't have much, see. Mostly their mothers can't afford to buy them fruit.'

'Morning, Dillie. How're you gettin' on down that posh 'ospital of yours, then?' A greasy-aproned fish-fryer hailed them from the doorway of his shop.

'Oh, not so bad, Alfie. Ask me again in four years' time!'

'An' how's your Auntie Mo?'

'Oh, she's fine. We're just off to see her now.'

'Well, give 'er me best. An' tell 'er I got some nice whiting in.' Alfie disappeared back inside his shop, whistling above the sound of bubbling fat and the whirring wheel of the knife-grinder on the pavement outside.

'Alfie's a good man,' explained Dillie. 'He keeps a lot of folk going round here. Gives tick, too. Leastways, he wouldn't sit back and watch anyone starve for want of a bit of fried fish.'

Lower Marsh blended almost seamlessly with The Cut, a wider road which seemed – if that was possible – to be even more tightly packed with stalls and shoppers. To Creena's right, a small girl was crawling about underneath the fruit and vegetable barrows, picking up the bruised and battered produce which had fallen off or been discarded. To her left, a thin, imperious-looking woman was selling second-hand clothes from a barrow.

'That's what they call a tot stall,' Dillie explained. 'Lots of the people round here get their clothes second-hand. In fact my cousin Jack has a stall a bit like that one, not that he spends much time on it. Here we are now – we need to turn left just here. Auntie Mo lives at number twelve.'

Just as they were about to turn into Bishop Street, they almost collided with a tall young man in a blue cashmere suit and black trilby. On his arm hung the fluffiest, most over-made-up young woman Creena had ever seen, and half a step behind trotted his runner – a boy in his late teens, with a fistful of paper scraps and a pencil tucked behind his ear.

'Well, if it ain't Dillie! It's bin a while, an' no mistake.' The tall young man tipped his trilby on to the back of his head and treated Dillie to a beaming smile. His blue eyes were as bright as periwinkles in his roguish but handsome face. Creena returned his gaze with interest. There was something both charming and a little dangerous about him – precisely the sort of man her father was always warning her about. Almost defiantly she decided to like him. He looked her up and down. 'So who's your friend then?'

'This is Creena,' Dillie told him. Creena thought she detected a slight note of reluctance in her voice as she introduced her. 'Creena Quilliam. She's one of my friends from the hospital. Creena, this is my cousin Jack. I think I may have mentioned him . . .'

Well, well, thought Creena. The famous – or should that be infamous? – Jack Doyle. Oh yes, Dillie had certainly mentioned him.

'Pleased to meet you,' said Creena, holding out her hand. Jack took it with a mischievous grin.

'Not as pleased as I am to meet you,' he replied. And the fluffy blonde on his arm gave him a venomous glare.

'Still running an illegal book, I see,' observed Dillie. 'You'll get caught one of these days, Jack Doyle.'

'Occupational hazard, ain't it?' Jack smoothed down the lapels of his rather exquisite suit. 'At any rate, with the profits I make I can easily allow for a few fines. Trouble is, with the war on there ain't so many punters, or much for people to place their bets on. But a man's got to make a livin,' ain't he, sugar?'

The girl on his arm giggled and gave him a peck on the cheek, the sleeve of her fur jacket riding up to reveal a rather nice silver bracelet which no doubt Jack had bought her with his ill-gotten gains.

'Oh yes, Jackie!'

Dillie regarded him with a sort of benign scepticism; disapproving of her cousin, yet never quite managing to dislike him.

'You should be in the army, Jack Doyle, not making a spectacle of yourself round here.'

'Ah well, I'd have liked to, course I would.' Jack turned his smile on Creena. 'But it's me asthma and me poor feet. They wouldn't have me, see. Dr Cohen turned me down flat, he did.'

'After you slipped him a backhander, I suppose,' suggested Dillie with grim humour.

'Now would I do a thing like that?'

Creena smiled to herself. She rather thought he might, scandalous though the idea was.

As they stood talking on the corner of The Cut and Bishop Street, Creena heard shouts coming from the other side of the road. A short, fat man in a dark overcoat was getting out of a big black car, and a woman in the uniform of a Salvation Army captain was shouting at him from the pavement.

'You're a filthy criminal, Sid Clayden! You and your sort bring nothing but shame and misery to honest people . . .'

Creena watched in astonishment as the man jammed his Homburg on his bald head and walked quickly away into the crowd, evidently anxious to avoid drawing any more attention to himself. She turned back to look at Dillie, and was in time to see that Jack had turned his face away, shielding it with his hand as though he was anxious not to be recognised.

'Who was that?' asked Creena, puzzled.

'Oh, nobody,' replied Jack uncomfortably. 'Nobody worth bothering about. Look, I 'ave to go now, but I'll be seein' you. Both of you maybe,' he added, casting another look at Creena, who felt her cheeks burn with embarrassment, not least because the girl on Jack's arm was definitely giving her the evil eye.

'See you then, Jack. And mind you keep out of trouble.' This was Dillie's parting shot as Jack and his small entourage disappeared into the throng on their way, no doubt, to run yet another illegal book on a bare-knuckle fight round the back of The Ring.

'Who *was* that man who got out of the car?' demanded Creena as she and Dillie walked together up Bishop Street.

'Oh, just the local nasty piece of work. Fellow called Sid Clayden.'

'And does Jack . . . ?'

'Know him? Good Lord no. He wouldn't be so stupid as to get mixed up with a man like that.' Or would he? thought

Dillie, instantly dismissing that thought from her mind. No, not even Jack would take that kind of risk.

Bishop Street was a good deal nicer than the roads around it, mused Creena. It was odd how the poorer streets and the better-off ones backed on to each other. In Bishop Street the big Victorian terraced houses looked well kept, with meticulously scrubbed and whitened front steps and dustbin lids so highly polished that you could see your face in them.

'Nearly there,' said Dillie, turning down a side alley which took them round the backs of the houses, where the odd bit of washing billowed in the November breeze and a group of small children were playing marbles along the gutter.

At their approach, a boy of seven or eight detached himself from the group and scampered over, dragging a smaller girl behind him.

'Auntie Dillie, Auntie Dillie!' The little girl leapt into Dillie's arms as she bent down to embrace her.

'Kitty, well, haven't you grown!' Dillie took an admiring look at her small cousin. Eddie's kids were certainly a credit to him – and Mo. They'd both shot up since the last time she saw them. 'And look at you, Micky. You'll be as big as your dad soon.' She turned to Creena. 'Micky, Kitty, I'd like you to meet my friend Creena. She's a nurse, too.'

Micky and Creena regarded each other with mutual interest and curiosity.

'Hello,' said Creena.

'You've got red 'air,' Micky observed, turning to his sister as if for confirmation. 'Ain't she got red 'air? Masses an' masses of it.'

'Creena's Manx,' volunteered Dillie by way of explanation.

'What's Manx?' asked Kitty.

'It means I come from the Isle of Man,' replied Creena.

'Oh,' said Micky. Then he asked hopefully: ''Ave you ever seen a dead body?'

Dillie took a swipe at him and he ducked.

'What sort of question is that, Micky Bates? And you'd better not turn up for your dinner with that tidemark, or Auntie Mo'll scrub your neck till the skin drops off.'

Micky and Kitty ran off back to their game, and Creena and Dillie continued on their way.

'Little horrors,' chuckled Dillie. 'But they're not bad kids, just . . . well . . . lively.'

Reaching a gate with 'No. 12' painted on it, Dillie pushed it open. A delicious smell wafted into Creena's nostrils, and her ravenous stomach grumbled its impatience.

'Here we are,' grinned Dillie. 'Best suet pudding in Lambeth – I'd know that smell anywhere.'

As they got halfway up the yard, the back door opened and a woman appeared in the doorway. Dressed in a cardigan, skirt and pinafore, she was in her mid-fifties, well built with pepper-and-salt hair scraped back into a bun; her face lined but her features strong, full of character. Her eyes were bright blue, just like Jack's.

'Dillie!' The woman's face lit up with pleasure.

'Hello, Auntie Mo.' Dillie rushed forward to receive her aunt's bear hug of welcome, but Creena hung back, feeling awkward.

'And you must be Dillie's friend.' Mo Doyle turned her blue eyes on Creena.

'This is Creena, Auntie Mo.'

Mo wiped her floury hand on her pinny and extended it in greeting.

'Pleased to meet you, I'm sure.'

'It's very kind of you to invite me...' began Creena; but Mo just laughed good-naturedly. Creena liked her instantly, responding to the warmth that radiated from her. There was something immensely strong and reassuring about Mo Doyle.

'If I can't welcome Dillie's friends, who can I welcome?' She regarded Creena for a moment, head on one side. 'Lovely hair she's got, Dillie, but Lor', she's skinny!' She took Creena's arm and led her up the steps into the back kitchen. 'Come on, girl, looks like I've got some feeding up to do!'

It was almost Christmas already! And here Creena was at the probationers' annual dinner dance, where even a humble first-year could enjoy herself and forget her aching feet. The weather outside might be damp, chilly and foggy, but in the grand hall of the Royal Lambeth Hospital all was warmth and merriment. It was quite difficult to believe that there was a war on – until you saw all the officer guests in their khaki and navy blue.

Creena could hardly believe that she had been a probationer for almost a full three months. If she passed PTS she would be able to discard her scratchy grey uniform for a scratchy lilac one; and she looked forward, a little apprehensively, to writing home and telling everyone that at long last she was a *proper* probationer nurse.

Almost Christmas 1939, and still London was waiting for

Hitler to unleash the might of his bombers on the capital. Everyone had said that the war would be over by Christmas, but then that was what they'd said in the last lot, as Frank had pointed out in one of his long letters.

Frank's letters made her feel a little wistful – not just because he wasn't here and they had always had such fun together at Christmas, but because she couldn't help feeling they had lost something which had been theirs, and theirs alone, since childhood. After three months away from him, she could hardly remember what he looked like.

She had to remind herself from time to time by looking at the photograph she kept in her purse; the one Padraig had taken of them with Máire at the Mhelliah. They all looked so young and carefree in that picture, naïve even. And now she was in London and Frank had given up his police job to volunteer for the army, just because Sergeant Maddrell had been rude about his mother. Things were changing so fast. Could they ever return to the way they were before? And even if they could, would she want them to?

'Not eating, Quilliam?'

Creena was jolted out of her reverie by Eleanor Howells, who was sitting next to her and taking very full advantage of the marvellous spread which had been laid out for them. After three months, Creena was just getting used to the rule about nurses addressing each other only by their surnames. It had seemed very peculiar at first, like being at a very strict young ladies' academy – which in a way, she supposed, was what the school of nursing was.

'I'm not terribly hungry.'

'Not hungry! After a day tramping up and down the wards?' broke in Jennie Daventry, one of the other first-years sitting around the huge table. 'They say rationing's going to start any minute now – so I say enjoy the grub while you can!'

'Just *look* at Clarke-Herbert,' sniffed Hester Frankenberg, toying with the food on her plate. Her attentions were entirely taken up with glaring at Marian as she whirled around the dance floor with her latest beau. 'Making an exhibition of herself.'

'I think he's *gorgeous*,' sighed Eleanor, biting off a huge hunk of bread and chewing it with gusto. 'What did you say he did?'

'He's the Canadian Air Force liaison officer to the Ministry of War,' replied Hester. 'And if you ask me, he's quite unsuitable for her. I mean, she's not even a good dancer.'

'Do I detect a touch of the green-eyed monster?' enquired Jennie Daventry. 'I mean, you wouldn't be at all jealous, I suppose?'

'Not at all,' sniffed Hester, taking a vicious bite at a piece of carrot. 'Why on earth would I be jealous of her?'

'Because you've set your sights on this chap and he's just not interested in you?' suggested Dillie innocently.

'Rubbish!' snapped Hester.

'Look,' said Creena, trying to be helpful and pour oil on troubled waters. This really wasn't a good time for arguments to break out – not at Christmas, when everyone was feeling homesick. 'Sometimes these things aren't meant to happen. I mean . . . if he's not right for you . . .'

Hester rounded on her with eyes that flashed a danger

signal, but Creena carried on, blissfully unaware of her *faux pas*.

'You know, sometimes it's better to wait for the right man . . .'

'And precisely what would *you* know about men?'

'I beg your pardon?'

'You, Quilliam. Little Creena from the back of beyond in the Isle of God-Knows-Where. What would you know about men? I mean, sweet twenty and never been kissed. It's not as if you've even got a boyfriend.'

'Well, actually, she has,' cut in Dillie on a reckless impulse.

This simple remark caused far more of a sensation than Dillie had bargained for. Suddenly all was silence around the dinner table, and half a dozen pairs of eyes focused on Creena with renewed interest.

'You? You've got a chap?' Eleanor leant closer. 'Where?'

'In the army. He's just joined up. But he's *not* my chap . . .'

The questions came thick and fast.

'What does he look like?'

'What does he do?'

'Are you going to marry him?'

'Well, well,' said Hester, dabbing her mouth with the corner of her napkin. 'Who'd have thought it? Little Creena Quilliam with a man of her own. This I must hear . . .'

Christmas had come and gone, and Robert Quilliam had hardly even noticed it. Three days into the new year, and

1939 seemed to have fused almost seamlessly with 1940. Even his birthday, just before Christmas, had seemed like something of an irrelevance, as though there really ought not to be anything worth celebrating until the war had been won.

The war might be unnaturally quiet – 'Sitzkrieg', the papers were calling it – but Robert had plenty to keep him busy. Here at the RAF station, somewhere in rural Bedfordshire, the days were filled with training exercises and gaining flying hours. In a matter of weeks, he would be a fully fledged navigator. Not a fighter pilot, it was true – he knew his father was secretly disappointed about that – but he was doing his bit, and that was what really mattered.

He stretched out his long legs under the rickety wooden table and wished for inspiration. Letter-writing was so difficult – there was such a lot you simply couldn't say because of the censors – and it was all the more difficult when you were living in a wooden hut in this icy weather, and the heat from the stove was little more than a feeble glow about your frozen fingers and toes.

Of course, in Ballakeeill it would be good and windy by now, with the smoke from peat fires pouring out of cottage chimneys, and the sheep huddled together for shelter under the hedgerows and dry-stone walls, in the lee of the biting gale. He missed it all, and yet he wasn't really a part of it, not any more. Much as he loved it, he had the distinct feeling that there wasn't anything left for him on the island of his birth.

He refilled his fountain pen and took a sheet of paper from his writing case. At least alone he could think more clearly. He really must write that letter to his sister. Plucky little thing she was; he honestly hadn't thought she had the guts to stand up to Ma and Pa like that, to tell them that she was going to London to be a nurse whether they liked it or not. Well, she'd passed her PTS examination, and that in itself was more than George Quilliam had believed she would ever be able to do. Yes, Robert was thoroughly proud of his sister.

Now, what could he say? He scribbled down a few encouraging words, telling her how delighted he was to hear about her success, and advising her to grit her teeth and take no notice of bullying Sister Meredith, snooty Hester Frankenberg or any of the other people who tried to make her feel small. She was a Quilliam, for goodness' sake!

He wanted to tell her something about himself, about what he was doing here. He started to write: 'I've almost finished my training and will soon be flying missions on Wellington bombers', but then wondered if he was allowed to say that. No, the censor would never wear it. So what *could* he say? Frustrated, he scratched out the sentence and started the paragraph again.

'Oh, you're in here. Fancy a few jars in the mess?'

Robert looked up into the handsome, tanned face of Terry Haines. He didn't know much about Terry, except that he was training to be a pilot and came from a rather well-off family somewhere in the Home Counties. In the weeks they'd been at the camp they'd found that they got along pretty well together, despite the difference in their backgrounds.

'Writing to your girl?'

Robert grinned.

'I suppose you could say that. My kid sister, actually. Hang on a mo, I've got a snapshot of her somewhere.'

He found his wallet, rummaged inside and took out a family photograph.

'That's her – second from the left. She's doing her nurse training at the Royal Lambeth Hospital. Red hair and green eyes she has. Quite a looker, by all accounts.'

'Yes, I suppose she is.' Terry didn't seem overly interested in Creena, but swung himself up on to the table so that he was sitting facing Robert. 'Anyhow, what about those few jars? I'm still waiting for an answer.'

'I don't know ... I've got this letter to finish...'

'It won't go till tomorrow now,' pointed out Terry.

'Well, I suppose...' Robert looked down at the half-empty sheet of paper, sighed and put down his pen. 'I can always finish it later. I was stuck anyway.'

'That's the spirit,' said Terry, and his amiable grin was infectious. 'No trueborn Englishman...'

'Manxman,' broke in Robert with feigned indignation.

'All right, no trueborn Manxman prefers writing letters to getting squiffy.'

'You can't get drunk on that stuff,' retorted Robert. 'They water it down.'

'Then you'll just have to drink twice as much. All the more reason for getting started early.'

'OK, you win.' Robert got up and wriggled his arms into his uniform jacket. 'Last one to the mess buys the first round.'

Creena stretched out on her belly on the bed, two of her mother's knitted bed jackets draped over her shoulders. It was freezing cold in the room she shared with Dillie, Marian and Hester, and she had long since left embarrassment far behind. The weather was practically Arctic, and now it seemed that the Thames was about to freeze over. Since she was already virtually a solid block of ice, Creena mused that she probably wouldn't even notice.

Christmas seemed ages ago now, even though it was only the first week of January. It was sad that she'd missed the festive season at Ballakeeill, and she did wish she'd been able to see Robert on his birthday. Still, she'd managed to scrape together enough to buy him a little present and he seemed pleased with it. She read his letter again, and a warm glow of reassurance spread through her frozen body.

'Stick with it, sis,' that was what Robert had written. 'Stick with it, and you'll make *everyone* in Ballakeeill proud of you. I'm proud of you already!'

Well, at least Robert believed in her, and the encouragement of just one person could move mountains.

She turned to pick up her mother's parcel and caught sight of the beautiful Christmas card that Frank had sent her. Tucked inside had been a ten-page letter, telling her all about what he was getting up to at his army training camp, but more than anything telling her how much he wanted the war to be over so that everyone could be together again. It was just like Frankie to join up when he could have had it cushy and stayed on the island. She felt a slight twinge of guilt. Work on the wards had been so hectic that she had hardly had the energy to write to Mother, let alone Frank. Her long letters had started to tail off into half-page notes. She must try harder.

'Letter from your boy?' enquired Marian, who was

trying to get some of the hard skin off her feet with a pumice stone.

'From my brother. You know, in the RAF.'

'Not heard from your boy then?'

'You mean Frank? He sent me that card – and a huge long letter.'

'Bet you can't wait to see him again.'

'Yes. Of course.'

Creena rolled over and slid her mother's parcel from under the bed. It was very heavy, very solid, rather lumpy.

'Good heavens, girl – haven't you opened that parcel yet? I'd have ripped the paper off as soon as it came.'

Creena grinned.

She had been dreading opening the parcel ever since it had arrived this morning. It would be bound to contain a letter – another of her mother's masterpieces of emotional blackmail. Ida Quilliam was taking an awfully long time to come round to the idea of her daughter's nursing career.

'It's from Mother,' she explained.

'Ah,' said Hester Frankenberg, the corners of her mouth twitching into a slightly malevolent smile as she anticipated her joke. 'So you think it's a bomb, then?'

To her surprise, Marian rounded on her.

'Do shut up, Frankenberg, and don't be such a bitch.'

Creena sat up on the bed and picked carefully at the well-knotted string which held the many layers of brown paper and cardboard together. Ida Quilliam believed in wrapping a parcel properly – and that meant sealing wax as well as string.

'Cut it,' said Hester. 'I would.'

'I'm sure you would,' replied Creena with unaccustomed

alacrity. 'But some of us are trying to do our bit for the war effort. If I'm careful, I can use this string and paper again.'

'Peasant,' sighed Hester, sinking back on to the lace-trimmed pillow she had sneaked into the hospital from home, and wiggling her silk-stockinged toes.

'Honestly, Frankenberg,' observed Marian tartly. 'Sometimes I wonder why you ever decided to nurse.'

'It's my vocation, darling,' replied Hester, her eyelids half-closed and her voice drowsy.

'Vocation!' Marian chuckled. 'You mean you wanted to wear a lacy cap and meet eligible young doctors.'

'Oh, do shush, you two!' said Creena. She unfolded the last sheet of paper and found the anticipated letter, a little grease-stained from the other contents of the parcel: a large round fruitcake, six mince pies – and a leg of roast goose.

'Good grief!' exclaimed Marian. 'Your mama must have heard about the awful muck they feed us at the hospital.'

'Here, help yourselves.' Creena put the box of mince pies on the dressing table, then returned to her bed to read her mother's letter. 'But save one for me!'

She opened the letter and smoothed it out.

Dear Creena,

I hope you are not faring too badly in London, though we do hear such terrible things on the news about mines and the weather, not to mention the threats of bombing.

Robert has almost finished his training and should be flying soon. Your father and I are so proud of him. Tommy is doing well at the High School, and Father is thinking of putting him in for a scholarship at King

William's. Your sister is a real treasure. She helps me in the house every day when she comes home from school, and has taken over looking after the chickens. Miss Pargeter says her needlework is coming along beautifully. She will make someone a wonderful wife.

Christmas was just as you would remember it, with the usual candlelight service at the kirk. You were much missed by the village choir.

The island is bearing up well in the hostilities, and all the servicemen and women should bring in a little extra business to make up for the lack of other visitors. Mrs Shimmin at the Stores always has a pound or two of dried fruit for her regular customers, so here is some cake etc, to remind you of home and keep the wolf from the door. Billy Callister at the inn sends his regards, as do the Reverend and his wife.

Your cousin Mona has had her baby, and irresistible he is too, fat as a mollag with Mona's blue eyes, and never a moment's trouble to his poor mother. She is calling him Douglas, after his father. You must come and see little Duggie, he is so adorable.

Are you sure that this life you have chosen is suiting you? In the photograph you sent you look very thin and pale. Why don't you give it up and come home? There is a great deal for you to do here, and I am sure Mr Gelling could find a place for you in the advocates' office.

Write soon,
Mother.

Creena sighed and put down the letter. All was pretty

much as she had expected. She contemplated the goose leg, picked it up and took an enormous bite of the juicy flesh.

Whatever her mother said, it was her brother's advice that she was going to take. Nursing might be hard – harder than she had expected it to be – but that didn't mean she was going to give up and go home with her tail between her legs. Stick with it, that's what she would do. Stick with it, no matter what.

Chapter 8

Creena tried to lie still on the hard tiled floor of the casualty hall, but her left leg had gone to sleep. She shifted uncomfortably, half on to her side, and resumed her low-voiced conversation with Dillie.

'It's hard work being dead, isn't it?'

Dillie chuckled.

'Thank your lucky stars it's only an ARP exercise. And it's better than being a "serious injury" – those poor blighters have to put up with being bandaged from head to foot.'

'Still, I don't see why we have to stay lying here like this,' grumbled Creena.

'They have to count us and suchlike. You know, go through all the proper procedures as if it was a real air raid.'

Creena propped herself up on one elbow.

'Do you think there will be raids?'

Dillie shook her brown curls.

'Doesn't look like it. If Hitler'd wanted to bomb us he'd have done it months ago, wouldn't he?'

'And the war at sea's starting to go our way now, too,' cut in Jennie Daventry. 'If you ask me, this is a waste of a perfectly good afternoon off. There's more chance of us being blown up by the IRA than the Germans.'

Creena had to concede that Jennie had a point. It was late March now, and Britain had been at war with Germany since the previous September. It was looking increasingly as if Hitler had neither the guts nor the resources to launch his threatened attacks on the British capital. But the thought of the IRA sent her thoughts winging back to the Isle of Man, and to poor innocent Máire and Padraig, who were having such a tough time of it because Padraig wouldn't compromise his pacifist principles and join up.

'How's Frank?' enquired Dillie. In the six months that she and Creena had been studying together, they had become firm friends; and each knew more than a little about each other's lives. Creena knew that Dillie idolised Mo Doyle, and that Mo regarded Dillie as the daughter she had never had. For her part, Dillie had listened to scores of tales about Creena's family, and not a few about a certain Frankie Kinrade.

'I'm not sure,' replied Creena. 'I had a letter from him a couple of weeks ago, saying he might be going abroad when he's finished his training. But nothing since.' She paused. 'I hope all this comes to an end and he doesn't have to go.'

'You and me both, chicken,' replied Dillie. 'Good men are hard to find.'

'Ooh – whoever's that?' Defying the possible wrath of Casualty Sister and the hospital ARP squad, Creena pulled herself up into a sitting position and tugged Dillie's sleeve.

'Who?'

'Him over there, putting Howells's arm in a sling.'

Dillie's face assumed a knowing grin.

'Oh, you mean our young surgeon with the film-star looks?'

'I'll say! I haven't seen him before, I can't have done. I'm positive I'd have remembered . . .'

'He's quite new,' Dillie told her. Dillie seemed to know all the hospital gossip. Having spent a couple of years as a nursing assistant helped, of course. Dillie knew everyone and everyone knew Dillie, and consequently not much got past her eagle eye. 'Came down from . . . oh, I'm not sure, Worcester or somewhere. He's a registrar, orthopaedics I think.'

Creena could hardly take her eyes off the young surgeon. Tall and broad-shouldered, with sandy hair and clean-cut features, he had the sort of compelling looks that were enough to turn any girl's head.

'What's his name?' she whispered.

'Can't remember. Tennyson, Trent, something like that.'

Creena hugged her knees, secretly fantasising about what it might be like to be kissed by a man like that. Not, of course, that a man like that was likely to want to kiss a girl like her; besides which, hospital romances were sternly discouraged.

'It's a good job your Frank can't see you staring like that,' observed Dillie cheerily. 'And you two practically promised to each other!'

'We are not!'

'Anyhow, the last I heard, love's young dream had his eye on that rather elegant staff nurse on Paediatrics.'

Creena allowed herself a quiet sigh of disappointment. 'Ah well.'

'Cheer up, Quilliam,' urged Daventry. 'It may never happen.'

'That's what she's afraid of,' observed Dillie laconically.

Daventry shifted position and rubbed the top of her thigh.

'I wish this was over and done with. I've got pins and needles in my backside.'

'Join the club,' muttered Creena, her mouth full of hairgrips as she struggled to anchor her slipping cap in place. 'And my feet are like two blocks of ice.'

'Oh look.' A wicked grin spread over Dillie's face. 'We're going to have a visitor.'

Creena almost swallowed a hairgrip as she watched the young registrar turn and stroll towards them across the crowded casualty hall, pausing here and there to step over prone and bandaged bodies. He greeted them with a smile and a nod.

'Good afternoon, ladies – I understand you're dead.'

'We will be if this goes on much longer,' grunted Daventry.

'Mind if I join you? Seems I'm surplus to requirements.'

'Be our guest,' replied Daventry with a supreme attempt at indifference.

Creena returned his smile with a look of wide-eyed astonishment.

'Temple's the name, Oliver Temple.' The young doctor shook hands with all three probationers in turn. 'Dreary business this, but I suppose it's necessary. You never know when Adolf may try something on.'

Now that they were at such close quarters, Creena could see that Oliver Temple was in his early to mid-thirties, with a friendly smile and the loveliest grey eyes, flecked with green. He was a complete contrast to the other doctors at the Royal Lambeth, most of whom seemed to be crusty bachelors of prehistoric vintage, or spotty juveniles barely out of medical school.

'Daventry,' butted in Jennie, trying to sound casual. She was quite starry-eyed to be in such close proximity to the gorgeous Dr Temple. 'And this here is Bayliss. And the mannequin with a mouthful of hairpins is Quilliam. She's Manx,' she added, as though that explained a great deal.

Creena jabbed the last grip into her hair – which she was sure must look lopsided and completely ridiculous – and glared at Daventry.

'Well, I'm very pleased to meet you all.'

It seemed to Creena that his eyes lingered on her for a fraction longer than they lingered on Dillie or Jennie – but that was probably just wishful thinking. She was still in the grip of that first, dizzying lurch of excitement.

Dr Temple surveyed the scene: stretcher-bearers moving in and out of the hall, ARP wardens and marshals wandering about with bandages and lists, and Casualty Sister doing her best to impose some kind of order on it all. 'Bit of a shambles, don't you think? God help us if the Germans do decide to attack – we'll be too busy making lists to get ourselves organised.'

Creena pretended to listen, but she wasn't taking in a single word he said; she was savouring the whole experience of him: his voice, with its lilting musicality, his refinement, his handsome features, his twinkling eyes.

A few moments earlier, she had been chatting happily about Frank, reliving the special friendship that they had known since they were children. But Frank couldn't have been further from her mind now. She had eyes only for Oliver Temple, this fascinating man who was so very different from any other she had ever met.

Dillie looked from Creena to Oliver Temple and back again. It didn't take an expert to work out that he was just as taken with Creena as she so obviously was with him.

It was about a month later that Creena found herself sitting in a café on the Kennington Road, taking afternoon tea. There was nothing particularly unusual about that – she often came here with Bayliss or the others on their off-duty days. It was cheap and cheerful, and they were always ravenous after long shifts on the wards.

But today was different. Today she was taking tea with Frank.

He looked at her across the tabletop and she thought how grown-up he looked, how very different in his army uniform. She hardly knew what to say to him.

'You should have let me know you were coming,' Creena repeated. 'I might have been on duty, or out somewhere with Dillie.'

'I'm sorry, Creena. I did try and telephone. You know how things are – one minute you're peeling spuds at the training camp, the next you're on embarkation leave.'

He reached across the table in hopes of taking her hand but she didn't reciprocate and so he drew back, disappointed and uncertain. He wasn't the only one who had changed, he told himself.

Frank took a swig of the stewed, sweet tea. He had only been in London for a day, but already he detested it, feeling uncomfortable with the crowds and the noise, and the insincerity and impersonality of the city. He couldn't for the life of him see how Creena coped with it all, let alone enjoyed it. But he could tell that she did – he could see it in the way her green eyes sparkled.

Creena took a bite of the scone on her plate. She wasn't particularly hungry, but eating gave her time to think of the right thing to say.

'When will you be going?'

'Monday, I think. I've got a seventy-two-hour pass.'

'Where . . . ? Or am I not supposed to ask?'

Frank shrugged. He didn't like lying to her, but he had no choice.

'I know I'm going somewhere, but I haven't a clue where. Nobody has.'

'I hope it's not Norway,' shivered Creena. 'They say the Nazis are going to overrun it any day.'

'Could be anywhere,' replied Frank. 'But somehow I don't think it'll be Norway.'

'At least at the hospital they tell us where we're going to be working next,' mused Creena. 'That's sort of reassuring.'

'What's it like, being at the hospital?'

'It's amazingly hard work.' She smiled, happy to have found a subject which she could chatter on about. 'I had no idea how hard it was going to be.'

'But you like it?'

'I *love* it. And I've made so many friends – there's Dillie, and Marian, and Eleanor. It's tough, but I'm determined to get through.'

Frank nodded.

'I know you will,' he said. 'You're strong. The way you stood up to your dad . . .'

'If I hadn't, I wouldn't be here.'

'So what do you reckon to London?'

Creena put her head on one side, thinking, considering, weighing things up.

'At first it terrified me,' she admitted. 'But you get used to it. It's exciting, there's always something new.'

Frank pulled a face.

'I'd never get used to this place! I don't know how you put up with it.'

'Oh, you know. You adapt. I suppose I've changed, grown up a bit since we were kids together.'

He caught Creena's gaze and for a few seconds they were looking straight into each other's eyes. Then she changed the subject.

'You're well?'

'Fine.'

'And your dad?'

'Couldn't be better. He's bought a couple of new heifers, oh, and Ailish and Gwen send their love.'

'Didn't you want to spend your embarkation leave with them?'

'Seventy-two hours isn't long enough to get to Ballakeeill and back. And besides . . .'

'What?'

'I wanted to see you. I wondered if maybe there was something wrong.'

She looked up in surprise.

'Wrong?' She laughed. 'There's nothing wrong.'

'You haven't written in a while, see.'

'Oh, I'm sorry, Frank. I've been very busy, what with the long hours and all the studying.'

Frank nodded.

'Yeah. Course.'

He had come down to London intending to ask her straight out if she was seeing somebody, but now he was here he just couldn't bring himself to do it. He was afraid of what her answer would be.

'Frankie ... If I don't go now I'll be in trouble with Sister. I'm on duty in half an hour.'

'I ... Right. You'd best go then.'

'It was lovely of you to come and see me, really it was. I ... hope everything turns out right.'

'Oh, I'll be just fine, don't you worry.'

'Well ... I'd better be off then.'

She leant over him, planting a chaste peck of a kiss on his cheek. Her smile seemed a thousand miles distant from the girl he had known and loved for so many years. He longed to take her in his arms and just give her a simple hug, the way he used to do when they were kids.

'So long then, Frankie. Take care of yourself.'

'Shall I walk you back to the hospital?'

'Best not. I shall have to rush as it is.'

He knew he had lost her – not that she had ever been his in the first place. But he had thought that, in time, her feelings for him might grow from friendship into love. Now he could see that he had been deluding himself. You couldn't make someone love you, just through the force of your own wanting. If only he knew how to stop loving her.

Walking back to the hospital past St George's Cathedral, Creena thrust her hand into her coat pocket and fingered the little silver lucky charm that Frankie had given her before she left the island – the charm which he had promised would always protect her.

There was a dull ache in her heart, and she didn't even know why.

'No, Padraig, no! You're mad to think of it, you can't do it.'

At the little cottage on the outskirts of Onchan, Máire O'Keefe sat white-faced in the late May sunshine.

'I have to, Máire. Joining the army was one thing – I couldn't do that, not to kill people. But this is something else, it's my duty, girl. If I don't do it, I'll just be proving all those people right – the ones who say I'm a coward.'

Máire's eyes were very dark in her pale face, her glossy black hair dishevelled from being raked back with tormented fingers. In the last couple of weeks, events had begun to take a very disturbing turn in France. The remnants of the British Expeditionary Force were being driven inexorably back through Belgium by the German army, and were making for the northern French coast. But once there, how would they escape? Their only hope was to be evacuated by boat.

On 22 May, the British Government had started mustering ships and boats of all sizes on the coast of England. In a few days' time they would be heading for the beaches of Dunkirk. And now Padraig was telling Máire that he wanted to be on one of those boats.

'The trawler *Mary Jane*'s coming over from Peel tomorrow night,' he told her, sitting close and taking hold of one of her hands. It felt cold and clammy. She turned her face away, not wanting him to see her panic, her fear, her resentment. 'They're short-handed, what with three of the crew being away in the merchant navy. They need anyone they can get who knows how to handle a boat.'

'But this is a fishing boat, Padraig,' she pleaded. 'What do you know about a boat that size? All you ever had was a tiny dinghy...'

'I know enough, Máire. I'm no hero, you know that. If I thought I'd be a liability to them I wouldn't go. But I *have* to go.'

Her anger and pain spilled out with the tears, unbidden.

'And what about me, Padraig? What will I do on my own? What if you don't come back?'

He put his strong arms round her shoulders and gave her a bear hug.

'I'll be back in a few days' time. Just as soon as we've got those poor beggars off the beach and brought them home.'

'It's an outrage! An absolute outrage!'

George Quilliam burst into the kitchen at Ballakeeill schoolhouse with an expression like thunder and a complexion as red as a boiled beetroot. Ida looked apologetically at her sister Bessie.

'You mustn't mind him. He works himself up into such a state.' Then she turned to her husband. 'Hush, George. The infants' class might hear. They're only outside in the yard with Miss McGregor.'

'It's the pupils I am concerned about, Ida!' George drew out a chair and sat down on it. His brow was beaded with sweat.

'Whatever is it now, George?'

'That irresponsible oaf John Duggan has thrown a load

of rusty farm machinery over the orchard wall – right into the school grounds. Little Henry Craine nearly cut himself to ribbons on it. I shall have to have words with that man . . .'

'Yes, yes, indeed you shall.' These days, there always seemed to be some fresh source of conflict, something new for George to get upset about. And with Robert in the RAF and Creena playing at being a nurse, there was so much to do just to keep the family together and the home running smoothly. Creena ought to be here, helping her mother, not running off to London like that. And now there was Bessie's news to contend with. 'Why don't you have a nice cup of tea? It's a fresh pot. Bessie's rather upset, you see.'

George grunted a greeting to Bessie. In his annoyance he had hardly even noticed that she was there. He had quite enough to do in his short lunch break without sorting out yet another family problem.

'Upset? What about?' He poured himself a cup of tea and peered at Bessie over the top of it. She did look rather red about the eyes.

'It's my house,' sniffed Bessie, her normally plump and cheerful face collapsing into a maze of lines and wrinkles as the tears came again. 'They're taking over my lovely house.'

George blinked in surprise at the unusual spectacle of his sister-in-law's distress.

'Taking it over? Who?'

'You know, George,' Ida reminded him gently, sitting down beside Bessie and topping up her cup. 'The Home Office are going to use some of the boarding houses in Port Erin for the internee women.'

'But I thought they only wanted the big hotels.'

Bessie dabbed her nose with her handkerchief.

'Now they're saying they need all the accommodation they can get.'

'That's disgraceful!' If there was one thing George Quilliam liked it was a moral crusade. 'Turning honest people out of their homes.'

'No, no, dear. It's not like the men's camps,' Ida explained. 'They're putting up wire fencing all around Port Erin and Port St Mary, so that the two villages and all the area around them will be cut off. But the owners will be able to stay in their houses, not like in Douglas.'

'They're billeting six on me, you know,' Bessie said. 'Six! All different races, and probably Nazis to boot. Me, with Nazi women in my house – whatever will happen to me?'

'I suppose you could come and live here,' hazarded Ida – more out of sisterly duty than enthusiasm. She got on best with her elder sister in small doses.

'Good heavens, no!' exclaimed Bessie. 'And leave my lovely guest house to those women? No, no, I shall just have to stay put and make the best of it, though goodness knows how. It's like being put in prison.'

'Bessie will need a permit to go in and out of Port Erin,' continued Ida, sipping her tea. The whole thing seemed rather unreal, like something out of a film. 'And we shall need a permit from the police in Douglas if we want to visit her. It's so complicated.'

'I shall write to the Home Office and complain,' declared George, already having visions of the whole island – *his* island – being turned into some vast holiday camp for Germans.

Things were not going well, not well at all. British soldiers were being killed on the Normandy beaches, and at the very same time the island was being forced to welcome Nazis on to its own soil. It wasn't right.

If there was any justice in the world these days, mused George Quilliam, he certainly hadn't noticed it.

Creena sat in the darkness of the cinema and sniffed. It wasn't fair, it just wasn't fair.

As soon as she got off duty, she'd gone down to Female Surgical to see May Perkins for one of their regular chats, and all she'd found was an empty bed.

'She's gone,' Staff Nurse Ridley had said.

'Gone home?' Creena had stupidly asked.

And Staff had put her hand on Creena's shoulder in an unaccustomed gesture of tenderness.

'You were fond of her, Quilliam, weren't you?'

Creena had nodded in mute grief, the shock of May's death not quite sinking in. Since May had been readmitted for a second operation, a week ago, Creena had visited her almost every day, chatting to her about life on the island, making her laugh, taking her mind off the pain.

'You'll have a lot more deaths to put up with before you're much older,' Staff had said. 'It's the nature of the vocation. The thing we all have to learn is not to get too involved with the patients.'

After that, Creena had turned tail and fled. She simply had to get out of the hospital. Dillie had been sympathetic, of course, but Dillie wouldn't have been silly enough to get so emotionally involved in the first place, would she? It wasn't even as if May was Creena's first death. It was the suddenness, and the way that Creena had willed May to make a miraculous recovery.

That'll teach me, she thought. That'll teach me to think that I can make something happen just by wanting it to. After all, I wanted to be a good friend to Frankie; but look what a pig's ear I've made of that.

Feeling distinctly sorry for herself, she sat in the comforting anonymity of the picture house and gazed up at the screen. A newsreel announced that all signposts were being taken down to confuse the enemy in the event of an invasion; holiday camps on the east coast were to be closed down, too.

Creena wondered if anyone could seriously be considering going on holiday at a time like this, and she thought of her own faraway green island, now home to thousands and thousands of enemy internees – men, women and children. The article she'd read in the paper made it sound as if life for the women interned at Port Erin was going to be pretty much like a holiday, what with the sea-bathing and the golf course and the run of all the shops. She wondered how Aunt Bessie would cope with it all.

Her attention was caught by grainy footage of the Dunkirk rescue; ships, big and small, battling enemy fire to take thousands of exhausted men off the beaches. And wasn't that . . . wasn't that the *King Orry*? Now painted in a blotchy camouflage pattern, it was hardly recognisable as one of the three splendid 'white ladies' which had been the pride of the Manx fleet before the war.

So the *King Orry* was at war. You and me both, thought Creena, blowing her nose loudly and thrusting her hanky back into her pocket.

Chapter 9

'But, Auntie Mo...'

Mo Doyle drew herself up, tucking a wisp of greying hair behind her ear with a work-worn finger.

'Any more of your nonsense, Micky Bates, and I'll give you a good hiding. Now, take what you've been given and be grateful.'

The small boy shuffled from one foot to the other, reluctant to leave. Mo dropped the pile of dirty sheets on to the stone-flagged floor, and sighed.

'What is it now?'

'Uncle Jack said...'

'Yes, well, Uncle Jack says a lot of things. You ought to know better than to go believing them.'

'But...'

'No buts. You've got your bread and marge and a bottle of tea. That's more than most have got round here. Now get down that park and take Kitty with you. I don't want to hear another word from you until tea-time.'

'Yes, Auntie Mo.'

'And while you're at it, don't forget to buy tuppence-worth of fried fish on your way home. You lose that tuppence, and you're for it!'

'Come on, Micky, 'Arry Lane's got a bag of marbles.'

As Micky and his little sister ran off down Bishop Street into the fine June morning, Mo Doyle straightened up with difficulty, easing her aching back. That Micky. More trouble than a barrel-load of monkeys. He knew perfectly well that today was wash day, and she needed him and his sister out of the way. He was a good boy really, but he had too many fancies in his head. She blamed it on his Uncle Jack. As she lit a wood fire under the copper, she mused on the events which had brought this ill-assorted family together.

Jack was Mo's only surviving son. His twin brother, Joseph, had died in the Lambeth Hospital a few hours after birth and since Mo's policeman husband, Patrick, had passed away, Jack was all she had left. He'd always been a clever boy, but a bit wild – getting in with the wrong set. His father had despaired of him when the lad had been caught running an illegal bookmaking business in the alleyways near Cleaver Square. On that occasion he'd got off with a caution – what with him only being sixteen, and a copper's son at that – but it hadn't done him a bit of good. Jack had just become craftier, more cunning.

No, Jack wasn't a *bad* boy; it was just that he wasn't, well, steady. He was greedy for something better, impatient to get away from the grimy streets of Lambeth Marsh where the best he could hope for was a job labouring at McDougall's on the Albert Embankment, or 11s.10d. a week at George Harrods the boxmakers. Jack was ambitious; and his ambitions kept on getting him into trouble.

When Paddy died they'd moved from the flat in Campbell Buildings to number 12 Bishop Street. Nice big house it was, though it was always a struggle to pay the rent – especially with Kitty and Micky to look after. Not that she begrudged them their keep, poor kids, with their dad taken prisoner somewhere in France and no one knowing if he'd ever come home. Anyhow, with Paddy's pension and the money she raised from subletting rooms on the top floor, Mo always managed to make ends meet. No one would go hungry in her house, and the front step was always kept immaculately whitened.

The money Jack brought in helped, of course. Last year he'd taken a 'tot' stall in The Cut, selling second-hand clothes for a few pennies. He did good business too, but Mo knew the money he was earning from the barrow couldn't have paid for the sharp suits, the nice bits of meat he brought home on a Saturday night.

Jack wasn't just an illegal bookmaker, he was a black marketeer – a spiv. In these days of rationing and short-ages, it was hardly surprising that business was booming for the backstreet trader. Jack Doyle was the man everybody loved to hate: the man who could supply you with anything you needed – at a price.

'Come on, Ma,' Jack would wheedle, leaning lazily against the door frame, watching Mo as her strong brown arms fed starched wet sheets through the mangle. 'I just give the public what they want, that's all. Anything that's a bit difficult to get – tea, booze, bananas, fags . . .'

'It's not right.' Mo would have her back to him, stiff and

hostile. 'You know what your dad would have said about it.'

'Dad's not here, Ma. But I am. I'll look after us all, don't you worry.'

And he would put his big, strong arms around her shoulders and she would melt, just like she always did, as she looked up into those twinkling blue eyes.

'You're a charmer, Jack Doyle,' sighed Mo as she sorted out the dirty washing. 'You're a charmer through and through, but you'll come to no good.'

She felt guilty, knowing that she was becoming Jack's accomplice in his dishonesty; but there was a war on, she had her brother's two growing children to feed, and, well . . . you just did your best, didn't you?

It was a blazing hot June day, and beads of perspiration were standing out on Mo's brow. Perhaps, if she got on well with the wash, she'd treat herself to half a pint of ale down the Royal George later on. She peered into the bubbling depths of the copper. At least there was none of the telltale red scum that always appeared after old Edna Tilley had been doing her weekly wash. The whole street knew that Edna Tilley used Mo's copper to boil beetroots in! She took them down to Lower Marsh market to sell; and Mo hadn't the heart to tear her off a strip about it. The old duck was only doing what she could, scraping together a few pennies. When all's said and done, sighed Mo, you have to do your best.

''Ere, Mo – you better come quick!'

Mo spun round to see Mrs Marshall from Number 3, drying reddened hands on her damp apron. She was a spiteful woman, and a terrible gossip. Mo groaned inwardly. Ena Marshall was always first with any bad news.

'What's up, Ena? Not Jack again, is it?'

Ena laughed, her fat red jowls wobbling to the rhythm of her own private mirth.

'Gawd, no. 'E's too quick for the Old Bill, your Jack. No, it's your Micky, ain't it.'

'Micky!' Mo dropped her wooden laundry tongs. 'He's not been hurt, has he?'

'Not exactly. But 'e was 'avin' 'is backside well an' truly tanned for 'im when my Eric were passin' Maxwell's just now. Old man Maxwell reckons 'e caught 'im thievin'. If you ask me, it's your Jack as put 'im up to it. Dunno what your old man would have said about it all . . .'

Mo was not listening to Ena's malicious prattle. Micky – caught stealing! It just wasn't like him. She couldn't believe it. And from Maxwell's, the chemist in The Cut! Drying her hands hastily, she donned an old cardigan and threw off her knotted floral turban.

As she strode off down Bishop Street, past the twitching curtains and the watching eyes, Mo thanked her lucky stars that Dillie had turned out like she had.

Dillie Bayliss was Mo's pride and joy – the daughter she'd never had. There'd never been much money to spare in the Doyle household, but Paddy and his wife were careful with what they had, and they'd put by enough to help Dillie finish her schooling. She was as bright as a button, that kid. Even though Dillie was a grown young woman now, and training to be a nurse, Mo still thought of her as a kid.

Dillie had made some nice friends at the hospital –

especially the pretty red-haired Manx girl. Lovely girl, that Creena Quilliam, a real credit to her ma and pa. Nice friends and a respectable job: that was what Mo wanted for Dillie – not Jack's shady dealings.

Rounding the corner of The Cut, Mo caught sight of Micky, red-faced and wriggling, in the grasp of old Mr Maxwell, who ran the chemist's shop with his two spinster sisters. The boy was squealing with what looked like genuine indignation whilst his little sister Kitty looked on, round-eyed with fascination and horror.

'I never, mister. I never, I swear!'

Instinctively protective, Mo rolled up her sleeves and strode more purposefully forward, pushing her way through the small crowd which had gathered in front of the shop.

'Ain't you got no home to go to?' she snapped at a thin, bony woman with a string bag full of greenish potatoes. At the far end of the street, she could just make out the distinctive navy blue of a constable's uniform.

Micky and Kitty struck up a chorus of protest as she emerged from the crowd.

'Auntie Mo, Auntie Mo. We never, honest, we never!'

Silencing them with a glare, Mo turned to the chemist. Why couldn't they all be like Dillie?

'Now then, Mr Maxwell. Whatever the boy's been up to, I'm sure we can sort it out.'

The mist had melted away and the hot June sun was beating down out of a flawless blue sky, but Máire O'Keefe was oblivious to it. She felt chilled inside and out, marble-cold like a statue; a stone thing from which every ounce of warmth had been drained.

The sun filtered through the stained-glass windows of the church, casting shifting coloured patterns on her closed eyelids, on her pale lips as they moved in silent supplication. Head bowed, she tried to pray, but always it came down to a single word, a question: why?

She had been coming to the Catholic church in Douglas every day since the telegram had arrived – the telegram telling her that half of her life had been torn away. It felt as though her heart had been ripped from her chest, leaving nothing but a void, an empty, bleeding hole.

'My child?'

Máire opened her eyes and looked up, crossing herself.

'Father Riley.'

The elderly priest sat down on the chair beside her and looked at her with helpless compassion. He wanted to reach into her heart and offer hope, but right now she seemed lost too deep for him to reach.

'He was a good man, Máire.'

She nodded, her eyes red-rimmed but tearless, worn out with weeping.

'People said he was a coward, Father. If they hadn't said he was a coward, he wouldn't have gone away. He might still be alive . . .'

'Padraig was a brave man, Máire. He died saving other men's lives.'

'But why, Father? Why did he have to die at all? I just don't understand.'

Father Riley placed his tired old hand on Máire's shoulder. There were a lot of things he didn't understand about this war, either. All he – and she – could do was trust, and pray, and have faith.

'We must both pray for understanding, child.'

'I'm so afraid, Father. I'm so afraid I don't know how to pray any more.'

'Shall we pray together?'

She looked up at the old priest's face and nodded. And together they knelt on the cold tiled floor and bowed their heads.

'Eat up, Dolly Daydream – or I'll eat it for you! I'm ravenous, aren't you?'

Creena yawned and rubbed her eyes.

'Sorry, Bayliss. I can hardly keep my eyes open.'

Dillie nodded sagely and chewed hard on a crust of bread and marge.

'Nights get everyone like that, first time around. Seventeen on the trot's an awful lot to cope with, specially when you're Junior Relief and the night superintendent's got you running all over the place. But look, Cree – you've got to keep your strength up.'

Creena peered down at her plate. The hospital authorities had decreed, in their wisdom, that night nurses should have their 'breakfast' in the evening; their 'lunch' in the middle of the night; and their 'dinner' in the morning, before going to bed. Today's offering would have been bad enough at six o'clock in the evening – but at half past eight in the morning? She pulled a face.

'Yellow peril again!'

'Yellow peril' – an unsweetened, canary-yellow blancmange – seemed to be the chef's favourite pudding. At any rate, it turned up three times a week, regular as clockwork. Creena pushed her plate away.

164

'I can't. Honest, I'll be sick.'

'You'll be hungry later,' Dillie chided her.

'Yes, I know. But not for yellow peril!'

She was thinking of home. Of Ida's home-made custard, thick with eggs from their own hens and farm-fresh double cream. Of apple pie, hot and crisp from the oven, and feather-light steamed puddings succulent with raspberry jam. And of her father's new pig, which would soon be transformed into delicious bacon and sausages and home-cured hams...

'Shove it over then, Quilliam. I'll polish it off for you. Some of us don't have such delicate appetites!'

Eleanor Howells was busily munching her way through a plate of cold pilchards.

'Pass the mustard, Bayliss. Perhaps if I smother it I shan't be able to taste it!'

Perpetually hungry, Eleanor regarded any food as worth eating. As she ate, she got out a detective novel and started reading it under the table.

'Not still reading that rubbish, are you?' joshed Dillie. 'It rots the brain, you know. Besides, if Home Sister catches you you'll be for it – she hates reading at table.'

'I have to know what happens next, I just have to!' explained Eleanor through a half-chewed mouthful. She was addicted to pulp detective fiction, the more lurid the better. This latest one was entitled *Body in the Basement*.

'So who dunnit, then?' enquired Creena.

'It was either the housemaid or the medical student, I'm sure it was.'

'Probably the medical student,' chuckled Dillie. 'I wouldn't trust some of 'em to take my pulse!'

'A holiday,' announced Creena. 'That's what we all need. A couple of weeks to sleep and sleep and sleep.'

'Well, we've fat chance of getting one,' observed Dillie. 'They cancelled Whitsun and now they've cancelled August Bank Holiday, too. Do you suppose they think the Jerries are more likely to invade if we're all out sunbathing?'

The thought of invasion made everyone fall silent for a few moments. The east coast was heavily guarded, the Home Guard were on alert, and – worst of all – the Channel Islands had fallen to the Germans. That had really brought the threat home to all of them.

'Never mind,' said Dillie, scooping up the last spoonful of food with an artificial cheeriness. 'Mustn't grumble, eh? At least this is better than those terrible fried fish-paste sandwiches they gave us last week. Gave me a bellyache for days, they did.'

Eleanor took a gulp of stewed tea.

'Ugh. This tastes like disinfectant.'

Dillie winked,

'You know what Home Sister's like about "inner cleanliness". It probably *is* disinfectant.'

'Ah well,' mused Creena, 'it's not as if we've got any more to put up with than they have back home.'

Dillie looked up.

'You heard from your folks lately?'

'I had a letter from Máire the other day – you know, the Irish girl I used to work with.'

'The one whose brother . . . ?'

Creena nodded. The news of Padraig's death at Dunkirk had come as a terrible shock to her. How badly it had affected Máire she could only guess.

'It's a tragedy. They were so close, and he was such a lovely man. You know, my cousin Mona was quite sweet on him.'

'So how's Máire managing on her own?'

'I'm not sure. She's gone off to Ramsey to work in a hotel, I can't think why.'

'You never can tell what people will do when they're upset,' observed Dillie. 'Look how Kitty and Micky ran away when they heard about their dad being taken prisoner. Still, they've settled down all right now. You can get used to pretty well anything if you have to.'

'I don't think Mother ever will,' laughed Creena. 'She's convinced Aunt Bessie's going to be murdered in her bed by her internees.'

Eleanor Howells gave a dramatic shudder.

'Can't say I'd fancy being stuck on an island with thousands of Jerries. I'll take my chances here with the bombs – that's if they ever come.'

'My friend Arnold in the ARP . . .' began Dillie, and everyone started giggling. Dillie had been going on about her new 'friend' Arnold ever since she'd met him on a visit to London Zoo, where he looked after the animals which were not being transferred to Whipsnade. Dillie insisted that she and Arnold were 'just friends', but the hospital grapevine had practically married them off already.

Dillie glared indignantly at her laughing companions.

'My *friend* Arnold in the ARP,' she repeated, 'reckons Hitler hasn't got the guts to mount any big raids on London, not with our Brylcreem boys giving him such a bloody nose. Speaking of which, Cree, how's your brother?'

'He's a navigator now. Says he's missing home, but I bet he's got all the WAAFs wrapped round his little finger. He looks so dashing in that photo he sent me . . .'

Instinctively Creena glanced down at her own uniform, the lilac dress rumpled and the starched white apron pockmarked with tiny, unidentifiable stains. She could feel her lacy cap sliding askew on her hair, the unruly auburn mop secured with dozens of impossible-to-obtain grips.

She exchanged glances with Dillie and both burst out laughing.

'More than they can say for us, eh, Quilliam? Do you think we'll make Bond Street mannequins when the war's over?'

'Not if she doesn't eat her pilchards,' commented Marian Clarke-Herbert as she slid into the seat next to Creena's and started tucking into her dinner. 'What's the matter, poppet – off your food?'

'Quilliam's in love, aren't you?' teased Dillie.

'Oh, I say! You made up with your boy back home then?' enquired Eleanor Howells, forever fantasising about other people's love lives.

'No, not him,' replied Dillie in a tantalising whisper. 'It's that new orthopaedic registrar, isn't it, Cree? Can't say I blame her either, he's a real dreamboat. *And* he can't keep his eyes off her . . .'

'Some girls have all the luck,' commented Howells dreamily.

Creena felt her cheeks burning.

'Don't!' she squeaked in protest, suppressing giggles of embarrassment. 'It's not true.' But how she wished it were . . .

'Come off it!' chided Dillie. 'I've seen the way he looks at you – and if you ask me, the feeling's mutual.'

At that moment Creena was saved from further embarrassment by the arrival of Home Sister, her voice ringing out with such authority that every starched cap in the Junior Dining Room sprang to attention.

'Eat up, girls! Bed in precisely thirty minutes' time. And I expect to see clean plates. Whilst you are on night duty, you must pay particular attention to proper rest and nourishment.'

Dillie returned to her food, munching thoughtfully on the last few mouthfuls of her bread and marge.

'Course, you're right,' she commented thoughtfully. 'The food here's diabolical. Not a patch on my Auntie Mo's bacon pudding.'

Creena closed her eyes and groaned. Crispy bacon and cheese with a hint of onion, all rolled up in a featherlight suet crust . . .

'Oh don't. You're making my tummy rumble!'

'She used to make it on a Friday, when Uncle Patrick brought his wages home. It's our Micky's favourite. Jack was telling me yesterday when I met him outside the Underground. Hey, you'll never guess what that little monkey Micky's been up to.'

'Go on, tell me.'

'Auntie Mo only caught him fighting with the chemist's shop boy. She'd given Micky tuppence for fried fish and this boy tried to take it off him, see – so he fetched him one, right on the nose. Well, old Maxwell – that's the chemist – he reckoned young Micky'd been caught stealing, what with the shop boy howling and shouting "It was him, it was him!" So old Maxwell grabs hold of Micky and gives him the hiding of his life – and all the time, the shop boy's got Micky's tuppence in his waistcoat pocket!'

Creena gave a slightly nervous giggle. The story reminded her of all the times she'd taken the blame for something somebody else had done. It was just like George Quilliam to use the cane first, and ask questions afterwards.

'Poor Micky! So what happened?'

'Auntie Mo marched into the chemist's shop and told old Maxwell he'd better listen to what Micky had to say – because Micky doesn't tell lies! Of course, the truth came out and the shop boy got a clip round the ear. Mind you, Micky caught it off Mo, for not staying out of mischief down the park with Kitty, like he'd been told to. He's got a real shiner, too.' She chuckled, remembering how Mo's determination to be stern always ended up melting. 'It must be weeks since you last saw Auntie Mo,' she added.

'Not since she came up to Cas with that old gentleman.'

'Old Bert? I wouldn't describe him as a gentleman!' Dillie pictured Auntie Mo's latest tenant, a crusty old codger who had fought in the Boer War and liked to make sure that everyone knew about it.

'Well, anyway, we didn't have a chance to chat. You know what Casualty Sister's like about talking to patients.'

Dillie screwed up her face into a passable imitation of Sister Edgerton's fierce expression.

'"Idle chitchat, nurses! The devil makes work for idle hands..." Tell you what – you've got some off-duty coming up, haven't you? How'd you like a proper meal?'

'What – go to Lyons Corner House, you mean? Funds are a bit low at the moment...'

'No, not that. Come home with me! Come to Mo's for tea.'

'Again? Won't your aunt mind?'

Dillie laughed.

'Mind? She'll be as pleased as punch. Auntie Mo's really taken a shine to you.'

'Nurse Bayliss! What is the meaning of this?'

Dillie swallowed hard and tried to hide the slice of pie behind her back, but it was too late and the dry potato pastry had stuck in her throat. Creena stared at her in panic as Sister MacCarthy's massive bulk loomed up in the doorway of the ward kitchen.

'This is disgraceful, Nurse! How many times have you been told that eating on duty is not permissible under any circumstances?'

Dillie hung her head, her face crimson with shame. Creena stared at her shoes. Only a minute or so earlier, she too had been gulping down the congealed remains of the patients' supper-time vegetable pie – mercifully left in the ward kitchen by a forgetful – or compassionate – day staff.

'Eating the patients' food is not only undisciplined, Nurse Bayliss, it is dishonest. Whilst such behaviour is perhaps not entirely unexpected in one of your ... background, it is certainly not acceptable in a Royal Lambeth nurse.'

Creena willed Dillie not to lose her temper. She breathed a sigh of relief as her friend clenched her teeth and forced herself to play the humble first-year probationer.

'Yes, Sister. I'm very sorry, Sister.'

'Three meals a day are provided for you free of charge,

Nurse. Whilst you are on duty, your sole care should be the wellbeing of your patients. Remember your vocation, Nurse – if you indeed have one. You are privileged to be allowed to train at the Royal Lambeth School of Nursing.'

'Yes, Sister.'

Sister MacCarthy's basilisk stare lighted on Creena.

'Nurse Quilliam.'

'Yes, Sister?'

'Why are you loitering in the ward kitchen? Have you no work to do?'

Without waiting for a reply, she continued:

'As soon as you have finished taking round the evening drinks, you are to make up a post-op bed in the side ward for an emergency admission. He should be up from theatre within the hour.'

'Yes, Sister. Right away, Sister.'

Creena turned to go.

'And Nurse Quilliam . . .'

She turned back to face Sister, suddenly and painfully aware that her starched apron had come unpinned on the left side of her bodice.

'Smarten yourself up. This is the Royal Lambeth – not some insignificant little island hospital.'

Ten minutes later, as Creena was folding back the blankets on the post-op bed in the side ward, Harry the orderly bustled past with a trolley of urine bottles. Days, nights, medical, surgical, they were all the same to Harry. Nothing ever seemed to get him down. He paused at the doorway and hissed a cheery greeting.

'What's up, Quilliam? You've got a face like a wet weekend. Sister on the warpath, is she?'

Creena nodded, shamefaced.

'Bayliss caught it for eating in the ward kitchen, but it was just as much my fault too.'

'Poor kids – they don't feed you right, that's the problem. Now if I had my way . . .'

Creena placed her finger on her lips.

'Sh! Someone might hear.'

Harry gave a big grin that almost split his jolly freckled face in two.

'Mum's the word, old girl.'

His trolley squeaked and rattled on the polished linoleum as he disappeared into the main body of the ward, and Creena found herself smiling. He was a likeable character, was Harry – and a born survivor too. She could learn a lot from him. When he was around she felt curiously safe, like she used to feel when she and Frankie were kids together.

Frank. She thought of the unanswered letter, still lying in the drawer in her room. She wished their last meeting could have been happier, but something had changed between them – as if their lives were a big jigsaw puzzle whose pieces didn't fit together any more.

They should have talked properly. But it was too late to do anything about it now. It was weeks since Frank's last letter – she didn't even know where he was.

'Nurse, Nurse!'

The voice was a hoarse, urgent whisper; and Creena hurried out into the ward, masking the beam of her torch with her hand so as not to wake up any sleeping patients. Fifty-two beds stretched away into the distance, in two dimly lit rows. Somewhere at the far end, Harry's tall, rangy figure was moving about, making a patient comfortable. The cool silence was broken here and there by the rustle of a crisp white sheet, the rasping cough of the old man with one good lung.

The young man in the bed nearest Sister's desk was scarcely more than a boy, his chin downy and beardless. Eighteen or nineteen, perhaps, at most. He was a casualty of the savage air battle now raging in the skies over southern England; the Battle of Britain, they were calling it. Day after day, more brave British pilots were giving their lives to defend their country against the evils of Nazi Germany. It was all Creena could do to suppress the tide of anger within her.

Most patients were taken to EMS hospitals in the country after initial treatment, but this boy was too poorly to be moved. Creena couldn't help feeling thankful that Robert was in bombers, and not a fighter pilot as George had hoped he would be. Robert would undoubtedly face other dangers, but at least he was spared this.

In the dull, yellowish torchlight, the boy's skin looked like ancient parchment: thin, shiny and translucent. It reminded Creena of how May Perkins's skin had looked, the very last time she saw her. She placed her hand on his forehead. He was still burning up, despite the tepid sponging he'd been given to reduce his temperature.

'What can I get you?'

'Drink . . . drink of water.'

Creena eased him up the bed a little way and helped him curl his shaking fingers around the feeding cup on his locker. She tried to look only at his face, not at the bandaged stump of his right arm or the bed cradle arching over the charred remnants of his legs. So young, so ill. Lowly first-year probationers were not told very much, but it had been clear from the hushed tones of Sister and the consultant that this was one patient who was not expected to recover.

'Better?'

'Yes, better. Thank you, Nurse. So hot ... can hardly breathe.'

'Do you need anything? Shall I fetch Sister?'

'No, no. Just want ... to sleep now.'

The boy's pale grey eyes closed, and his face relaxed, as Creena lowered him gently on to the softness of the pillows. He was no weight at all, just a thistledown of blond hair and wasted flesh. She marked up his fluid intake on the chart at the end of his bed, and tiptoed quietly away back to the desk, trying not to think about Robert, Frank and poor Padraig ... Padraig the gentle giant, who had drowned trying to save others who were fighting a war which had never been his to fight.

Despite the processions of pale, sad-faced evacuees from Dunkirk and the horribly burned pilots who had passed through the Royal Lambeth on their way to the EMS hospitals in Surrey, the war still seemed a curiously distant thing; something that was more of an inconvenience than a real danger to the people of London.

Certainly the ordinary folk of Lambeth Marsh seemed to have forgotten their initial panic, and were taking the invasion threat in their stride. In fact, they were now going about their business pretty much as normal. In the early days of the war, everyone had expected the worst. Gardens had been dug up for Anderson shelters, gas masks had been handed out and were taken absolutely everywhere, just in case; everyone was convinced that Hitler would soon launch an all-out attack on London.

At the Royal Lambeth Hospital, the wards on the upper floors had been evacuated and their windows bricked up, in readiness for the air raids. The old glass-roofed casualty department had been closed down, and relocated in Surgical Outpatients. Emergency operating theatres had been set up in the warren of cavern-like rooms which opened off the central corridor running almost the entire length of the hospital basement; and outpatients' clinics and non-emergency admissions had been suspended, in anticipation of a daily influx of 25,000 casualties in London alone.

But the air raids hadn't come. The Battle of Britain might be raging overhead in the English summer skies, but it seemed a world away – a spectacle to be observed from afar rather than participated in. Apart from the nightly 'nuisance' raids on the outskirts over the last couple of weeks, London had remained untouched; and not surprisingly the people of Lambeth had grown tired of waiting. Patients had begun drifting back to the hospital, and little by little, all the clinics had reopened. It was business as usual at the Royal Lambeth.

The ward doors swung open and a trolley glided towards the side ward, Staff Nurse Pemberton bustling around the moaning patient and a white-coated figure stooping over the trolley, murmuring words of calm reassurance:

'It will be all right now. Try to sleep, everything will be all right.'

Dr Temple's soft voice sent a shiver through Creena

from head to toe, the way it had done the very first time they met. There was such warmth in him, such compassion. Despite the long hours he worked, he always had time for his patients, never failed to put them first.

Their eyes met, briefly, as the trolley disappeared into the side ward, and Creena felt something inside her reach out to him, yearning and strong. Something that might be more than admiration, more than respect.

No, she mustn't fantasise; it could never be more than wishful thinking.

As the door to the side ward closed, she sat down at the desk again; and the whole city seemed to hold its breath, waiting for something immense and irrevocable to happen.

Mo Doyle sat in the kitchen at 12 Bishop Street, looking out of the window at the lightening sky. She'd half promised Jack that she'd go down the public shelter with the children, but instead she'd sent them off there with Edna Tilley and Gladys from the top floor. Bert hadn't wanted to go – old soldier that he was – but in the end Mo had managed to persuade him. To be honest, it was a relief to get him out of the house, what with him going on at Jack about 'doing the right thing' and 'King and Country'.

But tonight, of all nights, Mo couldn't face being away from Bishop Street.

She looked up at the sky, its velvety blue-black brightening to royal blue as the August night faded into early dawn. A light red glow to the north showed that, once again, the Luftwaffe had confined their attentions to factories and military installations on the outskirts of the metropolis.

Hitler wasn't interested in Lambeth Marsh; at least, not tonight.

Still, she was glad she'd sent the kids down the shelter. Almost a full moon it was – a bombers' moon – and it was better to be safe than sorry. She'd spent the night sitting in the kitchen, listening to the distant thud of the ack-ack guns north of London, watching the pale beams of the searchlights crisscrossing in the sky. There had been one or two bombs dropped somewhere a long way off, but nothing Bishop Street need worry about – despite Old Bert's intimations of doom.

In any case, it wasn't bombs Mo was afraid of. It was the waiting. Waiting for the raids which must surely come. Hitler had sworn to bring his enemies to their knees. He'd done it to Belgium, Poland, even France ... and now Britain stood alone. Goering hadn't yet managed to shoot the ill-prepared, outnumbered RAF out of the skies, but even if the Luftwaffe were sent home with their tails between their legs, that wouldn't be the end of it. Mo Doyle was a good judge of character, and she knew a nasty piece of work when she saw one. That Hitler was a man who hated failure. He'd be back, she knew it. But would London be ready for him?

Tonight, Mo had needed to be alone with her thoughts. She was thinking of Patrick, wounded in the Great War but brave and strong as a lion. Patrick who had upped and died on her, five years ago to this very day. The glint of a tear appeared at the corner of her eye but she wiped it away, swiftly and efficiently, with the corner of her ever-present apron.

'Now then, gel; buck up an' smile.'

That was what Patrick would have said, and she had to be strong for the kids. Micky and Kitty needed her more than ever now, what with their dad Eddie being a prisoner of war. She'd sent them down the shelter with a packet of bread and jam, fervently praying she'd be there to greet them when they came back in the morning.

Then there was Jack. He might think he was grown-up and independent, but he still needed someone to give him a good talking-to when he went too far off the rails. She sighed. Why hadn't he come home last night – again? She knew that money wasn't so easy for him to come by, what with the temporary suspension of horse-racing, but he always found a way. She pictured the shadowy figures under the railway arches, the goods exchanged without a word for fear of discovery. And in the morning he'd be back, hollow-eyed and unshaven, but with money in his pocket once again. Mo wasn't a timid woman, but sometimes it paid not to ask too many questions.

In the midst of all this chaos there was Dillie. Good, sensible, honest Dillie. Patrick would be proud of her if he could see her now – and Mo was sure that he could.

It was getting quite light now. Danger over for another night, Mo closed the window gently, turned back to the old scrubbed wooden table and started cutting thick slabs of bread. The kids would be back home from the shelter soon, and they'd be clamouring for their breakfasts. There might be a war on, but Mo Doyle didn't see any reason to change her daily routine for the sake of some jumped-up Austrian corporal.

Lambeth was waking up, just as it had always done; and Mo shrugged her shoulders as she dragged a thin scraping of margarine across the doorsteps of bread. Lord Haw-Haw was doing his best to terrify them all with his daily messages of doom, but there was no sense in fretting about a disaster that might never come.

Already there were signs of life in Bishop Street; the whistling of the milkman, bottles and churns clinking as he led his horse and cart through the pinkish-blue of the dawn light. The old man next door was coughing and wheezing as he shuffled down the yard to the communal privy. A baby was crying somewhere in one of the flats opposite. New life; and a new morning.

Chapter 10

'Cockles, winkles, shrimps – tuppence a pint!'

'Git yer 'earthstones 'ere.'

'Cow 'eel an' tripe, ladies. Lovely jellied eels.'

The cacophony of stallholders' cries forced Dillie to raise her voice as she pursued her cousin Jack down the street.

'I wish you'd give it up, Jack, really I do.'

Dillie had to quicken her pace to keep up with Jack as he strode down The Cut, hands thrust into the pockets of his blue chalk-striped suit and fedora pulled down at a rakish angle over his eyes. She couldn't help wondering how much it had all cost: the double-breasted suit, the handmade shirt, the shiny two-tone shoes – and where Jack had got the money.

'It worries Auntie Mo. She can't sleep at night.'

Jack wheeled round and stopped abruptly, almost knocking over a small, gap-toothed boy who was selling carrots and potatoes from a barrow.

''Ere, watch where yer goin', mate!'

Jack's blue eyes glinted with defiance.

'Look, Dillie, how I earn my money's my own business.'

'But...'

'I suppose you think you're better than all the rest of us, now you've got your fancy friends up at the hospital.'

His voice was tinged with bitterness. Saddened, Dillie reached out and touched his arm. They'd been so close when she was a little girl, orphaned and alone. Now it was as if Jack wanted to build a wall between them.

'No one's been better to me than you and Auntie Mo, you know that, Jack. But it doesn't mean I can just stand by and say nothing. You don't have to do this – you could get a proper job.'

Jack let out a dry, humourless laugh.

'Oh yeah. Washing flour sacks down McDougall's? Where's the future in that, Dillie? You bettered yourself, why shouldn't I?'

'You could always join up,' said Dillie quietly, wishing instantly that she'd kept her mouth shut.

There was a brief moment of awkwardness before Jack replied.

'It's always the same thing, ain't it? You *know* the army won't have me. Turned me down flat.'

Dillie knew all right. Jack's convenient ill-health was no secret down Bishop Street, though none of Mo's neighbours had seen much evidence of the flat feet and chronic asthma which apparently afflicted him. As far as Dillie was concerned, the only time she'd ever heard Jack coughing was when he had his first cigarette of the day.

She sighed.

'It's not just Mo, Jack. I'm thinking of you too. Don't want you getting yourself into trouble.'

'I can handle myself, Dillie.' Jack's voice was firm but

there was no longer any anger in it. 'Just stop goin' on at me and askin' damn fool questions, will you? I'm doin' all right.'

He sincerely hoped Dillie hadn't been around to spot him ten minutes earlier when he was concluding a little deal with Sid Clayden, the local Mr Big. That could lead to some very awkward questions indeed. Rummaging in his pocket he pulled out a thick wad of notes. Dillie's eyes widened. On her probationer's pay of £30 per year, she was lucky if she ever saw a pound note, let alone a whole bundle of crisp white fivers.

Jack peeled off a ten-shilling note and stuffed it into the top pocket of Dillie's old coat.

'You're lookin' peaky – not bin takin' care of yourself, have you? Here's ten bob. Get yourself somethin' nice.'

Dillie's conscience told her she ought to protest, but at that moment a middle-aged woman pushed past, chivvying along two grubby boys in cut-down trousers secured with string around the waist. A few steps behind trudged a shabby, dispirited-looking man who might once have been a stevedore. His hands were roughened with work, and his now flabby frame retained the last vestiges of an impressive musculature. He growled irritably as he disappeared between the rows of tot stalls and costermongers' barrows.

'Git a move on, or you'll feel the weight of my 'and.'

As they strolled on together through the street market, towards George's pudding shop at the end of the street, Jack turned back to Dillie.

'Is it so bad, not wantin' to be like him? Whatever else happens, I'm not endin' up with the backside hangin' out of my pants and kids who won't give me the time of day.'

'No – but there's other ways, Jack. Legal ways. I wish you'd settle down, get yourself a wife, maybe, instead of all those girlfriends of yours...'

Jack's eyes twinkled with sudden mirth.

'Me – married? Who to?' He gave a laugh. 'Tell you what – how about that friend of yours, eh? The one with the red 'air and the daft name.'

'Creena?' Dillie was astonished.

'Yeah, that's the one. Little red-haired Creena. Bit spindly, but she's a real looker, that one.' He grinned broadly. 'Reckon she'd take me on? Or has she got a bloke back 'ome?'

They reached the end of the street and Jack hailed an old man selling newspapers outside Mrs Grundy's café.

'Wotcha, Fancy. What's today's latest score then?'

Fancy Edwards – so nicknamed because of his taste for lurid painted ties – squinted knowledgeably up at the sky where vapour trails marked the passage of many aircraft – both British and German. It was early August now, but there was no sign of the Battle of Britain ending. He indicated figures chalked on a blackboard propped up against his stand.

'It's gorn quiet but it'll soon be 'ottin' up, Jack. Four-one to us so far. Ours come dahn north of the river somewhere, but I saw 'im bail out safe.'

'That's what I like to hear,' said Jack, rummaging in his pocket for change and tucking a *Daily Herald* under his arm. 'Let's hope Jerry gets the message quick and buggers off 'ome.' He took a dubious squint at Ma Bates's café. Every kid in Lambeth knew that Iris Bates's kitchen was running with rats the size of small terriers, but she did do a nice meat pie. Jack looked at Dillie and raised a quizzical eyebrow.

'Cup of char?'

'Why not?'

As she pushed open the café door, Dillie couldn't help chuckling to herself as she pictured the peculiar combination of Creena Quilliam and Jack Doyle.

'Creena did use to have a bloke,' she told Jack as she sat down at a battered wooden table with folded-up paper under one of the legs to stop it rocking. 'Frank Kinrade, his name was. She'd known him since they were kids. Sent him off with his tail between his legs when he came to see her on his embarkation leave, though.'

''Ad a big bust-up, did they?'

'No, not really. Poor girl's all mixed up – she doesn't really know what she wants. And Frank was really cut up about it, by all accounts. But that's the war for you. It changes people.'

Jack took a swig from the tin mug of hot, sweet tea.

'So there's still a chance for me, eh?'

For a moment Dillie stared at him, almost thinking he was serious. Then she giggled.

'You are a tease, Jack. Besides, looks like there's a new man on the scene, or there soon will be.'

'Is that so?' Jack took out an engraved silver cigarette case and selected a slender Russian cigarette. 'Want one?'

Dillie wrinkled her nose and shook her head.

'Don't care for those funny foreign fags.' She bent over the table and lowered her voice. 'If you ask me, she's set her cap at one of the doctors – Oliver Temple, his name is.

He can't keep his eyes off her, and she goes all trembly and silly every time he speaks to her.'

'Don't worry me,' replied Jack dismissively, blowing smoke rings and winking roguishly at a couple of factory girls sitting at a neighbouring table. 'There ain't no woman I've ever met who can resist me if I put my mind to it.'

Dillie shook her head and laid her gloved hand on his.

'Take it from me, Jack. This one's right out of your league.'

The Battle of Britain raged on through the middle of August, bringing with it new terrors, new suspense; a feeling that if this crucial battle were not won – and swiftly – all would be lost. Everyone knew that Hitler's armies were ranged across the Channel, simply waiting for the signal to invade once the Luftwaffe had crushed the life and spirit out of the Royal Air Force. And London held its breath, waiting to see if Hitler would carry out his threats.

It was about half past three on a sultry August afternoon, and Creena and Marian were working together on Female Surgical, under the watchful eye of Sister Meredith. On this particular afternoon Creena was showing one of the very newest probationers how to give out the patients' afternoon teas.

'That's right, Jamieson. Just the one slice of bread and marge per patient. And watch you don't give Mrs Oldroyd any sugar in her tea, she's diabetic . . .'

The sound of distant gunfire floated in through the open windows, vapour trails crisscrossing the skies. Another dogfight was being acted out above London, two planes locked in a deadly battle, two mothers' sons fighting to the death. But no one dared look in case it went badly for the British boy.

'Bit hot in 'ere, ain't it?' observed Gloria Bradley loudly, her arms and chest almost indecently bare in her insubstantial nightdress.

'It's a wonder you ain't freezin' to death,' retorted Mrs Lawlor in the next bed. 'Dressed like that – or should I say *un*dressed?'

Several small explosions overhead were followed by a louder bang, and then there was only one aircraft engine droning across the London sky. The other one had been replaced by the unmistakable whining, coughing drone of distress.

'It's ours,' said Mrs Eversleigh, her pale face grown still paler.

'No it ain't.' Mrs Lawlor stopped knitting and listened intently. 'It's one of theirs.'

'For Gawd's sake shut it, will yer?' Gloria Bradley entreated them. 'I'm tryin' to listen. Go an' ave a look out the winder, will you, Nurse?'

Creena left Nurse Jamieson in charge of the tea trolley and pushed open the doors which led to the balcony. In peacetime these had been clear glass, but now the glass had been taken out and replaced with thick plywood as a precaution against bomb blasts.

Creena was just in time to see a fighter plane – its entire tail end a ragged, smoking mess – go screaming through the air above her head, missing the roof of the Royal Lambeth Hospital by what seemed, in her terror, like mere feet.

Hands over her ears against the deafening sound, she

watched as the plane's nose dipped in a final dive, ominous black smoke pouring from its rear as it plunged towards the river and its final nemesis.

Although she had heard dogfights before, this was the first time that Creena had seen any of the planes at such close quarters. She felt shivery.

Walking back into the ward she closed the balcony doors behind her.

'It was one of theirs,' she said.

Harry the ward orderly was walking along the Embankment when he saw the Messerschmitt.

One minute it was the epitome of Nazi menace, the next a torn and broken toy, its fuselage ripped through by bullet holes and the tail section blown clean away.

As he watched the plane plummet through the air in a plume of oily black smoke, he found himself feeling sorrow rather than elation. Poor bugger of a tail-gunner, he thought to himself. Just one more unlucky kid who drew the short straw.

The wrecked plane belly-flopped in the mudflats at the edge of the Thames, its nose burrowing some way down into the soft, smelly mud and the smoking tail end hissing as the river water lapped against the hot and blackened metal. And then there was silence. Nothing moved, save the gently lapping river water, murky with debris.

Moments later, AFS fire tenders were rushing to the scene, uncoiling hoses to play jets of water on to the wreckage; policemen and ARP wardens appearing as if from nowhere, self-important and loud, holding back a gathering crowd of ghoulish onlookers.

Slightly sickened, Harry turned away and walked slowly back towards the hospital, his thick-soled right boot heavy and awkward on his aching leg.

Poor buggers the lot of us, he thought.

It was a couple of hours later, as Creena was heading towards the Junior Dining Room for a belated break and a quick listen to the news on the wireless, that she met Eleanor Howells half walking, half trotting down the corridor.

'I say, Quilliam!'

'Where's the fire, Howells? If Matron spots one of her nurses running she'll have your guts for garters.'

Eleanor paused, red-faced and bright-eyed with excitement.

'It's that Jerry plane,' she said. 'The one that came down in the river. You must have heard the crash.'

Creena nodded.

'Well, the AFS have managed to cut the crew out. The gunner was dead – shot to pieces, they said. The wireless operator's lost an arm but he's going to be all right. They've taken him to a military hospital. But the pilot . . .'

'What about him?'

'The pilot has severe spinal injuries. He can't be moved under any circumstances – so guess what? They're bringing him here and putting him in one of the private rooms!'

Creena stifled a yawn and resisted the urge to lean her aching, sweating back against the cool metal of the radiator. Her starched apron and cuffs were going limp in the heat. This August weather was sweltering and soporific, but it would never do to be caught napping –

especially on Female Surgical. Sister Meredith was a real tartar, and Staff Nurse Ridley wasn't all sweetness and light, either.

Creena took a crafty peek at the ward clock. Still only mid-morning. Another round of obs to do, Mrs Eversleigh's dressing to assist with and absolutely ages until lunch.

Being bright, breezy and efficient all the time wasn't easy – unless you were Marian Clarke-Herbert, of course. Everyone knew that Marian was a born nurse.

'Chin up, old thing!' she hissed encouragingly as she strode towards the sluice, a vision of invincible English womanhood in snowy starched apron and lilac skirts. 'Dillie's treating us all to the flicks on our next day off.'

'Really? How come?'

'Seems that no-good cousin of hers – Jock is it?'

'Jack. Jack Doyle.' Creena smiled inwardly as she pictured him in his sharp suit and two-tone shoes.

'Yes, well, Jack's slipped her some more of his ill-gotten gains, and to salve her conscience she's taking you, me and Hester to the flicks to see George Formby's latest. So you'd better get out your glad rags and gas mask!'

As she took Mrs Eversleigh's temperature, Creena wondered what on earth had possessed Dillie to accept more money from Jack. Dillie was always going on about what a bad lot he was, and how the whole family was suspicious about how he made his living. Mind you, a trip to the pictures would be nice ...

'You look all in, duck,' observed Mrs Eversleigh as Creena took the thermometer out of her mouth, shook it down and replaced it in the little vial of antiseptic at the head of the bed. 'They work you girls too hard.'

Once a huge and motherly woman, Mrs Eversleigh had shrunk by degrees to a shadow of her former self. As the disease within her had caught hold, it had turned her skin to the colour of old vellum. Last week's exploratory operation had confirmed the worst: the surgeon had removed a huge malignant tumour, and the prognosis was doubtful. It broke Creena's heart to see her, for she reminded her so much of May Perkins. The death of people she cared about was something that Creena was still having difficulty coming to terms with. It wasn't easy, looking after patients without getting emotionally involved.

Creena replaced Mrs Eversleigh's TPR chart on its hook at the foot of the bed and rearranged her stack of pillows.

'Oh, I'm right as rain, Mrs E. And how are you today?'

'Hell of a bleedin' bellyache, to be honest, Nurse. You couldn't...'

Creena consulted the chart.

'I'll ask Sister if we can give you something for the pain.'

'Thanks, duck. You're a good gel. You know, what you an' me both need is a decent bit of kip. Bit bloody close that bombing last night.'

'Yes, I suppose it was.' Creena wasn't quite sure what to say, having – rather embarrassingly – slept through last night's Orange Alert. Jerry was still targeting only the periphery of the city for his night raids, and Creena had learnt to sleep through the air-raid siren. She straightened the castors on the bed-legs and smoothed down the white bedspread. 'Anyhow, no need to worry. Jerry's only interested in our factories and airfields. You'll be quite safe here.'

'Until 'e sends 'is bleedin' tanks over,' commented a heavily built woman balanced painfully on a rubber ring. 'We'll all be killed, you mark my words. Just look what 'e done to Poland and France.'

'Please don't talk like that, Mrs Paterson . . .' pleaded Creena, but Mavis Paterson was in full spate.

'They say them SS men kill kids and turn 'em into soap,' she said with relish. 'I read it in the paper.'

A young woman in the next bed gave a stifled sob.

'Shut yer face, Mavis, you stupid mare,' snapped Mrs Eversleigh. 'Now look what you've done. You've upset our Gladys.' She contemplated Creena, then turned to her companion in the next bed. 'So, what do you reckon to Nurse Quilliam, Mrs Lawlor? She lookin' under the weather, or what?'

'Too skinny by 'alf,' replied the docker's wife, looking up from her interminable knitting and wincing as she pulled her cholecystectomy stitches. She had two sons in the navy and a daughter driving lorry-loads of explosives for the army, so she liked a diversion to take her mind off her own worries. 'A bit down in the mouth an' all – could do wiv a bit of slap an' tickle. Well, it works wonders wiv my Stan!'

Her throaty chuckle infected all the patients down the left side of the ward, and Creena was sure that Staff Nurse Ridley must be able to hear the commotion from the ward office. Hastily she moved on to the next bed, thrusting a thermometer into a surprised patient's mouth and seizing hold of her wrist.

'Got a boyfriend, have you, luv?' interjected Gloria Bradley, who was busy titivating her eyebrows with a pair of tweezers and a pocket mirror. 'Pretty girl like you should have a boyfriend – someone to buy you nice things and stuff. Some rich geezer to get you out of this bloody awful hole.'

Gloria was by far the most interesting character on the ward, but it wasn't until Marian had enlightened her that Creena realised what a colourful life she led. Apparently, Gloria was a well-known lady of the night, a regular in all the wharfside pubs. Bottle-blonde and brassy with it, she didn't give a damn what anyone thought of her.

'Yes, go on, tell us,' teased Mrs Lawlor. 'Courtin', are you?'

'Really, ladies, I don't think this is quite the place . . .' began Creena, embarrassed beyond belief.

'Leave her alone, girls,' said Mrs Eversleigh. 'Can't you see she's shy? Bet she has got a fella, though – she's blushing all over her face!'

'Mrs Eversleigh, if Sister gets to hear . . .'

A sudden shout in the corridor outside the ward made conversation draw to an abrupt halt.

'Whatever is that?' Creena turned, and started walking back down the ward towards the office.

'Sounds like a bulldog wiv a bellyache,' commented Mrs Lawlor, dropping a stitch.

'No, no, no, no!' It was a young woman's voice, hysterical and shrill. 'I won't let it happen. Give her to me, I want my baby! I want my baby now.'

The doors of the ward burst inward and a woman in her early twenties ran in, her eyes wild and her dark hair in tangled disarray. Creena froze in mid-step, her mouth suddenly dry and her palms wet with perspiration.

Staff Nurse Ridley emerged from the ward office with a face like thunder.

'What is the meaning of . . . ?'

Her voice tailed off as she saw the knife in the woman's hand. It was a kitchen knife with a six-inch blade, pitted with rust but nonetheless wickedly sharp. She was clutching it so tightly in her right hand that her knuckles had turned bone-white.

'She's here,' wailed the young woman. 'I know she's here. Give her to me.'

'No, you give that knife to me,' said Staff Nurse Ridley with cold emphasis. 'At once.' She stretched out her hand but the woman jerked the knife-blade towards her, forcing the staff nurse back against the wall. 'Nurse – find a porter, a policeman . . .'

Marian slipped out of the linen room and tried to make for the ward door, but the woman was too quick for her, jabbing the knife, making her retreat towards Ridley.

'You can't go till I get my baby. I want my baby.'

'Give me that knife,' snapped Ridley, impatient for this frightening but foolish incident to end. 'How dare you . . .'

'My baby,' repeated the woman, her red-rimmed eyes wide and bright. 'Blue eyes she has. Blue eyes and blonde hair. She's such a pretty girl.'

Her heart thumping, and very much aware that all eyes were on her, Creena edged a little nearer the woman. At the far end of the ward Nurse Jamieson stood like a terror-stricken statue, a brimming bedpan in her hand.

'Get away from me,' hissed the woman.

'What's your name?' began Creena in a very quiet, very shaky voice. She could hardly believe what she was saying.

The woman spun round to face her, and the knife-blade glinted a warning.

'What's it to you?'

'My name's Creena. What's yours?'

There was a long, tense silence; and then:

'A-agnes. My name's Agnes.'

'And what's your baby called?'

'Josephine. Little Jo-Jo, I call her. She's only two and a half, she doesn't understand.'

'My cousin's got a little boy,' said Creena, desperately searching for something to say but finding only a meaningless jumble of words. 'His name's Duggie. He's not quite a year old.'

'They're coming and I can't let them have her, can I, Nurse? Better if I do it myself, it's only right, I'm her mother...'

'Your baby – little Jo-Jo,' said Creena, hardly able to speak for the dryness in her mouth. 'Where is she? We can't help you if we don't know where she is, can we?'

'She's here. In this hospital. My neighbour brought her here, didn't she? Trying to take her away from me, but I have to find her.' She gripped the knife more tightly and sunlight picked out the dark pits of rust along the blade. Her wiry body was a mass of knotted tension. 'I have to kill her. If you keep her from me I'll have to kill you too.'

'For pity's sake, woman...'

Losing patience, Staff Nurse Ridley made a sudden grab for the knife but the woman slashed out wildly with it, catching Ridley on the back of the hand. A small, thin cut appeared, and a few drops of blood sprang into fat red beads. Ridley gave a low curse of anger and fumbled for a handkerchief to press over the cut.

'You want to *kill* Jo-Jo?'

Creena wondered vaguely if this was some sort of horrible nightmare. She was silently measuring the distance between the corridor and the ward telephone in Sister's office. No, it was hopeless. Somehow, she wasn't sure how, this would have to be talked through.

'I have to. When the Germans come they'll kill her. Pretty little girl she is, blonde with blue eyes.'

'Why would they want to kill her, Agnes? I don't understand.'

'Because she ain't perfect. They only let the perfect ones live.'

'But she sounds so lovely . . .'

'She's deaf, Nurse. Born that way, like her grandma. Won't never hear nothing. The Jerries are coming, and do you think they'll let her live? They'll kill her, like they killed their own deaf and blind and sick kids.'

Through the mist of Creena's fear, understanding dawned. This was what terror could do; terror made more acute by sensational stories in the papers and scurrilous gossips like Mavis Paterson. She didn't know how much of it was true, but she did know that she would fight it.

She reached out, very slowly, but made no attempt to take away the knife. Her fingers touched the woman's bare arm. It felt clammy in the August heat, drenched in sweat.

'I don't believe you really want to kill your daughter,' she said quietly.

'I have to.'

'But you don't want to, do you, Agnes?'

The woman's eyes glistened brightly and her voice shook with emotion.

'No. Course I don't. But I have to, don't you see . . .'

'I think you just want to keep her safe. And that's what we want to do, too. Won't you let us help you?' Creena's fingers settled lightly on the woman's bare shoulder, fear joining with fear. 'Please trust us, Agnes. Let us help you.'

And Agnes Tressel – married and a mother and widowed all before she was twenty – hung her head and began to weep, very softly, in the eerie silence of the ward.

Marian darted into the ward kitchen on her way to the Path Lab with a blood sample.

'How's our heroine of the hour?' she grinned.

'Oh, do give it a rest, Clarke-Herbert,' urged Creena, busily cutting thin slices of bread and marge. Her dramatic encounter with Agnes Tressel had been the talk of the Royal Lambeth for the last week, and quite frankly she was getting fed up with all the teasing. She hated being the focus of attention. 'It was just beginner's luck and you know it.' She paused. 'How are mother and baby, anyhow? Any news?'

'Agnes is in the mental wing at St Gregory's,' replied Marian. 'The child's being looked after by friends until her mother's better.'

'Poor Agnes,' sighed Creena. 'She trusted us, too. I feel sort of . . . responsible.'

'It's the papers I blame,' said Marian grimly. 'And all that BUF propaganda. It's a good job they've put Oswald Mosley in jail – he's a nasty piece of work. Anyway, chick,' she beamed. 'Life goes on and it's your turn to make coffee for Sister and Mr Beresford. Now, doesn't that gladden your heart?'

'I'll say,' replied Creena with mock enthusiasm. Now that she'd been here almost a whole year she'd hoped to have progressed beyond coffee-making, but with the ward maid joining the AFS and Nurse Jamieson off with influenza, it was all hands to the pumps. 'Anyhow, I've already boiled the milk, so it should only take a jiffy.'

She took down the huge tin of coffee from the cupboard, then stood on a chair to reach Sister Meredith's very own special tin of chocolate biscuits. Where she got them from, no one dared ask, and if a junior nurse should dare to sneak one she would be sure to be found out – Marian was convinced sister counted them every evening when she went off duty.

Creena arranged four biscuits on a plate, then fetched out two of the nicer cups and saucers and made the coffee. It was pretty awful stuff, a sickly concoction of evaporated milk and water, but it certainly helped to keep the medical and nursing staff going through long days and nights on the wards. And right now, Creena longed for a sit-down and a reviving cup herself.

In a tearing hurry to deliver the tray, Creena did not notice Dr Oliver Temple's athletic figure striding towards her down the corridor, his white coat flapping behind him.

They collided outside Sister's office with a tremendous crash as tray, cups and biscuits all tumbled to the floor and scattered messily in every conceivable direction.

'Oops! Someone's 'avin' a smashin' time!' Mrs Lawlor called out gaily from halfway up the ward.

'Oh, my sainted aunt!' Creena clasped her hands to her mouth. There were shards of broken china and splashes of coffee everywhere – all over the floor, all down the front of her clean apron . . . and all up one side of Dr Temple's crisp white coat. The chocolate biscuits seemed to have rolled away to the four corners of the ward.

A split second later, the door of Sister Meredith's office opened with an ominous click, and Sister herself appeared in the doorway.

'Nurse Quilliam! What is the meaning of this!'

Creena felt suddenly faint, and longed for the ancient floor to swallow her up. She opened her mouth to speak, but no sound came out. Then, to her immense surprise and gratitude, Dr Temple turned to Sister Meredith with a dazzling smile.

'My dear Sister Meredith! I think apologies are in order.'

'Apologies? Indeed they are, Dr Temple. I shall ensure that Nurse Quilliam is reprimanded severely for this latest episode of clumsiness.' Creena cringed, remembering the thermometer that she had broken last week, and the shilling deducted from her wages as a result.

'No, no, I'm afraid you don't understand, Sister. This little mishap was entirely my fault. I came rushing into the ward and simply wasn't looking where I was going. Nurse Quilliam did her best to avoid me but . . . well, these things do happen, I'm afraid. I really am most terribly sorry.'

'I see.'

Creena could see that Sister Meredith wasn't at all convinced, but she wasn't the type to contradict a doctor. 'In that case, kindly clear up this mess, Nurse Quilliam, then go directly to the home for a change of clothing. Nurse

Tregowan will make the coffee when she returns from her break.'

With an angry swish of royal-blue skirts, Sister disappeared back inside her office and the door closed behind her.

Oliver Temple turned to Creena with an impish grin. There were coffee stains on his clean white shirt and tie.

'I ... look, I'm really sorry, Dr Temple. And very grateful too. You really didn't have to defend me like that, you know. It was all my fault, after all.'

'What – and leave you to the tender mercies of that dragon? I couldn't. Besides, from what I hear Sister owes you a favour. You're quite the heroine of the hour!'

'Oh please, don't ...'

'Giving you a hard time over it, is she?'

Creena thought of all the floors she had scrubbed since last week, and Staff Nurse Ridley's constant carping.

'You could say that.'

'Anyhow, fair's fair,' Oliver went on. 'If I hadn't popped in for a quick word with Mr Beresford, you'd never have bumped into me!'

Creena knelt to scoop some of the larger fragments of broken china on to the tray.

'Well, it's very kind of you, and of course I'm grateful ...'

'There's really no need to be. But I tell you what ...'

'What?'

Oliver took hold of her arm, drew her to her feet and led her back into the deserted ward kitchen.

'When's your next off-duty?'

'Er ... Saturday afternoon. Why?'

'How about coming out with me on Saturday, in return for my small act of chivalry? How does that sound? Will you come?'

Creena gazed up into Oliver Temple's piercing blue eyes and felt a frisson of delicious excitement run through her. But friendships between junior nurses and doctors were, if not absolutely forbidden, then certainly frowned upon. And besides, she and Oliver Temple came from different worlds. She couldn't possibly go out with a well-heeled orthopaedic registrar, she really couldn't. No, she'd quite made up her mind . . .

Turning to leave, she looked back at him and broke into a smile.

'Well,' she said, 'if you absolutely insist . . .'

'Which I do.'

'I'll come.'

Chapter 11

It was 4 September, but it was so hot you'd never have known. Creena wiped the back of her hand across her forehead as she pushed the empty wheelchair along the corridor which ran between Casualty and the large ward block where Female Surgical was situated.

She wasn't actually due on duty for another half an hour, but she had given up trying to concentrate on her books. Everyone found it difficult, even Dillie, having to fit all the lectures and studying into those few, precious off-duty hours; and Creena had never been what you'd call academically inclined. Passing the all-important intermediate and final exams was going to be a challenge, to say the least.

As she passed the end of the short corridor which led to a line of private rooms, a uniformed constable stepped in front of her.

'Miss . . . I mean, Nurse.'

'Can I help you, Constable?'

She noticed with a start that he was wearing a handgun – this was the first armed policeman she'd seen since the Government had brought in a special regulation allowing the Metropolitan Police to bear arms.

'PC Greaves, Nurse. If you could just come with me a moment. It's the prisoner.'

'The prisoner?' Realisation dawned. 'Do you mean the German pilot?'

'That's right, Nurse. You see, he will keep on moaning and groaning and me and Stan can't hardly make out a word of what he's saying. Gawd knows he don't deserve all this looking after, what with what his lot are doing to our brave boys, but . . . if you could just look in on him and sort him out . . .'

'He's not my patient, Constable. I'm very junior and I really shouldn't interfere. Have you rung the bell for a nurse?'

'Three times, miss, but nobody's come. If you could just see your way. I mean, he's not violent or anything – and he can't do much with a broken back, can he?'

'Well . . . I'll just find out what he needs, but your colleague must go and fetch someone.'

Putting aside her misgivings, Creena followed the constable down the short corridor. She wasn't at all sure that she wanted to encounter the enemy face to face. She thought of the poor, legless airman on Male Surgical, who had lived a few paltry weeks after his nineteenth birthday, his body shattered and his innocence burned away, and anger rose in her throat. It was hard to think of this German as just another suffering human being who must be nursed with impartiality and compassion.

The constable pushed open the door and stood aside for Creena to enter.

'I'll be right outside, Nurse,' he said. 'If he tries anything, just you call out.'

'Thank you, Constable.'

The German pilot lay immobile on the bed, his whole body encased in a plaster jacket designed to prevent all movement and protect his shattered spine. He might walk again; he might not. He might even die. Creena had the distinct impression that PC Greaves hoped he *would* die, if only to relieve the tedium of sitting in hospital corridors for hour after hour, day after day.

'Mr . . .' She glanced at the chart at the end of the bed. It read: 'Lothar Menz'. 'Herr Menz?'

The body on the bed did not move, but the eyes flickered open. They were a clouded sea-green. Creena did not want to look into those eyes. They didn't look like the eyes of some Aryan monster. He was older than she'd expected, too – at least forty and prematurely lined. There were flecks of grey in his brown hair.

'Bitte . . .'

Creena reached up for the bell and pressed it. Hopefully another nurse would be along in a moment, but it seemed clear that Lothar Menz was a long way down the nursing staff's list of priorities. She scoured the deepest recesses of her mind for any remembered fragments of German, but her mind was a blank.

'Can I get you anything, Herr Menz? Are you in pain?'

'Ja. Schmerz. Much pain in my head.'

Creena checked his dressing. The injury – a small facial burn – was trivial in comparison with the terrible spinal fractures he had suffered. But Herr Menz could not feel any pain in his back or legs. It was quite possible that he would never feel anything there again.

'I'm afraid I can't . . .' For the first time, she wished that she had paid more attention to Robert's *ad hoc* German lessons. 'Ich kann nicht, aber . . . look, I'll fetch someone, verstehen?'

'Ja, ja. Verstehe. I understand.'

As she straightened the bedclothes her eyes flicked across to the pathetic jumble of Menz's personal possessions, lying on top of the bedside locker: keys, a handkerchief, a singed leather wallet, a few coins and an old photograph showing a man, a woman, a baby, two smiling children. Menz caught her looking and spoke again.

'My wife Elise. Sie ist tod. Dead, many years. Meine Kinder . . . I have only my children now.'

Creena did not want to know any more. She felt uncomfortable and confused. Why couldn't Lothar Menz be what she wanted him to be – a hard-faced young zealot exuding hatred and contempt? His eyes didn't look mad or filled with loathing; they just looked sad. She was profoundly grateful when the door opened and Staff Nurse Jeanette Reid took over; her detached and efficient manner as she attended to Menz's needs was everything that Creena's was not.

'I must go now,' said Creena, escaping with immense relief from the sad green eyes.

'Danke schön,' replied Lothar Menz, and Creena hated him for his gratitude.

It was Saturday at last. Saturday, 7 September 1940: a date which was to be engraved on Creena's heart.

Heart thumping, she raced down the stairs, out into the courtyard and across to the nurses' home, running full tilt into Harry the ward orderly, who was placidly pushing a linen trolley towards the hospital laundry.

'Steady on, sweetheart!' laughed Harry, catching Creena and preventing her from falling over. 'More haste, less speed.'

Creena stood panting for breath. In her hurry to get back to her room, she had forgotten Matron's cardinal rule: that no nurse must ever run, except in case of fire, haemorrhage or cardiac arrest.

'Sorry, Harry,' she panted. 'But I can't stop – I'm dreadfully late. Mr Beresford's round took twice as long as it usually does, and then Mrs Lawlor had to be prepped for emergency surgery. It's been quite a morning! I really must dash. I'm meeting someone.'

'Afternoon off, is it?'

Creena nodded.

'Well, whoever he is, I hope he's worth it!'

Pushing open the door of the nurses' home, Creena ran up to her room, taking the steps two at a time. Was it really so obvious that she was off on a date? She suppressed a girlish giggle, wondering what could be making her feel so light-headed and excited. After all, she was only meeting Dr Temple for 'a stroll in the park and a spot of afternoon tea', as he'd put it. That wasn't anything to get herself in a dither about, was it? In fact, he probably wasn't interested in her at all – or at least, not in *that* way.

Hester Frankenberg was stretched out on one of the four narrow beds crammed into the shared bedroom.

'My feet,' she groaned as Creena bustled into the room. 'They feel as if they're on fire. I swear that ward gets longer every day. I don't suppose you've got any spirit I can rub into them?'

'In my overnight case,' replied Creena, taking off her cap. 'You should try wearing more comfortable shoes.'

'We can't *all* look dowdy, darling,' replied Hester witheringly.

Everyone knew that Frankenberg was a martyr to fashion. What was more, as the daughter of one of the Royal Lambeth's most senior consultant surgeons, she was accustomed to getting exactly what she wanted, on demand. Less charitable spirits – Dillie among them – were apt to conclude that Frankenberg was just plain spoilt.

Initially, Hester's father had been horrified at his daughter's decision to nurse; then relieved that she had chosen to train at the Royal Lambeth rather than sign up as a 'common' VAD. Naturally Hester had to have the best of everything. And even after almost a year's training, she had yet to learn that having stylish duty shoes was less important than having comfortable ones. Hester fervently believed that a girl had to suffer to be beautiful.

As Frankenberg rubbed her blistered feet with spirit, Creena took off her cloak, wriggled out of her crumpled uniform and took out the forest of grips which held her hair in a tight, uncomfortable bun. Once freed, it cascaded over her bare shoulders in glossy auburn waves.

'Nice hair you've got,' conceded Frankenberg. 'But you really ought to *do* something with it, you know. Have it bobbed or permed or roll it up or something. I could take you to this little salon I know up West . . .'

Creena gave Hester's short, rather severe cut a doubtful glance. Even in her uniform, Hester Frankenberg looked as though she had just stepped straight out of the fashion pages of some society magazine.

'Oh no, I couldn't. Besides, I like my hair long.'

Hester sniffed.

'Please yourself, darling. You're quite pretty, I suppose, in a country sort of way. But in my experience, men like Oliver Temple prefer their women sophisticated and chic.'

Creena seethed inwardly, but did not rise to the bait. Reflectively, she drew a brush through her thick hair. Was Frankenberg right? If so, it was a bit late to do anything about it now – she was supposed to be meeting Oliver in half an hour's time. She wished Dillie were here to give her some moral support. Or Marian, even. She'd tell Frankenberg to put a sock in it, and they'd all have a good laugh. But Dillie and Marian were both on duty this afternoon.

Hastily she dabbed a little loose powder over her pale skin, masking the faint, childish freckles she hated so much. No rouge, and just the merest hint of lipstick. At times like this, she could hear Uncle John's voice in her head: 'Be yourself, gel. Only fools try to be what they're not.'

She slipped into the artificial silk camiknickers which she'd saved up for ages to buy – the ones that made her feel like a film star – and followed it with her one good summer dress: a sleek but modest green rayon with glass buttons and a starched Peter Pan collar. She hoped Oliver would not find it too provincial. It had been the most expensive tea dress at Miss Curphey's fashion house in Victoria Street, but that was two years ago and Douglas fashions were hardly up to Bond Street standards, were they? Yet Frank had always said the green in it enhanced the colour of her eyes, made them 'shine like the sea at Santon Head when the sun's on it'. Poor Frank. She wondered where he was now . . .

'By the way,' yawned Frankenberg, picking up an envelope from her bedside locker, 'this came for you this morning. Clarke-Herbert picked it up at the porter's lodge.' She tossed the envelope across to Creena.

Creena gave up wrestling with an uncooperative suspender and picked up the envelope. The postmark was illegible, but the handwriting was unmistakable. Robert! She ripped open the envelope. Inside was a scrawled note on a sheet of flimsy, war-quality paper, and a photograph.

'Dear Sis,' the note read. 'Sorry I haven't written. Hope Ma and Pa have stopped giving you a hard time. What do you think of my haircut? Terry says his is better. Love, R.'

The photograph showed Robert with a dark-haired young man. They were holding pint glasses of beer and laughing into the camera. On the back of the photo was written: 'Terry and Robert, working hard, summer 1940.' Creena smiled. It was just like Robert to clown about with his pals when everyone else was talking doom and gloom.

As she slipped on her shoes and picked up the white leather clutch bag which Cousin Mona had given her for her twentieth birthday, Creena purposely avoided Hester's critical gaze. There was no sense in making herself more nervous than she already was.

'I'll see you tonight,' she said as she paused before opening the door on to the landing.

'Mind you do!' replied Hester, now curled up on her bed with a copy of *Picture Post*. 'Home Sister locks up at ten, remember.'

As the door swung shut behind her, Creena felt a thrill of anticipation. Questions tumbled around in her brain. What shall we talk about? Will he find me boring? Or ignorant? Or just naïve? She took a deep breath and a pace forward. Her first step down the old wooden staircase was her first step into a brand-new adventure.

Jack Doyle sat in the kitchen of his mother's house, chain-smoking. In front of him on the scrubbed wooden table lay a plate of faggots and pease pudding, virtually untouched.

'You not want your dinner then, Jack?'

Mo's gaze was concerned – and searching.

Jack shook his head.

'You ill?'

He sighed.

'No, Ma. Just not hungry. Probably this hot weather. Let the kids 'ave it, eh? Kit and Micky's always starving.'

But Mo was not one to be fobbed off with vague excuses.

'There's something on your mind, ain't there? Edna Tilley's sure she saw you with Sid Clayden the other day, down The Cut. She was worried . . .'

'Damn her,' hissed Jack under his breath. That Tilley woman was a real liability – nosy *and* public-spirited.

Mo turned round from the sink where she was washing out empty beer bottles. The noonday sun was streaming in through the polished window, revealing a kitchen which was shabby but spotless. Mo Doyle was the most house-proud woman in a houseproud street.

'What d'you say?'

'I said "is that so?"'

'What were you doin' with Sid Clayden, anyhow? You

been gettin' into some shady deals? You know that man's downright evil, don't you? You want to watch yourself, my boy . . .'

Jack sighed. This was exactly what he'd been hoping to avoid. He was in deep and he certainly didn't want to be reminded of it.

'Course I haven't been doing any deals with him, Ma. Sid Clayden's well out of my league, you know that. Big-time crook, he is. What would I have that would interest the likes of him, eh?'

'So what were you doing talking to him?'

'Just passin' the time of day, Ma. It don't do to go upsettin' a man like him. Could turn nasty. I won't get in with his sort, don't you worry.'

'Well, mind you don't.' Mo's face was turned away from him, an expressionless mask. She couldn't let him see how concerned she was. 'And if you want to get back in my good books, you can take the kids down Archbishop's Park this afternoon.'

'But Ma! I got things to do . . .'

'Been under my feet all morning, they have. And Edna Tilley won't have them no more – reckons it's like the monkey house at the Zoo, once they get going. No, you take 'em down the park and wear 'em out. It'll give me a chance to clean this place up a bit.'

Jack could not suppress a snort of mirth.

'Clean it up? Ma, this house is cleaner than Buckingham bloomin' Palace already! Why don't you take some time off? Take the kids down the park yourself . . .'

Mo shook her head.

'You've been promising them for weeks, Jack. Besides,

I've got my nets to wash. Now get a move on – and don't go letting 'em spoil their tea. I'm makin' a stew out of that nice piece of scrag-end you got me.'

As he slipped on his jacket and went into the yard to collect Micky and Kitty, Jack fought hard to conceal his anxiety. He felt guilty, lying to his mother, but how could he tell her the truth? Yes, he had been doing a deal with Sid Clayden – but not willingly. Far from it. The trouble was, Clayden had called in a debt from the days before Jack had learned how to keep one step ahead of the law. He had also eased Jack out of his recent financial troubles by helping him to set up a book on the dogs. Now it was the day of reckoning and it was a foolish man indeed who refused to settle a debt with Sid Clayden.

Clayden was arguably the most important man in the whole of Lambeth. There wasn't a racket south of the river that he wasn't involved in – and the war had brought interesting new business opportunities. When Sid had demanded Jack's help to store a few boxes of stuff 'till the heat dies down', Jack knew refusal wasn't an option – even though he could guess what the stuff was and where it had come from. Drugs and medical supplies, looted from a factory north of London that had taken a direct hit in a recent 'nuisance' raid.

It wasn't until he'd borrowed a mate's van and stashed the drugs in a disused warehouse down Surrey Docks that Jack really started sweating. How long was he supposed to look after them for? What would happen to him if the police caught him in possession? And worse – what would Sid Clayden's heavies do to him if anything happened to his stuff?

Jack had intended to go down the warehouse this afternoon, move the drugs somewhere a bit safer. Eric Coates's cellar, maybe. It was preying on his mind. They would be better kept away from his own stuff – a few boxes of watches, oranges, tins of corned beef and butter, that sort of thing.

But now Mo had put a spanner in the works. Ah well, it would have to be tonight, after blackout. In this last year he had become adept as an alleycat at moving about under cover of darkness.

He stepped out of the back door and strolled down the yard to the gate. Micky and Kitty were in the back alley, playing ball with an old sock filled with dried peas. Jack watched them for a few moments, torn between contempt for the shabby respectability they were living in, and envy for the innocent joy shining in their bright eyes. Guilt pricked his conscience, and he recalled everything his mother had done to give him a happy childhood. His late father Paddy, too.

He squinted up at the cloudless blue sky. It looked like being the perfect afternoon for a kickabout on the grass.

'Get a move on, you two!' he shouted. 'I'm takin' you down the park.'

Creena spotted Oliver long before he saw her. He was standing outside the York Hotel by Waterloo station, hands in his pockets and leaning casually against the wall. In his tweed sports jacket and grey flannels, he looked every inch the country gentleman – and even more romantically handsome than Creena remembered.

Her heart was in her mouth as she straightened the folds

of her green frock and prayed that she did not look too
dowdy. Then she walked towards him, not quite sure what
to say.

'Dr Temple ... I mean, Oliver?'

'Creena!' He straightened up and swung round to greet
her with a dazzling smile that turned her legs to jelly. 'You
know, I was beginning to think you'd changed your mind
and decided not to come after all.'

'Sorry I'm late.' Creena held out her hand awkwardly
and Oliver reciprocated with a grin. His grip was firmly
reassuring, his hand warm and dry and seductively strong.
'Mr Beresford's round didn't finish until ten to, and then I
had to get changed.'

'And very nice you look too, if you don't mind my saying
so.' The twinkling grey-green eyes appraised her in an
instant.

'Really?' Creena couldn't keep a note of disbelief from
creeping into her voice.

'Really. That's a simply charming dress. Sets off that
lovely red hair of yours.'

Creena shifted from one foot to the other. After so long
on duty in flattish black lace-ups, her white wedge shoes
were pinching her toes and making her calves ache. What
happens next? she wondered, wishing she had a little of
Hester's worldly wisdom.

'Lovely afternoon, isn't it?' she said, breaking the
awkward silence.

'Perfect. How about a stroll in the Archbishop's Park?
Afterwards, we could have afternoon tea. I know a
wonderful little hotel in the Strand – far better and far
classier than the Savoy, too.'

'Well ... yes, that sounds lovely.'

'And then what about a show? A pal of mine's in a revue at the Dominion. I'm sure I could get us a couple of good seats.'

'I'd love to, only I have to be in by ten ...'

Oliver smiled.

'Don't you worry about that. We'll get you back before Home Sister turns you into a pumpkin.'

Side by side, they walked along the Embankment, taking that exaggerated care that strangers take not to touch. It must surely have been a trick of the imagination, but Creena was sure she could feel a furnace-like heat radiating out of Oliver; a magnetism that drew her towards him, making her long to press against him, feel his touch on her hand, her face, her lips. She had watched him so often with his patients, sensed instinctively how gentle his touch would feel on her willing skin. It was all she could do not to stare at him, he seemed so beautiful. And to think he had chosen to spend this afternoon with her!

As they walked along, they made small talk as though each wanted to avoid voicing the real, compelling questions which burned within them. The river was busy but its waters were placid and oily. There was little sign of the chaos which had ensued on the day when Lothar Menz's Messerschmitt had plunged into the Thames.

'Creena,' mused Oliver thoughtfully. 'Is that a Manx name?'

'Manx as they come.'

'It's charming. Sort of ... exotic. You know, I don't think I've ever met anyone from the Isle of Man before. What's it like there? You must tell me all about it.'

'I don't know what you'd make of it. It's beautiful, but it's terribly quiet.'

'If you come from there, I'm sure I'd like it.'

Creena hoped fervently that she wasn't going to blush.

'I'm from a little village called Ballakeeill,' she told him. 'Hardly anything ever happens there. I suppose that's one of the reasons I wanted to come here. I had *such* a boring office job.'

'I can imagine. But you've picked a fine time to visit the great metropolis. Weren't your parents reluctant to let you go?'

Creena chuckled.

'They absolutely forbade me to come. I don't think either of them has forgiven me yet.'

'Forgiven you? What for?'

'For having a mind of my own. Mother wants to marry me off to the vicar's son, and Father thinks that just because he's the village schoolmaster, people should do whatever he says.'

'Ah,' said Oliver knowingly.

'He's a bit ... well, old-fashioned.'

'Yours and mine both,' commented Oliver. 'Mine's a magistrate in the depths of Hampshire, but he used to be something big in the Indian army before his health gave out on him. Hang 'em and flog 'em, that's his motto. Spare the rod and spoil the child.'

'Still, he must be pleased to see you doing so well as a doctor.'

'Not a bit of it!' Oliver tossed his head and his wavy sandy-blond hair caught the sunlight like a thousand fine strands of corn-yellow glass. 'He was dead set on my going to Sandhurst and becoming an army officer like my two brothers. Ironically, it looks as if I may well end up in a uniform after all.'

'Why's that?'

'The RAMC are crying out for qualified men, and I'm well up in orthopaedics, as you know. I really ought to be doing my bit. That's why I wanted a word with Beresford the other day – he was in the war last time around. Thought he could give me a spot of advice.'

They passed Lambeth Palace and entered the Archbishop's Park – a large stretch of the palace grounds set aside for public use. This was the only expanse of greenery that some of the Lambeth children ever saw, mused Creena – quite a difference from Ballakeeill, where gorse-covered hillsides tumbled down to a clear sea and the nearest small town was a good five miles away.

Oliver stood back politely to let Creena enter the park first, and she brushed lightly against his hand. A cold shiver of pleasure rippled through her as she turned back for the reassurance of his smile. What on earth was happening to her? She'd never felt like this before. How could she feel like this about a man who was almost a stranger to her?

Oliver flopped down on the grass and took off his jacket, spreading it out on the ground for Creena to sit on. The park was a leafy oasis of laughter and sunshine amid the grimy streets of Lambeth, a broad sweep of green dotted with children and dogs and prams. Apart from the odd splash of khaki and a few gas masks in their cardboard carrying-boxes, the war seemed to have touched Archbishop's Park remarkably little. But Creena felt that it had touched her to the quick.

'You're joining the RAMC? Leaving the Royal Lambeth?'

'Oh, not for ages yet, I shouldn't think. Maybe I shan't have to go at all. Depends what happens in this damn war, really. But I can't stand by and watch other chaps fight it for me. My brother Archie's in Intelligence, and Clive's a regular in the Royal Artillery.'

'If you go overseas will your father be proud of you?'

'I suppose he might. You know what it's like with fathers and sons.'

She did indeed. She thought of Robert, and wondered if Mother and Father were glad now that he wasn't a fighter pilot after all.

'But what about your mother? Wouldn't she be upset if you were in danger?'

'Mother died when we were living in India.'

'Oh. I'm sorry.'

'It was ages ago, long in the past.' Oliver paused. There was a lilt of sadness in his voice. 'Water under the bridge.' A man trundled past with a hand-cart, laden with cold drinks. 'Fancy one?'

Creena shook her head.

'Sure? Could be the last bottle of pop you get, what with rationing. Filthy stuff, that cherryade, but I'd miss it. You know, it beats me where Sister Meredith gets her chocolate biscuits from.'

Creena thought of Dillie's cousin Jack, and felt she had a fairly good idea.

'Oh, I think you can still get pretty much anything, if you're willing to pay for it. But it's not right really, is it, what with so many people having to go without?' She looked at a gaggle of skinny-ribbed children, sharing handfuls of broken biscuits out of a paper bag.

'No, you're right, of course. It isn't.'

Oliver stretched out his long limbs on the sun-bleached grass.

'Creena?'

'Hmm?'

'I'm so glad you agreed to come out with me today. I thought you might turn me down flat, you know?'

Creena stared at him, incredulous.

'No!'

'Yes, really. A smashing girl like you, well . . . you're bound to have scores of other admirers.'

'Well . . . hardly,' replied Creena in some confusion. Her heart was pounding as she got to her feet and brushed imaginary blades of grass from the skirt of her dress. 'Shall we walk a little further? It's so nice to be out in the fresh air when everyone else is inside, working hard.'

'Right-ho.' Oliver stood up and put on his jacket. He was so tall and tanned and good-looking, thought Creena in silent admiration. 'Let's take a stroll. I want everyone to see me with the prettiest girl in the world on my arm.'

''Ave you got another piece of chocolate, Uncle Jack?'

'Yeah, go on, Uncle Jack, give us some! Just one more bit, please!'

'Well, I dunno.' Jack glanced at his watch. Time was getting on and it would soon be five o'clock. 'Don't want you spoilin' your tea. Auntie Mo's makin' a stew.'

'Aw, Uncle Jack!'

Jack relented. He usually did. He knew treats were few

and far between at the house on Bishop Street, and chocolate was like gold dust now that sweets were disappearing from the shops. Since his father had died, Mo Doyle had worked hard to maintain a decent standard of living for the family – but there wasn't much left for frills. Jack knew how much she hated taking money from him, as if it was some sort of betrayal of Paddy and all he had stood for. But Jack wanted to help her out. After all, on bad days, tea might consist of nothing more substantial than bread and marge, washed down with a pot of tea.

'Well – only if you don't go blabbin' to your Auntie Mo. She'll 'ave my guts for garters.'

Micky's urchin face was a picture of angelic sincerity.

'We won't – promise! Don't we, Kitty?' He nudged his small sister in the ribs and she nodded vigorously. 'Cross me 'eart an' 'ope to die!' His fingernail described an arc across his throat with bloodthirsty relish.

Jack rummaged deep in the pockets of his jacket, now slung over his arm, and extracted a couple more squares of Fry's Five Boys, wrapped up in shiny silver paper. He hesitated for a moment, tantalising the bright-eyed faces before him; then slapped the chocolate into Kitty's open palm.

'Go on then. But if you throw up, your Auntie Mo'll tan your hide, and so will I.'

Kitty devoured her square of chocolate in a single gulp, then licked each sticky brown finger in turn.

'Uncle Jack?'

'What is it now?'

'Uncle Jack, look – there's Auntie Creena.'

Jack's gaze followed Kitty's pointing finger. In the

middle distance, a young woman with a long sweep of flame-red hair was laughing and joking with a tall, sandy-haired man in well-cut sports jacket and flannels.

He recognised Creena instantly. There couldn't be two girls with hair like that, not in the whole of London. Couldn't be two with a boyfriend like that one, either.

He observed them from a distance, interest acquiring a tinge of envy as he watched the man slip his arm around Creena's slender waist, pulling her close against him. And for a brief moment Jack imagined that it was he who was holding Creena, he who was smiling and laughing with her.

He might have stood watching them for longer, had an all-too-familiar sound not rent the air of that peaceful September Saturday afternoon. A thin, wailing cry, rising to an angry, baleful screech.

The air-raid siren? On a Saturday afternoon, in broad daylight? No, surely not.

There was silence for a moment: uneasy, disbelieving silence as whole families stopped in their tracks, as though this were a children's game of statues. Then the exodus started – parents scooping up children in their arms and heading for the nearest public shelter.

'Kitty, Micky – come here!'

Wide-eyed but unafraid, Kitty grabbed Jack's hand. Her pudgy pink paw felt sticky from the chocolate, and there was a brown circle round her mouth.

'What's 'appenin', Uncle Jack?'

Micky came running up, breathless and excited.

'Are they goin' to drop bombs on us, Uncle Jack?'

'Will they kill us?'

Jack's mind was working overtime. He cursed himself for

not knowing all the public shelters round here. Maybe they could get under the railway arches? No, a tube station, that was their best bet. Never mind what the Government said about not using the Underground to shelter in. Anyway, this was probably a false alarm – God knows, there had been plenty, and Hitler had never yet launched a daylight raid. Still, better to play it safe.

'Course not, Kitty. No one's going to get killed. But just do as I say. Understand? And that goes for you too, Micky.' He hoisted Kitty up and slung her over his shoulder, taking an indignant Micky firmly by the hand. The screwed-up ball of silver paper fell from his fingers on to the yellowing grass. 'Now, get a move on!'

As Jack joined the crowds making for the shelters, dragging Micky behind him, he heard a distant droning and looked up. He could hardly believe his eyes.

Dorniers. Heinkels. Messerschmitts. Not one, or two, or a dozen. Hundreds of the bastards, coming up the estuary. Was this the beginning of the invasion – the beginning of the end for London? Images flashed through his mind: Mo, vulnerable and alone in the house on Bishop Street; Creena and her beau, strolling across the park; Dillie on duty at the Royal Lambeth. And Sid Clayden's illicit 'stuff', still sitting in the bonded warehouse at Surrey Docks.

For a split second, he froze in his tracks; then he gripped Micky's hand very tight, and ran as he had never run before.

It was just five minutes past five when Creena half ran, half fell into the public shelter in the basement of the hotel on Lambeth Road. Her lungs were almost bursting with exertion, and only Oliver's iron grip on her wrist had kept her going.

'Good job I knew about this one,' gasped Oliver as they dived inside. 'Are you OK?'

Creena nodded, scarcely able to speak.

'Good. Then I think I'd better try and get back to the hospital – they're going to need me.'

Creena's eyes widened in horror.

'But . . . !'

'Hurry up, ladies and gentlemen, please,' urged the shelter marshal, a harassed-looking clerk in a blue suit with shiny trousers, and a tin helmet jammed on his bespectacled head. 'I must close the gates.'

Creena shuddered at the distant thudding sound of a bomb exploding. A second . . . and then another, and another. Distant, and yet much, much too close.

'You can't go – you'll be killed!'

Oliver gave Creena a big hug – much like the hugs that Robert had given her when she was a little girl.

'I'll be fine.'

'Then I'm coming back with you. They'll need me, too.' She thought of Dillie and Marian, working on the wards. Of Mo Doyle and the children, at number 12 Bishop Street.

'I'm leaving you here, where it's safe.'

'Oh no you're not.'

Oliver stepped forward to talk to the marshal.

'If you could just let me out. I'm a doctor. I need to get back to the Royal Lambeth Hospital right away.'

'I'm very sorry, sir, but I'm afraid you're going nowhere,' replied a burly ARP warden. He glanced at Creena, still trembling violently. 'And neither are you, madam. You're both going to stay right here until the all clear sounds. And if you're a doctor, sir, might I suggest you attend to some of the ladies and their children?'

Oliver turned to survey the jumbled mess of humanity gathered together in the shelter. Shocked faces looked back at him: the faces of people who, only minutes before, had been enjoying the languid warmth of a September afternoon.

He gave Creena's hand a squeeze. His grip was strong, warm, strength-giving; and as Oliver's lips brushed her hair, very briefly, Creena almost forgot the terrible truth which every man, woman and child in the shelter understood.

That above them, London was burning.

Chapter 12

Ida Quilliam glanced at the clock on Aunt Bessie's mantelpiece. It was a little after five o'clock.

'Time is getting on,' she observed. 'I shall have to go soon.'

'You'll take another scone first, though?'

Ida accepted another scone from the flower-patterned plate.

'I'll bring you some more sugar, next time I come,' she said, spreading rhubarb and ginger jam on her scone. 'Nancy Shimmin gets it from a farm over Crogga way – they used to feed it to their cattle before the war, but it's perfectly all right.'

Bessie poured Ida a second cup of tea and topped up her own cup before settling in her favourite armchair. To look at her, thought Ida, you'd never guess what she'd been through.

Staying in her precious boarding house in Port Erin had meant all sorts of inconveniences for Bessie. Not only did she need a special pass to get in or out of the village; she had also been obliged to accept a houseful of internees. Dame Joanna Cruickshank, autocratic commandant of the women's camp and a formidable organiser, had spared no one's feelings in her determination to get all four thousand women promptly billeted and settled. But it seemed that Bessie was determined to make the best of a difficult situation.

'You're looking tired,' remarked Ida, sipping her tea.

'Oh, don't you worry about me – I'm strong as an ox,' said Bessie. 'But these internee women do keep me on the go, what with having to make sure they do their chores. Some of them seem to think they're only here to laze around and make life difficult for everyone else.'

Ida nodded, thinking of the smiling women she'd seen strolling along the promenade, sunbathing on the beach and swimming in the bright blue sea. Why, some of them even played a daily round of golf! To think that every one was a potential enemy. Nazis, Fascists, goodness knows what else – they were all here. It gave her the shivers. And you had only to read the papers to know that the internees were getting the best of everything. An extended holiday, thought Ida to herself, that's what it is for these wretched women.

'So where are they, then? These women you've got billeted with you? I could only see two when I came here – sitting outside with their sewing.'

'Oh, that would be Rebecca and Olya. Jewesses from Galicia – I'm not sure where that is, somewhere out east. I can't understand much of what they say, but they're nice girls and they work hard. They came here with hardly a stitch to their names, poor dears. The dark-haired one's expecting – it's due any day now. I don't envy her – or the poor mite.'

228

'Have you only got the two girls now then?'

Bessie shook her head.

'Lord, no! Dame Joanna's billeted six on me, even though I've only got the three spare rooms. And an ill-assorted lot they are too. Nasty tempers they've got, the Nazi girl and the Austrians. And as for that Italian, well . . .' Bessie lowered her voice and assumed an expression which was half shocked, half amused. 'She's a member of the oldest profession, if you know what I mean.'

'Heavens!' exclaimed Ida, her cup halfway to her mouth. 'How dreadful.'

'Needless to say, the women don't get on with each other and it's no good my trying. Now the German and the Austrians have applied for a move to another house, and good riddance I say. Still, I'm sure Dame Joanna will send me another three to make up the numbers.'

'I wonder you put up with it,' exclaimed Ida.

'I don't have much choice,' pointed out Bessie. 'It was either stay here with the women or get out of my beautiful house.' She looked lovingly around her sitting room. 'And I couldn't leave the Ben-my-Chree, now, could I? At least now they've got the women working, the three troublemakers are out of the house for most of the day. They get tenpence a day cooking at the Hydro, you know.'

'Really! I'd have thought they ought to be grateful just to be living in such luxury.' Ida put down her cup. 'Very nice scones, Bessie. I wish I had time to bake more. Tommy and his sister do love their home-made bread, and it's just not the same from the Stores.'

'I hear you're doing war work now?'

'Oh, just a couple of days a week at a WVS canteen. I'd do more, but George is on Civil Defence duty at night – and someone has to stay at home to take care of the children. Besides, George is so tetchy these days, since Robert and Creena went away. He just sits there in his armchair, reading his paper and looking like thunder, hardly saying a word to anyone. Honestly, he talks to that wretched pig of his more than he talks to me!'

Ida's voice faltered, her mind assailed by images and imaginings she had tried to suppress for months.

'Doesn't he realise that I worry, too? Poor Robert, he's so far away. And the dangers . . .'

Bessie reached over the table and patted Ida's hand.

'I know, dear. So many on the island have lost husbands and sons. But Robert's a brave boy. He wouldn't want to be safe here while other people were doing his duty for him, would he?'

'No, of course not, but . . .'

'And then there's Creena.'

Ida paused, her cup halfway to her mouth.

'Creena's a foolish, headstrong girl,' she said bitterly.

'But she's doing her duty too.'

'She could have stayed at home and done her duty, Bessie. She didn't have to go traipsing off to London. We expressly forbade her to go, you know.'

Bessie watched Ida closely.

'It takes a girl with guts to stand up to your George,' she said. Not to mention you, Ida, she thought grimly. 'Besides, she's needed in London, and I'm sure she's big enough to take care of herself. And surely even the Germans won't bomb the hospital...'

'That's what I thought too,' replied Ida, setting down her empty cup very carefully on its saucer. 'Until I heard what happened the other night – that direct hit on the hospital in Kent. All those casualties...'

'She'll be all right, just you wait and see.'

Ida picked up her handbag.

'I suppose you're right.' She looked at the clock again. Twenty past already. 'I really must go now. It's a long walk to the bus and you know what George is like if I'm late.'

She got up from her chair and Bessie fetched her coat. Together they walked out into the evening air. The two Galician girls were still sitting there, sewing blouses from cheap print fabric, and they smiled and nodded as Ida passed. They didn't seem too bad, she supposed. For internees.

But looking down Shore Road to the promenade, she could see other women laughing and splashing in the sea. Well, at least the seafront itself remained much as it had always been: the broad sweep of the bay, lined with hotels, and the magnificent swell of Bradda Head rising at the northern end, with Milner's Tower atop it, silhouetted against the sky.

Seagulls wheeled in a pale blue sky, as they had done every September for as long as Ida Quilliam could remember. Even at tea-time the beach was thronged with bathers, and chattering groups of women walked arm in arm along the seafront. The only difference was that these were not tourists, these were three-bob-a-day internees – some of them enjoying the benefits of hotel rooms which had cost a guinea a day before the war. It didn't seem right to Ida, really it didn't.

Ida and Bessie walked together through Port Erin, up Station Road and past the pretty red-brick railway terminus to the double row of wire-festooned posts which marked the perimeter of the camp. They stood together for a few minutes on the inside of the wire, looking out to the dark roundness of the hills beyond. Was this what it felt like to be a prisoner? wondered Ida.

'Identity card and pass please, madam.'

The blond guard at the camp gates seemed far too young to be a soldier. Ida looked him up and down and thought of Robert, her Robert, so far away and so brave. She prayed that the war would end soon, so that neither he nor this boy would have any further need of the deadly skills which they had been taught.

She rummaged in her bag and brought out the permit she had had to obtain from the police in Douglas. Lord help anyone who had to make the journey in and out of the camp on a regular basis.

'Thank you, madam.'

The first set of gates swung open and Ida stepped through.

'Goodbye, Bessie.'

'Goodbye, Ida – and don't worry yourself so.'

The second set of gates clanged shut behind her and she was free again, walking down the road to the bus stop. The sound of an aeroplane passing overhead made her start momentarily, until she realised that it was just a training plane out on a sortie from Ronaldsway or Jurby aerodrome. Surely Bessie was right. Not even the Germans would bomb the Royal Lambeth Hospital.

The last Dornier moved slowly back up the Thames estuary, a fat, droning bluebottle glimpsed only fitfully through the dense black pall of smoke drifting over London. A few minutes later, at 6 p.m., the all clear sounded.

Scrambling up the steps from the public shelter, Creena and Oliver coughed and blinked in the choking air, hotter than an August noon and reeking of cordite. It was like stepping straight into hell. The black smoke had created an artificial night, illuminated by the ferocious reds and oranges of the fires blazing out of control all over London. And through the smoke burned the angry red glow of the setting sun, hostile as a malevolent eye.

Through the crackling of flames, Creena could hear voices shouting, screaming, sobbing, calling through the noise of falling masonry. The voices mingled in a strangely subdued cacophony, occasional words and phrases more distinct than the rest.

'Alfie! Where the hell are you, Alfie?'

'What's old Winnie doin' about our guns? Tell me that. Why didn't we 'ear no ack-ack guns?'

'Hoses are running dry again, Bill. How can we fight a bleedin' fire without water?'

'It's all right, lady. You just tell me where you last saw your little girl.'

'Oh, Oliver, we have to *do* something!' Creena felt sudden, intense guilt that she had been off duty during the raid, as if simply wearing her uniform would have endowed her with miraculous powers. At least it might have made her feel more confident. Standing here in her best green dress and inappropriate shoes, she felt ludicrously out of place. Somewhere nearby she could hear a baby wailing and a man roaring in impotent rage. *Could* she do anything to help these people? On impulse, she set off blindly into the smoky darkness to her right, following the source of the baby's cries.

'Steady on, old girl.' Oliver gripped her arm and held her back. 'It would be best if we got back to the Royal as soon as poss. We'll be more use there than here. And you'll be no use at all if you break a leg.' He took hold of her hand and his calm strength seemed to flood into her. 'Now, stay close to me and be careful.'

Eyes smarting, feet crunching on piles of broken glass, they edged along in the semi-darkness, dodging huge lumps of masonry that crashed around them as buildings crumbled and blazed to blackened shells.

'Out the way, for Gawd's sake – and mind your step. This lot could go any minute.'

A fireman with blackened face and red-rimmed eyes loomed up out of the gloom, pushing Creena and Oliver away from the margin of a huge crater in the middle of the street.

'Is there anything I can do? I'm a nurse,' blurted out Creena. But the fireman shook his head and shouted above the noise of the water jet.

'Bloody chaos, that's what it is. We're all just doing what we can.'

Creena and Oliver stumbled on a little further, Creena only dimly aware of the direction in which they were heading. Ragged groups of shocked civilians were wandering about, marshalled by ARP wardens and policemen. All wanted to go home; but for many that would not be possible. This first daylight raid of the war had scored deep wounds on the face of London.

'We'd best get a move on,' shouted Oliver over the general hubbub. 'Jerry's bound to have a second go when it gets dark – and with fires all over the place to light his way, it'll be a piece of cake for him.'

'But we can't just leave all these people!' protested Creena, kneeling to comfort an elderly woman with cut hands, who was sitting on what had once been a wall, shaking uncontrollably as she tried to drink the cup of water a warden had just given her. 'Drink what you can – it will help you feel better.' She held the bandaged hand steady about the cup, but the woman's eyes seemed to look right through her. She was sunk irretrievably deep in shock.

As Creena and Oliver emerged coughing and spluttering around the corner, an ambulance rolled past them, its whitened sides now smoke-grimed. It came to a halt a few yards away and two men in tin helmets jumped out of the back.

'Seriously injured man over there,' a policeman shouted, clambering over rubble with the ambulancemen in tow. 'Wife dead, child shocked but I think that's all . . .'

Oliver headed towards the ambulance and Creena followed him. The hem of her green dress caught on a piece of hot, jagged metal but she didn't even notice the tear. Stretchers were being carried towards the ambulance: the white face of a child gleamed in the flickering red from the flames, its father's face drenched in blood from a massive head wound.

'I'm a doctor,' announced Oliver. 'And this is Nurse Quilliam.'

'There'll be plenty of work for you tonight,' observed the stretcher-bearer grimly. He was sweating copiously in the heat from the fires. 'Can you do anything for this poor blighter? He don't look as if he's going to make it to the Royal Lambeth.'

Creena looked at the man. She could see he was very badly hurt. Thank goodness Oliver was here and they weren't far from the hospital. And then a curious thought hit her: what if the Royal Lambeth Hospital wasn't there any more? What if Hitler had simply wiped it off the map?

Oliver felt the man's pulse. It was weak and thready. He didn't look as if he would last much longer – and that head wound was a real mess, the whiteness of smashed and splintered bone showing through the pulpy red.

'I'll do all I can,' he replied. 'Quickly, get in,' he ordered Creena, and she obeyed him automatically, jumping up into the cavernous interior of the ambulance where a massively pregnant woman was already lying on a stretcher, her hands clasped in agony to her swollen belly.

With a crash the doors swung shut and slowly, almost dreamily, the ambulance swung round the corner, taking its place in a long, dismal convoy heading towards the Royal Lambeth Hospital.

Kitty and Micky were still sound asleep on the platform of

Lambeth North Underground station, but sleep was a long way from Jack Doyle's mind. All he could think about was how stupid he'd been.

Stupid to stash that iffy stuff so far away, down Surrey Docks. Stupider still to let his mother bully him into taking the kids to the park. If he'd stuck to the original plan, he could have borrowed the van, moved the stuff to the relative safety of Eric Coates's cellar, and still been back in Bishop Street in time to get Mo and the kids to the shelter when the alert sounded. Now he was stuck down here, listening to the distant thud and crump of Jerry bombing the heart out of London.

As he fingered the tuppenny platform ticket in his pocket, a soft Yorkshire voice close to his ear made him start.

'Want a fag, mate? You look like you could use one.'

Jack turned to look into the friendly face of a middle-aged corporal with his left arm in a sling. Accepting a cigarette from the crumpled pack of Player's Weights, he nodded his thanks and proffered his lighter.

'Ta very much, mate.' The soldier lit up and sat back on his haunches. He smiled as he looked at Kitty and Micky, curled up peacefully beside Jack.

'Your kids?'

'Me ma's brother's. Their dad got took prisoner overseas.'

The soldier nodded his commiseration.

'Ah've got three – two girls and a boy. Bit too young for this lot, thank God. Let's hope it's all over before they're old enough to understand what's going on.' He indicated his bandaged arm. 'Copped this one at Dunkirk. Bullet went right through and left a bleedin' great 'ole. Still, it's got me a nice bit of home leave – if I ever make it back to 'Uddersfield, that is. Bit of a bugger, this lot.' He drew deeply on his cigarette, inhaled and considered Jack with friendly curiosity. 'You waitin' for your call-up then?'

Jack squirmed inwardly, a raw nerve cut and jangling.

'Yeah . . . bit of trouble with me asthma, though, an' me flat feet. Doc says he don't think they'll 'ave me.'

'Tough luck, mate. Bet you can't wait to get out there and kick Hitler right in the Anschluss.'

'Yeah . . . Course I can't.'

He looked at the soldier's wounded arm, and couldn't help his thoughts wandering to Sid Clayden's looted medical supplies. To Dillie, too – hard at work at the Royal Lambeth and no doubt crying out for bandages and syringes. Not normally given to attacks of guilty conscience, Jack found it unexpectedly difficult to look the soldier in the eye.

Seconds later, a distant wailing of sirens announced the all clear, and Jack heaved a sigh of relief. All around him, people eased themselves to their feet, dusted themselves down. The soldier too got to his feet, nipped the end of his cigarette and put the remainder back into the packet. Waste not, want not.

'Ah well, best be off to me billet, eh? If it's still there, like.'

Jack cleared his throat.

'Look, mate. You need anythin' while you're in London, any help or whatever, you come straight to 12 Bishop Street. It ain't far from 'ere, anyone'll tell you. I'll see you right. Jack Doyle's the name.'

The soldier wiped his palm on the seat of his battledress pants and held out his hand.

'John Hebden. Much obliged, I'm sure. Well, ah'll sithee around then, Jack.'

Hoisting his kitbag on to his good shoulder, the soldier turned and walked away up the steps to the ticket hall. Jack stooped and shook Micky by the shoulder.

'Come on, kids,' he said, more gently than usual. 'Time to go 'ome.'

If it's still standing, he thought. If it's bleedin' well still there.

'How many casualties?'

Mr Beresford stood in the middle of the casualty hall at the Royal Lambeth Hospital, sleeves rolled up, perspiring profusely. It was only 7.45 p.m., but already he felt exhausted, mentally and physically drained. Casualties had been arriving in dribs and drabs for the last hour or so, and were lining the long wooden benches which ran down the length of the hall, but Edward Beresford could tell that this was merely the tip of a very large iceberg.

His registrar, Dr Amschewitz, shook his head.

'No official figures yet, sir, but I've had Civil Defence on the blower and they estimate at least five hundred dead, maybe as many as two thousand seriously injured.'

'Ah.' Intellectually, Beresford had no difficulty in coping with such numbers; but picturing them mentally, in terms of mangled flesh and bone, was unthinkable. Trying to think of two thousand desperately injured human beings might make even an experienced surgeon like Edward Beresford lose his sanity.

'No figures at all for our zone, I'm afraid,' Dr Amschewitz continued, 'but we're expecting a convoy of ambulances from the southern sector any time now. Half London's ablaze out there, and they say he's made a terrific mess of the Surrey Docks.'

'What about the fire in the lab block?'

'Under control, but still smouldering. The AFS reckon it must have been a five-hundred-pounder, at the very least, to have caused such damage. Luckily we'd just finished evacuating the block when the bomb hit. Mind you, one of the probationer nurses had a bit of a narrow squeak. Silly girl went back in to fetch something – had to make a run for it at the last minute.'

Edward Beresford mopped the cold perspiration from his brow. It didn't seem right to him that young girls – some of them scarcely older than his own daughters – should be risking their lives in this inferno. Jacob Frankenberg must be mad to let his daughter train at the Royal Lambeth. She'd have been far better off playing nurses at some cosy little hospital in the country.

'I'll patch up this next lot of stretcher cases, then I must go and assist Mr Andrews in the emergency theatre. There are already ten waiting for surgery, and I've a notion some of 'em won't wait much longer. Besides, Hitler's bound to have another go at us later tonight.'

Wearily, he moved off towards a curtained-off cubicle where a young mother lay, filthy with blood, soot and plaster dust and so shocked that even kind, sensible Dillie Bayliss couldn't persuade her to give up the body of her dead child, clasped tightly in her arms.

By now, the casualty hall had become an ordered jumble

of bodies – some standing, some lying on the floor, some sitting or stretched out on the wooden benches. Procedures had been laid down, of course – and they were being followed as closely as possible – but even the best-thought-out procedures were apt to go awry under the sheer weight of numbers.

Over all presided Casualty Sister Winifred Edgerton, something of a martinet in her crisply starched apron and the razor-sharp lace bow tied tightly beneath her chin. She had been nursing for years, and had no intention of letting Hitler succeed where the Kaiser's Zeppelins had failed. If one thing was anathema to Sister Edgerton, it was panic.

An unnatural quiet reigned over the assembled throng, broken only by occasional groans and coughs, Sister Edgerton's abrupt commands, and the squeaking of trolleys being wheeled down to the emergency operating theatres which had been set up in the basement. The distant thuds and crashes of falling masonry provided a disturbing but curiously unreal counterpoint to Sister's enforced calm.

It was fortunate indeed, she told herself, that the Royal Lambeth had such a rigorous and well-rehearsed emergency drill. As soon as the air raid had been confirmed as a Red Alert, all the upstairs wards had been evacuated to the safety of the main basement. Those critically ill patients who could not be moved had had their beds pushed into the middle of the ward corridors and protected from any bomb blast with spare mattresses. At this very moment, trolleys were queueing all along the corridor which ran the length of the hospital basement; patients waiting for essential surgery which might or might not save them.

'Nurse, Nurse! It's my old man – he's hurt bad.'

Dillie trotted over to help the woman in the blue coat, once probably her Sunday best but now soaked through with blood where she had clasped her husband's almost severed hand to her chest. The woman's face was so streaked and caked with dust that it looked like a mask, brittle and starkly expressionless as the features beneath.

The elderly man had lost so much blood that he was grey-faced and only semi-conscious. How his wife had managed to get him here, Dillie could scarcely begin to understand.

'Come with me, Mrs...'

'Evans. Mary-Ann Evans.'

'Come with me, Mrs Evans, and we'll make your husband more comfortable.'

She led them into a cubicle just vacated by a stretcher case which had gone down to theatre, and helped Mrs Evans to lay her husband down on the examination couch. There clearly wasn't much time to lose. If the bleeding wasn't stemmed right away, he could die within minutes. She put her head through the curtains.

'Doctor – quickly, Doctor.'

Dr Amschewitz was on his way, but Dillie couldn't wait for him. Seizing a wad of gauze, she laid the clean cloth over the horrific wound and exerted a firm pressure, all the time talking as calmly as she could to reassure Mrs Evans.

'You're quite safe now. We'll get you a cup of nice strong tea just as soon as we can.'

'To be honest, Nurse, I'd as soon have a half-pint of ale. But me local ain't there any more, is it? Just a bloomin' big 'ole where it used to be. It's gone, and 'alf the street with it.'

* * *

It was just after eight o'clock when the ambulance carrying Creena and Oliver finally reached the hospital. It had been a long, slow process and they had picked up three more casualties along the way – two young girls with minor leg injuries and a middle-aged man who had been shocked half out of his senses when the Anderson shelter his wife and daughters had taken refuge in took a direct hit. He, it seemed, had been spared only because he had gone back into the house to make a flask of tea.

The condition of the man with the head injury had deteriorated. His complexion was ashen, his lips bluish, and now he had lost all control of his bodily functions. The interior of the ambulance was rank with the stench of human misery. But still Creena kept on talking to him, in the faint hope that he could hear her, that her words might keep him hanging on just that little bit longer.

'If only I'd had my bag with me,' hissed Oliver in frustration. He had bandaged up the girls' leg injuries but the little blonde one was sobbing and sobbing with pain. A shot of morphia was the least he could have done for her.

'You were off duty,' Creena pointed out. 'We both were.' That sunny Saturday afternoon seemed an awfully long way off now.

She knelt down beside the pregnant woman, whose jaw was clenched shut with pain. Her only visible injury seemed to be a small gash on her arm, but her hands were still clasped about her belly.

'It's all right. It's going to be all right,' Creena repeated, using her lace hanky to wipe the woman's sweat-streaked face. Dark, deep-set eyes followed her every movement, pleading with her to take the pain away and replace it with reassurance.

'My baby,' gasped the woman in heavily accented English. Creena couldn't quite place the accent, though it was guttural, vaguely Germanic.

'Everything will be all right.' Creena wished she could think of something more specific to say. Telling this poor woman that everything was all right seemed ludicrous in the midst of all this mayhem.

'Your baby's fine,' Oliver told her. Without his equipment he couldn't be sure that was true, but worrying the woman would only make things worse. She looked very young. He glanced across at Creena. 'You're in excellent hands.'

'Do you think...' Creena looked from the woman's immense stomach to Oliver and swallowed hard. 'You don't suppose the baby might be on its way...?'

'Bit early to be sure,' Oliver replied. 'Probably just a false alarm.'

Creena could have wept with relief as the ambulance turned through the hospital gates and rattled to a halt outside the entrance to the casualty department.

The back doors of the ambulance opened and Oliver sprang out, helping the ambulance driver and his mate to lift out the most seriously injured patient.

'Serious head wound, pulse weak, possible fractured femur and internal injuries,' Oliver rattled off. 'I have to leave you now, Creena – do what I can. Sorry the theatre didn't work out. Next time, eh?'

'Next time.' Creena met his smile with a rather lopsided

one of her own, and had the strangest urge to hug him. Just a few hours ago they had been almost strangers; now she felt as though adversity had bonded their lives together.

'Next time, *for sure*.'

He was gone, disappearing into the darkness through the blacked-out doors of the casualty department and leaving Creena to help the ambulancemen with the rest of the injured. Curiously, she realised that she felt no fear.

Something had changed inside her. Maybe it was just the adrenaline pumping through her veins, but she felt distinctly different. She felt as if, at long last, she was growing up.

'Thank God, Quilliam! I was beginning to think Jerry'd got you, really I was.'

Dillie Bayliss rushed forward to greet her friend like a mother hen as Creena, dazed and grimy, followed the last of the stretchers into the casualty hall.

'Are you all right? You look like you've been dragged through a hedge backwards.'

Creena blinked in the light, with difficulty taking in the organised chaos around her. Nurses were bustling with quiet-voiced efficiency among the wreckage of dazed humanity, the grey-white faces smeared with blood and caked with soot and dust. The air smelt odd, too: the familiar smells of carbolic acid and soap, floor polish and boiled cabbage were all mixed up with the scents of war – of dust, urine and blood.

'Yes, yes, I'm fine.'

'You're very pale. In fact you look an absolute fright, Cree.'

'I'm fine, really,' said Creena firmly. 'Shouldn't you be off duty by now?'

'I shouldn't think anyone's going to be off duty for a long time,' replied Dillie grimly. 'There's so much to do here . . .'

'Yes, I must report to Sister Meredith,' said Creena suddenly, as though waking from a daze. 'She'll want me up on the ward.'

'Sister M's in the basement with the rest of Female Surgical. They were evacuated down there as soon as the Red Alert was confirmed.' Dillie looked at Creena's drawn face and felt a deep concern for her. This was a nightmare, but at least two years as a nursing assistant had given Dillie a certain resilience. 'Report to Sister Cas – she'll tell you what needs doing. Must go now – have to assist Dr Amschewitz.'

Dillie bustled away and Creena shook herself into shape. Casualty Sister was marshalling her troops and it was quite obvious that everyone, absolutely everyone, was needed here. Remember your training, Quilliam, she told herself and with head held high she walked across the hall towards Sister Edgerton.

'Sister?'

The ramrod-stiff sister turned on her heel, peering at Creena through horn-rimmed spectacles. Despite the disarray around her, Sister Edgerton's steel-grey hair was scraped back into an immaculate bun with not a strand out of place, her cap and apron a perfect, shimmering white under the subdued emergency lighting.

'And you are . . .?'

'Quilliam, Sister,' Creena explained breathlessly. It

dawned on her that she must not look very much like a probationer nurse, what with her ripped stockings, tousled hair and the dried bloodstains on the hem of her dress. 'Probationer nurse, first year. I was off-duty...'

Sister Edgerton's severe features softened just a fraction.

'I can see that, Nurse. Well, we are grateful for your help. Which ward are you seconded to?'

'Female Surgical, Sister.'

'Very well. You may report to Sister Meredith in the basement.'

'Yes, Sister. Right away, Sister.'

'But first...'

Creena swung round.

'Sister?'

'Go straight to the home and get washed and changed. This may be an emergency, Nurse Quilliam, but there is no excuse for slovenliness. As a Royal Lambeth nurse, you have a certain standard to maintain.'

Washed, brushed and changed more quickly than ever in her life before, Creena trotted at top speed down to the emergency surgical ward in the basement. She was shaking a little after her ordeal in the ambulance, but shock had not yet taken its toll and she felt hyped up, ready for anything. Right on cue, as she descended the stairs to the basement, she heard the sirens sound a second air-raid warning. Her heart sank.

Oliver had been right. Jerry was back for a second bite of the cherry.

Patients had been carried down from the first floor on

their mattresses, which had then been set up on old bedsteads arranged along the corridor. Sister Meredith and Staff Nurse Ridley had made their ward office in one of the alcoves.

It was an odd scene; dozens of beds arranged along a dimly lit, rather musty corridor through which ran the massive central heating and water pipes for the whole hospital. Almost eerie, really. But Creena remembered what she had been taught in PTS, and forced herself to breeze into the makeshift ward with a smile on her face.

'Good evening, ladies!'

''Well, if it ain't our very own Manx Maid!' exclaimed Mrs Lawlor, glancing up from her knitting.

'Nice to see you again, ducks,' added Mrs Eversleigh. 'Still lookin' a bit pale, I see.'

'We all are,' pointed out Gloria Bradley with acid humour, 'what with that lot goin' on up there.' She nodded in the vague direction of the ceiling and as if in answer there was the distant rumble of detonating explosive. 'But what really gets me is havin' to miss out on me tea just 'cause of him.'

'It would only 'ave bin pilchards agin,' interjected Mavis Paterson mournfully. 'It ain't as if we're missin' anythin'.'

'I'd feel easier if I could hear our boys answerin' back,' commented Mrs Lawlor. 'Not a peep out of our guns. It ain't right, just lettin' Jerry get away with it like that.'

'I'm sure our boys are doing all they can, Mrs L,' observed Sister Meredith, emerging from her improvised office with a kidney bowl covered with a white cloth. 'Well! If it isn't Nurse Quilliam.'

'I'm reporting for duty, Sister.'

'You may assist Nurse Clarke-Herbert with the obs. Then there will be at least five post-op beds to prepare. Admissions could start coming in from the emergency theatres at any time.'

'Yes, Sister.'

Marian Clarke-Herbert, seconded from her placement on Male Medical, greeted Creena with even more warmth than usual.

'Am I glad to see you!' she exclaimed as she fetched a bedpan for old Mavis Paterson who – true to form – hadn't stopped moaning since she'd woken up that morning. 'The ward maid told everyone she'd seen you heading for the park and of course Mavis said she was sure you'd bought it. She's a regular Jeremiah, that woman.' She lowered her voice. 'Is it truly awful up there?'

'Like hell,' replied Creena soberly. 'Only worse. I still can't believe the things I saw.'

'How on earth did you get back?'

'Hitched a lift with Oliver in an ambulance with some of the casualties. Oh, Marian, if you'd seen some of the injured ... It's enough to break your heart ...'

'Well, I heard from Harry that Jerry's had a field day out there. Lambeth Marsh has taken a real pasting – hundreds injured, maybe even thousands. Lord knows how many poor innocent people that monster's made homeless tonight. And there's a few pubs won't be serving any more pints too, by the sound of it. Harry says the Royal George went down with a tremendous bang ...'

Creena felt the hairs on the back of her neck stand up.

'The Royal George?'

'That's right. You remember ...'

Of course Creena remembered. How could she forget? The Royal George was on the corner of Bishop Street, just a few doors down from Mo Doyle's house. It was Mo's favourite pub. Or, at least, it used to be . . .

A full eight hours later, mind and body fighting the great grey blanket of tiredness that threatened to descend and swamp her, Creena emerged from the basement. It was four o'clock in the morning and it felt as though the air raid had been going on for ever.

She had been summoned to Casualty by a cryptic message to Sister Meredith, brought by a breathless VAD: 'Please may Nurse Quilliam be released, as she is required to assist Sister Hambleton.'

Sister Hambleton? But that made no sense at all. Sister Hambleton worked on Maternity, and Creena didn't know the first thing about babies. Frankly, she found them rather terrifying – fragile, squalling bundles of incoherent vulnerability. What ever could Sister Hambleton want with her? she wondered as she reported to Sister Edgerton.

Without further illumination, she was sent to one of the side wards along the corridor which led out of the casualty hall. She hesitated outside for a moment; and at that moment a land mine exploded, shaking the whole building and making the emergency light flicker wildly on the end of its bare flex.

She pushed open the door and went in.

Sister Hambleton glanced up from the woman writhing on the bed. Clara Hambleton was a small woman but she had immensely strong, gentle hands, and her common-sense manner endeared her to all who worked with her.

There was no bitchiness or snobbery about her – her only concern was to get the job done and do what was best for the patient.

'You're Quilliam, right?'

'Yes, Sister.'

'Pop on a gown and gloves, Nurse. Sorry I had to summon you like that. This is Anna Van Heest, a Dutch refugee, the poor lass. She'd got herself in such a pickle I thought she might do herself an injury. You've met, I believe?'

Mrs Van Heest turned her head towards the door and – although her face was paper-white and contorted with pain – Creena instantly recognised the woman from the ambulance. Her arm wound had been bandaged, but she was still in her clothes and lying on the bed with her eyes hugely wide and her knees drawn up to her swollen belly.

'Y-yes,' replied Creena, her eyes meeting the woman's. She thought she saw Mrs Van Heest relax, just a fraction, heard her breathing become slightly less hoarse.

'Mrs Van Heest, this young lady is Nurse Quilliam. You know, Quilliam, she wouldn't let me do a thing for her, and kept saying "I want the red-haired nurse in the ambulance." Your friend Nurse Bayliss told me who you were. Ever assisted with a delivery before?'

Creena shook her head slowly.

'No, Sister.'

'Never mind, there's a first time for everything. Whatever it was that you did for this lady in the ambulance, I'd appreciate it if you could do it again. Not that it'll take long. If I'm not very much mistaken, the poor girl's almost there.' She listened to the foetal heartbeat. Regular and strong. Good. 'As you can see, it's all been so quick that there hasn't even been time to prep her properly. Must have been the shock of the raid that set her off.'

'My baby – is good?'

Mrs Van Heest looked up at Creena, and Creena was alarmed to see the degree of trust in those dark, deep-set eyes. She didn't know anything, not a thing! She felt like a complete fraud, but she took hold of Mrs Van Heest's clammy hand and nodded.

'Very good. Everything's fine.'

'Please – stay with me.'

'I will. I shan't go.' Creena turned to Sister Hambleton. 'What should I do, Sister?'

'Give her plenty of moral support, sponge her brow – and stop any more of those damned blackout screens from falling down. I've no intention of switching off the light, and we don't want Jerry taking a pot shot at us while we're hard at work.'

Right on cue a bomb came whistling down and seemed to lift the whole building off its foundations for a split second before depositing it back on solid ground in a fine mist of plaster dust and a clatter of falling bottles and dishes. Another of the wooden blackout screens came tumbling down, followed by a tinkling of broken glass. Creena rushed to jam the screen back into its frame.

'Damn those Jerries,' said Sister Hambleton under her breath, gently examining her patient. 'That's the ticket, Quilliam. Now come back here and hold Mrs VH's hand whilst I . . .' Mrs Van Heest gave a dreadful, blood-curdling screech and Creena felt every muscle in the young woman's body tense as she strained; pushing, pushing, pushing with all her might. The Dutch girl's eyes were screwed tight shut, rivers of sweat trickling down her face and plastering her hair to her scalp.

'Yes, *good girl*, Mrs Van Heest.' Sister Hambleton felt gently for the child's head, then took Creena's hand and placed it on the smooth, domed hardness. 'Feel that, Quilliam?'

'Yes, Sister.'

'That's the infant – so you see, we're almost there.'

Creena felt a dull excitement ripple through her at the realisation of what she could feel under her fingers – the sticky, slimy dome that was the top of a real, living child's head.

'Hell of a night to choose to get yourself born,' observed Sister Hambleton. 'But infants never did have a very good sense of timing. I delivered my first in the middle of a thunderstorm, you know. So not much changes, really!' She looked down at the tired face of the Dutchwoman. 'You all right now, dear?'

Anna Van Heest nodded and tightened her grip around Creena's fingers, gathering up her strength for what she sensed would be the big push, the final effort which would bring her child into this world of noise, danger and pain. She had never given birth before, but her instincts were driving her now; her instincts and her instinctive trust in the red-haired girl with the gentle green eyes.

Crump. Crump. Thud. Hitler's bombers were taking out a few final targets. From time to time, the sound of gunfire or the sudden cut-out of an engine suggested that, at last, the boys in blue were putting up some resistance.

'Hear what I hear?'

'Sister?'

'I swear those planes are getting further away. Pray God I'm right.'

At that moment, Mrs Van Heest gripped Creena's hand for dear life and gave a terrible, shuddering cry which cut right through the fading sounds of battle beyond the blacked-out windows.

'That's right, dear. Push. Push hard. You're so nearly there. Good *girl*.'

A single bomb whistled past the window with a piercing shriek, but for the moment, at least, Creena was beyond caring about bombs.

She was simply stunned and enchanted by the speed of it all; the head and then the body, shooting out of the fat round belly and into Sister Hambleton's waiting hands. It was a baby, a real baby girl . . . Yet another blackout screen had shifted slightly in its frame, but Creena didn't notice.

'Aah,' gasped the new mother, falling back on to the stained and crumpled sheets as the all clear sounded. To Creena, it was every bit as beautiful as a choir of angels.

'A lovely little girl, Mrs Van Heest. Perfect in every way. Nurse will just give her a bit of a wash and brush-up, then you can hold her. Good work, Nurse Quilliam. Just the ticket.'

'But Sister . . . I didn't do anything . . .'

'You did perfectly well, Nurse. You kept your head and that's more than a lot of girls your age would have done.'

It was just as Creena was holding the bowl to receive the placenta that there was a tumultuous knocking at the door and a red-faced medical student peered into the room.

'Sister Hambleton?'

Sister stared back at the medical student, momentarily struck dumb with astonishment that anyone should dare to invade her patients' sacred privacy.

'Yes?' she replied with acid precision.

'There's a policeman outside, Sister. He's frightfully shirty – says you're showing a light . . .'

Sister Hambleton cursed softly under her breath.

'Does he now? Well tell him . . .'

'Yes, Sister?'

'Tell him there's a war on. And while you're at it, tell him to go to hell.'

Chapter 13

It had been another bad night for the Royal Lambeth Hospital.

For the ninth night in a row, Hitler's bombers had shown Lambeth Marsh neither mercy nor respite. Black Saturday – just over a week ago – now seemed years and years in the past, the beginning of a dark and sinister new world in which carefree walks in the park had no place.

Creena and her contemporaries, just beginning their second year as probationers, were having to grow up very quickly indeed. Grumbles about food and tyrannical sisters seemed petty and insignificant now. It was all hands to the pumps – and if that meant no off-duty and hardly any sleep, well that was all part of Doing Your Bit. There were shattered bodies to mend and any one of them could be your own brother, father, mother, child.

'London can take it' – that was what the signs said, chalked defiantly on the doorways of bombed-out shops and houses. And perhaps London could, after all – though how the Royal Lambeth Hospital was going to cope with the nightly influx of casualties was beyond Creena's powers of reasoning.

Down in Female Surgical, now permanently removed to the reinforced basement, the air raid had been reduced to a series of faraway rumbles and thuds. The only tangible sign of any damage up above had been the sound of the emergency generators cutting in, and a few puddles appearing on the corridor floor, the result of one or two cracked water pipes. Each new sound – whether ack-ack or bomb blast – was interpreted with gloomy relish by Mavis Paterson: 'That'll be the private patients' block if I'm not mistaken'; 'Now the sisters' home 'as copped for it, you mark my words'; 'I'll bet there's not much left of the old pile come morning.'

In the event, when the all clear sounded and the smoke of a thousand new fires began to clear, it transpired that the hospital had escaped with relatively slight damage, though Outpatients had taken another pounding and one of the other blocks had lost its top storey.

Creena slung her cloak over her shoulders and walked back across the rubble-strewn courtyard towards what had been the Junior Dining Room. With admirable pragmatism, Matron had decreed that the ground-floor dining room and the basement beneath should be turned into a temporary dormitory for those probationers with rooms on the upper storeys of the nurses' home, and that in future all probationers would take their meals in the Senior Dining Room.

On this particular morning Creena had little interest in food. The certainty that a plateful of congealing leek and bacon fritters would be waiting for her in the dining room only quickened her steps towards the makeshift dormitory and the luxury of a mattress on the floor. She wasn't on again till two and the lecture on theatre procedures had been postponed, so this was a golden opportunity to catch up on lost sleep.

Wriggling gratefully out of her uniform, she folded it and slid into bed. On the adjoining mattress, Hester Frankenberg was slumbering peacefully, immaculate even in the midst of chaos. Snuggling down and clutching her pillow, Creena drifted off into sleep.

What seemed like mere seconds later, she was being roused by Dillie.

'Shake a leg, Sleeping Beauty.'

Creena grunted and tried to turn over.

'What time . . . ?'

'One thirty. Time to get up.'

'It can't be!'

With an effort of will, Creena threw back the blankets and rubbed her eyes. Dillie was just off duty after an eight-hour stint in Cas, but she looked fresh as a daisy. Creena's brain felt like mud. She yawned.

'What's happening out there?'

'Beresford and Andrews have finished operating but Cas is packed out. They're hoping to get those that can be moved shifted down to the EMS hospital this afternoon to make room for the next lot . . .'

Creena did not answer as she put her hair up – once a lengthy and fiddly process but an automatic reflex now – and pinned on her starched cap before stepping into her dress. They all knew what Dillie meant. There was no reason to suppose that tonight would be any different from last night, or the eight nights of hell before that. There seemed no sign at all of this 'blitz' letting up.

'Speaking of moving patients,' piped up Howells, who was stretched out on her mattress with the inevitable whodunnit, 'did you hear about that German?'

'What?' Dillie slipped on her nightdress and got into bed. 'The one who was shot down?'

'That's right. Lothar Menz.' Howells drew herself up into a sitting position, hugging her knees with her arms. 'They're moving him to a military hospital today.'

'But I thought he couldn't be moved,' said Creena, puzzled. 'His spinal injuries . . .'

'They haven't got much choice,' replied Howells, her eyes bright with scandal. 'Someone tried to . . . you know . . . do him in!'

'No! Who?' Dillie and Creena forgot their tiredness for a moment and stared at her.

'You're fantasising again, Howells,' said Dillie.

'No, no, I'm not, honestly,' insisted Howells in the face of such scepticism. 'I'm not sure of the details but it seems some patient or other tried to get into his room when it was left unguarded for a few minutes and smother him with a pillow. Might have done away with him, too, if Sister hadn't come along in the nick of time.'

Dillie shook her head in disbelief. She couldn't help thinking of Micky and Kitty's dad, who was probably in a POW camp in Germany by now. Would he fare any better than Lothar Menz?

'Look, I really must dash,' said Creena, pinning on her fob watch and checking her black lisle stockings for crooked seams and wrinkles. She would have to do. 'Daren't be late for Sister M.'

She hurried across to the main hospital building. The

private patients' block had a crack up the side wall and the lab block was a real mess, what with its roof gone and half the top storey with it. In the afternoon light it looked dark and sad, like a blackened and rotting tooth in a once-perfect smile.

Descending the stairs to the basement she met Staff Nurse Ridley, looking somewhat flustered and carrying the dangerous drugs book under her arm.

'It really is too bad, Nurse Quilliam,' she commented. 'First our supplies are disrupted, and now the chief dispenser tells me that controlled drugs are being stolen from the hospital. To think that there may be thieves among us at a time like this. Whatever is the world coming to?'

Without waiting for Creena's opinion on the matter Staff Nurse Ridley bustled on, leaving Creena speechless in her wake. Hastily she smoothed down her apron in readiness for her first encounter of the day with Sister Meredith.

Meredith was sitting at the ward desk, discussing the latest intake of patients with a junior house surgeon. She scarcely glanced up as Creena approached.

'Cap crooked, Nurse Quilliam. And when did you last polish those shoes?'

'Sorry, Sister. Yesterday, Sister.' Surreptitiously buffing up the toe of her right shoe on the back of her left stocking, she readjusted her cap as best she could without a mirror. She knew it was still not straight, but Sister Meredith did not press the issue any further.

'You are to report to Dr Amschewitz in the casualty hall,' Sister Meredith announced. 'You will assist with a patient transfer.'

'Yes, Sister.'

Meredith tilted her head back and gave Creena a long, hard stare.

'You are looking tired, Nurse. Tired student nurses are a liability on any acute ward. On your return, you will take at least three hours' sleep before returning to duty. Is that clear?'

'Yes, Sister. Of course, Sister.'

Dr David Amschewitz was waiting for her when she reached the casualty hall, his curly black hair looking lank and dishevelled after seventy-two hours on duty with virtually no sleep.

'Doctor? Sister Meredith sent me. She said you needed me to help with a patient transfer.'

'Ah yes, Nurse. We had a young chap brought in with severe eye injuries last night, and I don't give much for his chances of seeing again without specialist treatment. I have his notes and X-rays here.' He handed two folders to Creena. 'All you have to do is deliver him – and these – to the Royal Eye, then report straight back to me. Think you can do that?'

Creena nodded.

'Yes, Doctor.' She felt proud to be entrusted with such a responsibility, and wished that Oliver were here to see that she was coping, doing so much better than she'd thought she ever would. But Oliver had been called up, posted to a military hospital near Aldershot, and she had no idea when – or even if – she would see him again.

She followed the stretcher out to the ambulance. The patient was heavily sedated but lapsing in and out of consciousness, mumbling a few incoherent words. Almost the whole of his face was obscured by bandages and thick, soft dressing pads over his injured eyes. As she settled him down, Creena noticed that he had also lost a hand; but after all that she had seen over the last few days, that seemed a minor, almost inconsequential injury. What mattered now was saving his sight.

'Hold on to your hat, Nurse,' said the ambulance driver – a jolly, middle-aged lady who had never imagined her duty would extend beyond bringing up her four daughters and looking after her engineer husband. 'This could be a bumpy ride – Jerry's made a terrific mess of Westminster Bridge Road.'

And just about everywhere else too, mused Creena, surveying the devastation around her as the ambulance swung out of the hospital gates. When was it going to stop?

Dr Oliver Temple put his stethoscope into his pocket and sat down on the edge of the bed.

'Chin up,' he said, but the soldier turned his head away, ashamed of the tears in his sightless eyes.

'It's no use, Doc. It's good of you to try and cheer me up but I wish I'd died out there, honest I do.'

'That may be how you feel now, but later on . . .'

The soldier gave a dry laugh.

'Later? What do I care about later? I'm blind, my girl's given me the push, what is there to look forward to?'

'There'll be other girls.'

'No girl's going to look twice at a blind man.'

'Listen.' Oliver pushed back his mop of sandy-coloured hair, searching for the right words. 'There'll be someone out there for you, you mark my words. There's someone special for us all.'

It was Thursday, 26 September 1940, and as far as Micky and Kitty were concerned, the world might as well be coming to an end.

'Don't make us, Auntie Mo! Don't make us go!'

Micky's face was screwed up in a final, all-out plea for clemency. He looked so comical that Mo Doyle almost laughed out loud, in spite of the heaviness in her heart.

'You know it's for the best,' she said firmly, tying a brown luggage label on to the small cardboard suitcase which contained two changes of underwear, brand-new pyjamas and a toothbrush. It had not been easy, finding the money to kit out the kids for their trip, but Mo Doyle was a proud woman and she wasn't sending Eddie's kids away to be made a mockery of. 'Half the kids in Bishop Street are going. It's not as if you'll be on your own, now, is it?'

'Auntie Mo, Auntie Mo – it's not fair!' Kitty joined in Micky's chorus of protest but it was no good. Mo's mind was made up and she had to harden her heart.

'You're going, an' that's all there is to it,' she said, tying Kitty's shoelaces with a firm finality which concealed the upset she too was feeling at this parting. 'Uncle Jack agrees, don't you?'

She threw Jack a look that would freeze a volcano, and he nodded vigorously.

'Do what yer Auntie Mo says, or else,' he said with as much menace as he could manage. Actually it wasn't too difficult to profess enthusiasm. He was glad the kids were being evacuated to the country. He'd never been big on responsibility, and Micky and Kitty were a very big responsibility indeed. You only had to turn your back on them for five minutes and they were into everything: playing on bomb sites, falling into craters, you name it.

'Or else what, Uncle Jack?' asked Kitty innocently.

'Or *else*.' He too half wanted to laugh, half wanted to sympathise. At their age he'd have been inconsolable, too. Falling bombs and fizzing incendiaries must seem exciting when you were too young to understand what those bombs and incendiaries could do to living flesh.

'What about me shrapnel collection?' demanded Micky, wriggling furiously as Mo forced him into the good second-hand coat with the velvet collar from Jack's tot stall. 'Why can't I take it wiv me?'

Jack suppressed a smile. Micky's shrapnel collection would fill several large suitcases.

'I'll look after it for you,' he replied, tapping the side of his nose in an all-men-together sort of way. 'But if I 'ear of you gettin' into any mischief . . .'

There wasn't much point in sticking around to see them off. They'd only blub, and then Mo would blub too and – Gawd help him – he might get all emotional as well. Couldn't have that. So he left them to their aunt's tender mercies, slipping a half-crown surreptitiously into each coat pocket before he went.

He stepped out into the warmth of the afternoon sun, turned left into The Cut and walked along in the direction of The Ring, on the corner of Charlotte Street. The poor old Cut had taken a bit of a pounding, these last three weeks. They'd bombed the chemist's where Micky had got his backside tanned, and the blown-in front of the iron-monger's was all boarded up, with a crookedly painted sign: 'More open than usual'. Still, at least they hadn't bombed his favourite pub yet, and the boxing ring on the opposite corner was still intact.

Jack wished he could run away from his troubles as easily as Micky and Kitty could. Life was a lot easier when you were a kid. Pushing open the door of the public bar, he acknowledged friends and acquaintances with a nod and ordered a pint.

'Bloody awful racket agin last night, Jack,' observed Ernie the barman, pulling the pint and setting it down on the bar. 'My Hattie didn't sleep a wink.'

Jack shrugged and pushed his money across the polished bar top.

'Yeah, well, bombs is the least of my worries.' He picked up the pint, sipped it and then held it up to the light. 'See yer still waterin' down the beer then.' It was more of an observation than a criticism. Another casualty of war.

It was Ernie's turn to shrug. Polishing a glass on a greying towel, he leant across the bar. 'Flamin' Government, ain't it?' he growled. 'Can't git the good stuff any more, can yer?'

'Need anythin', do you?' Jack never missed an opportunity to be of service to one of his many customers.

'Got any dried fruit? Hattie's sister's kid's gettin' spliced but she can't get the makin's for a cake. Best the baker can do is supply one o' them cardboard jobs to stick over a sponge cake. 'Ardly the same, really, is it?'

Jack made a note on a scrap of paper.

''Ow much you want? Two pound? Three?'

'Two should do it.'

'I'll see what I can do. I'm seein' someone tonight about a bit of business . . .'

Hardly had the words escaped from his lips when he felt an iron-heavy hand on his shoulder.

'Bit of business, Jack? What about *our* bit of unfinished business?'

Jack hardly dared turn round, but he forced himself to. He knew it was Sid Clayden even before he found himself looking into those pink-rimmed piggy eyes and that fat red face beneath the black Homburg. The overcoat had a real astrakhan collar and when Sid took off his leather gloves Jack saw he was wearing half a dozen heavy gold rings. Dead men's rings, he thought with a shudder . . .

'Hello, Sid,' he said uneasily. This was the moment he'd been dreading. He'd been avoiding Sid Clayden ever since Black Saturday, when Sid's investment had gone so inconveniently up in smoke. 'Buy you a pint?'

'Double brandy,' replied Sid. 'Take it out of that bottle you keep under the counter, Ernie – Jack here's payin'.'

Jack forked out handsomely for the brandy and went to sit at a quiet table with Sid Clayden.

'See that picture?' Sid jerked his head and Jack's eyes wandered up to a picture of a prize fighter, massively built, muscles rippling, fists up and stance threatening. The caption underneath read 'Jack Doyle'. 'Now that's what I call a *real* fighter, Jack, not like you.' He sniggered unpleasantly. 'You, you're just a ducker and diver.'

'I . . .' The words stuck in Jack's parched throat. He took a swig of watery beer and wished it were something stronger. 'That stuff you left with me . . .'

Sid's unpleasant smile left his face. It was almost a relief.

'I heard, Jack. And I wasn't pleased. That was careless, Jack, very careless.'

'I know, Mr Clayden. And I'm really sorry – but how was I to know Jerry'd choose that night to bomb the Surrey Docks? I was goin' to move the stuff that afternoon...'

Sid silenced him with a dismissive wave of his hand.

'I'm not interested in excuses, Jack. I don't want to know the whys and the wherefores. I gave you a little job to do and you let me down. You owe me double now.'

Jack's heart sank. He'd known all along that it was a big mistake to get involved with Sid Clayden – but what could he do? And now he was doubly indebted, and Sid never, ever failed to call in a debt. Not that he couldn't afford to write off the loss – Sid had done very well indeed out of looting and racketeering – but it was the principle of the thing. Let one get away, and his power might be seen to be slipping.

'Yes, Mr Clayden.'

Sid finished his brandy, wiping a fat pink paw across his mouth.

'Good brandy, Jack. I'll have another.'

'Right away, Mr Clayden.' Jack nodded to Ernie at the bar.

'And while Ernie's getting me that, you can start telling me how you're going to pay me back. Because you'd better make good this debt, Jack, otherwise you're going to find out just how angry Sid Clayden can get. And Jack...'

'Mr Clayden?'

'I shouldn't bother thinking of running away. These are dangerous times, you might have a little accident. Even shelters aren't safe, you know.' His piggy eyes narrowed to malevolent points of light. 'People can drown in shelters...'

Hester Frankenberg was not in one of her happier moods.

'Trust you!' she sniffed, buttoning on a freshly starched uniform collar and stiff cuffs. 'Trust you to get sent to some cushy hospital in the country, whilst the rest of us have to stay here and get bombed to smithereens.'

Marian Clarke-Herbert exchanged exasperated glances with Creena and Dillie. All of them wished it had worked out differently, but Matron's edict had been quite clear: all first-years, and all probationers under twenty-one, were to be evacuated to an EMS hospital in leafy Surrey.

Marian was still six months away from her twenty-first birthday, and had been 'jolly well peeved' to be sent packing to the country – why, hadn't she applied to the Royal Lambeth precisely because she wanted to get away from her father's rural estate and do something really useful? At twenty-one and twenty-two respectively, Creena and Dillie were grateful to have escaped this enforced evacuation from the danger zone; frightened though they might be, they were determined to stay in London and do their bit.

Hester, however, was furious. She had just had her twenty-first and had been celebrating her elevation to adulthood when Matron had made her announcement. Never one for inconvenience, discomfort or danger, Hester would have been frankly overjoyed to have been sent to the EMS hospital until the heat died down. But it was not to be, and Marian was going instead. Creena and Dillie weren't sure who was the most dismayed – themselves, Marian or Hester.

'Do dry up, Frankenberg,' Marian urged. She was the only one of her set who could handle Hester's uppity moods. 'I shall only be going for a few months anyway, till I'm twenty-one. At least I'm not poor Philomena Clarke – married in secret and now she has to pretend he's only her fiancé or they'll both get the sack.'

'Tough luck that,' agreed Dillie. 'But if you ask me, anyone who gets married in this lot has a screw loose.'

'I don't see why they can't evacuate *all* of us,' said Hester coldly.

'Because then they'd have no one to run the hospital, would they, you silly goose,' retorted Marian, packing her case. 'Without the likes of us to skivvy, the whole place would fall apart. And what would all the poor souls who've got themselves injured do then, eh?'

'All I can say is, I hope you don't get yourself blitzed, Frankenberg,' observed Creena. 'You'd make a rotten patient.'

She cast her mind back to the young woman, about Frankenberg's age, who had been admitted to Cas only yesterday. A few hours before, out dancing with her beau at some society party, she must have been strikingly lovely. Now she had lost an eye and almost half of her face. So far, the nursing staff had kept her away from mirrors, but sooner or later she would be bound to find out what had happened to her . . .

'Well, I'd swap with you any day, Frankenberg,' Marian cut in, bouncing up and down on the lid of her suitcase to force it shut. 'If only Matron'd let me. It'll be deadly dull out in the country, *and* I shall have that dreadful Mavis Paterson to contend with.' Marian was accompanying some of the patients from Female Surgical to the EMS hospital, and Mavis Paterson had become something of a legend at the Royal Lambeth.

'It won't be so bad, Clarke-Herbert,' volunteered Creena. She had no desire to leave London, not now. It was her duty to stay. But she did think a little wistfully of Ballakeeill and of leafy green lanes, far from the sound of ack-ack fire and falling bombs. 'It'll be nice and quiet and peaceful. Regular shifts and plenty of sleep. Bliss . . .'

'Hmm,' grunted Marian, unconvinced.

'Look at Waverley,' pointed out Dillie, folding her cap and pinning it to her curly brown locks.

'Who's Waverley?' demanded Marian.

'Oh, you know, staff nurse on Gynae. Qualified last year. She's always droning on about the delights of the provinces – Warwickshire she's from, isn't she? Coventry or thereabouts. I bet she'd go to the EMS like a shot if she had the chance.'

'Warwickshire? Wasn't it Warwickshire that your Kitty and Micky were evacuated to?' enquired Eleanor Howells, who had just entered the improvised dormitory.

'No, that was Wiltshire,' replied Dillie. 'And don't they just hate it! Auntie Mo had a letter from Micky the other day. It said . . .'

But Creena wasn't really listening. She had had a letter too – from Oliver. At last he had managed to get a couple of days' leave from the military hospital, and was coming up to London. Better than that, he had asked her to go to the pictures with him. She couldn't wait to see him again . . .

At that moment the telephone rang and Marian picked up the receiver.

'Nurses' home? Yes, Sister. Right away, Sister.' She replaced the receiver on its hook. 'Who's on first call for Casualty? Seems a bomb's gone off at Balham tube station and taken half the street with it.'

Creena and Oliver came out of the cinema around tea-time. At the start of the Blitz the Government had closed all theatres and cinemas 'for the duration' but now the picture houses had reopened for afternoon performances, and London life was getting on as best it could. The good news was that the bombing raids had eased off lately. It had been almost a whole week since the last serious raid. Could it possibly be true that Hitler had decided to focus his attention elsewhere?

Oliver turned his collar up against the chilly, drizzly weather and popped his trilby on his head.

'Third time lucky!' he observed. 'You know, I was beginning to think I'd never get another evening off to take you out!'

'I'm glad you did,' replied Creena, trying hard not to betray *how* glad.

'Am I worth the wait then?' demanded Oliver, his grey-green eyes twinkling. 'Have you forgiven me for having to rush off back to the hospital like that?'

'Oh . . . perhaps . . .' teased Creena. But she knew he was worth it all right. He was more than worth it.

'I really am sorry,' said Oliver. 'It was all so sudden. One minute I was sawing through some fellow's femur in theatre, the next, I was being measured for my uniform.'

'It's all right, I understand.'

'Pax?'

Creena giggled nervously as Oliver took her hand and, very gently, planted a kiss upon it.

'Pax.'

His smile was purest electricity. He looked so handsome in his uniform; tall and broad and the perfect English gentleman. He slipped a protective arm about Creena's waist and she made no attempt to draw away. His fingers felt hot and strong through the too-flimsy fabric of her raincoat and second-best dress. Paradoxically, the heat of his touch made her shiver, suddenly aware of the chill around them.

'Cold?' he asked.

Creena nodded.

'Foul weather, isn't it?'

He drew her closer.

'Tell you what. Why don't you come back to my place for a while? It's only a few steps from here.'

'Well . . . I don't know that I should.' She was thinking of what Matron and the senior tutor would have to say about young probationers accepting invitations to doctors' private quarters. But then again, she was off duty, and it wasn't as if Oliver still worked at the Royal Lambeth. 'In fact, I know I shouldn't. It'd be death by a thousand cuts if Matron got to hear of it.'

'You won't even come back for a cup of tea?' He lowered his voice. 'I've got some chocolate biscuits too, but don't tell Sister Meredith.'

Creena burst out laughing and so did Oliver; and for a few moments they stood on the pavement just gazing into each other's eyes whilst the crowd from the cinema pushed their way past in the twilight.

'Bleedin' lovebirds!'

'Oh shut up, Henry. We were like that once.'

'If you stand there much longer, mate, you'll get pigeons roosting in yer 'at.'

Creena gave a little sigh of capitulation.

'It'll have to be just for half an hour. The thing is, I've got some lecture notes to write up . . .'

'You've passed your prelims,' Oliver pointed out. 'Couldn't you ease up on the studying a bit?'

'I suppose . . . but I'm not keen on finding my way back in the blackout, raids or no raids.' She hesitated. 'Half an hour?'

'Half an hour, and I'll see you back to the home myself. A boy scout's word is his honour.'

Arm in arm they walked down the street in the gathering gloom, laughing and chattering together like school-children. The respite in the bombing raids had released the girlish gaiety within Creena. And there was something about Oliver, something ebullient and irrepressible, which awakened new and intoxicating feelings in her. It was too early to know just how much she cared about him; certainly too early to know if she loved him. But she knew that she had to know more, had to take another step with him into this new adventure.

As they rounded the corner, Creena's eye was caught by two figures huddled in a doorway on the other side of the road. Wasn't that Jack? Jack Doyle? His face was half turned away, but she recognised the blue suit, the sharp features and the tall, spare frame. The man with him seemed familiar, too: shortish, pudgy, well dressed in a black overcoat and Homburg.

The memory came flashing back – that day in The Cut with Dillie, on their way to see Mo Doyle. That was the man Dillie had said was a bad lot, she was sure it was. But hadn't she also said that Jack Doyle would never have anything to do with Sid Clayden?

'Penny for 'em.'

Oliver's voice roused her from the brief reverie, and she swung round to smile at him.

'Sorry, Oliver. Thought I recognised someone then. Must have been mistaken.'

'Well, I can see I'm going to have to try a bit harder, aren't I?'

'Sorry?'

'To be fascinating and irresistible. I mean, I'm not having much luck, am I?'

They stopped outside the door to Oliver's apartment building, and his arm tightened about her waist.

'Do you find me boring, Creena?'

'Boring! No, no, of course not,' she gasped.

'I'm glad.' He lowered his face to hers and she felt his breath on her cheek. 'Because, Creena Quilliam, I think you're the most beautiful and exciting woman I've ever met.'

His lips touched hers only briefly but the feeling lingered far longer than the kiss. The heat, the moisture, the softness of his lips remained with her long after he had drawn away to take the keys from his pocket and led her into the hallway.

Her head was still reeling as Oliver unlocked the first

door on the right, reached inside and clicked on a light switch.

'A small thing, but mine own,' he announced, ushering her inside. 'I don't think I shall keep this place on much longer – not a great deal of point with my being away. Don't know when I'll be back again.'

Creena stood in the living room and surveyed the scene. He had good taste, though a bachelor's untidiness.

'Sorry about the clutter,' he said, removing a pile of books from the settee. 'It needs a woman's touch. Can I take your coat?'

'I can't stay long.'

'No, no, of course not. Just half an hour.'

'Well, all right then.' She surrendered her raincoat and he carried it over to the ornate Indian coat stand by the door.

Oliver went off to make the tea and Creena wandered round, trying to figure the man out from his possessions, the things he liked to have around him. There were books – loads and loads of them, everything from Greek poetry to astronomy; a pair of riding boots; Indian clubs; a portable gramophone with an assortment of classical records. And on the mantelpiece there was a large collection of framed photographs.

'Is this you?' she called out, and Oliver's head popped out of the kitchenette.

'Oh, that one! Yes, I was only eleven at the time – it was our prep school production of *Hamlet* – guess who got to play Ophelia!'

'And these here?' She picked up a group portrait in a decorative silver frame.

'Er ... let's see.' He brought the tray out of the kitchen and set it down on the low table in front of the sofa. 'Mum, Dad, Clive and Archie, and that's Auntie Belinda, when we all lived in Simla. That's a hill station in northern India.'

Creena worked her way along the whole row of photographs until she reached a small one at the back; a picture of a tall, elegant young woman with a long cigarette holder and a tiny fluffy dog tucked under her arm.

'That?' Oliver's brow furrowed for an instant, then cleared. 'Oh – that's my kid sister Lucinda. We don't see each other much now – what with the war. To be honest, we don't really get on.'

Seeing that Oliver didn't want to pursue this line of conversation, Creena accepted his invitation to sit with him on the sofa. It felt strange, sitting next to this man she knew so little about and yet to whom she felt irrevocably, irresistibly drawn.

His arm slipped behind her, pulling her a little closer. Creena could feel her heart pounding so fast and so loud in her chest that she was sure Oliver must be able to hear it.

'I've missed you, Creena.'

'I ... I've missed you too.'

The tea lay forgotten, stewing in its silver pot. Their lips met in a joining of such passion that nothing else seemed to exist. Creena had known no kisses, no embraces like these before; and she was almost afraid of her eagerness to respond in kind. A thrill of guilty, forbidden pleasure ran through her as Oliver's tongue tip pressed its way between her parted lips and explored the moist, willing interior of her mouth.

'Oh, Oliver!'

She drew back in sudden alarm, scared of her own passion, her own need for this sophisticated, enigmatic man.

'You mean so much to me, Creena. You truly do.' His fingers were entwined about hers, willing her to come back into his embrace, offer herself more completely to the need and desire he felt for her. His voice became quieter, a little quavery. 'You could stay.'

'Stay!'

'No, don't turn away, Creena. Don't be afraid. It's just . . . just that I don't want to lose you, I don't want you to go. I'll be posted abroad soon. I don't even know when we'll see each other again.'

The words cut into her heart like a knife. The fear of losing him, the fear of doing something wrong, the fear of not understanding her own needs and desires, the fear of somehow betraying the childish affection that she had once known with Frank . . . Feelings met and mingled, fought and struggled within her.

'Stay with me tonight, Creena.'

And suddenly her mind was made up. Gently she withdrew her fingers from his. He made no attempt to stop her, but his eyes were full of sadness.

'I can't, Oliver. It's too soon – it just wouldn't be right.'

'But Cree . . .'

'No, Oliver. It doesn't feel right.' She took her raincoat from the stand, put it on and felt for the torch in her pocket. 'Please, Oliver – you promised. See me home.'

* * *

'Sit straight, Jessie. Oh, Voirrey, do eat up your cabbage and stop complaining.'

Cousin Mona gave a sigh and went on spooning pureed carrot into little Duggie's ever-open mouth.

'I'm sorry, Ida,' she said. 'They're a little restless today. I expect it's the pig.'

'Oh, that pig.' Ida's eyes rolled heavenwards and, as if on cue, loud squeals rent the air. 'I'm surprised George doesn't move in with her and have done with it.'

'Can we go and see her now, Mum?' Voirrey's eyes were every bit as round and as blue as her mother's had been at six years old.

'Please?' echoed her eight-year-old sister.

'Well . . . I don't know,' replied Mona doubtfully. 'You'd better ask your Auntie Ida.'

Ida shrugged. She supposed it might be considered educational for Mona's children to see Maisie farrowing, and besides, they were country children, farm born and bred. Nature was unlikely to remain much of a secret to them for very long.

'Very well then,' she sighed, though she didn't approve of children leaving the table before they had finished their dinners. 'But don't get in your Uncle George's way.'

'We won't,' the two chorused in unison, and they wriggled off their chairs, racing into the kitchen and exploding into the great outdoors like corks out of a bottle.

'And put on your coats,' called Mona after them. 'It's cold out there.' But it was too late; they were gone.

More squeals announced the arrival of another piglet. Since George had acquired Maisie the Middle White sow, back in August, her progress had been the talk of Ballakeeill. What was more, she had become George's pride and joy. Maisie was the biggest, fattest, best-scrubbed, most spoilt and in all probability would become the most productive sow in the south of the island. And now the big day had arrived: the day when Maisie would prove her worth and George would be able to show off her newborn offspring with all the pride of a new father. More, in fact, pondered Ida resentfully. He'd never shown this much interest in the births of any of his children.

'So how are you getting along?' enquired Ida, pushing away her plate. Really, the sounds of Maisie's squealing and George's shouts of encouragement were enough to put anyone off their Sunday lunch.

'Pretty well,' replied Mona, wiping little Duggie's face with the corner of a napkin. 'What with the Italian internees I've got working for me now, the farm's ticking over nicely. Better than it ever was when Duggie was running it,' she added darkly.

Ida's brow furrowed. Whilst she didn't approve of Duggie Mylchreest and his thuggish ways, she wasn't sure that she approved of internees being allowed to wander about the island either, supervised or not.

'Do you trust them then, these ... these Italians?' Mona chuckled.

'Of course! And if you were to meet them, you'd soon see why.'

Ida recoiled visibly at the very thought.

'Two of them are fifty if they're a day,' continued Mona. 'Good, steady men with a farming background. They stayed on in England after the last war – they only got interned because they never bothered getting themselves naturalised. And then there's big strong Giacomo – he used to sell ice cream in Glasgow; and Antonio – he's a lovely boy, only eighteen and gentle as a lamb with the stock. He has a real gift with the animals.'

'I see,' said Ida, who didn't. She couldn't imagine how Mona, however hard pressed, could bring herself to practically abandon herself and her children to the tender mercies of four cut-throat Eyeties.

'I see you've got another broken window, then,' remarked Mona, speedily changing the subject. 'What happened – one of the schoolchildren kick a ball through it?' Unbeknown to her, she had hit on another raw nerve.

Ida's eyes closed in a brief moment of controlled fury.

'It's those Duggan children again,' she said. 'The little wretches. I wouldn't care, but they're hardly ever at school. They just run wild! That John Duggan's going to be the death of George.'

'Oh, I think George is more than a match for John Duggan,' Mona said reassuringly. She had never been in George's class at Ballakeeill School but she had known plenty who had; and the squeals coming from Maisie's farrowing were not so very different from the squeals George produced with the aid of a cane on a child's backside.

'I had a letter from Alexa the other day,' said Ida, getting up to clear away the half-eaten food from the plates. She didn't know why she bothered to cook proper meals any more, really she didn't. No one ever seemed to be home at the right times to eat them. No doubt Maisie would get the benefit of all these lovely leftover vegetables.

'How is she?' Mona looked up from baby Duggie with sudden interest. She knew Alexa Powell well – probably even better than Ida did. Alexa had been a great support to her that time she'd run away from the island and got herself a job in the Adelphi Hotel. 'How are things in Liverpool?'

'Bad. Half the street went in the last raid, and they have to boil all the water before they use it. It can't be good for her or the children.'

'We should help her,' said Mona.

'Help her? How?'

'Well, we could always invite her to come over here.'

'To the island? Oh, no, we couldn't. Anyway, she'd never come. And where would she stay if she did?'

'You've got plenty of room here, what with Robert and Creena away,' pointed out Mona. 'Surely you could squeeze Alexa and Albie in. And Kenny would be no trouble. Think of the little ones . . .'

Ida's jaw tensed for an instant. This wasn't something she had foreseen, and quite frankly it wasn't something she would welcome. She and Alexa might be related through George, but they hadn't always seen eye to eye and thoughts of having to share her beloved kitchen with another woman made Ida feel quite ill. On the other hand . . .

'Yes, you are right. We *should* help her,' she said. 'And I'm sure we'll find a way.'

'She's a woman on her own,' Mona pointed out. 'It's been difficult for her since her Albert died.'

'Speaking of which,' said Ida, 'you haven't told me how Duggie's faring.'

As if I cared, thought Mona. To hell with all his

contrition and his assurances that things would be different when he got home. As far as she was concerned he was gone and if she didn't see him for twenty years it would be twenty years too soon.

'Oh, he writes once in a while,' she replied. 'He seems all right – from what's left after the censor's been through his letters. Don't know where he is, though, but it must be somewhere hot.'

'What makes you say that?' asked Ida, suddenly curious.

'His last letter was full of sand.'

It might be early December, but you'd never know it, thought Frank as he hung over the rail of the ship and the sun beat down on the back of his bare brown neck.

The sea beneath him was blue; not the cool, greeny-blue of the sea off Maughold, or the bluey-grey of the cold, watery fingers that crept so stealthily up the shore at Grenaugh on sunny summer days. No, this blue had a hint of tropical indigo to it. It wasn't the sort of colour you ever saw in the sea off the island, and Frank Kinrade knew all the colours in the ever-changing patterns of the Irish Sea.

'Where do you suppose we are?' asked Bob 'Mac' McKenzie, joining him at the rail.

'Beats me,' replied Frank, squinting up at the sun. 'But it's getting pretty warm. We must be heading south.'

It was only mid-morning but already there was a warmth and strength in the sunlight, and the sky was a curious turquoise blue. Frank felt a very, very long way from home.

The old troopship slid on through the ocean. She was a long way from home too. Frank wondered if she knew where she was going any more than the quiet huddle of soldiers below decks – bored with the sun and sea now, and whiling away their time playing cards whilst they waited for a first glimpse of land.

Frank knew where he was going all right. He knew that his and Mac's paths would soon diverge, but these days it was best to keep quiet about what you knew.

'Bit different from the Isle of Man, at any rate,' observed Frank. 'I'd give anything for a plate of prithers an' herring.'

'Prithers?'

'Potatoes, you cook them with the herring. And a pint of Castletown ale to wash it all down.'

'Wish I was back in Scotland wi' my girl,' said Mac softly.

'You got a girl?'

'Used to have,' replied Frank. 'At least, I thought I did. But I lost her.' He looked down into the water. The blue swirling patterns of light and shade made him feel dizzy, and for a second he thought he saw Creena's face smiling up at him, her arms reaching out to him as they had done when they were children together.

In a flash he remembered that evening – was it five years ago, or six? – when he and Creena had sneaked off to the annual Bachelors' Ball over Braaid way. George Quilliam would have been wild with fury if he'd known about it, but Creena had arranged to stay the night at Cousin Mona's, and what the eye didn't see the heart couldn't grieve.

After the supper and the entertainment were over, Frankie and Creena had followed the giggling mass of local youth to the crossroads and watched as, underneath the moonlight, they formed the traditional Kissing Ring.

Frankie had wanted to kiss Creena, and *only* Creena. He remembered that feeling very distinctly. But he had been painfully shy in those days, and so had she; and in any case, back then he had been so sure that they would always be together, that one day she would love him the way that he loved her.

And now he couldn't be sure of anything – not even whether he'd be alive tomorrow.

Chapter 14

Creena sat in the buffet at King's Cross station. She didn't care about the lukewarm tea in the cracked cup, or the hard, dry crusts on the sardine sandwiches. She didn't care that it was a freezing March afternoon and the wind had blown her carefully brushed hair into ragged knots and tangles. These last two days had flown by; almost two whole days of glorious, unexpected leave. And best of all, Oliver had been there to spend them with her.

He sat opposite her, and she was all too aware of the big old mahogany clock ticking away the seconds on the wall behind him.

'I have to go soon,' he said. 'I don't want to, but...'

'I know.'

'They're expecting me at the military hospital in York tonight, and the trains are so damned unreliable – you just have to get on the first thing that's heading north and hope for the best.'

He sighed, and Creena knew why. There was still a barrier between them, and she felt a dull ache of regret for the pain that she was causing him.

'I wanted to,' she said quietly, her voice hushed as

though she felt everyone in the buffet must be watching and listening. 'I just couldn't.'

She cast her mind back to the previous evening, when they had gone out dancing and afterwards back to Oliver's hotel for supper. There was a raid on, and it would have been so much easier and pleasanter for her to have stayed the night in his bed, but no; she had insisted on joining other stranded guests on mattresses in the ballroom. She hoped Oliver understood, but was afraid that he might not.

'I just wish you trusted me,' replied Oliver, his handsome face clouded and serious.

'I do trust you,' protested Creena, but he took hold of her hand and she stopped speaking, hanging on his every word.

'If you trusted me, Cree, you'd know I wouldn't ever hurt you, or do anything you didn't want me to.' His grip was warm, strong, reassuring, sensual as his kisses.

That's just the problem, thought Creena to herself. I *do* want to; but I'm afraid too, and perhaps a little guilty.

'It's not that boy of yours from back home, is it?' asked Oliver, his grey-green eyes searching her face for some sign or explanation.

'No, no.'

Creena shook her head. No, it wasn't Frank. Her feelings for Frank belonged to a simple, childhood world without pain or passion. Frank seemed to understand that, too. He didn't sign his letters 'Love, Frankie' any more, just 'All the best'.

'You're sure?'

She turned her face to his, a sudden smile lighting up

her prettiness, the wild waves of her flame-red hair catching the light from the lamp above the table.

'Couldn't be surer, Oliver. You're the one for me. I just need more time.'

'Time.' Oliver's eyes were downcast and sad. 'If only we could see into the future.'

'It would be different if we were... you know... properly engaged.'

Oliver set down his cup and pushed back his sandy-coloured hair with his free hand.

'Oh, Cree – marriage, I don't know . . .'

'Don't you care about me enough to marry me?' Creena felt a stab of wounded pride.

'Oh, sweetheart, you mustn't think that! Of course I care about you. I care about you more than anything else in the world. I desperately want to marry you.'

'Then why . . . ?'

'Look, Cree, cards on the table. We're in the middle of this damn awful war and nobody knows when it's going to end. I'm going off to the hospital today, but tomorrow they could send me God knows where. I might not come back.'

Creena's fingers tightened about his hand, as though she were trying physically to hold him back, prevent him from leaving her.

'Of course you'll come back.'

'But I might not. If we got married now, and Matron found out, you'd be sacked on the spot from your job and you're not even halfway through your training. The next thing, I might get myself killed. What would you have left then, eh?'

'I'd have what we'd shared together,' replied Creena quietly. 'I'd have your ring on my finger.'

'Creena – don't, please don't. If you could only be patient ... wait until this damned war's over.'

'Then *we* have to wait,' repeated Creena, looking into his eyes and summoning up all the courage of her crumbling convictions. 'Please try to understand.'

She bought a platform ticket and walked to the train with him, and he leant out of the carriage window to kiss her goodbye in the swirling clouds of steam.

'I don't know when I'll see you again,' he said sadly. 'But I'll write.'

'Come back to me ...'

The train started to move and Oliver's hands were pulled from hers, his face receding into the distance as the train glided out of the station.

'Come back to me.'

It wasn't until it was too late that Creena realised how deeply, how desperately she loved him; and how, if he had begged her just one more time, she might well have given him everything he had asked for.

It was April 1941, and by some miracle London had learned to acclimatise itself to life in the Blitz. Every day, at four o'clock prompt, the Underground stations were opened for use as shelters, and some Londoners had even reserved themselves a regular bunk or draught-free piece of platform. The following day, as soon as the all clear sounded, they emerged into the gloom of the early morning to go home for a couple of hours' kip, a quick cuppa and to get on with their daily lives.

In the casualty department at the Royal Lambeth Hospital, life was also settling into some sort of routine, with as many casualties as possible being patched up and moved out to the EMS hospital during the daytime lulls between raids. The department itself had sustained some damage in a recent raid, and part of the large hall had had to be boarded off, but – like the citizens of Lambeth Marsh – the Royal Lambeth was getting on with life.

From inside Cubicle 3, Creena could hear Staff Nurse Harrington barking out orders.

'Porter? Oh, there you are – take this patient to X-ray.'

'Right you are, Staff.'

'Nurse Grey.'

'Yes, Staff?'

'Sutures – Cubicle Four.'

'Yes, Staff.'

'Nurse Quilliam.'

Creena apologised to the patient and emerged from behind the screen.

'Staff?'

'When you have finished there, you may go for your break – and try to find something for that VAD to do, all she does is clutter up the place.'

'Right away, Staff.'

Creena returned to the cubicle to prepare her patient for examination.

'That's right, Mr B. Is that more comfortable? Now if you could just wait here a moment, Doctor will be with you shortly.'

Creena replaced the fabric screen which served as a

curtain and walked back to the desk. As she passed Cubicle 2, young Dr Harris emerged, rather blue about the chin after eighteen solid hours on duty.

'Varicose ulcer and a bump on the head for you in Three, Doctor.'

'Varicose ulcer? Shouldn't he be in Outpatients?'

'Poor chap took a bit of a knock in last night's raid,' explained Creena. 'It looks as if the leg's been bleeding quite badly – and the ambulance people said he was confused.'

'Fair enough,' sighed Dr Harris. 'All in a day's work. Couldn't get someone to brew up, could you? If I don't get a strong cuppa sharpish I think I shall fall asleep over this chap's leg.'

'I'll see what I can do,' promised Creena with a smile, as she spotted VAD Carol Coates, dejectedly mopping up a sticky puddle of vomit.

'Fancy a change when you've done that, Coates?'

Coates straightened up painfully.

'Ra-ther! My back feels like an elephant's been sitting on it.'

'Dr Harris is bushed and Mr Andrews has been in theatre all night. They'll love you for ever if you brew up.'

'Right you are, Nurse Quilliam.'

It was awkward managing without first-years, mused Creena as she headed towards the dining room for a much-needed break. It meant second-years having to do the work of the junior pros as well as their own, and in some cases third-years were having to take on the responsibilities of staff nurses. And to think that the Royal College of Nursing had complained at nurses being offered a small pay rise, in case it attracted 'the wrong sort of girl'! Hester Frankenberg had commented that in any case the only sort of girl who would want to be a nurse was a pretty peculiar one – and for once Creena and Dillie had had to admit she had a point.

Passing the dispensary, Creena thought she caught sight of a familiar figure emerging from one of the empty offices.

'Jack? Is that you?'

The tall figure stopped in its tracks, wheeled round slowly and finally faced her. His smile seemed half genuine, half uneasy.

'Hello, Creena.'

'What on earth were you doing down there?'

'I, er . . .'

'Were you looking for Dillie?'

'Yeah. Yeah, that's right, I was lookin' for Dillie, only I got lost. You ain't seen her, I don't suppose?'

'I think she's off till two today. I'll be seeing her later – shall I give her a message?'

'Well, if you could just say I called for a chat. Only Mo likes to keep in touch and she ain't heard from our Dillie in a while, see.'

Creena nodded. There was an easy, roguish charm about Jack Doyle, something in those periwinkle-blue eyes that reminded her of her Uncle John. But Jack looked worried today, uncomfortable and maybe just a touch guilty. She didn't entirely believe his story about looking for Dillie, either.

'There's nothing wrong, is there? Mo's all right?'

'Mo's fine. Bit shook up, o' course, what with number

three copping it the other night. It's our Micky an' Kitty what's drivin' everyone round the bend.'

'But I thought they'd been evacuated.'

'Oh, they 'ave!' Jack chuckled. 'An' I reckon we ain't never goin' to hear the last of it, neither. Kitty's took to it like a good un, but our Micky ain't one for the country. Never stops moanin' – he says Wiltshire stinks of pigs an' there ain't nothin' to do.'

Creena smiled.

'I expect he'll get used to it. Like I got used to London.'

'Yeah.' Jack suddenly took an interest in the mirror-shiny toecaps of his two-tone shoes. 'Er, I was wondering . . .'

'Yes?'

He looked up and treated Creena to the Jack Doyle smile.

'Fancy a trip up West tonight? Only a customer of mine gave me a couple of tickets to a show an' I just thought . . .'

'Thank you.' Creena was smiling too, Jack's grin was infectious. 'But I'm on duty this evening. It's a pity.'

Jack nodded, concealing his disappointment.

'Ah well, never mind, eh? Some other time, maybe?'

'Some other time, maybe. Give my best to Mo.'

'I'll do that.'

He watched her bustle off down the corridor and his smile couldn't help coming back. He was no fonder of the country than Micky was; but if all country girls were like Creena Quilliam he might just be converted yet.

Early May sunshine flooded the hillsides above Ballakeeill,

lighting up the great yellow drifts of gorse and awakening their warm, sweet, biscuity smell.

Lessons were over for the day, and George Quilliam was sitting in the kitchen, writing up the school log. Warm, dry weather had brought the usual spate of spring absenteeism but that wasn't the reason for the tensions within the Quilliam household.

Three days ago, Alexa Powell had arrived with her two children on the night boat from Fleetwood – and not so much as a telephone call in advance to let them know what time they'd be arriving.

Ida had known it was a big mistake right from the moment that Cousin Mona had suggested it, but she hadn't been able to think of any good reason *not* to extend the hand of hospitality. Besides, Alexa would be sure to turn down the invitation; she and Ida had never been the closest of friends and on one memorable occasion Alexa had even been rude enough to call George a 'stuffed shirt'.

But the unthinkable had happened. A stick of bombs had dropped right on 42 Crocus Lane, with the result that Alexa, Albie and Kenny had been made homeless. With nowhere else to go, it stood to reason that they would make straight for the Isle of Man – and Ida Quilliam's jealously guarded home.

Sleeves rolled up, arms floury to the elbow, Ida Quilliam was making angry pastry on the old scrubbed-oak table. She knew it wouldn't turn out well; it never did when she was in a mood. It was the same with bread dough; it seemed to sense that she was angry and refuse to rise. It was all Alexa's fault – and Hitler's.

'Can I help, Ida?' asked Alexa, walking into the kitchen. She looked tarty in that dress, thought Ida, even if it was buttoned up to the neck. War economies or no war economies, that skirt was far too short.

'Not really,' replied Ida, turning her attentions to the pastry, which – true to form – was sticking to the rolling pin.

'Bit wet, that pastry,' observed Alexa.

Ida gritted her teeth. It wouldn't do to have a row, not here and not now. After all, she had no idea how long they were going to be forced to live under the same roof. She didn't mind so much letting Kenny have Creena's room – it wasn't as if she'd even come home for her twenty-first birthday – but putting Albie in Robert's had been a real wrench. Robert might be home any time on leave. She wanted his room to be just the way he liked it.

'It'll be all right,' she said.

'Shall I lay the table in the dining room?'

'No, no need. We'll eat in here.' Ida hated the thought of Alexa's working-class offspring being let loose on her nice damask tablecloths and napkins. And she'd probably have to boil the good china afterwards too – what was left of it – in case of germs. 'There's more room.'

'Why don't you come out for a spot of fresh air?' suggested George, sensing undercurrents of tension. 'We could see what the children are getting up to,' he added. George Quilliam's educational philosophy centred on the maxim that children should never be left on their own – especially if they were being quiet. Quiet children were invariably up to no good.

'If you like.'

Alexa picked up her jacket from the back of the chair and slung it over her shoulders. She had nothing against walks in the country – she'd spent her early childhood in Douglas and she and Albert had shared a mutual love of the island – but ever since she and the kids had arrived she'd been sent out on endless walks or errands, particularly by Ida. It was as though Ida couldn't stand having her in the house, and Alexa was starting to feel unwelcome. That was something she and Ida would have to have a little chat about before too long.

She followed George out past the classroom where young Kenny had just experienced his first two days of Manx schooling. He hadn't been too impressed – but then Kenny had never been keen on school, and like most city kids he was bored to death without German planes to spot and bomb sites to play on. Well, he'd have to get used to it – they all would.

Albie was outside with Amy and Tom, all three of them leaning over the wall of Maisie's sty. George and Alexa joined them.

'How many piglets did she have, Uncle George?' asked Albie.

'Six.'

'Is that a lot?'

'It's not bad for a first farrowing,' replied Tom knowledgeably. He was turning into quite an authority, noted George approvingly. And there was no one in the whole of Ballakeeill more devoted to that pig's needs than Amy Quilliam. The three of them made a very serviceable team.

'What happened to them?' asked Albie. He was a very innocent young lad, thought Alexa, and soft with it. Where he came from, pork came from the butcher's, not from pigs. And there'd been precious little of it anyway. They'd never been well off.

'When they were fat enough the butcher came and slaughtered them,' explained Tom cheerfully. 'We kept a carcass and shared it out with our neighbours. It made smashing sausages.'

'Oh.' Albie looked a touch green as he contemplated the huge, friendly sow who was looking back at him with disturbingly intelligent pink eyes. Country ways were going to take some getting used to.

'Where's our Kenny?' asked Alexa. It had suddenly registered that her younger son was nowhere to be seen.

'Dunno,' replied Albie. 'One minute he was feeding the chickens, the next minute he'd gone.'

Alexa was just thinking that there wasn't much mischief a boy could get up to in Ballakeeill when a loud shout erupted from somewhere behind the schoolhouse, followed by the sound of boyish squeals and running feet.

'What the . . . ?'

A few moments later, young Kenny came haring across the rough turf behind the schoolhouse, his face a white mask of absolute terror.

'Kenny!' exclaimed Alexa. 'What on earth's happened?'

'It's that Mr Duggan,' replied Kenny, half panting, half sobbing.

'What have you been up to?' demanded George sternly, instinctively assuming the worst.

'Just climbing over 'is wall, like. Me ball went over so I went in after it.'

'I told you to stay away from Mr Duggan's orchard,' George reprimanded him.

'But Uncle George, I was only gettin' me ball. An' when 'e saw me, he said he'd take a pot shot at me if he saw me again, didn't 'e?'

'Did he now!' said Alexa grimly. 'Well, we'll see about that!'

'I'm really sorry it's taken so long to get to you, Flight-Lieutenant. Mr Beresford's just finishing up after last night's road accident. Honestly, I sometimes think the blackout's causing more injuries than Jerry is!'

Creena checked the airman's temporary dressing, and was relieved to see that the bleeding seemed to have stopped. It was a nasty compound fracture of the femur, though; the sooner it was attended to, the better.

'That's OK, Nurse,' laughed the airman, shifting slightly on the trolley to make himself a little more comfortable. 'Reckon it's my own fault anyhow, getting my parachute stuck in that tree. Never did have much sense of direction.'

'Is that a Canadian accent?' enquired Creena, checking the airman's obs.

'Nope. Yankee through and through. Name's Cal Handley.'

'An American! But your lot aren't even in the war!'

'Not yet – but soon maybe, if Roosevelt gets his way. I'm in the American Eagle Squadron. We got together to help out the little guys back in the Spanish Civil War, and when this lot broke out we reckoned maybe you Limeys could do with a hand too.' He laughed again, then winced. 'Reckon I'm more of a liability than a help now, though. Mind if I smoke?'

'Sorry, Mr Handley, not in here. You'd probably blow all our oxygen cylinders sky-high, and then where would the poor old Royal Lambeth be? I can't even get you a cup of tea, I'm afraid – not whilst you're waiting for surgery.'

'Tea!' Cal wrinkled his nose in disgust. 'Give me a cup of coffee any day, coupla pancakes, maple syrup . . .'

''Fraid you'll have to wait a while for that.' Creena smiled. 'The best you can look forward to here is stewed tea and salt cod – now, isn't that worth getting better for?'

'I thought hospitals were supposed to make folks better, not kill them,' commented Cal.

Glancing across the casualty hall, Creena noticed a small girl sitting alone on one of the benches, her legs, too short to reach the ground, swinging idly to and fro.

Lone children weren't a rare sight at the hospital. The people of Lambeth Marsh had always regarded the Royal Lambeth as their local surgery, and quite small children often brought themselves in to have their cut fingers and grazed knees treated for free. Since the Blitz had speeded up evacuation, there had been fewer children; but still they came in in dribs and drabs, with or without their parents.

But this little girl didn't look quite right, somehow. A sixth sense, developed over the long months of her training, sent a warning message to Creena's brain. She turned to Cal with an apologetic smile.

'There's something I need to do. Will you be all right here?'

'Right as rain, Nurse.'

'If you need anything – a bottle or whatever – just you shout and a nurse will be with you. OK?'

'OK. Be seein' you around, Nurse.'

Creena crossed the casualty hall swiftly, her eyes never leaving the child for a moment. She was a pretty little girl but somewhat gaunt, thought Creena, with dark circles under eyes that should have been a merry, carefree brown but which were deep-set in her pale face. How old would she be – seven, eight? It was so difficult to tell with these Lambeth children. Some of them were so undernourished that they looked four or five years younger than they really were.

'Hello,' said Creena quietly, getting down on her haunches so that she and the little girl were virtually eye to eye. 'My name's Creena. What's yours?'

The child avoided her gaze, and when Creena took hold of her small, cold hands, she flinched slightly. At the touch, the brown eyes flicked upwards, as if in surprise or alarm.

'It's all right, sweetheart,' said Creena with the utmost gentleness. 'Nobody's going to hurt you. Did you come here on your own?'

The child looked at her blankly for a few moments longer, then opened her mouth like a baby bird and uttered a single word:

'Mam.'

'Your mother? You want your mother? Is she here?'

The child clammed up again. Creena was at a loss to

know what to do. It wasn't as if the child seemed injured, or very deeply in shock – simply withdrawn, defensive. Perhaps if she made enquiries of the police, or asked Sister Edgerton ... But Sister was very strict in her application of the rules; people who were not sick or injured had no place in Cas. And yet, Creena was convinced that something was wrong – otherwise, why would the child have come here?

'Oh Grace! Not here *again*. I've been looking all over Lambeth for you.'

Creena looked up to see a tall and very respectable-looking woman of middle years striding towards her, cutting a swathe through the assembled throng, the feather on her hat bobbing up and down furiously as she walked.

Creena got to her feet.

'You're this little girl's mother?'

'Unfortunately not, Nurse.' The woman turned to Grace with a sad but exasperated smile. 'Grace's mother was killed in the bombing last October, but Grace just doesn't seem to be able to come to terms with it. She's run away from more foster homes than you and I have had hot dinners, and she always ends up coming back here.'

'Why?'

'Because this is the last place she saw her mummy.' The woman held out her hand to Creena. 'Millie Duval's the name. I run the shelter group over at Long Wall Yard. Grace has been living with me in Kennington for the last few weeks – no one else would take her in, poor child, and she won't stand to be evacuated with the others.'

'I'm very pleased to meet you,' said Creena, shaking Millie's hand. 'And you, Grace.' The little girl's eyes followed her every movement, but she made no sound. It was obvious that she no longer trusted anyone but Millie Duval.

Poor kid, thought Creena as Millie took Grace by the hand and led her back to Long Wall Yard. And she thanked her lucky stars for her own good fortune.

Chapter 15

Up to their arms in disinfectant, Creena and Eleanor Howells were busy cleaning out one of the Royal Lambeth's mobile operating theatres, ready for its next outing. Everyone at the hospital hoped that there wouldn't have to be one.

'You know, I think Jerry's actually given up this time,' Howells commented cheerfully, scrubbing hard in a dizzying haze of carbolic. 'We haven't had a proper night raid since the tenth of May – that's over a month ago.'

'Don't tempt fate,' said Creena. 'As I recall, that's what we all thought last November, and then back he came to give us that special Christmas present.'

'That's what I like about you, Quilliam – you're such an optimist.'

'It's being so cheerful that keeps me going,' laughed Creena.

'Unlike Staff Nurse Waverley,' muttered Howells.

'Waverley?' Creena looked up. It had been Doreen Waverley who'd helped her settle in at the Royal on her very first day.

'Such a temper she's got – and it's getting worse.

Jamieson says she had a stand-up row with the Gynae registrar last week.'

'I wonder why,' mused Creena. She'd been quite looking forward to working with Waverley again, but now she wasn't so sure.

It was getting warm, Creena thought as she helped Eleanor clean and prepare the operating theatre. Too warm to be scrubbing walls and floors. She could feel an unpleasant moistness around her middle, where her un-yielding uniform belt clung too tightly, making her perspire. It would be summer soon. If she closed her eyes, she could smell not carbolic but the sun on the gorse above Ballakeeill.

With thoughts of summer came hope. London was slowly being tidied up, rubble shifted, being set to rights as much as any city could be when it was still under imminent threat of destruction. Some bombed-out busines-ses had moved three or four times, but still they kept on going. If anything, the severity of the bombing had stiffened London's resolve to resist. The thought of defeat now seemed an unthinkable obscenity which no one would dare speak.

'Do you know what I fancy?' sighed Eleanor.

Creena stifled a laugh.

'Yes, I do!'

'What's that supposed to mean?' demanded Howells indignantly.

'It means I saw you mooning over that American airman with the fractured femur,' retorted Creena.

'Yes, wasn't he *gorgeous*?' agreed Howells dreamily. 'Such a pity they sent him to a military hospital, I could have soothed his fevered brow ... But that wasn't what I meant.'

'What then?'

'I thought we might have a trip up West – a bit of shopping, tea and buns at a posh tea shop.'

Creena laughed.

'You and your buns!' She thought for a moment. 'I'd love a new dress, but I just don't have the coupons ...'

'Then treat yourself to a new hat. That'll make you look as if you've got a new outfit, even if you haven't.'

'I suppose it might.'

'Look, Clarke-Herbert's coming back from the EMS soon,' pointed out Eleanor. 'She's bound to be dying to see her old haunts again ...'

'What's left of them.'

'... and we ought to do something to welcome her back. What do you say you, me and Bayliss take her out for the day?'

'What about Frankenberg?'

'What about her?'

'We really ought to ...'

'Oh all right, we'll let Frankenberg come too – seeing as Marian will be there to calm the savage beast.'

'Talking of savage beasts,' observed Creena, 'Dillie was talking about her "friend Arnold in the ARP" the other day.'

Howells pulled a face.

'Arnold's hardly a savage beast! More like a big floppy Labrador.'

'He's in charge of the big cats now,' continued Creena, vaguely aware of a lank strand of hair slipping slowly down over her nose. She pushed it out of the way with the back of her arm. 'You know, all the zoo-keepers have been armed, in case any of the dangerous animals escape. Can you imagine that – Arnold with a gun?'

'It's a terrifying thought,' replied Howells, trying to picture steady, soft-hearted, dependable Arnold Watkins holding the forces of evil at bay. 'I don't know why Bayliss is so smitten; he's almost old enough to be her father.'

'Nice, though,' Creena pointed out.

'Hmm, yes, he's *nice* enough – he's just not my type. I prefer Clark Gable myself . . .' She grinned. 'Or your Oliver.'

'Shh!' hissed Creena. 'Someone might hear.'

'How *is* love's young dream?'

Creena went back to scrubbing the floor of the operating theatre.

'Your guess is as good as mine. I've had one or two letters but he's not allowed to say where he is. I just hope he's all right.'

'He will be,' said Howells with energy. 'He's so irresistible, no one could bear to harm a hair on his pretty head!'

Creena smiled, but her smile concealed a persistent anxiety. Oliver might be a non-combatant, but even non-combatants could get themselves killed. If only this war would finish so that he could come home, and they could get married and have done with all this cloak-and-dagger nonsense.

But mooning about and fretting wouldn't serve any useful purpose. In any case, there were plenty of other things to worry about – like passing her exams and getting through the rest of her training. Pull yourself together,

Quilliam, she told herself, and went back to scrubbing the floor.

Jack Doyle stood in front of the mirror and admired himself in his new suit. He looked good. Pity it wasn't a full-length mirror, so he could get the effect of the hat and shoes too; but it was definitely a winner. Financially, at least, things were looking up.

On Jack's bed lay Smudge the cat, one eye half open just in case. Since he'd been bombed out of a house in Theed Street, Smudge's world-view had taken a bit of reshaping, but now that he'd been taken in by the Doyles he'd fallen on his feet. At Mo's house, the regular supply of fish-heads and table scraps was quite often supplemented by the odd titbit of butcher's meat – when Jack was in a good mood or Mo thought no one was looking.

The cat stretched its black and white body – noticeably sleeker after two weeks at Mo's – and Jack tickled it under the chin.

'You just keep yer fleas to yerself, you 'ear? Or you'll be straight back on that bomb site.'

Jack went down the stairs two at a time. You had to be careful around the middle two or three, because that land mine at number 3 had left some of the treads a bit unsteady. He took a long stride over them and made a mental note to get someone round to sort them out. Couldn't have Mo risking her health on a dodgy staircase – nor Old Bert for that matter, though the thought was a seductive one.

In the back kitchen, Mo was listening to Edna Tilley rambling on whilst Old Bert smoked a pipe of foul-smelling tobacco by the open back door.

'So Ena says to 'im, Mo, she says, "You ain't got no right, stoppin' folks goin' into their own 'omes." An' 'e says, the ARP, 'e says quick as a flash, "It ain't yer 'ome no more, Ena, it's a bleedin' 'ole in the ground." And it were an' all, Mo – flat as a pancake number three were, and hardly nothin' left of five or seven neither.'

Mo peeled the vegetables as thinly as she could, reserving the carrot and potato peelings, which would later be dried out in the oven for rabbit feed.

'She always was trouble, that Ena Marshall, and I daresay she always will be.'

Mo felt some sympathy for Ena, bombed out of her house and deprived of most of her possessions, but at least Ena had a daughter and son-in-law to go to – and it was hard to feel very much for a woman who'd done her best to make your life a misery for years. Spiteful, Ena was; spiteful and malicious.

'ARP should've let her through,' observed Old Bert from his ringside seat. 'If she wanted to get 'erself killed for a few bits and pieces, 'e should've let her.'

'What – an' make more work for 'isself?' retorted Edna Tilley. 'The size she is, it'd take a week to dig 'er out!'

Jack sauntered into the kitchen, hands in pockets, three crisp white fivers safely secreted in his wallet.

'Afternoon, Ma, Edna,' he said, helping himself to a piece of raw carrot from the table. 'Bert,' he added with less enthusiasm, darting a glance at the old soldier in the doorway to the back yard.

'You off out again?' demanded Mo.

'Just for 'alf an hour, Ma.'

'You'll be back for your supper, mind.'

'Yeah, yeah, course. Well, probably.' It was an early July day, nice and fine, good for business. Jack had it in mind to check up on the stall, then maybe visit a few of his regular customers to offer them first pick of the new merchandise. Clothing coupons were as good as gold bullion these days, and Jack had tapped into a regular and reliable supply.

'Mind you are. I'm not cookin' this pie for me own amusement, you know.'

'Yeah, I know, Ma. Get you a bit of mutton tomorrow, if you like. I know a man who knows a man . . .'

Old Bert gave a snort of derision which turned into a cough as he sucked in a mouthful of ropy tobacco smoke.

'It's about time that son of yours got 'isself a proper job,' he commented to Mo. 'Or joined up. You ought to be ashamed of yourself, Jack Doyle – profiteering while better men are dyin' for their country. It's a good job young Micky an' Kitty ain't 'ere to see you.'

'Give it a rest, Bert,' snapped Jack. 'I didn't 'ear you complainin' when I got you that baccy.'

'And bloody awful muck it is too,' retorted Bert.

'Got any more of them onions, Jack?' enquired Edna Tilley.

'And you ought to be ashamed of yourself an' all, woman,' cut in Old Bert.

There was a knock at the front door.

'I'll go,' said Jack, grateful to get away from Bishop Street's very own Siegfried Line. It was probably one of Mo's cronies on the scrounge. She might not be well off, but Mo was thrifty and always had a little something left over that she could lend to her neighbours. Pity they hardly ever paid back the favour, thought Jack. Mo was too generous by half, that was her trouble.

He reached the front door and gave the handle a good wrench. Ever since the bomb down the road, none of the doors seemed to fit properly in their frames any more.

A short man with a thick neck and bushy eyebrows was standing on the doorstep.

''Ello, Jack.'

'Jim.'

Jack regarded the new arrival with distinct unease. Jim Brandon was rarely the bringer of good tidings.

''Ope you ain't got nothin' special planned for tonight, Jack.'

'Why?'

'Because our mutual friend Mr Clayden 'as another little job lined up for you.'

Alexa Powell sat at the table in Ida Quilliam's kitchen and breathed the sweet air of freedom.

At last – at long, long last – Ida had condescended to go back to her WVS canteen, leaving Alexa and the children with George. As it was the school summer holidays and George was busying himself with Civil Defence exercises, that effectively meant that Alexa, Albie and Kenny had Ballakeeill schoolhouse to themselves for the morning. It was quite a diverting prospect. Later on Mona Mylchreest was coming round and they would have a good gossip, unimpeded by Ida's impeccable manners and best china tea service.

'Dear Creena,' wrote Alexa. She paused, chewing the end of her pen. What should she say? She wouldn't mention the general daggers-drawn atmosphere at the schoolhouse; didn't the poor girl have enough to upset her already, what with her mum and dad still acting so cold towards her, and the terrible things that had been happening in London? Creena was a brave girl, and Alexa at least was proud of her.

She continued slowly, out of the habit of writing long and newsy letters.

'I hope you are well.' She crossed it out, and started again.

Dear Creena,

We all hope you are well.

The weather is good on the island – not windy and wet like it usually is! – and me and the boys are settling in just fine. Kenny is glad it's the school holidays. He's picking up the local lingo and says that school is 'middling dreary'. Your dad doesn't approve. Albie is a bicycle messenger for the Civil Defence. He's a big lad now, you'd hardly recognise him. But he's still clumsy, mind!

Billy Callister says . . .

She didn't finish the sentence, because just as she was about to begin the next word, she heard the sounds of a heated argument. It seemed to be coming from somewhere behind the schoolhouse – somewhere near John Duggan's orchard.

Alexa threw down her pen in exasperation. Not *more* trouble with the Duggans. She could hear Albie's voice, a great gruff rumble in his wiry, boyish body, and a higher counterpoint that might have been Kenny's. The third voice was all too recognisable. There was no mistaking John Duggan's uncouth shouting – though she had met many others like him in Liverpool. Bullies, the lot of them. And bullies needed teaching a lesson.

Right, she thought to herself as she stalked out of the schoolhouse, that's the last time you tell me to keep my nose out of your business, John Duggan. If you don't leave my children alone, I'll poke *your* nose so far into your business that you'll never see it again . . .

Dillie found Creena in the sluice, rinsing soiled sheets before putting them into the 'wet linen' bag for collection. It was an unpleasant job, usually done by the most junior of junior pros, but with all the first-years away in the depths of Surrey, even the loftiest of second-years – like Hester Frankenberg – were having to do their fair share of floor-mopping and bedpan-scrubbing. On these hot summer days, picking through the laundry was an even smellier job than usual.

'Ready for the off, Quilliam? I know you can't bear to leave this place, but Sister says we can go for our lunch now.'

'I'd better just finish doing these sheets.'

'Gloria Bradley again?'

Creena nodded.

'They're trying everything to get her temperature down, but I don't think it's working.'

Gloria – a familiar face from Female Surgical all those months ago – had been admitted to the Gynae ward the previous evening, with infection raging through her body.

Rumour had it that she was the victim of a botched abortion. The sight of screens going up around her bed had confirmed that she was very seriously ill indeed.

'They're not moving her then?'

Creena rinsed the last of the linen and straightened up, her hands red raw from day after day spent immersed in cold water and disinfectant. No amount of lanolin cream, it seemed, could return them to their former silky softness.

'Shouldn't think so – she's too ill. Sister's watching her like a hawk.'

'I wish Staff Nurse Waverley would stop watching *me* like a hawk,' observed Dillie, rinsing out a bedpan.

'She's not had another go at you?'

'Oh, I don't think it's anything personal. These days she's being an absolute cow to everybody – and she used to be so nice, too. Can't imagine what the matter is. Frankenberg's sure she smelt drink on her breath . . .'

'No!' Creena washed and dried her hands, tucked a wisp of hair under her cap and stared at Dillie in incredulity. 'Surely that's just Hester being a bitch.'

'Mind you, I could hardly blame Waverley if she did turn to drink,' remarked Dillie as they collected their cloaks and walked together down the stairs from the ward. 'I felt like a double gin myself when I heard about Arnold.'

'What's he been up to now?'

'Nearly getting himself killed, that's what! Remember I told you the zoo-keepers had guns, just in case?'

Creena nodded.

'In case of air raids?'

'Or invasion, or whatever. Well, I thought the worst of it was over, didn't I? Then last night a UXB went off near the large animal compound. Only took the corner off the tiger house!'

'Was anyone hurt?'

'No, thank God. But no thanks to Arnold. He loves that tigress so much, she's like a kid to him. Couldn't bring himself to shoot her, could he? Just stood there like an idiot with his pistol in his hand and the tiger licking her lips and thinking her ship had come in.'

'So what happened?'

'The head keeper turned up in the nick of time and shot her in the leg. And you know, Arnold's more upset about that tiger than he is about nearly being eaten!'

They walked down the stairs and out into the courtyard, crossing it and heading towards the dining room. It was a hot day but there was a slight breeze, and the fresh air was a welcome relief after the stuffiness of the wards.

On Sundays the food was usually marginally better than on other days of the week, and as they walked past the hospital kitchens Creena savoured the aroma of pot-roasted brisket. It could only be an improvement on the previous day's offerings – marrow surprise and beetroot pudding.

'Hello there, Harry,' called out Dillie as they passed the ward orderly, hanging around just inside the kitchen doors with his hands in his pockets. Unusually, he hardly acknowledged them, giving them barely a grunt instead of his usual cheery grin. Dillie looked at Creena with raised eyebrows. 'What's the matter with him?'

'Probably come to complain about the food!'

Eleanor Howells caught up with them just outside the dining room.

'I'm starving, aren't you? Hope there's seconds.' Perpetually hungry, Howells lived in eternal hope of second helpings. 'Oh, Quilliam, this arrived for you.' She hiked up her apron and rummaged in her dress pocket for a crumpled envelope. 'It came by hand so I said I'd bring it over.'

'Thanks, Howells.' Creena took the envelope and looked at the front. It read: 'Student Nurse C. Quilliam (Yr 2).' She didn't need to open it to know that it was from Oliver.

'Oh, Oliver...'

'What, darling?'

'You shouldn't have, not really.'

'Shouldn't have what?' He stroked her hair with gentle fingertips.

'Sent me that note. Someone might have opened it. And as for inviting me to supper in your hotel bedroom... Whatever would Matron say?'

'Aren't you pleased to see me?'

'You *know* I am. I've missed you so much. It's been so long, and I didn't even know where you were.'

'I've missed you too, Creena. More than I can say.' He took her in his arms and devoured her tenderly with his kisses; his lips brushing her cheeks, her closed eyelids, her waiting mouth. 'I'm sorry. I couldn't tell you where I was or what I was doing. I was working in a field hospital in North Africa, and then I copped a bullet in the shoulder and got wheeled off to some bloody awful fly-infested clinic in Cairo.'

'A bullet! You never told me you were wounded...'

'I didn't want to worry you. You've had enough on your

plate with the Blitz, from what I hear. And besides, it really wasn't much of an injury. I'm better now.'

'Oh, but Oliver . . .'

'Anyhow, soon as I got home leave, I headed straight for the hospital. I thought if I handed the note to that Howells girl, she'd be bound to make sure you got it. And she did. And now you're here!'

They embraced, and the happiness bubbled and fizzed inside Creena like a waterfall. To think . . . to think she had let him go, and he had been wounded, and she might never have seen him again. And now, miraculously, he was back and they were together once more, the way they were meant to be. How could she bear to let him out of her arms a second time?

'I nearly lost you,' she whispered, a cold thrill of realisation chilling her, despite her exhilaration. 'I might never have seen you again.'

'I'm fine,' Oliver reassured her. 'And I'm so much happier for seeing you again. You do understand now . . .?'

Her green eyes looked up beseechingly into his.

'Understand?'

'That I love you, Creena. That I love you and I want you; and that the wanting is *because* I love you, because you mean the whole world to me?'

'Yes. Yes, I understand now.'

His strong and gentle arms drew her down so that she was sitting on the bed beside him. The last time he had told her that he wanted her, it had felt wrong, she hadn't been ready, she'd been afraid. Now things had changed. She was beginning to trust her instincts, to understand that all her doubts and fears were as nothing compared with the wanting inside her. And she so wanted him, wanted him more than anything in her life before.

'Trust me, Creena. I'll never, ever do anything to hurt you.'

Oliver's kisses traced the soft curve of her cheek as his fingers unfastened the top button of her dress, a second, a third; slid down the silky crêpe de Chine to bare one smooth, creamy-white shoulder. She trembled as his lips and tongue touched her flesh, the moist trail of his saliva cool and thrilling in the sultry August heat.

His hands peeled down the bodice of her dress and then the loose straps of her slip. To her surprise she felt no shame or embarrassment, only a passionate, raw excitement which longed to respond to his caresses. Beneath the slip her breasts were bare, her nipples erected into rosy crests which had so long yearned for his kisses, his soft and subtle caress. He cupped one firm, white globe and at the touch she ignited, her untutored body caught in the white-hot inferno of their shared hunger.

'Oliver, please . . .'

'Let me. Trust me.'

And as his left hand crept from her knee to her thigh she felt all her tension and resistance melt away, her legs softly parting to welcome him in. Instinctively she knew that there would be a little pain; a tiny, insignificant pain. And then there would be pleasure. Nothing but pleasure for ever more.

Chapter 16

'Oxford Street's got a few more holes in it than it used to have,' commented Marian Clarke-Herbert. 'But it's still nice to see it again.'

Marian, Creena, Dillie, Hester and Eleanor were all sitting in a café sipping the worst coffee that Creena had ever tasted. It certainly wasn't a patch on Callister's in Douglas, but since none of the others had ever been anywhere near Douglas, the comparison was rather lost on them. And in any case – who cared about bitter coffee and buns with no currants in them? Suddenly life for Creena Quilliam was happier than it had ever been.

'Don't you miss the country?' enquired Eleanor, who had been brought up in a middle-class semi in Metroland and still cherished romantic notions about bucolic living.

'Miss it!' Marian grimaced. 'All that fresh air is positively bad for you, I'm convinced it is. Rows and rows of draughty wooden huts, and nothing to do on your off-duty but count the cowpats. You know, I had more colds whilst I was down there than I've had in my entire life. I'm jolly glad to be back, I can tell you. *And* I don't have to contend with that dreadful old Jeremiah Mavis Paterson!'

'"The 'ole 'ospital will be gone by mornin', just you mark my words",' quoted Creena.

'But oh – poor Gloria Bradley. Do you remember her?' Dillie asked, recollecting another former inhabitant of Female Surgical.

'Bradley?'

'You know,' cut in Hester, blowing out smoke from her cigarette. Creena had always found smoking faintly unpleasant, but Frankenberg managed to make it look elegant every time. She looked just like a film star sitting there, with her perfect ankles crossed and her svelte body encased in a couture suit she'd somehow managed to acquire in defiance of clothing coupons and shortages. 'Bradley – that dreadful brassy tart. She was discharged just before your lot were evacuated to the EMS.'

'Oh, I remember,' nodded Marian. 'Blonde woman, bit of an acid tongue but talked a lot of sense. What about her?'

Dillie threw Frankenberg a venomous glare, but it was a waste of effort. Frankenberg could have made a basilisk think twice.

'She's dead,' said Dillie. 'Septic abortion. Terrible, it was.'

'Poor woman.' Marian sipped her coffee. 'I rather liked her. Still, there's one bit of good news at least. Mrs Eversleigh's bucked up quite a bit since they sent her down to Epsom. Sister was convinced she wouldn't last the month out, you know. I can't imagine why, but I think our Mrs E's developing a taste for the country!'

It was good to laugh, thought Creena. Good to laugh

after the horrors of the last year. In that year she had seen things she had not even known existed – things that she prayed she would never have to see again.

The war had been going on for two years now, but the air raids had eased off considerably since May, with Hitler turning his attentions to the Eastern Front. It was difficult not to feel that things were on the up.

And then there was Oliver. Oliver, who had changed her life, turned her at last from a timorous, naïve girl into the woman she had always yearned to become. Oliver, who filled her every dream. Oliver, whom she loved to absolute distraction.

Right on cue, Marian's curiosity got the better of her.

'How's the love life, girls? What about you, Bayliss – still with the same chap?'

Dillie reddened to the roots of her hair – something she positively *never* did. But everyone could see that her friendship with Arnold had become something more permanent.

'If you mean my friend Arnold in the ARP...'

A chorus of delighted laughter greeted Dillie's now famous catch phrase.

'Come on, Bayliss, admit it,' teased Howells. 'He's a bit more than a friend now, isn't he?'

'Well...'

'And the poor chap nearly got himself eaten by a tiger the other week,' added Creena, breathless with merriment. 'Perhaps you'd better snap him up before another tiger does!'

At this, all eyes turned on Creena.

'What's this I've been hearing about you, you dark

horse?' demanded Marian with a knowing smile. 'Something about handsome doctors rushing back from Cairo . . .'

'Please!' protested Creena, squirming with embarrassment yet almost bursting to bore her friends with every last detail of her lover's virtues. Yes, *her* lover! Oliver Temple was hers at last and when the war was over the whole world would know that they belonged to each other for always.

'Don't forget the assignations in hotel bedrooms,' cut in Frankenberg drily.

'Oh shut up, Hester,' snorted Dillie. 'Frankenberg's just jealous,' she explained, 'because the only rich doctor who's shown any interest in her is Denman-Hart, and he's sixty if he's a day!'

Marian laughed.

'So where is this paragon then?'

'Oliver? He had to go back to his unit,' sighed Creena. 'I had a letter from him yesterday.'

'Poor lovelorn creature,' chaffed Howells good-naturedly. 'I'm almost glad I'm on the shelf. All this mooning and letter-writing would wear me out.'

Creena sat back in her chair. If she was honest with herself, she didn't care one jot about the teasing, not any more. Let Frankenberg be a complete bitch if it made her happy. Creena felt cushioned from the world and all its injustices by the wondrous certainty of her love.

'I hope he's worth it,' commented Marian as she bit into a bun.

'Oh yes,' smiled Creena. 'He's worth it all right.'

Not much further now. Not too much further.

ACROSS THE WATER

There was nothing left for Robert to do, just watch and hope. The course was plotted, the Wellington's nose pointed in the direction of home; now it was up to Skip to get them there.

Robert felt more angry than afraid. It had been a stupid raid, a botched job all round. Contrary to what Bomber Command might think, not all of Jerry's fighters were busy on the Eastern Front. A healthy contingent had met them over the coast, long before they got anywhere near the target, and they'd had to jettison their bombs over the sea in the frantic rush to cut and run. Pocklington and Smith had been lucky – Robert had seen them brolly-hop into the Channel, but poor old Chipperfield's crate had gone up like a Roman candle. What a bloody awful mess. He could think of a hundred better ways to spend a fine September Saturday.

The tail-gunner had bought it good and proper in the fight to get away. Tomkins the wireless op had stopped a bullet in the shoulder but he ought to be all right. The other two were OK too, so things could be a lot worse. Robert had flown enough missions to know that that roaring noise in the right engine wasn't a healthy one, but they'd been shot up before and made it back. They could do it again.

'You OK, Skip?'

The pilot did not reply immediately. His features were set into a grim mask of determination. Below, sea turned to cliffs then to open fields and they were heading home, home across the English downlands. Down on the ground, people – ordinary, good, honest people – would be looking up, craning their necks to see the ailing giant

325

lumbering overhead, willing its occupants to make it, seeing the telltale black smoke and praying it would not turn to flame.

'Can't hold her steady much longer, Rob. The wing's going, it's half sheared through. Better help Tomkins strap on his 'chute.'

'Not far now though.' Back at the airfield, Terry would be strolling back from breakfast, nursing a sore head after too many beers the night before. Waiting for the sight of the returning bomber squadron. 'You can do it, Skip.'

'No, Rob.' The aircraft shuddered, faltered, the throbbing drone of the engines turning quite suddenly to a shrill scream. 'She's going, Rob. Time to bail out.'

'But Skip . . .'

There were flames. Little yellow lapping tongues; crackling, bursting, greedy tongues of flame. Robert thought of all those pictures of London burning; the Royal Lambeth Hospital and his kid sister Creena in the middle of it all. Why hadn't he made her stay at home, like Dad had wanted? He ought to persuade her to go home now, home where she would be safe.

'I said bail out! I'll try to keep the nose level while you jump. I'll be right behind you.'

This was it, thought Robert as he got Tomkins strapped into his chute then reached for his own. And he'd promised Terry he'd be careful, too. Terry would kill him when he got home.

Creena flipped up the hem of her apron and re-read the notes she had scribbled on the underside of the starched white fabric. She had a memory like a sieve, and it didn't do to forget anything when Sister had sent you on an errand.

'Crêpe bandages, tulle gras, and I've brought some hypodermic needles for sharpening...'

The assistant dispenser looked doubtful.

'We're very low on stock,' he said. 'Deliveries aren't as reliable as they might be, and then there's the pilfering.'

'Pilfering? I thought it was just morphia they were after.'

'Drugs, bandages, equipment, anything they can get money for. These people have no moral scruples, Nurse. They wouldn't think twice about stealing the sheets from a patient's bed if they thought they could get away with it.' He surveyed the half-empty shelves. 'I can let you have a couple of tins of tulle gras but that's about it until tomorrow. Can't you borrow from another ward?'

'I'll try.' Sister Gynae abhorred borrowing from other wards as it upset her nice orderly administrative records, but an emergency was an emergency after all.

It wasn't a bad day for late September, she thought to herself as she walked back along the corridor composing conciliatory explanations for Sister. One of those September days that seemed more like the tail end of summer than the beginning of autumn. The breeze that blew in from the river hadn't yet acquired that raw, damp chill that heralded the slow, sad decline into winter.

The sea at Port Grenaugh would be at its warmest now – warm enough for the intrepid to go swimming in the clear grey-blue waters. Creena tried not to think about

Grenaugh too much, because each image she called to mind had Frank in it. Somehow Grenaugh had become the symbol of their happy childhood times, a place which belonged to both of them, together.

Last week's news about Frank had left her deeply shocked. 'Missing': that was all Don Kinrade's letter had told her, and apparently all the authorities had seen fit to tell him. Poor Frank had been posted missing in action – and no one seemed to know anything more than that, not where, or when or how. Could he be a prisoner of war? Then why was there no more specific news about him?

Dead; everyone knew that was what it meant. Frankie Kinrade was dead.

Creena could scarcely remember a time when Frank had not been part of her life. They had grown up together, shared everything together – and suddenly, he was gone. It was almost as if he had never existed at all.

But he *did* exist, thought Creena. And you couldn't wipe out half a lifetime of memories without wiping out a part of yourself too. Whatever had happened to him, Creena knew that there would always be a part of her that belonged to Frankie Kinrade.

Turning into the ward Creena almost collided with Sister.

'Only two tins, Nurse Quilliam? I ordered six. And where are my crêpe bandages?'

'I'm sorry, Sister. These are all the dispenser had.'

'Really! I will not have my patients suffering because of a lack of organisation, Nurse.'

'He suggested we borrow some bandages from one of the other wards, Sister.'

Sister gave an impatient sigh.

'If needs must, Nurse Quilliam. But I shall be having words with the chief dispenser. And Nurse—'

'Yes, Sister?'

'It seems that our ward maid has deserted us for the ATS and *both* our VADs are on sick leave, so we shall all need to work a little harder. Check our linen stocks thoroughly before you go off duty. This ward *must* have an adequate supply of laundered sheets.'

'Yes, Sister.'

Cursing silently, Creena directed a mental dagger between Sister's retreating shoulder blades. She had been supposed to get off duty ten minutes early to attend a lecture, but obviously that would have to go by the board. Wearily she pushed open the door of the linen room and clicked on the light.

'Oh! I'm sorry, I . . .'

Creena blinked in the light, perplexed and embarrassed. Staff Nurse Doreen Waverley was slumped on a hard-backed chair in the corner of the linen room, head in hands, lacy cap crumpled and slipping on her unbrushed hair. She barely looked up at Creena's approach, but Creena could see that her eyes were red-rimmed and her cheeks streaked and puffy from crying.

'I'm sorry, Staff, I didn't realise you were in here. I'll go.'

'You don't know, do you?'

'Staff?'

'You just don't know, any of you. You don't bloody know anything at all, do you?' Waverley's voice came out in savage sobs of bitterness, the tears springing up afresh and coursing down over her face. A handkerchief was twisted round her contorted fingers.

Shocked and slightly embarrassed, Creena crouched down beside Staff Nurse Waverley. The reek of alcohol hit her full in the face. So the rumours were true after all.

'Staff ... Waverley ... I can't understand if you won't tell me. Would it help if you told me?' She thought about putting her arm round Waverley's shoulders to reassure her, but even though Waverley was only a couple of years older than she was, it seemed unthinkable – staff nurses and probationers lived scrupulously separate existences.

She remembered her first day at the hospital, when Waverley had seemed so calm and authoritative and unshakeable. This felt all wrong. The roles ought to be reversed: the calm, experienced staff nurse should be comforting the humble probationer.

'I hate myself, you know, Quilliam. I truly do.'

'No, no, that's silly, you can't hate yourself. Why would you want to do that?'

'I do, believe me I do. I hate myself for being alive. *They* aren't alive, are they? So why am I?'

Still not understanding, Creena risked Sister's displeasure and laid her hand on top of Waverley's. It was trembling.

'Please tell me. It's all right. Everything's all right.'

Waverley's dull eyes flashed anger.

'How can you say that? How can you say everything's all right when they're all dead and I just have to carry on? You don't know anything, you're just a silly kid. They're gone and I have to carry on, but I can't. Don't you see? They're all gone. What's the point of anything any more?'

'Surely ... there's always hope. There's always a reason to go on.'

'Oh yes – our *vocation*.' Waverley's voice was filled with quiet bitterness. 'There's always our vocation to keep us going. Mustn't let the side down by showing our feelings, must we?'

Creena said nothing. Something had stirred in her memory – something about Waverley. Warwickshire she was from, wasn't she? Coventry, she was sure Dillie had said Coventry – and everyone knew what had happened to Coventry. Her mouth dry, she floundered for something to say, sure that whatever it was it would be the wrong thing.

'Is it ... is it something to do with your family?'

Waverley looked away, as if she couldn't bear to meet Creena's bright eyes. Those eyes were so full of life. What real sorrow had they ever known?

'They were all down the shelter,' she said, her voice suddenly flat as though she were reciting something she had learned by rote. 'Just like the Government said – go down the shelter and you'll be safer there. Mum and Gran wanted to stay at home in the cellar, but Dad said no, come down the shelter, it's much safer there.

'They all went – Mum and Dad, Gran, my two sisters, Auntie Grace. All of them except Uncle Clive – he was away on fire-watching duty. Nobody's quite sure when the bomb fell – so many bombs fell on Coventry that night. But in the morning they found the shelter had taken a direct hit.'

'And your family ... ?'

'Dead. All dead. Every single one of them. And do you

know what's *really* funny?' Waverley turned back to Creena and the tears were spilling out of her eyes, unchecked, sparkling on her lower lashes like huge, pendulous dewdrops.

Creena did not reply. Her heart felt like a lead weight in her chest.

'The house – our home – it wasn't even touched. If they'd stayed there, they'd have been all right. Isn't that funny?' She bent double, her whole body racked with sobs. 'But what would you know? What the hell would you know . . . ?'

Watching her in silence, Creena felt the full force of her own helplessness and inexperience. Frank might have been posted missing in action, but her family had been scarcely touched by the ravages of war, and she was ridiculously happy in her love for Oliver. She knew the hollowness of her words. How could she even begin to share Doreen Waverley's pain when her own heart was filled with hope for the future?

It didn't hurt at all, not one bit. Which was amazing really, because Robert knew he had been badly burned. He could see that from the expressions of the people gathering round him as they stretchered him into the ambulance.

He had a vague recollection of getting Tomkins and the others out of the plane and turning back to get Skip, but Skip was trapped and all of a sudden so was he. The world had turned to flames and the old crate was a mass of hot, twisted metal when it came down in the stubble field.

'What's your name? Can you tell me your name?'

For a moment he couldn't quite remember. Funny, that. But the well-meaning faces hovering over him would keep going out of focus, and he was distracted by the pictures in his head.

'Quilliam. 524876 Quilliam, Robert, Flying Officer . . . How's Skip? And Tomkins?'

'Everything's going to be all right, Robert. Everything's fine.'

And that was odd, too, because Robert had been so sure that things weren't going to be all right, what with the ground rushing up like that and Skip trapped behind a wall of flame. But these people sounded so sure, so reassuring. And the morphia was making him very drowsy.

'Am I going home now?'

'Soon. We're taking you to the hospital.' The girl's voice was kind and bright, a bit like his sister Creena's.

'Hospital. Yes.' The picture in his head changed and he saw his kid sister in her uniform. He was so proud of her, had he ever told her that? He couldn't remember. There were a lot of important things he'd wanted to tell her about but there didn't seem to be time any more. 'Creena . . .'

'There's someone you want to talk to, Robert? I can pass on a message.'

'Creena. My sister Creena.' He wanted to sit up but he didn't seem to have the strength. 'Please tell my sister . . .'

And then, quite suddenly, he ran out of time.

Creena was a little worried about Oliver. The last time she had had to wait this long for a letter, he had got himself wounded. And, of course, if he *had* been wounded he wouldn't tell her. He'd want to spare her the worry. If he only realised that not telling her made her worry even more – it was the not knowing that really made things difficult.

Like the not knowing for sure about Frank, thought Creena. It was as if someone had switched his whole existence off like a light, and she found that not only upsetting but peculiarly disturbing. What was more, that incident with Doreen Waverley a couple of weeks back had brought the horror of war back into focus with a disturbing clarity. She had even started to feel anxious about her family back in Ballakeeill, though everyone said that the island was quite safe, what with there being so many internees there: Hitler wouldn't bomb his own, now, would he? These days, Creena wasn't quite so sure.

'Not still scribbling, Quilliam?' Howells popped her head around the door of the common room and gave a jocular grin. 'What is it – another practice essay for Sister Tutor?'

'She's such a swot,' commented Hester, still smarting from a bad ward report.

'It's not an essay, it's a letter,' retorted Creena.

'Ah! *Another* letter?' Howells smirked knowingly. 'I bet it's to the divine Oliver.'

'It might be.'

'Let's have a look then.'

'Not a chance!' Laughing, Creena slid the letter under a sheet of blotting paper.

Pouting in mock indignation, Howells left with a parting shot:

'You could at least ask him if he's got a rich friend for me.'

Creena tried to settle down to writing her letter. She managed a couple more sentences, then put her pen down. She knew that the military hospital where he had been based before would forward her letters, but it wasn't the same as writing to a proper address, knowing that her letters would go straight to him. If he's overseas again, she thought to herself, goodness knows how long it takes my letters to reach him.

'I miss you so, my darling,' she wrote. 'I long to be with you again.' She wanted to write something more intimate, but thought of what the censor would make of it, and it didn't seem right to share her yearnings with a third party. 'Just think, I've started my third year now, so it's less than a year until I take my state finals, then one more year for my hospital badge. Who knows? Perhaps the war will be over by then and we can be together for always.'

She was gazing out of the window into the courtyard below, thinking about Oliver, when there was a knock at the door. That was odd – people didn't knock at the common-room door. They just barged in.

'Come in.'

The door opened and Home Sister was standing there, very stiff and straight in her navy-blue uniform with its crisp starched collar and cuffs. Her normally smiling face was serious, emphasising the lines about her eyes and mouth.

'Nurse Quilliam,' she began.

Creena jumped to her feet.

'Is something wrong, Sister?'

'This telegram has arrived for you, Nurse Quilliam.'

Creena accepted the buff-coloured envelope with shaking fingers. A telegram. Telegrams never brought good news, not ever. What if ... What if Oliver ... ?

Taking a deep breath she tore open the envelope and took out the telegram. The words seemed to swim before her eyes as she forced herself to read them.

No. No, please, not that, it couldn't be true. Anything in the world but that.

But she knew that there could be no mistake.

Creena stood, white-faced and shaking, in front of the mirror. She was glad the others weren't here to see her like this. She'd have to try to put on a brave face, and right now she wasn't at all sure that she could do that.

She'd broken down in Matron's office, but Matron hadn't seemed to mind. In fact she had been very good about it. Creena supposed she must be used to breaking bad news by now.

'Take one week's compassionate leave,' she had said, and her warm brown eyes had seemed to understand. But could anyone really understand how Creena felt at this terrible moment? 'A little longer if you need it. You should be with your family at a time like this.'

Walking back along the corridor to her room, Creena had wondered if just possibly this might be a horrible dream, something her own subconscious had conjured up as a punishment for being too happy, too much the optimist. But it was real all right; she still had the telegram in her hand: ROBERT KILLED IN ACTION STOP FUNERAL WEDNESDAY STOP G. QUILLIAM STOP.

ACROSS THE WATER

With clumsy fingers she took off her cap and slid the grips from her hair, letting it fall down over her shoulders. She wasn't Probationer Nurse Quilliam any more, she was just plain Creena; and it was time to go home. Whatever else she did, she mustn't let Robert down.

Chapter 17

'Get a move on, you lot. I haven't got all day.'

The middle-aged lance-corporal gestured half-heartedly with his rifle and the loose assortment of men moved on up Douglas promenade towards Hutchinson internment camp, collars turned up against the stiff October breeze coming in off the Irish Sea. Some were dressed in working clothes, two were carrying rolled-up newspapers and several were smoking or chatting. One or two offered up rude comments in their own language, but their significance was lost on their escort.

All seemed cheerfully resistant to any suggestion of discipline, much to the frustration of the lance-corporal. He was not best pleased to be nursemaiding a bunch of internees on their weekly outing to the town. Cinema? He'd give 'em bloody cinema.

The long, curving sweep of the promenade – so handsome before the war – was now interrupted at intervals by double rows of barbed wire. These were slung between posts, which extended halfway across the carriageway, obliterating the horse-tram tracks and cordoning off large blocks of hotels for use as internment camps.

'Oi! You – yes, you, Hermann bleedin' Goering. Pick yer ruddy feet up, will yer?'

Creena stood on the promenade in the drizzle and watched the column of internees turn up Broadway, straggling on towards their camp. They might not look very menacing but they certainly did look alien. The island had changed. Or was it just that Creena had changed and left the island behind?

She fought the memories that welled up, so strong and vivid, from her subconscious. In her mind's eye she saw a tiny red-haired girl walking along the shingle beach, her ice-cream-sticky fingers gripping her brother's hand very tightly. Then that same brother, grown into a lanky blond youth now, laughing merrily as he taught his young sister how to play French cricket. And if she turned her head and looked down towards the harbour she knew that she would visualise a tall, athletic young man in a smart black jacket with striped grey trousers, striding along the promenade to meet his proud sister after his first day in the advocates' office.

The associations were so strong in this place; too strong to bear. Every stone, every grain of sand held a memory, evoked a picture she would rather not see. It was her duty to be here and yet she had dreaded the thought of returning – to Douglas, to Ballakeeill, to this island she loved so well. Her instinct had been to hide herself away in London, like Waverley had done, somewhere where her pain need not be exposed for all to see. If only Oliver could be here, by her side, to hold her hand and give her the strength she so sorely needed.

Lost in thought, she almost forgot the meeting she had

arranged. And then she saw the graceful, dark-haired figure walking up the Loch promenade towards her.

'Máire! I was afraid you might not come.'

'Oh, Creena. Creena, I don't know what to say. First Frankie gone, and now Robert...'

They stood and looked at each other for a few moments and then Máire opened up her arms, so that Creena could hang her head and weep, just a little, on Máire's shoulder. The Irish girl thought how thin and pale Creena looked, with those great dark circles under her lovely green eyes and that sickly pallor to her normally rosy complexion.

'He's gone, Máire, I know Robert's gone but I just can't believe it. And it's the funeral tomorrow and I don't know how I shall bear it.'

Máire smoothed her hand over Creena's mane of red hair, searching for the right words that refused to come. She, at least, could understand what Creena was going through, feel what she was feeling. Hadn't she been through it all with Padraig, and didn't she still shed tears whenever she thought of him?

'Hush now, Creena. The pain doesn't go but in the end you learn to live with it.'

'But he was my brother, I loved him so much. How can I ever forget him?'

'You don't forget, Creena. It's just ... in time, you realise it's good to remember, not bad. I think about Padraig all the time, you know.'

'Oh, Máire, I'm sorry. I'm being selfish.' Creena dried her eyes and sniffed away the last of the tears. 'It's hardly any time at all since you lost your brother. And then you went away. You never did tell me why.'

341

Máire sat down on one of the benches overlooking the sea and gazed out towards the Tower of Refuge.

'I needed to get away for a little while – away from the memories.'

'That's why you took the job in Ramsey?'

Máire nodded.

'I did think about going back to Ireland, but me and my dad . . . well, let's just say we don't get on. There's nothing for me there now. I thought it was about time I faced up to things, so I went back to Onchan. The cottage is my home now.'

Máire's eyes fixed on a point in the middle distance; a small boat bobbing perilously on the choppy waters. She thought how cold it was, how the autumn chill was sinking into her bones. She pulled her coat more tightly around her.

'Families,' she sighed.

'All Mother and Father have done is argue since I got home,' said Creena, wiping a salty ooze from the corners of her eyes. She'd had enough of crying. 'Father keeps flying into rages, and then Mother . . .'

'What?'

'You know, I think she blames it all on me. It's little things she says . . .'

'Blames you? For what happened to Robert? But that's nonsense!'

'Perhaps, but I'm still here and he's not. And Robert was always her favourite.'

'Oh, Creena, don't talk like that. Of course your mother doesn't blame you, she wouldn't do a thing like that.'

Máire looked at her friend with frustrated compassion. She wanted to believe that this was all in Creena's imagination. But hadn't she seen with her own eyes how George and Ida Quilliam undervalued their brave, loyal, spirited daughter?

'I don't know how I'm going to go through with it,' whispered Creena. 'The funeral . . . I just don't.'

'You will,' replied Máire firmly, drawing on every resource of strength she had. 'Because I'm going to be right there by your side.'

A cloak of mist was closing about the south of the island, from Langness to Cass-ny-Hawin, rolling over Arragon Veg and into the little valley of the Grenaugh River towards the hamlet of Ballakeeill.

The kirk's single bell tolled in the damp October air. It made a slow and mournful sound, strangely muted in the grey blanket of mist which made sea and sky indistinguishable. But in the distance Creena could hear the gulls crying as they flew in from the sea, crying like lost souls.

Creena's head throbbed and she felt sick with exhaustion and grief as she walked through the churchyard with Máire and took her place at the graveside. How the others felt she could only guess. George Quilliam was tight-lipped in his stiff white collar and black suit; Ida had been fussing non-stop all morning about the arrangements, as though talking all the time were the only way she could stop herself thinking.

The whole village was there, of course: Don Kinrade, still shell-shocked by the news of Frank's disappearance; Nancy Shimmin from the Stores and old Billy Callister, his briar pipe deferentially unlit. Even the Duggans had come, hanging around at the back as though they were not entirely sure that they ought to be there at all. And one of Robert's friends from the RAF camp – a young pilot called Terry Haines. Creena had recognised him from the photograph Robert had sent her: 'Terry and Robert, working hard, summer 1940.' They had both seemed so happy, so carefree.

There were many red-rimmed eyes and quiet tears in the churchyard; brought down to this scale the war seemed that much closer, that much more real. And George Quilliam and Don Kinrade were not the only inhabitants of Ballakeeill to have a son or daughter in the forces.

It was the children who broke Creena's heart, though. They looked so out of place in their new black clothes: young Kenny Powell and Euan Duggan in stiff suits, their hair plastered down with water; Mona's little girls, so blonde and frail, like china dolls in black velvet and lace. By contrast, Amy looked very grown-up; not tall but with a woman's wise face on her adolescent body. Amy would never cause her parents any grief, thought Creena with the faintest twinge of resentment.

Over there was little Duggie – such a good-natured toddler, snuggled in the crook of his mother's arm and watching everything with his wide blue eyes. One thing was for certain; Duggie Mylchreest junior was nothing like his father, and that was one thing to be thankful for.

'... we commit the body of our dear brother, Robert Thorkell Quilliam, to the ground ...'

Somewhere behind her Nancy Shimmin sobbed once, twice, and then was silent. Creena peered down at the coffin as it was being lowered into the grave. It was so blank and anonymous, as though it had nothing whatever to do with her brother. Why hadn't Father let her see Robert's poor, burned body? Hadn't there been far worse sights to bear through the long nights of the London Blitz? All she'd wanted to do was say goodbye.

'. . . earth to earth . . .'

She looked up and saw her mother staring fixedly in front of her, her eyes very wide and unblinking and tearless, her lips pressed tight shut against all emotion.

'. . . ashes to ashes . . .'

Creena willed her mother to look at her, to give her some sign that all was forgiven, but none was forthcoming. Silent now after all her fussing, Ida seemed unaware of anything but her own private grief.

'. . . dust to dust.'

'Goodbye,' Creena whispered, and dropped the single, thornless rose on to the coffin lid. A few seconds later it was obliterated by the first spadeful of dark, wet earth.

''Tis a powerful bad thing now, powerful bad.'

In the front parlour at Ballakeeill schoolhouse, Don Kinrade sipped lukewarm tea out of one of Ida Quilliam's best china cups. He would have preferred a nip of potheen, to 'keep out the cauth', but George Quilliam had a hatred of strong drink and it had seemed disrespectful to bring the hip flask.

Creena nodded, unsure of what to say – especially to Don Kinrade. She was only too aware of the expectations that he – and most of the village – had had for her and Frank.

'It was good of you to come,' she said.

'Come now, Creena-gel. You don't think I'd let your boy go without a proper send-off? I haven't forgotten the time he got me out of that bother with the pheasants over Arragon way. He were a good friend to me an' the girls – an' our Frankie.'

'I . . . I'm so sorry about Frank.' Creena felt dizzy with sadness – not just for herself but for Don. Don loved his two daughters, Ailish and Gwen, to distraction; but since his wife Elena had died, almost a decade ago, Frank had been his reason for living.

'I know, Creena-gel.' Don set his empty cup down on the table. Somehow he didn't have any appetite for Ida's potted salmon sandwiches, or the very impressive sponge cake that dominated the Quilliams' carved-oak sideboard. 'I know how close you were, you two. Time was,' his rheumy eyes fixed Creena's and she thought her heart would burst, 'time was when we all thought you an' he . . .'

'He'll come back,' said Creena. 'He *will*.' She wanted to believe it as much as Don did. She and Frank might not be childhood sweethearts any more, but that didn't mean she didn't care.

Don patted her shoulder. He was fond of Creena, had often chided Frank for not being more open about his feelings for the girl. ''Tis no use bein' backwards in coming forwards,' he'd told him time and again. 'Else some other fellow worth half of you will go an' snap her up.'

'Well, maybe it's just as well you didn't tie the knot,' he said. 'For to be sure there's enough widows been made by this war already. I'll be off an' have a word with your mother now,' he added. 'An' then I must be away. Don't want to outstay my welcome.' His rough chin brushed her cheek. 'You're always welcome at the cottage, Creena-gel. Frankie would be proud of you if he could see you now.'

He left and Creena felt lost in the sea of chattering bodies around her. The dark solemnity of the funeral service had transmuted into a sort of forced cheerfulness, each mourner trying to outdo the others in colourful anecdotes about her brother.

'An' do you remember the time the l'il feller fell out the back o' John Cregeen's stiff-cart?' Billy Callister bit into a home-cured ham sandwich.

'Proper little ruffian, he was,' recollected John Duggan, waxing nostalgic after years of grumbling. 'Had half the apples out o' my orchard, but you couldn't hold it against him.'

'Wonderful scholar, that Robert,' sighed Nancy Shimmin. 'Knew all the Latin an' the Greek, he did. Could've been a doctor if he'd wanted.'

Creena could hardly bear to listen. It wasn't as if she was needed here. She felt superfluous. Amy was busying herself with a huge brown pot of tea; George was accepting commiserations with a grave and white-faced dignity; and even Tommy and Kenny were making themselves useful handing round trays of sandwiches. She thought of going over to talk to Cousin Mona, but Mona was in deep conversation with Aunt Alexa and it seemed unmannerly to intrude.

Making her apologies to Máire, she pushed through the throng and went into the kitchen. Ida Quilliam was standing at the earthenware sink, scrubbing so hard at a bone-china cream jug that Creena half thought the pattern would come off.

'Mother . . . ?'

Ida half turned but did not smile. Her eyes were dry but Creena saw the haunted look in them. She wanted to give her mother a hug, to ask her if they could share this pain together, but Ida seemed far away, locked in her own hermetic world of silent, resentful grief.

'You should be talking to our guests, Creena.'

'I wanted to see how you were. Can I help?'

Ida rinsed the jug and set it down on the draining board, then turned her attentions to an almost spotless plate.

'There is no need.' She was silent for a few moments, then: 'You're not looking at all well.'

Creena sat down at the kitchen table.

'I'm still getting over the journey. Nine hours on the train, and then the sea crossing. Mother . . .'

'Mmm?' This time Ida did not look round. Why was it so difficult? Why couldn't they just tell each other what they truly felt, get it all out into the open? Surely Robert's death ought to bring them closer together, not drive them further apart.

Creena thought of Doreen Waverley, and hoped with all her heart that her mother would not let grief eat away at her like that, like a worm in the soft white heart of a rosy apple. A stand-up row would be better, far, far better, than that. Creena would try to explain why she had defied them and gone to London; why it was so important to make her own destiny, away from Ballakeeill.

She took a deep breath.

'I just wanted to say...'

A light, rather tentative knocking at the kitchen door brought an abrupt end to Creena's attempts at conversation.

'Excuse me, I hope I'm not intruding.'

Ida and Creena looked round simultaneously, Ida's hands dripping soapy water that glittered diamond-bright in the wintry light from the kitchen window. Terry Haines was standing in the doorway, looking as abjectly awkward and apologetic as Creena felt. Her heart went out to him.

'No, of course not. Come in.' Creena got up from her chair and extended her hand in greeting. 'I'm Creena, Robert's sister. You must be Mr Haines.'

'That's right, Miss Quilliam. Terry Haines.'

'Mr Haines is a pilot,' cut in Ida. She was glad that Terry had come. Through him it felt as if she retained some link with all the ebullient young life that had epitomised Robert. 'He and Robert met during their training, isn't that so?'

Terry nodded.

'We were pretty close.'

Creena filled the big heavy kettle and dragged it over to the hob.

'Tea?'

'Thank you, no. I really ought to be going – I could only get a forty-eight-hour pass.' He turned his uniform cap round and round in his hands. 'There was just something I wanted to say before I went. Well, it was something Robert said really. I thought you'd want to know.'

Ida dried her hands on a towel, then hung it neatly on the wooden drier suspended over the kitchen table. She sat down slowly, her eyes never leaving Terry's face. She was spellbound.

But Terry's eyes moved from her to Creena.

'The VAD in the ambulance asked me to tell you that Robert's last thoughts and words were of you,' he said softly. 'You meant a lot to him, you know. He wanted you to know that.'

'Me? But . . .'

Creena caught Ida's expression. It was one of mingled pain, anger, and deepest jealousy. How could it be that her beloved first-born son's last thoughts were not of his mother, but of Creena? Creena, of all people! Creena, who had distanced herself from the family through her head-strong defiance. Terry could not have said a worse thing.

Creena saw that he was puzzled by her mother's silence, and intervened.

'Thank you, Mr Haines. It was very kind of you to come and tell us.'

'Yes, thank you, Mr Haines,' said Ida, getting up from the table. 'If you'll excuse me . . .'

Lips pursed, she took off her apron, smoothed down her neat black dress and went back into the parlour, leaving Creena and Terry alone in the kitchen.

'Did I say the wrong thing?' asked Terry. He certainly had the impression that he had.

'No, no, of course not,' replied Creena. 'She's just upset, that's all. You know how it is.'

But Creena knew how it really was, and a wave of despair and bitterness washed over her. No matter what she did, no matter how she tried, Ida would never love her as much as she had loved Robert, and that was all there was to it. She was being punished simply for being herself and that was just plain unfair.

She would go and find Máire right away; and the two of them would go – anywhere, just as long as it was away from the schoolhouse at Ballakeeill.

Sitting in the living room of Máire's cottage, Creena reflected on the day. Quite possibly, it had been the worst day of her life – worse even than those nightmare days and nights of the Blitz when hell had rained from the skies. This was just turning out to be a different sort of hell.

'You feeling any better now?' enquired Máire, setting down a bowl of soup on the little table in front of her. She was concerned about Creena. The girl was looking so pale and drawn, and she hadn't eaten a thing all day.

'Yes ... no ... I'm not sure. But I won't eat anything, thanks. I feel a bit sick.' She pushed the soup away, feeling like an ungrateful wretch. 'I'm really sorry – it's so kind of you to let me stay the night with you.'

'Nonsense, I'm glad of the company. But I don't like to see you looking so poorly.'

'Oh I'm fine, really I am. Just a bit off colour.'

'Do you want to go to bed? I could bring you a cup of tea and a hot-water bottle.'

'No, really, I'll be fine,' she repeated. At the Royal Lambeth, nurses were left in no doubt that they were there to look after sick people and should never, ever dare be sick themselves. It was a habit that was difficult to break.

Creena's head was still throbbing, her back aching and

that uncomfortably nauseous feeling hadn't left her ever since she'd got off the night boat from Fleetwood. In fact, if she was honest with herself, it was getting worse.

'I expect it's just the shock and the worry,' she sighed. 'You know, bringing on my monthly. It's such a wretched nuisance.'

'How about a couple of aspirin then?'

'Yes – all right, that might help.'

Creena rubbed her lower belly with the flat of her hand. The nausea was turning into that familiar heavy, drawing pain. Her periods had been irregular and often painful ever since she'd started her training – practically everyone else's were too, what with the odd working hours and not eating properly. Howells's had actually stopped completely for six months, and the poor girl had been frantic until the doctor had examined her and told her it was nothing to worry about.

'What you need is rest,' commented Máire. 'You look worn out.'

'Perhaps you're right – I'd best get an early night. I could always go over to Ballakeeill tomorrow and see the family – they'll most probably be in a better mood now the funeral's over.'

She stood up. Dizziness hit her with a devastating suddenness and the pain followed a second later, like the savage stab of a blade to the stomach. Doubled up, she stumbled and slumped forward, clutching at the edge of a chair.

'Creena!' gasped Máire in horror. 'Whatever is the matter?'

Scarcely able to speak for the stabbing pains that

convulsed her, Creena crouched on the stone-flagged floor, arms crossed across her belly, knees drawn up to her chest. Her face was white as chalk, her mouth open in a continuous O of astonishment and pain.

'Please . . .' she gasped. 'Fetch someone . . . a doctor . . .'

Máire's head was spinning. Creena needed a doctor . . . but there was no telephone in the cottage and the nearest doctor was several miles away. She looked down at Creena's white face and saw the pain in her eyes. What could she do?

Euan McPherson . . .

He wasn't a qualified doctor, of course, and admittedly he wasn't the sort of person you'd call upon unless you had absolutely no other choice. But this was an emergency, and McPherson only lived a few doors away.

'Hold on, Creena,' she said. 'Hold on. I'm going to fetch Euan McPherson.'

Old Euan McPherson put on his jacket and looked down at the frightened, white-faced figure on the bed.

'By rights, of course, you ought to go up to Noble's.'

Creena stared back at him, horrified.

'Hospital? Oh no, not hospital, I couldn't.'

'Well, when you go to see your doctor, you'd better not tell him I took a look at you first. He might not like it, see.'

'Will she be all right?' Máire perched on the edge of the bed, her overcoat still wrapped round her shoulders after her dash to McPherson's house.

'Should be, with a bit of rest. Of course, you have to understand . . . and in her position it's probably just as well . . .'

'Understand what?' demanded Creena, angry that she was being talked about as if she wasn't there.

'I've stopped the bleeding, Miss Quilliam, but I'm afraid you've lost the baby.'

Three days later, Creena stood on the deck of the *Snaefell*, watching the island recede into the distance as the boat turned to make for Fleetwood.

She felt numb, inside and out. How could she possibly not have realised that she was pregnant with Oliver's child? How could such a terrible mistake have happened when he had been so careful? Later, she knew, the numbness would fade and grief would take over; but for now she could not see beyond the next few hours – the need to get back to London and hide behind the anonymity of her nurse's uniform.

The previous day, she had returned to Ballakeeill to say her farewells to the family. Looked at objectively, the meeting had not gone too badly – but how could she look at anything objectively any more? There were times when the only way to survive was to do your duty and forget about your dreams, when there was no option but to close your aching heart and put on a brave face.

Mother had kissed her on the cheek and even cried a little when she said she had to go. Father had been even stiffer and more formal than usual, but at the last minute he had pressed a pound note into her hand – and Amy had baked a cake for her to take back to London.

Creena had smiled and said thank you, and on the face of it everything had been back to normal – or as normal as it ever could be after what had happened. But inside Creena had felt like dying, forced to bear the weight of a secret sorrow she could never tell.

Except, of course, to Oliver – and when would she next get a chance to talk to him? She didn't even know where he was.

Chapter 18

The year was moving steadily towards a close. The nights were drawing in, the breeze taking on a new and bone-deep chill. But Lambeth – 'bombed but not beaten' – was putting a brave face on things, readjusting to the damage it had sustained since this time last year.

For Creena, too, this was a time for damage limitation. The last three weeks of October passed in a dull haze. Still deeply shocked by what had happened, she found hard work a comfort. It distracted her from the thoughts that crept in on her in quiet moments, the terrible anxiety of when – and what – she was going to tell Oliver. Would he understand? Don't be a fool, she told herself, of course he'll understand.

The worst part of it all was keeping the secret. The others in her set had noticed that something was amiss, and kept asking questions she couldn't bring herself to answer. And then there was Dillie's Auntie Mo, who had practically adopted her since she'd come to Lambeth Marsh. Good-hearted, straight-talking Mo Doyle, whose bulldog determination refused to let go when she sensed trouble – and her sixth sense had had plenty of practice, what with Jack still living at home.

On this cold October afternoon, Creena was sitting by the fire in Mo's parlour, soaking up warmth. At her feet, Smudge the cat was playing with a piece of old rag, pouncing on it and tossing it into the air as though it were a mouse – not that there were any mice in Mo Doyle's house, they wouldn't dare.

'What is it, ducks?' Mo was concerned about Creena, sensing more to this than a family bereavement. 'You can tell me.'

'Nothing's the matter, Mo, honestly. I'm just a bit tired.'

'Somethin' botherin' you, is it?'

'No, really, I'm fine.'

'Hmm.' Mo regarded her with arms folded, head cocked on one side as though weighing up the evidence for and against. 'Well, you look like you got somethin' on your mind, if you ask me.' She nodded in the direction of Jack, who was sitting at the table, reckoning up his takings. 'Ain't that so, Jack?'

Jack glanced up from his books and Creena found herself looking into his bright-blue eyes.

'Leave 'er be, Ma,' he urged. ''Ow about another pot of char?'

'Char! You'll end up lookin' like a pot of char, Jack Doyle.'

'Go on, Ma. Nice pot o' char an' a piece of that cake . . .'

'Shall I make the tea?' volunteered Creena, getting half out of her seat.

'You'll do nothin' of the sort.' Mo pushed her firmly back into the depths of the battered old armchair and Smudge the cat took the opportunity to jump up on to Creena's lap.

''E likes you,' observed Jack with a grin. And so do I, he thought silently to himself. So do I, Creena Quilliam. 'Big soft lump, 'e is. Ma feeds 'im too well.'

Creena smoothed Smudge's coat from nose to tail and he arched his back in pleasure, purring like a furry dynamo.

'Thanks,' she said quietly.

'What for?'

'For . . . you know.' She nodded in the direction of the kitchen, where Mo was singing to herself as she waited for the kettle to boil.

'Well, I could see you wasn't keen on answerin' no more questions,' shrugged Jack. 'She's a diamond, is Ma, but she will keep on.'

He went back to scribbling for a few moments. Unusually for him, he was at a loss for words. He'd have tried asking her out to the flicks again, but she'd only tell him she was 'spoken for'. Bloody shame that. Bloody shame her bloke couldn't put a smile on her face.

He looked up.

''Course . . .'

'Hmm?'

'If there is anythin',' you know, a problem or anythin' . . .'

'I'm fine, Jack, really I am.'

'Yeah, sure, I know. But if there's ever anythin' you need, you'll know where to come, right?'

'Right.'

Creena gave a fleeting smile and it was like watching the sun come out from behind a big black cloud. Gawd, it wasn't like him to get soft over a girl. But then he'd never met a girl quite like Creena.

'I'll see your twenty,' said the man with the slicked-back grey hair.

'And I'll raise you another forty.'

He pushed the wad of notes into the centre of the table, and Jack felt quite dizzy to be in the presence of such recklessness. Poker had never been his game. He'd always thought he had a cool head, but he hadn't got the nerve for poker – and this wasn't playing for pennies or matches, this was the big time. He was glad he was only watching from the sidelines, learning the ropes.

'See, Jack,' said Sid, topping up his glass from a dusty bottle of cognac. 'I told you it would work, didn't I? You bring in the punters, I fix the venue and organise the rest.'

'Er . . . yeah, Mr Clayden. That's right.'

'You *know* people, Jack. That's a very useful commodity to me.'

Jack was beginning to wish he didn't 'know people' – and in particular, that he didn't know Sid Clayden. Every little favour he did for Sid, every errand he ran and racket he helped set up, was digging him deeper into the dark world of Sid's Lambeth 'firm'. He longed for the days when he was a freelance operator, a small-time wheeler-dealer whose success was measured simply in terms of how fast he could leg it when the Old Bill turned up. PC

Paddy Doyle was probably spinning in his grave to see what his only son had sunk to.

Even in his anxiety, Jack had to admit that the house on Coade Walk was just right for what Sid Clayden had in mind. It was sturdily built and had avoided any major structural damage, although the houses on either side had been badly blitzed and were uninhabitable. That suited Sid's purposes down to the ground. He didn't want anyone around to poke their nose into his very private business.

During the daytime, the upper floors were used by the Red Cross for packing food parcels; but the house was empty after six o'clock, and the woman who lived in as caretaker was a long-time friend of Sid's sister. She was perfectly happy to turn a blind eye to whatever went on in the basement at night – in return for a small consideration. And Sid's considerations were seldom small.

Five men sat around the table, deep in concentration. One of them was Sid's man, Jack knew that. He wasn't stupid enough to think that the game was fair. The cards were marked and the odds were loaded, but Sid would work the con slowly and subtly. Let the poor bastards win a couple of hands, then take them for everything they'd got.

'Three queens,' said the grey-haired man, throwing down his hand. Jack saw hatred, despair and hope in the eyes of the other four men. If they played another hand, they were thinking, just one, they would win back all they had lost, and more besides. Gambling was an addiction for them; they were easy prey for Sid Clayden. And so am I, thought Jack.

The sound of a knock at the front door floated down the steps into the basement, freezing the gamblers in mid-deal, and Sid Clayden's expression darkened. It couldn't be the cops – hadn't he bought them off, to make sure there'd be no trouble? But he didn't like this; he didn't like it at all.

'Should we ignore it?' whispered Jack. 'We ain't supposed to be 'ere.'

'Nah – we're just friends of Mary's, come to visit her, ain't we? Get rid of 'em. It's probably the soddin' ARP.' Sid grimaced. 'Charlie – get them cards put away, just in case.'

Jack took the steps two at a time, switched off the hall light, then opened the front door a couple of inches, keeping the chain on.

'What d'you want?'

'It's me, Jack. For God's sake let me in.'

It was hard to make out the man's features in the impenetrable darkness of the blackout, but the voice was unmistakable. With a Chinese sailor for a father and a Lambeth Irish girl for a mother, Benny Chung had developed an accent all his own.

'Benny? What the 'ell you doin' 'ere?'

'I been looking everywhere. Jack, you got to help me, let me in . . .'

'' 'Ang on a mo, Benny. I can't let you in, we got a bit of business on, see . . .'

'They after me, Jack.'

'Who? Who's after you?'

'The police, Jack. I get home, find they're waiting for me. They raid the club. I get away, but . . .'

Benny's face was pressed right up against the two-inch gap in the door. In the slight glimmerings of moon-light Jack could see that fear had turned his almond eyes round and shiny as marbles. Benny was strictly amateur, and small-time amateur at that. He had never had the stomach for ducking and diving, and if Jack hadn't introduced him to it in the first place, he wouldn't be in this mess. That pricked Jack's conscience with uncomfortable sharpness. He and Benny went back a long way.

'What you after then, Benny?'

'Money, Jack, somewhere to stay. Maybe a bribe . . .'

'Well, I dunno. Let me see what . . .'

The sudden heaviness of the hand on his shoulder stopped Jack in mid-sentence. He didn't need to look round to know that it was Sid Clayden. He could *smell* that it was Sid Clayden; a sickly miasma of hair pomade and brandy surrounded him like a malevolent cloud.

Sid's other hand pushed the door shut in Benny Chung's face with a crash which seemed to shake the whole house.

'You don't know him, Jack.'

'But Mr Clayden, it was only Benny Chung . . .'

'I said, you don't know him.' There was not only authority in Sid's voice, there was menace. 'He's nothing – just a dirty little half-breed Chink who's got himself in shtuck. That ain't none of your business, and it certainly ain't none of mine.'

Angry as he felt, Jack sensed that arguing would be futile – maybe even dangerous.

'Whatever you say, Mr Clayden.'

'You might as well cut your own throat as hang around with no-hopers like him, Jack. So when the police come calling, you don't know him, you never have, you don't know *nothing*. Understand?'

Jack swallowed. There seemed to be a great, unyielding lump in his throat that simply refused to go down.

'Yes, Mr Clayden.'

Jack understood all right. Understood that somewhere along the line, he had been careless enough to sell his freedom to Sid Clayden. And now the price of loyalty was soaring way, way too high.

Sixteen year-old Albie Powell – soon to be seventeen, as he was at pains to tell everyone – hovered in the kitchen doorway and tried to think of an excuse not to go out.

It was a chilly November Saturday at Ballakeeill, and the wood-burning range in the schoolhouse kitchen offered a glow of comforting warmth; but that wasn't the reason why Albie was so reluctant to face the outside world. Albie had a crush on Máire O'Keefe.

'Shall I make a pot of tea, Ma?' Albie cleared his throat and tried to look taller.

Alexa regarded him quizzically, banishing the smile from her lips.

'But you've only just made one, Albie. I'm not surprised there's a milk shortage – I reckon it's you that's causing it!'

'Shall I wash the dishes then?'

Alexa sighed.

'If you're that keen to help, you can go to the village shop with Tom and fetch another couple of sacks of logs.'

Albie's face fell.

'Do I have to?'

'I thought you wanted to help.'

'Yes, but...'

Máire set down her tea cup and looked at Albie, her head tilted slightly to one side.

'This is a lovely cup of tea, Albie,' she said.

'Really?'

'Really.'

'It's not too strong then?'

'It's just right.'

The radiance of adolescent pride spread across Albie's face.

'Should I go and get the logs, or shall I make you some more tea?'

Máire considered for a moment.

'Oh, I should go and get the logs if I were you,' she said. 'Your Auntie Ida will be pleased when she gets home tonight.'

'Oh. Oh, all right then.'

Apparently satisfied, Albie fetched his coat from the hall and disappeared out into the yard.

Alexa gave a huge sigh of relief, sprawled back in her chair and chuckled.

'Honestly, I never thought he'd go.'

'I ... rather think he likes me,' suggested Máire wryly. The thought was both ludicrous and rather touching. She was a good five years older than Albie.

'Likes you!' Alexa shook her head. 'The lad's daft about you. Ah well, that's first love for you. Speaking of which...'

'Hmm?' Máire looked up.

'Creena dropped hints about a nice young man in one of her letters, but that was ages ago. She mentioned he was a doctor, I think . . .'

'Really?' Máire was cagey. In the years since she'd left home to escape her father's violence, she'd learned to respect secrets, never to give anything away.

'You don't know anything about him, then?'

Máire shook her head. She trusted Alexa, but there was too much at stake. You had to be so careful with other people's secrets, other people's pain.

'She didn't really say anything.'

'Ah.'

Máire wondered if Alexa believed her. If not, it couldn't be helped.

'Only . . . I was thinking it would be nice for Creena if she had someone,' Alexa went on thoughtfully. 'Her mother's not been exactly warm towards her lately, and you know what George is like. I mean, we all know how terrible it is for poor Ida, losing a son like that, but why take it out on your daughter?'

'Grief can change people,' replied Máire. 'All I wanted to do when Padraig died was find someone to blame.'

'You know, Mona Mylchreest had a stand-up row with Ida at Robert's wake,' commented Alexa. 'It was after you and Creena had gone to the cottage. "Why are you taking it out on Creena?" she says – and half the village can hear, though they're in the pantry and the door's shut.'

'And what did Ida say to that?'

'She let fly at Mona, poor girl – asked her what made

her think she could tell Ida how to run her family, when she couldn't even keep her own husband from drink!'

That was the trouble with Ida, thought Máire; she always put moral judgements before love. So what on earth would she say if she ever found out about Creena?

'How about the pictures then?'

Dillie stood, hands on hips, staring in exasperation at Creena. This was the first afternoon off they'd had together for ages, and normally they'd already have made plans for it – window-shopping perhaps, or a proper tea in a tea shop, or even a trip to the Zoo (admission free, courtesy of Arnold).

But Creena had changed since her return from the Isle of Man. And there was more to that change than just grief at the death of her elder brother, Dillie could tell. She'd seen grief often enough to know that.

'No . . . no, not the pictures, not today.'

Dillie gave a sigh of frustration.

'I just wish you'd tell me about it,' she said.

'I don't know what you mean.'

'I thought we were supposed to be friends. *Best* friends.'

Creena looked up from her textbook. Dillie noticed how the dark hollows under her eyes seemed deeper, like blue bruises against her white skin. She looked worn out.

'Oh, Dillie, don't say that. You *know* we're best friends. And you're worrying about nothing.'

'Then stop swotting and come to the pictures with me. I hate going on my own, and Howells is sulking after that dressing-down by the Assistant Matron.'

'I can't. There's something I have to do.' Creena paused for a moment, thought, then reached into her overnight bag and took out a letter. Dillie recognised the handwriting on the envelope instantly.

'Oliver! You've had a letter from Oliver and you never said . . .'

'He's back in Aldershot, and he's coming to London next week,' explained Creena. 'He wants me to meet him at a restaurant next Wednesday evening.'

'But you're on duty then.'

'I know,' she sighed. 'And it's been so long since I saw him. I desperately need to talk to him.'

'Can't you ring him?'

'I tried. You know what the phone lines are like, and it's impossible to get messages passed on without them ending up garbled.'

'So – what are you going to do?'

'I'm going to go round to his new flat this afternoon – it's not very far – and leave a note for him. At least he'll get it as soon as he gets back to London.'

'And if there's time when you've finished this errand of mercy . . .'

'What?'

'Why don't you come to the flicks with me? Cheer yourself up. You can make eyes at Ronald Coleman and pretend it's Oliver.'

Creena looked at Dillie and burst out laughing.

'All right then,' she said. And her heart allowed itself a first fluttering of real optimism. These last weeks had been hell; but at last Oliver was coming home. She didn't know how she had managed to get through it all without him.

Creena got off the bus and pulled Oliver's letter out of her pocket. She checked the address: Beaumont Court. 'It's not bad for a *pied-à-terre*,' he'd written. 'A couple of quite nice rooms in a purpose-built apartment block overlooking a neat little square.'

Turning the corner into Beaumont Square, she saw what he had meant. It was a very pleasant square – the very epitome of smart London living – and it occurred to Creena that Oliver must be earning a lot more from his RAMC post than he had been at the Royal Lambeth Hospital. Funny, she hadn't thought army doctors would be so well off.

All the railings had been taken away for scrap, but the small central garden remained and even on this chilly early December afternoon, there were a couple of old ladies sitting on a bench, sharing their sandwiches with the pigeons. They wished her a cheery good afternoon as she walked across the square towards the front steps of the apartment block.

Beaumont Court must have been built around 1890. It was a squat, five-storey building in red brick embellished with coloured tiles and terracotta mouldings. Creena hurried up the steps, pushed her way through the swing doors and found herself in a spacious, high-ceilinged entrance hall.

To her right, an ancient man in a concierge's uniform was dozing on a chair. He was well past the normal retirement age, but had no doubt been pressed back into service because of the acute labour shortage.

'Er . . . excuse me.' Creena reached out and touched his arm. He jolted into a sort of indignant wakefulness.

'What . . . yes? What is it?'

'Excuse me,' repeated Creena, reaching into her shoulder bag for the note she had written for Oliver. 'I was wondering if I could leave this message with you.'

The concierge fumbled for his glasses and jammed them on the end of his nose.

'Who's it for?' he demanded, squinting at the writing.

'Oliver – I mean, Dr Oliver Temple.'

'Temple? Temple – Flat Fourteen, that'll be. Why don't you take it up to him yourself?'

'Take it up? But he's away – he isn't back yet.'

The old concierge scratched his head and looked at Creena as if she were mad.

'Not there? Of course he is. I saw him this morning.'

'Thank you.' Creena's heart was in her mouth. Oliver was back? Oliver was back!

Ignoring the lift, she raced up the stairs, undaunted by the climb after two full years at the Royal Lambeth – where lifts were for patients, porters and dinner trolleys, but definitely not for probationer nurses.

Pausing on the third landing, her heart thumping, she thrust her hand into her pocket and touched the envelope. If Oliver really was at the flat, there wouldn't be any need for the letter. She hesitated for a moment, suddenly terrified, then took the last flight of stairs almost at a run.

There it was: Flat 14.

Creena reached up and pressed the bell. She waited.

Nothing happened – but of course it wouldn't, because Oliver wasn't there. He wasn't back yet after all. Maybe she should just push the letter through the letter box and go back to the hospital. Well, just once more. She reached for the bell, but before she had time to press it, she heard footsteps in the hallway beyond the door.

The latch clicked free and the door swung inwards.
'Yes?'

Creena blinked in astonishment. The woman stared back at her, dispassionate, slightly bored.

'I ... er ...'

'Did you want something, dear?'

Creena looked at the woman. Didn't she recognise her from somewhere? That wavy blonde hair, immaculately permed; that athletic frame clad in tailored woollen jersey; those pale eyes ... She couldn't quite place her, somehow.

'I was hoping to give Dr Temple a message. I'm from the Royal Lambeth Hospital,' she added as an afterthought, taking the letter from her pocket. Panic was setting in; what on earth was this woman doing in Oliver's apartment? All sorts of horrible, ridiculous imaginings were spinning around in her brain. She shouldn't have come, she knew she shouldn't have come.

'If you give it to me I'll see he gets it,' said the woman with what Creena thought was a rather supercilious smile. Who *was* she?

At that moment, a small, fluffy dog raced along the hallway of the flat and the woman bent to scoop it up, tucking it under her arm. The picture was complete, and Creena suddenly remembered where she had seen the woman before – in a photograph; a photograph in a silver frame, on Oliver's mantelpiece. The sigh of relief which shuddered through her was palpable. How could she have been so silly?

'You ... you must be Lucinda – Oliver's sister!' said Creena brightly.

The woman's expression did not change; her smile did not slip, even for an instant.

'I'm afraid you're quite mistaken, dear,' she replied. 'I am Oliver Temple's wife.'

Creena stared blankly back at her, for a few moments quite incapable of taking in what she had heard.

'You're ... ?'

'That's right, dear, I'm his wife. And you are ... ?' Creena thought she detected just the faintest hint of a tremor in the woman's voice. But it was her own voice that was shaking, her whole body quivering with horror and disbelief.

'I ... Just a colleague, we worked together ...'

'Is that so?'

Creena felt hot, cold, faint. She had to get away, had to get away from this place, this nightmare, this humiliation.

She turned to leave, sick with shame and anger and grief.

'The message, miss ... ? You said you had a message for my husband.'

Creena half turned back, unable to meet those pale, accusing eyes. There was bitterness as well as pain in her voice.

'If you ... if you could just tell him Nurse Quilliam called.'

As Creena descended the stairs, Lucinda Temple stood in the doorway of the apartment, watching her with perfect impassivity; watching as though she were ticking yet another name off a very long list.

It was only when Creena had disappeared from sight that Lucinda Temple cursed the man she could never stop loving, and permitted herself the frailty of tears.

Chapter 19

Why?

That was the one question that kept thundering into Creena's thoughts as she knelt in the church and tried to pray. She hardly noticed the priest's voice, or those of the congregation as they followed the Advent service in their prayer books. All she could hear was that same question again and again, as she struggled to frame a prayer for forgiveness.

Today – 14 December 1941 – would have been Robert's twenty-eighth birthday. But now he was gone, taken from her as all those she cared about seemed to be taken. Uncle John; Frankie; Robert. Was her mother right – could it in some way be her fault?

She kept telling herself that life didn't work like that; but at least if it worked like that it would make sense. The arbitrary horrors of war were beyond her fathoming. If all of this wasn't a punishment, then what was it? Why was it happening?

Why?

And now look what had happened. Look what her silly, romantic dreams had brought her to. Every time she closed her eyes and tried to pray, all she could see behind her closed eyelids was the blonde woman with the pale eyes and the red lips, looking at her half in scorn, half in pity.

No, not 'the blonde woman'. She must give each thing its proper name. And this one's was *Mrs Oliver Temple*.

She was glad, profoundly glad, that Dillie and Marian and the others weren't here to see her like this. By the time she got back to the hospital she would be dry-eyed, efficient, Probationer Nurse Quilliam again. But for now she was just a silly, disobedient girl who was paying the price for her foolishness.

Young Micky Bates wriggled like an eel on the bum-smoothed oak of the church pew and told himself that Auntie Mo must really hate him and Kitty. If she didn't, then why had she sent them to Wiltshire?

Beside him, Kitty stood very still and sang along breathlessly to 'O come, O come, Emmanuel'. Micky preferred to make up rude words to songs – and hymns were, after all, songs of a sort – but he'd soon discovered that Wiltshire offered little scope for a budding lyricist. Uncle Jack might have appreciated his efforts, but Mrs Davenport definitely didn't.

Mrs Davenport was the woman who had taken them into her house as evacuees, and she took her duties very, very seriously. Micky and Kitty had been scrubbed to within an inch of their lives, had their hair doused with foul-smelling anti-nit lotion (and they didn't even have nits!) and been forced to eat fish without chips for the first time in their young lives. It hadn't been a happy experience, particularly for Micky.

It was Mrs Davenport who had made them come to Midnight Mass. 'It's traditional at Christmas,' she'd said, and that was that. Well, no doubt it might be traditional in a small Wiltshire village, but it certainly wasn't in Bishop Street – Lambeth Palace or no Lambeth Palace. Micky had never been forced to sit still for so long in his entire life, and he was convinced it was going to do him long-term damage.

The worst thing of all about Wiltshire was that it was *boring*. Now, who would ever have thought that living in a pub – even a village one – could be boring?

''Ere, I've 'ad enough.' Micky nudged his sister in the ribs and she gave a little yelp of surprise.

Mrs Davenport's huge flowery hat instantly loomed into view.

'Do settle down, m'dears,' she said, 'And don't get your nice new clothes crumpled.'

Her beatific smile struck terror into Micky's heart. Auntie Mo would have dealt him an almighty wallop across the backs of the legs, and that he could cope with; but *smiling* like that – well, in his book it was a cruel and unusual punishment and definitely not in the Geneva Convention.

'What is it, Micky?' whispered Kitty.

To Micky's consternation she had taken to Wiltshire better than he had, but then again girls always did go in for having ribbons stuck in their hair and all that sissy nonsense. He'd soon knock it out of her once they got back to Bishop Street.

'I said, I've 'ad enough of this,' he replied. 'I want to go an' play in the snow.'

'You can't,' hissed Kitty. 'Mrs Davenport says you'll catch yer death.'

Micky grunted his frustration. Three days and nights that snow had been falling. Half an inch of the stuff in Lambeth and they'd have been out in the streets, making the most of it – with or without their coats. He'd never caught his death there, had he?

And here there were eight whole inches of snow to mess about in! All the other kids in the village had been out in it, chucking it about, stuffing lumps of ice into snowballs and half killing each other with them – but oh no, not Mrs Davenport's evacuees. Her evacuees were going to stay nice and safe at home and drink warm milk.

They'd been the laughing stock of the village! And then the final straw had come when that old man with the dewdrop on the end of his nose had said Micky was 'so well behaved – for an evacuee'. Hah! He'd show them who was well behaved . . .

'I want to go 'ome,' he said to Kitty.

'You can't.'

'I can if I want.'

'How?'

Mrs Davenport threw them a quizzical glance.

'Do behave for Auntie,' she said soothingly, then turned back to her hymn book.

Auntie indeed! Mo Doyle was his aunt, thought Micky, not Mrs Davenport. And he wasn't going to put up with this any longer.

'I'm goin' 'ome,' he said. 'You can come too if yer want.'

Kitty's round blue eyes grew noticeably rounder.

'Home!'

'I said, didn't I?'

'When?'

'Soon as yer like.'

'Can't we 'ave our presents first? It's Christmas tomorrer. Mrs Davenport says there's presents.'

Micky considered and took the pragmatic option.

'All right, after presents.'

'Auntie Mo'll never let us,' protested Kitty. She recalled how very keen Mo had been on keeping them down in Wiltshire when she'd come to see them on that special excursion train. They'd begged her to take them back with her, but she wouldn't have any of it. All she could say was 'Ain't you getting fat!' – and that had seemed to please her no end.

'Auntie Mo won't know,' replied Micky enigmatically. At least, not until it's too late, he thought to himself, and began singing 'The First Nowell' with renewed gusto.

The barrage balloon loomed over the Royal Lambeth Hospital like a fat silver cloud, its edges iridescent in the cold January sunlight. As the wind caught it it pulled at its tethering hawser, as though only the solid stones of the hospital were stopping it from floating away.

The gap between the ward blocks – the space that had once been occupied by the original lab block – had lain empty and unused for over a year, since Hitler had come back to finish it off, leaving nothing but a heap of rubble.

That site had been cleared and then left empty with an almost superstitious observance. Nurses, doctors, patients, all skirted round the area like children stepping over the cracks in the pavement. But you couldn't leave a prime site like that unused for ever, and a couple of weeks ago the barrage-balloon crew had arrived: jolly, friendly girls in siren suits and 'tin lids', raising and lowering their balloon by means of a winch on the back of a large wagon. *They* hadn't been bothered by the empty site, or the memories and fears that it evoked in the people of Lambeth Marsh. Not a bit of it. They had simply set about getting on with their jobs.

'Afternoon, Nurse!' a short-legged, sturdy girl called out to Creena as she walked back to her study bedroom.

'Good afternoon.' Creena enjoyed passing the time of day with them. She pulled her cloak more tightly around her, but the icy January breeze still cut right through it. 'Rather you than me,' she observed, looking at the group of shivering girls drinking mugs of tea.

'Oh, you get used to it.' The girl wrinkled her turned-up nose. 'Personally, you wouldn't get me within a mile of a hospital if it weren't for that thing.' She nodded up at the balloon. 'Just the thought of blood makes me come over all peculiar.'

'You get used to that, too.'

'I wouldn't!' The girl produced a packet of cigarettes from her pocket. 'Fag?'

'I don't, thanks. Tried it once, and it made me throw up. Besides, if I got caught smoking in uniform I'd be for the high jump.'

'Don't know how you stand it. It's only the booze and fags that keep us going, isn't it girls?' The others broke into peals of laughter. 'Oh, and the blokes of course.'

A blonde girl broke in: 'Wishful thinking.'

'Bet you nurses get the pick of the doctors,' grinned the first girl, taking off her tin hat and scratching her head.

Her words cut through Creena like a cold steel blade.

'Oh . . . there isn't much time for that sort of thing,' she said. 'I've got my state finals coming up in the autumn. I seem to spend all my time swotting.'

'Might just as well join a convent,' remarked the blonde girl.

'Oh, it's not that bad.'

Or perhaps it was, thought Creena as she exchanged pleasantries and moved on towards the home. Over these last four or five weeks she'd made a point of being on her own as much as possible, because when she was on her own she could let down her guard. It helped that the third-year students had been moved into study rooms – but she still had to share with Bayliss, and Bayliss wasn't stupid.

Dillie had stopped asking questions, but it was pretty obvious that she knew something was wrong. All of Creena's set knew that she wasn't seeing Oliver any more, but she hadn't told anyone why. How could you explain that your trust had been betrayed? That you had been a naïve, self-obsessed little girl who had mistaken lust for love?

Talking about it was unthinkable, even to Dillie, her best friend. All Creena could do was bury the hurt and anger deep inside – and go on punishing herself, because she had no way of punishing Oliver.

Work was the answer. You could lose yourself in work, let it carry you along. If you worked hard enough, it could give rhythm and shape and purpose to life – even become life itself. And right now the hospital needed every nurse, every doctor, every penny it could get.

She would work until she dropped if that was what it took to forget.

Creena was vaguely aware of the distant ringing of the ward telephone, but scarcely registered it as being important. Staff Nurse Thompson was in the office to answer it, and besides, Creena was busy showing one of the new probationers how to measure and chart fluid output properly. It seemed scarcely five minutes since she'd been the hopeless, fumbling probationer, convinced that she would never learn the simplest of nursing tasks.

'That's right, Nurse Holloway. Now, just mark the amount down on the fluid balance chart and I'll be back in a mo with the . . .'

'Nurse Quilliam!'

Staff Nurse Thompson's voice rang out from the office just as Creena was emerging from behind the screens.

'Staff?'

'Come into the office at once.'

Puzzled, Creena followed Staff Nurse Thompson into Sister's office.

'You do realise that personal telephone calls are absolutely *not* allowed?'

'Yes, Staff, of course.'

Thompson sighed. She knew what it was like, being young and in love. It wasn't so very many years since she'd been a probationer herself.

'Go on, Quilliam – you can take the call, but keep it brief

and you'd better not let Sister catch you.' She nodded towards the telephone receiver.

'A call – for me?'

'Get a move on – I'll cover for you, but it had better not be for long!'

She left the office and, baffled, Creena picked up the receiver. Would it be bad news from home? No, please, not that – not another tragedy after all that she had gone through.

'Nurse Quilliam speaking.'

'Creena, darling – did you get the roses I sent you?'

Creena's heart seemed to miss a beat, as though it had momentarily frozen into a solid block of ice.

'Oliver . . .'

'I had a devil of a job tracking down red roses – but nothing but the best for you, sweetheart.'

'How dare you!' Inarticulate with rage, Creena gripped the telephone receiver as though she wanted to squeeze the life out of it. How could he do this to her? 'After what you've done to me . . .'

'I'm sorry, Creena, really I am. If you'd only let me, I can explain.'

'Explain!' She wanted to scream and shout at him down the telephone, but she had to keep her voice down to a barely controlled whisper. 'You betrayed me. You told me you loved me and wanted to marry me, and all the time you were married to that . . . that . . .'

'Steady on . . .'

Steady on. Is that all he can say? thought Creena. Is that all he can say after practically destroying my life? She hadn't told him about the baby – why should she? Why should she give him the satisfaction of sharing her private grief with him? He had stolen away her love and her trust, and now she owed him nothing but her cold, hard hatred.

'I never want to see you again,' she said with icy clarity, and dropped the receiver back on to its stand.

Chapter 20

Just behind the Red Lion Brewery and the old round shot tower, a stone's throw from the south bank of the Thames, lay Long Wall Yard.

You could hear it long before you saw it, even above the general hubbub of river traffic. Once a timber yard, now the site of several public shelters, Long Wall Yard had recently taken on yet another lease of life. Generally shunned by the locals in favour of Underground stations and cellars, the brick-built huts had gradually been commandeered for use by Millie Duval's shelter group.

On this drizzly February day, the voices of the children rose above the shouts of lightermen like raucous birdsong.

'Bill's 'ad two, miss, Bill's 'ad two – I saw 'im.'

'No I ain't.'

'I saw 'im, miss!'

Millie Duval ladled soup into yet another bowl and scowled at the boy over the top of her horn-rimmed spectacles.

'I shan't call you a liar, Cyril Grimes,' she said, not without a trace of humour, 'but you're certainly a stranger to the truth.'

She peered into the giant soup tureen. There was plenty for everyone today. It wouldn't hurt to offer seconds, just this once. In any case, this was probably the only meal Cyril would get today. Everyone knew he and his sisters lived in one filthy room, and Mrs Grimes had hardly enough to feed one of them, let alone all five. 'Go on then,' she said, and refilled his bowl.

Millie turned to Creena.

'You've been a great help today,' she said. 'Honestly, though, I don't know where you find the time. And giving up your off-duty like this...'

'Oh, that's all right. I enjoy it.'

Creena certainly found that working at Long Wall Yard had given her a new sense of direction. She'd omitted to mention to Millie that Matron would be apoplectic if she knew that one of her third-year probationers was 'freelancing' on her off-duty. Tiring though it was, this was what she wanted to do right now, not sitting in the pictures or going out dancing.

'I don't think people realise what it's like, trying to feed sixty hungry kids all at once,' observed Millie, glancing down at little Grace who was standing very close beside her – still afraid that this source of comfort might also be snatched away, just like her parents, her house, her world had been. 'You know, some of the big ones will steal from the little ones, given half a chance.'

Creena felt no great surprise at this. As she cleared up, she watched the children eating their soup and bread. A few were sitting at the long wooden table, but many were standing about or alone in corners half scooping, half pouring the soup into their mouths. Some looked just the right side of starvation.

At the hospital she had seen many children like these – thin, dirty, old before their time. Sawing off great chunks of bread and handing them out to the children, she had already noticed how malnourished many of them were, and how underdressed for this damp, chilly weather. Some had the telltale marks of impetigo and scabies, most had sores that would not heal. These were not the warmly dressed, relatively well-fed children of Bishop Street – these were virtually street urchins, left to fend for themselves.

'Give it back! Miss, he's nicked me fucking spoon.'

'I fucking never!'

'Give it back! Miss . . .'

Creena raised an eyebrow but did not react with shock or anger. That was probably exactly what Cyril wanted.

'Take another one from the drawer,' she said quietly.

'He's just showing off,' commented Millie. 'They all do, whenever anyone new comes. It's as if they're testing you out. Once they realise they can't shock you they get bored and stop it. Well – all except Cyril. He's a terror, I'm afraid. You'd think at ten years old he'd have better manners, but it's the same with all of them, they hate any sort of discipline.'

'Ten!' Creena looked across at Cyril. He was osten-tatiously ignoring her now. He looked about six – seven at most.

'Ten – and as illiterate as the day he was born. His mother keeps him home to look after his brothers and sisters, so he's had virtually no schooling.'

'Miss?'

Creena looked down. A slightly built girl of perhaps nine or ten was standing looking up at her.

'Yes?'

'I know summink.'

'Oh yes? What do you know?'

'The big boys 'as got a new game.'

Millie surveyed the girl, hands on hips.

'The boys have a lot of games, Joanie. I'm not sure Miss Quilliam wants to hear about them.'

'They go an' collect up all the milk bottles, miss,' continued Joanie, apparently unperturbed by Millie Duval's disapproving stare. 'An' when it's dark they nick a couple of bicycles, and they race 'em an' drop the bottles on the pavement, in front of all the people. Just like bombs, it is! It ain't half a lark.'

'They got a den, an' all,' cut in Cyril Grimes, warming to this subject. 'It's the cellar in a bombed-out 'ouse. Alec Fuller takes 'is tart there. I seen 'em doing it.' His eyes flicked up to Creena's and he grinned, in anticipation of maximum embarrassment. 'Whose tart are you, miss? Got a feller, 'ave you?'

'No,' she replied softly. 'I don't have time for boyfriends.'

'Buck up, Frankenberg,' urged Eleanor Howells, swallowing a generous forkful of Spam fritter.

'Would *you* buck up if Matron had just practically given you the boot?' demanded Hester, pushing her lunch dejectedly around her plate.

'Oh, come on, old thing, it isn't that bad.' For once, Marian was feeling very slightly charitable towards Hester

Frankenberg. Over these last few months, Frankenberg had been making an effort, and she'd thought that effort was paying off. Now, only months before their state finals, Hester had been hauled up before Matron and given a strict warning about her attitude.

'It's worse,' retorted Frankenberg. She really did look quite deflated, thought Creena. 'Matron's bound to have it in for me now. I might as well give up and leave.'

'Oh, don't talk rot.' Howells wiped a slice of bread round her greasy plate and – much to the disgust of her fellow diners – munched on it with gusto. 'Look, Frankenberg. You've as much chance of passing as anyone if you pull your socks up. At least your essays are half decent.'

'That's true,' agreed Creena. 'On the strength of my last one, I'll be lucky if I scrape through.'

Marian gave Creena a sidelong look.

'You've been overdoing it,' she said.

'What makes you say that?'

'You're as thin as a rake, and all pasty-faced, for starters,' replied Marian. 'And Bayliss says you've been up all hours swotting – not to mention rushing around Lambeth in your off-duty doing all manner of good works for the poor of the parish. Matron'll be livid if she ever finds out.'

'If I don't work hard, I shan't pass,' protested Creena.

'And if you don't get any sleep you won't pass either.'

Howells pushed away her plate, patting her stomach. 'I'm stuffed.'

'Well there's a novelty,' remarked Hester, with a resurgence of her former acid sarcasm. 'And to think you've only had *two* people's lunches besides your own.'

'Cheek! I've just got a healthy appetite, that's all.'

'Then I hate to think what constitutes an unhealthy one.'

Creena ate her lunch mechanically, not really noticing the taste or texture of the food. She was thinking about home; about what it would be like when she went back to the island on her next leave. Would this feeling of guilt ever go away? Sometimes she even imagined that it had left physical marks upon her flesh.

'Did you hear about Arnold?' Howells wiped her mouth on her napkin.

'What – Dillie's Arnold in the ARP?' Marian chuckled. 'What's he been up to now? Not been eaten by one of his tigers, I hope.'

'I saw him in Cas the other day. White as a sheet, he was, and covered in blood. He'd come in with a casualty. This poor girl had been buried under a heap of rubble for two days and Arnold and his ARP chaps had dug her out.'

'Quite the little hero, our Arnold,' sniffed Frankenberg, who had a secret soft spot for Arnold but would have died rather than admit to it. He was, after all, a very common little man.

'Dreadful state she was in,' Howells went on, ignoring Frankenberg's interruption. 'Looked like an old woman, but she couldn't have been more than nineteen. Her young man was with her, and do you know what? Arnold told me that boy hadn't slept for two days and nights. They'd tried to get him to go home, but he wouldn't leave his girl under that bombed-out house. They had to stop him trying to dig her out with his bare hands. His fingers were cut to ribbons

– and would he let go of her hand? Dr Amschewitz practically had to prise him away so he could examine her.'

'He must love her very much,' said Creena very quietly, and Marian threw her a searching look. But Creena just kept on looking down at her plate.

'Man troubles, ducks?' asked Marian.

'Not any more,' replied Creena, and went on eating.

Dillie walked briskly down Waterloo Road, past the fire station, glancing once or twice at her watch. Time was getting on, and dusk was falling over Lambeth Marsh.

Sunday off or not, she really oughtn't to have stayed quite so long at Auntie Mo's. There was studying to do and sleep to catch up on before tomorrow's early shift. But the lure of Mo's bacon pudding had been irresistible, and of course she'd had to stay to hear the latest about Kitty and Micky. Those two little ruffians had been found at Swindon station a few days after Christmas, trying to buy railway tickets to London – would you credit it? They were back with Mrs Davenport now, but Dillie fully expected to hear that they'd been up to more mischief before many more weeks had passed. With Jack Doyle for a role model, a boy like Micky could hardly be expected to stay out of trouble for long.

It was a pity Creena had decided not to come with her today. Auntie Mo would have welcomed her with open arms, and perhaps this time Creena might have felt able to talk about whatever it was that was troubling her so much. It hurt Dillie that Creena couldn't talk to her about her problems, but it hurt her infinitely more to see her suffering in silence.

Dillie was just about to turn right into Lower Marsh when she heard heavy footsteps behind her. Instinctively she quickened her step. The footsteps behind her quickened too. No nurse from the Royal Lambeth had ever come to any harm around here, but it was getting dark and she was in mufti. You heard such stories . . .

'Nurse Bayliss?'

At the sound of her name she stopped and turned round. A tall, broad-shouldered man was standing a few yards behind her, his hands thrust into the pockets of his belted raincoat and his collar turned up against the March wind.

'Terribly sorry, Nurse – did I startle you?'

'Dr Temple? Oliver Temple?' Dillie gaped at the sandy-haired young doctor. He was as handsome as ever, as urbane, as desirable. For the umpteenth time she wondered what could possibly have happened to drive him and Creena apart. If only Creena wasn't so secretive. 'What on earth are you doing here?'

'I . . . er . . . followed you,' confessed Oliver.

Dillie eyed him with faint suspicion.

'Followed me? Why?'

'It was the only way I could think of to get to talk to you.'

Dillie moved on, walking quickly towards the hospital.

'OK, you've found me – talk away.'

Oliver's long legs easily kept pace.

'It's Creena . . .'

'Ah.'

'You know we . . .?'

'I know you two aren't seeing each other any more. I don't know why.'

Oliver's expression relaxed very slightly.

'Look, Nurse Bayliss, we had a silly disagreement. If I could just get to talk to Creena, but she won't see me . . .'

Dillie shrugged.

'If she won't see you, that's her decision.'

'But you're her friend,' protested Oliver.

'I still don't see what I can do.'

Oliver paused.

'I'm only on leave for a few days. I have to rejoin my unit soon, and I really do need to see Creena before I go. I was thinking . . .'

'What?'

'I was thinking . . . couldn't you sneak me into the nurses' home? I only need a few minutes with her.'

Dillie stared at him in disbelief.

'You've got a cheek. Have you any idea what Matron would do to me if I got caught?'

'But you won't.' Oliver's lips curled into that irresistibly charming smile which had melted so many hearts. 'And you'd be doing me the most tremendous favour.'

'I'm sorry, but I can't do it,' replied Dillie; but already she knew that she would.

Creena sat back in her chair and eased the tension out of her tired shoulders. It was her day off – her precious Sunday off – but she had spent it working. In the morning she had gone down to Long Wall Yard to help Millie, and after lunch she had forced herself to get out her notes and study.

She knew, deep down, that this punishing routine wasn't doing her any good. There wasn't an ounce of spare flesh on her, and there were bluish circles under her eyes. Not that she really noticed the tiredness any more. Adrenaline had taken over as it had done at the height of the Blitz, driving her on, forcing her to work harder and harder.

And everyone was having to work harder now. With the first-years all away in Surrey and the hospital having to take on conscript nurses who thought the Royal Lambeth would offer an easier ride than the QAs, third-years like Creena and her set were in many cases shouldering all the responsibilities of full-blown staff nurses. In some ways Creena was glad. In these last few months, her nursing career had come to mean more to her than it had ever done. Being a good nurse seemed the best – perhaps the only – way to make things right again.

She put down her pen and picked up Aunt Alexa's letter once more.

Dear Creena,

If I don't get out of this house soon I'll go mad, I swear I will. Albie is halfway there already. He is driving poor Máire to distraction with his mooning about.

Your mother can't stand having me in the kitchen – she says I get under her feet and make her Yorkshire puddings go flat. I ask you! It's very good of her and your dad to take us in, but sometimes I could throttle Ida. It would be nice to have our own place again. In a way I almost envy your cousin Mona – with that big farmhouse all to herself, and those Italians doing all the farm work for her. One of them is *really* good-looking!

Hope you are eating properly, but I suppose that's

too much to hope for, what with the rations so low and that horrible National bread. Billy Callister sends his best. Tommy's doing well at King Billy's College, and your Amy is turning into a regular mother hen.

Don't take too much notice of your mother. What happened to your brother hit her hard, and our Ida never was one for showing her feelings. Chin up, kid, and I'll send you another fruitcake if Ida'll let me in the kitchen for five minutes.

Much love,
Alexa.

Creena wished her mother's letters were as chatty as Alexa's. Robert had been the only one of her children that Ida Quilliam could really talk to; and now that he had gone her letters had become more formal than ever.

She turned back to her books. Had she really made these notes herself? They seemed so jumbled and disjointed. That was the trouble with having to attend lectures between shifts and during off-duty – half the time you were barely awake, let alone alert.

A knock on the door made her look up. It couldn't be Dillie – Dillie wouldn't bother knocking, and the others generally just barged in.

'Yes?'

The door edged open a few inches and Dillie's face peered in.

'Dillie? Whatever are you playing at?'

'I've got a visitor for you.'

'A visitor?'

'I had the devil's own job smuggling him in here, so

you two lovebirds had better kiss and make up pronto. Look – I'll wait outside, never was any good at playing gooseberry.'

Creena's mouth fell open, her complexion draining of all colour.

'Hello, Creena.'

She got to her feet, very slowly, very unsteadily.

'How did you get in here?'

'Your friend Dillie ... She was very understanding.'

'Oh, I'm sure she was!' Creena's eyes flashed a warning. 'After you'd told her a pack of lies. You used me, and now you're using my friends.'

'I needed to talk to you, Creena – to explain.' Oliver held out his arms as though to embrace her.

'Explain!' hissed Creena, taking a step backwards as he approached her. 'How dare you come here?'

'But Cree, just listen to me ...'

'I listened to you before, do you remember?' She was shaking like a leaf, her heart thumping so hard and so fast in her chest that she thought it would burst. 'I loved you – I gave you everything. Everything I had. And now you have the audacity to come here and say that you can *explain*. You're a married man, Oliver Temple – are you telling me you can explain *that* away?'

'N-no,' Oliver admitted.

'That woman – that woman at the flat. She's your wife?'

'Yes, but ...'

'No buts, Oliver.'

'Look, Creena, I'm sorry if I hurt you. I didn't mean to. Yes, I'm married, yes, Lucinda's my wife – technically speaking – but she means nothing to me ...'

'And you mean nothing to me, Oliver. I told you never to contact me again, and I meant it.'

'Why won't you listen . . . ?'

'I won't listen because you're a liar and a cheat and I hate you. Almost as much as I hate myself for letting you do what you did to me.'

'It's not that simple, Creena.'

'It's very simple. Either you get out of here right now, or I scream the place down.'

'Creena, calm down.'

'Get out!' For the first time, Creena's voice rose above a hiss and became a shout.

'OK, OK . . .'

'Get out. Now!'

The door opened, framing Dillie's shocked face.

'What's the matter?'

'Get him out of here, Dillie. Get him out of here right now.' Pale and trembling, Creena was clutching the back of a chair, her knuckles white with tension.

'You heard.'

'OK, OK, I'm going.'

With a parting glance of utter scorn, Oliver strode out of the room and his footsteps disappeared down the corridor towards the back entrance of the home.

But Dillie wasn't listening. She didn't give a damn about Oliver Temple, only about her friend, white-faced and deeply shocked. Gently she put her arms around Creena's shoulders.

'Oh, Cree, Cree, I'm sorry. I thought it was for the best, really I did. He said he just wanted a chance to explain.'

'Explain? Oh, Dillie, if only you knew.' Creena gave a humourless laugh, dry as a twig snapping underfoot.

'How can I know if you won't tell me?'

Dillie hugged Creena very tight and Creena laughed again, great, hacking sobs of laughter.

'Tell me,' Dillie begged her. 'You have to tell someone. You can't keep this pain to yourself for ever. If you don't share it, it's going to make you ill.'

Quieter now, Creena sank down on the edge of her bed and Dillie sat beside her, holding her hand tightly now, unsure of what to do even though she had dealt with grief and shock many times over the past few years. Treating a patient professionally was very different from helping a friend.

'I hate him,' whispered Creena.

'Oliver? You hate Oliver? But why?'

Creena's dry, bright eyes searched Dillie's face, looking for comfort, for answers.

'I went to his flat to leave him a message – do you remember? It was back in December, just before he was due back on leave.'

'I remember. I wanted you to come to the flicks with me, but you were dead set on going round to Oliver's.'

'I should have gone with you,' said Creena. 'In fact, I should never have had anything to do with Oliver Temple. Frankenberg was right – his sort aren't for me.'

'But why? I still don't understand.'

'Oliver wasn't at his flat, but someone was. His wife.'

Dillie's expression changed from puzzlement to astonishment and then horror.

'His *wife*!'

'I've been a stupid little kid, haven't I? Do you know, I'd even seen her picture, and he'd told me she was his sister.'

'Oh, Cree. But you couldn't have known. How could you possibly have known?'

'If I'd been you, or Hester, or Marian, I'm sure I'd have known. I've been behaving like a stupid child.'

'That's not true. Anyone could have been taken in by him – we all were! Howells was besotted with him. He's just a rat. But it's all over now, Cree. Just put it down to experience . . .'

Creena gave a single sob that seemed to wrench her very soul out of her body, and then the tears came in a great flood.

'How can I? How can I forget? I gave him everything. Do you understand? Everything.'

'I understand. He was special. He was the first.'

'It was worse than that, Dillie, much worse. You see, I didn't know it, but when I went back to the island for the funeral I was pregnant – pregnant with Oliver's child. I miscarried . . .'

'Oh, Creena, I had no idea.' Dillie was lost for the words of comfort she longed to speak. 'Poor, poor Creena.'

'I wanted to tell you, truly I did,' sobbed Creena. 'But I just couldn't. It hurt so much, and I feel so ashamed. But I loved him more than anything . . .'

'There's nothing to be ashamed of,' said Dillie firmly. 'Listen to me, Creena; there's nothing to be ashamed of and you've done nothing wrong. The only one who's done anything wrong is Oliver bloody Temple.'

And if I could get my hands on him, thought Dillie

grimly, nurse or no nurse, I'd cheerfully wipe the smile off his cheating face.

April came to the island, with bluebells in the glens and yellow gorse covering the hillsides above Ballakeeill. Tiny brown trout wriggled in crystal-clear streams, and gulls cried as they followed the fishing boats home from the sea.

Even in war-torn London, spring seemed to touch the city and its inhabitants, bringing an irresistible atmosphere of hope. 'Down but not out' read the sign on the sandbags outside the Royal Lambeth Hospital; and the collecting boxes bulged with donations from patients who had scarcely enough money for themselves. London *could* take it. How could anyone doubt it, with the spring sun shining and the dome of St Paul's still rising, undaunted, above the defiant city?

Creena walked along the Embankment in a dream. She had read her mother's curt note a dozen times, but still the words refused to sink in, though they went round and round in her head, jumbling themselves up the more she thought about them.

'You are no daughter of mine,' that was what her mother had said. No daughter of mine, no daughter of mine . . .

How could she have found out? Who could possibly have told her? How much did she know? There were no answers to Creena's questions, only the angry words that dismissed her from her mother's life and love: 'No daughter of mine would commit such a wicked act. You are not welcome here. You are no daughter of mine . . .'

Robert and Frankie; Oliver, and now even her own mother. All gone.

Now she really was alone.

Chapter 21

'I still say you're anaemic,' said Millie Duval as she scraped a little leftover cabbage into the pig bin. The kids at Long Wall Yard were too ravenous to leave much on their plates. 'You could do with a good rest and a few square meals on your off-duty, rather than rushing down here and doing enough work for two.'

'I *like* coming to the shelter group,' insisted Creena, buttoning up her coat. 'And besides, if I was back at the hospital I'd only be swotting for my dratted finals.'

Millie looked up.

'How's it going?'

Creena shrugged.

'Difficult to tell really. I've never been red-hot at exams. I shall have to work hard if I'm going to scrape through.'

'Not *too* hard, I hope.'

Creena smiled.

'Not *too* hard, Millie, I promise.' She picked up her handbag. 'I'll be off now before it gets dark. Shall I come on Thursday?'

'If you're sure you have the time.'

Creena looked at little Grace, her round face peeping out from the folds of Millie's skirt.

'Oh, I've got the time, don't you worry.'

It was Millie who emerged first from the shelter and into the now deserted yard, just as a tall figure in a dark suit was slipping out of the shadows.

'Evenin', Mrs Duval.'

Millie's face registered welcome.

'How good of you to come.' She turned to Creena. 'Creena, this kind gentleman here is . . .

Creena blinked in astonishment. Jack Doyle looked very faintly disconcerted.

'Jack!' Creena exclaimed. 'What on earth are you doing here?'

'You two have already met?'

'Jack's my friend Dillie's cousin,' Creena explained.

Jack switched on a smile. To be honest, he hadn't expected Creena to be here, not on a Monday night.

'Blimey, Creena.' He tipped his hat on to the back of his head. 'Don't you never stop workin'?'

'No, she doesn't,' cut in Millie, giving Creena a long, hard look. 'But she ought to.'

Jack felt in the inside pockets of his capacious raincoat.

'I . . . er . . . got somethin' else for you, Mrs D,' he said. 'For the kids.' He fetched out an orange, then another, then two more from the pockets that had concealed everything from watches to day-old chicks. This was a bit embarrassing, not quite in keeping with the image he liked to project. 'It ain't much, I know, only oranges is 'ard to come by just now.'

Millie accepted them with exclamations of delight.

'Oh, how kind, the children do so need fruit . . . you must tell me how much I owe you . . .'

She reached into her handbag but Jack stopped her.

'No need for that, Mrs D. You don't owe me nothin'.'

'You're sure?'

'Just keep it to yerself, eh? Don't want people thinkin' Jack Doyle's gone soft.'

Jack jammed his hat squarely back on his head.

'Best be off. Got a bit o' business on tonight.' He looked quizzically at Creena. 'Goin' my way? I could walk you back down the 'ospital.'

Creena and Jack left Long Wall Yard together, Creena more than a little surprised by what she had seen. Everyone in Lambeth Marsh knew Jack Doyle was an adroit businessman, a wheeler-dealer, but now she was seeing a whole new side to him.

'It was good of you,' she began, 'getting those oranges for Millie.'

Jack shrugged uncomfortably.

'I got 'em cheap,' he said. 'Bit of a thank you from a satisfied customer.'

'All the same . . .'

'No big deal.' Jack couldn't wait to change the subject. 'Dillie says I have to cheer you up,' he volunteered, waiting to see what Creena's reaction would be.

'Oh she does, does she?' Creena sounded half amused, half indignant.

'Says you've bin a bit down in the mouth.' Jack scrutinised her pale face in the half-light. 'You're lookin' peaky, an' all. 'Ow's about I take you for a slap-up meal, somewhere up West?'

'Oh, Jack, I don't think so. It's very kind, but ...'

'What about that trip to the flicks then?'

'Jack ...'

'Or 'ow about a show?'

Creena couldn't help laughing at Jack's efforts.

'Jack, please, stop!' She laid her hand on his arm. 'I'm just ... not really in the mood for that sort of thing right now. I've got things on my mind.'

Jack looked into her green eyes, perplexed. Things must be bad if he couldn't tempt her with an evening up West. He wished he knew what was bothering her – probably something and nothing. He could have it sorted for her in no time, if she'd only tell him.

'Tell you what though.'

'What?'

'Least you can do is let me show you the sights.'

'Where?'

''Ere – in Lambeth. Just a stroll around the old place on yer afternoon off. What d'you say?'

His look was so insistent, his smile so persuasive, that she found herself saying:

'Yes, all right, Jack, why not?'

'Look, Ida, I'm hardly being unreasonable.'

Alexa Powell stood in the kitchen at Ballakeeill schoolhouse and watched Ida Quilliam charging about like a human tornado. Anger and pain seemed to surround the schoolmaster's wife like crackles of static electricity.

'I have told you before, Alexandra, my family's business is our own.'

'For goodness' sake, Ida, I *am* family.'

Ida glanced up and gave a disdainful sniff which made Alexa's blood boil.

'You are one of George's second cousins. I would hardly count that as family.'

Alexa glanced out of the kitchen window and counted to ten silently. The rain thundering down out of a blustery, leaden sky seemed a perfect match for the atmosphere within the house.

'All I want to know, Ida, is why you are treating your own daughter like dirt.'

'Creena is no daughter of mine.' Ida rolled her sleeves up and set about blacking the range. 'By her own actions she has forfeited that right.'

'*What* actions?' demanded Alexa in exasperation.

'I am not under any obligation to discuss them with you.'

Alexa heard the catch in Ida's voice, as though beneath the coldness and the anger there was a deep pain threatening to break through to the surface, only ever held at bay by an immense effort of will.

'Look, I've got a letter from her here.' She took the sheet of paper out of her pocket and unfolded it. 'She's terribly upset, Ida. She doesn't understand why you won't answer her letters – and neither do I.'

'Understand!' snapped Ida. 'Of course she understands. She knows what she has done.'

'Let me read it to you,' pleaded Alexa. 'If you could just hear what she has to say . . .'

'I have heard quite enough lies and defiance from that girl. I do not wish to discuss her any further.'

Alexa tried a different tack.

'What does George think about all this?'

Ida drew in breath sharply, and rounded on Alexa.

'And what exactly is that supposed to mean?'

'What it says.'

'George is in full agreement with me.'

Is he now? thought Alexa. She had noticed how George, usually every inch the blustering schoolmaster, had grown more and more withdrawn in recent weeks. All his attentions seemed focused on his school, his garden and his pig, and at mealtimes he hardly said a word to anybody, except to snap some ill-tempered remark. Even well-behaved Amy had suffered the rough end of his tongue, and as for Kenny – well, George was making his life a misery in class.

Something was horribly wrong with this family, and Alexa was convinced it had little or nothing to do with Robert's death. She was beginning to wonder if poor Creena wouldn't be better off without the lot of them. Then she relented. Ida and she had never been what you'd call close, but – whatever Ida might say – family was family, and she ought to make another effort, if only for Creena's sake.

'Oh, Ida,' she sighed. 'I wish you'd tell me what the matter is.'

She touched Ida's shoulder, but Ida shrugged her hand away, turning all her attentions to the gleaming black kitchen range.

'Nothing is the matter, Alexandra, I've told you.'

Alexa's temper flared again. She hated it when Ida called her Alexandra, which she only did when she was angry or wanted to score points off her.

'For God's sake, Ida – if you don't pull yourself together, you'll soon have no family left!'

'How dare you!' Ida's face was a picture of rage.

'It's true. Whatever Creena's done, she doesn't deserve to be treated like this.'

'This is my family and my house, Alexandra. How dare you try to tell me how to bring up my own children?'

'She's not a child any more, Ida, that's just the point. She's a grown woman. And she's your daughter. You owe it to her at least to tell her why you're doing this.'

'I owe her nothing. And I don't see how you can talk about obligations, Alexandra Powell. You who I took into my own house when you didn't even have a roof over your head! You and your badly behaved children . . .'

'I see.'

Alexa felt icily calm now. She could stand back from her own anger and take the measure of the situation with surprising clarity. Living at Ballakeeill schoolhouse had never been a picnic, but lately things had grown perceptibly worse, with Ida's tight-lipped unpleasantness and George's sudden outbursts of temper. Alexa had thought it her duty to stay around, offer Ida whatever support she could; but this inexplicable business with poor Creena had put the lid on it.

'Well, you needn't put up with us any longer, Ida. Mona Mylchreest has offered to let us move in with her at the farm, so I and my badly behaved children will be leaving you just as soon as I can arrange it.'

'Creena.'

A voice penetrated Creena's dream and suddenly she was surfacing towards consciousness.

'Creena, Auntie Creena, wake up.'

As she blinked in the late afternoon sunlight, the first thing she saw was a pair of large green eyes, peering unblinkingly into her own.

'Miaow. Miaow-wow-wow.'

Smudge the cat was hanging unceremoniously by his armpits from Kitty's determined embrace; his soft black and white belly dangling like a furry scarf down Kitty's front, the tip of his tail swishing ever so gently in protest.

'Are you all right, Auntie Creena?' lisped young Kitty. 'Micky said you was dead.'

'She might've bin,' insisted Micky. 'I seen a dead body once,' he added.

'For Gawd's sake, put that poor animal down, Kitty,' scolded Mo Doyle as she bustled into the front room with a huge brown earthenware teapot and a plate of bread and marge. 'It's been through enough without you squashin' the life out of it.'

Sleepily, Creena swung her feet down on to the floor and sat herself more decorously on Mo's ancient and battered sofa. She yawned.

'I'm ever so sorry, Mo. I must've dropped off.'

'You needed it,' said Mo, setting down the tea. 'After our Jack 'ad walked you halfway to Brixton an' back.' She tut-tutted over her son, who had now taken himself off down The Ring, no doubt to conclude another of his 'business arrangements'. 'Showin' you the sights, indeed!'

Creena rubbed her eyes, still a little groggy.

'Actually I enjoyed it,' she said. And she had, too. It was surprising how Jack Doyle could joke away your troubles.

Dillie laughed.

'A day out with our Jack? You're not serious!'

'No, really. I'd no idea there was so much to see. Did you know that Captain Bligh's tomb is in St Mary's churchyard? He got married on the Isle of Man, you know.'

'Ain't it a small world?' agreed Mo.

Dillie, sitting in the old armchair and scraping carrots into a bowl, gave Kitty and Micky a meaningful look.

'Creena needs a bit of peace and quiet,' she said. 'Which means you two can stop pestering the life out of her,' she added.

'We ain't doing no harm,' protested Micky.

'Well, you can go an' do it outside,' replied Mo, wiping her hands on her apron.

'Aw, Auntie Mo!'

'I said outside,' repeated Mo firmly. 'Or would you rather I sent the both of you back to Mrs Davenport?'

'Come on, Kitty,' said Micky. 'Billy Wiggins 'as got a pet rat.'

Dillie watched in amusement as the two fell over each other in their haste to get out. A moment later she heard the back door bang shut behind them.

'Micky'll do anything to avoid being sent back to Wiltshire,' she observed. 'Little ruffians – running away like that. Mo was hopping mad when they turned up on the doorstep, but she hasn't the heart to send them back.'

Creena chuckled. Since she'd got to know Dillie's family, she'd become very fond of Kitty and Micky. The house had seemed empty without them, and she could easily understand how Mo might not want to be parted from them again.

As she sipped her tea, she cast her mind back to the days, not so very long ago, when she and Frank had been kids together. Like Micky Bates, Frank had been into everything, getting into countless scrapes, and never an ounce of bad in him.

'Frankie fell asleep in the back of Tossie Taggart's lorry once,' recollected Creena, remembering the day so vividly that there was no room for sadness. 'He must've been about eleven then. You know, that lorry took him all the way to Ramsey before Tossie found him, and half the folk in Ballakeeill thought the Little Folk had taken him! His dad didn't half give him a sore behind when he got home. And then there were all the times he and Don were caught poaching . . .'

'He sounds like a real tearaway!'

'Oh, he was, Dillie! You'd never have guessed he'd end up as a policeman. But he was such a kind boy, especially to me.'

Dillie settled herself back in the battered old armchair, for once vacated by Old Bert, and curled her legs up under her.

'No news of Frank, then?'

The laughter of childhood remembrances faded in an instant from Creena's face.

'Not a word. He's gone, Dillie, I know he is. I just wish . . . I just wish we'd not parted the way we did.'

'You can't go blaming yourself for everything,' Dillie pointed out.

'But I never even got round to answering his last letter. I was so besotted with Oliver . . .' She hung her head, the weight of shame and anger heavy on her shoulders. 'What a fool I was, to be taken in like that. It's no wonder my parents won't speak to me.'

Dillie reached forward and took a slice of bread and marge, then held the plate out to Creena.

'Come on girl, eat up.' She paused. 'Just give your parents time, they'll see sense. And you don't know for certain *why* they're so angry with you. You can't be sure it's about . . . you know . . .'

'Yes I can, Dillie. I *know*. I should have realised I could never hide a secret like that. Not from my own mother.'

Creena toyed with the slice of bread on her plate.

'How did she find out, Dillie? How could Mother have found out about the baby?' Her green eyes searched Dillie's face, desperate for an answer to the question that kept her awake night after night, long into the cold, dark hours before dawn. 'Máire would never say a word, I know she wouldn't. And even old McPherson . . . well, he told me himself he knows how to keep his mouth shut.'

Dillie shook her head.

'I don't know, Cree, I wish I did.'

'But how am I ever going to find out, if they won't answer my letters?'

Mo Doyle, round and motherly in her floral print overall, bustled in from the kitchen with another tray. The appetising aroma was enough to tempt even Creena's jaded appetite.

'Jack managed to get a bit of stew beef,' she said triumphantly, 'so I made a pie. Now you won't let it go to waste, will you?'

'Well, I . . .' Creena looked from Mo's expectant face to Dillie's. 'Thank you,' she said. 'It looks lovely.'

Mo doled out the pie with a generous hand. Old Bert would be peeved that there wasn't any left for him to scavenge, but some things were more important than Old Bert's capacious stomach. Things that needed putting right. Rich folks might try to do it with money or influence; Mo Doyle did it with food.

'You not heard from your ma and pa then?' she asked Creena as she watched her eat, counting every mouthful with silent satisfaction.

'I've written – I even tried telephoning the school, but they wouldn't speak to me, neither of them. I've not heard a word from them since my mother's letter. Nothing. I don't know what I should do.'

Mo folded her arms over her ample chest and pursed her lips in anger.

'It ain't right,' she said. 'Cuttin' off your own daughter like that.'

'Mother and Father are very strict,' said Creena. 'If they really have found out about . . . you know . . . well, perhaps they just can't forgive me. I can see why . . .'

'I've never heard such nonsense in my life,' retorted Mo, now well into her stride. 'Round here, if a girl gets herself into trouble, well, her family might get a bit stroppy but they'll rally round quick enough.' She gave a dry laugh. 'Just as well, ain't it, Dillie? Half the girls in Lambeth Marsh are expectin' before they get married.'

'You don't understand . . .' began Creena.

'Oh, I understand right enough.' Mo perched her bulky form on the arm of the sofa and laid a large, protective hand on Creena's shoulder. 'Seems to me your ma and pa have been angry with you ever since you left home. They never wanted you to leave and be a nurse, now, did they?'

'No, but . . .'

'You went against what they wanted, and they didn't like that. Felt like they were losin' you, see. Then they lost your brother too. And when they found out about your trouble, well . . .'

'We don't know that,' cut in Dillie. 'It might be something else.'

'I'd lay odds it ain't,' replied Mo. 'But whatever it is, all they can see is that you went against them. They can't see their poor girl's goin' through hell.'

'It's nobody's fault but my own,' said Creena quietly. 'Perhaps they're right to punish me.'

'They don't need to,' observed Dillie. 'You haven't stopped punishing yourself since it happened.'

Creena set her half-empty plate down on the table. In the corner by the fireplace, Smudge the cat eyed the remains of the meat pie with sly covetousness. Patiently, he judged the exact moment for his next felony with a street cat's artless precision.

'Listen to me,' said Mo with authority. 'The worst thing you've done is believe a man's lies, and Gawd knows, girl, we've all done that in our time. You meet a man – he's good-lookin', well off, pays you a lot of attention. He gets himself wounded, and it stands to reason you're going to fall for him, give him what he wants. You're flesh and blood, girl, it's nature!'

'But I should never have done it,' said Creena with a slow shake of the head.

'That's as maybe,' replied Mo. 'But if you're in the wrong, what about him? Never told you he was married, did 'e? Didn't give a damn that he'd got you in the family way . . .'

'He doesn't know about the baby. I didn't want him to know . . .'

'And if he did know, and you hadn't lost the baby? What then? He'd have scarpered, that's what, you know 'e would. You ain't done nothing wrong, Creena. If there's anyone who should be ashamed, it's that Dr Temple, not you. And if your ma was here now, I'd tell her so to her face!'

The back door had opened and closed so quietly that no one but Smudge heard Jack returning to the house from his little bit of business. And Smudge gave no sign that he knew. They understood each other perfectly, Jack Doyle and the black tom cat with the ragged ears. In embattled London, stealth was more than a stock in trade for both of them; it had become an instinct, a means of survival.

After slipping his takings under the kitchen lino, Jack had intended to make a grand entrance, flourishing the small string bag of lemons he'd got in exchange for a set of tyres. You couldn't get lemons. *Nobody* could get lemons. Mo would be pleased as punch.

But then he'd heard Creena's voice, and something had made him wait, watch, listen. Over these last couple of weeks he'd known darn well that something was eating away at her, but Mo had been as aggressively protective as a mother cat with her kitten, and there was no getting the truth out of Creena.

Jack didn't like to be kept out of the picture, and besides, he didn't like seeing Creena unhappy. He couldn't resist eavesdropping. But what he'd just heard hadn't only surprised him – it had made him very, very angry.

'Oh, Mo,' Creena said, very quietly. 'You're so kind to me. But my mother . . .'

'Your mother's a silly woman whose pride's took a knock.'

'Will things ever be all right again?'

'It'll mend, girl. Things always mend.'

Mo put her arms round Creena's shoulders and hugged her tight. On the other side of the kitchen door, Jack Doyle cursed himself for a bloody fool.

He'd known the minute he saw him that Oliver Temple was up to no good – Jack had a spiv's sixth sense for these things – but how could he have warned Creena? She wouldn't have believed him even if he'd tried – and why should she? Why should she have thought Jack Doyle would be any better friend to her than treacherous Oliver Temple?

Chapter 22

'Hello, Harry!'

'Oh. . . er, hello, Nurse Quilliam.'

Walking down the corridor towards the dining room, Creena almost tripped over Harry the ward orderly, kneeling on the floor amid a jumble of boxes and their spilled contents.

'Let me help you pick those up.'

'There's no need, really. You'll be late for your dinner . . .'

'No, let me help.'

Creena knelt down on the floor beside Harry and helped to reassemble the boxes.

'What happened?'

'Oh, I . . . er . . . I was just giving one of the porters a hand, Nurse. Said I'd carry this little lot down to the stores. Anyhow, Nurse Quilliam, how're you keeping? Don't see much of you these days.'

'Oh, I'm just fine, Harry.' The hospital was no place to air her private troubles. 'How are you?'

'Top-notch, Nurse, top-notch. Though that Sister Meredith keeps us all on our toes, and no mistake.

Terrible about that UXB at Elephant and Castle, though.'

'Tragic. Nineteen dead and three hundred homeless. And to think the bomb had been there over a year, and no one even knew.'

Harry finished tidying up, stepped back and surveyed Creena from head to toe. 'Looking a mite tired, if you don't mind my saying, Nurse. Too many nights on the tiles?'

Creena smiled.

'Swotting for my finals in September, more like. Only four months to go now. I can't believe it's nearly three years since I started here.'

'Well, don't you go overdoing it, Nurse,' Harry chided her, loading the boxes back on to his trolley. Creena noticed a half-empty pig bin in among the boxes, but thought little of it. 'Mind you take care of yourself.'

'And you, Harry.'

As she watched Harry's overloaded trolley squeaking away into the distance, Creena couldn't help wondering why, if he was supposedly heading for the stores, he was pushing his trolley in the opposite direction...

Creena's Aunt Bessie was adapting to the exigencies of war rather better than she – or anyone else – had expected.

Once the initial shock had worn off, and those annoying Nazi women had been moved into one of the larger boarding houses, life at the Ben-my-Chree had settled into a daily rhythm. With the approach of the finer weather, many of the women spent most of their time out of doors, swimming or sunbathing, or making things to sell in the camp shop on Station Road.

Of course, one or two of the locals remained furious that 'enemy' women should be enjoying such privileges. But as time wore on, Bessie had come to see that the situation wasn't quite so clear-cut as some might like to believe.

For a start, despite the establishment of a married camp, many of the women were still separated from their husbands and lovers – for only those of 'proven good character' were to be allowed to move into the married camp. And then there was the sheer monotony, the awfulness of being cooped up like a caged animal and not knowing when – if ever – the Home Office board would declare you eligible for release. Over the last couple of years of sharing life behind barbed wire, Bessie had come to feel a curious kinship with the shifting population of internees who shared her guest house.

'Keep in the garden, and don't let little Duggie out of your sight!'

She watched Olya's young daughters playing in the garden with little Duggie Mylchreest, and turned back to Mona with a smile.

'Goodness knows what language they talk to each other in, but they seem to get along all right.'

'I'd have thought Rebecca and Olya would have gone with the other mothers to the married camp,' remarked Mona, watching in amusement as one of the girls picked little Duggie up off the grass and planted a huge wet kiss on his cheek.

'They asked the commandant if they could stay here as they're up before the Release Board next week,' Bessie explained. 'If all goes well, they'll be free.'

'Where will they go?'

'Back to London, I should think. Rebecca used to work as a cook for a rich Polish family, and they've offered to take Olya in as well.' She shook her head sadly. 'There's nowhere else for them to go. So far from home ... And all the welfare nurses and resettlement officers in the world can't bring back Olya's poor dead husband.'

Mona was uncomfortable with too much solemn reflection. She tossed back her blonde curls and patted down the skirt of her new powder-blue dress.

'Do you like it?'

'It's lovely, dear,' observed Bessie. 'But where on earth did you get the material? It looks like pure silk!'

Mona's still-pretty face developed two girlish dimples as she laughed.

'Giacomo's sister sent it to him from Italy, as a present for me.'

Bessie's eyebrows arched almost to her hairline.

'Is that allowed?'

'I haven't the faintest idea, Bessie. But if I'm given four whole yards of beautiful Italian silk, I'm not going to ask too many questions.' She grew more serious. 'Things aren't easy, you know, what with Duggie being away ...'

And I hope he stays away, she thought to herself. Wherever he is, I hope he stays there and never comes back. We're managing fine without him, just fine.

'I know, dear.' Bessie poured a dab of milk into Mona's cup. 'But at least you won't be lonely now, what with Alexa and her boys to keep you company.'

Mona thought it best not to say that she hadn't been

lonely anyway, what with the delicious Giacomo and the other Italians from Onchan camp. She hadn't been lonely since the first day the internees came to work on the farm. But it was nice to have Alexa around – and besides, she could hardly turn her away, not when Ida was giving her such a terrible time. Ida was giving *everyone* a terrible time at the moment.

'Oh, we're getting along very well,' said Mona. 'To be honest, I don't think Alexa could have stood it a moment longer at Ballakeeill. Ida's so po-faced all the time, and George hardly says a word except to shout at some poor child.'

Bessie sat herself down in her favourite armchair. Her sister Ida was proving to be something of a problem – much more of a problem, indeed, than the internees whose arrival she had so feared.

'Is she still refusing to have anything to do with Creena?' Mona nodded.

'I can't understand it. The whole village knows Ida's fallen out with Creena – and of course George is going along with it – but no one seems to know why. And Ida won't tell anyone. She almost tore Alexa's head off when she tried to ask her about it.'

Bessie murmured her concern. She, better than anyone else, knew just how obstinate Ida Quilliam could be. And she also knew how terribly vulnerable Ida was. Something must have cut her very deep to make her behave like this.

She remembered how it had been when they were girls together, Ida, Bessie and Ida's best friend Jeanie. Even then Ida had been the dominant one, domineering even. Only Jeanie had known how to get through the barrier of

Ida's dreadful moods, though later on Robert had also had that gift.

But Jeanie was long gone, and as for poor Robert . . .

'She took Robert's death very badly,' observed Bessie.

'I don't think it's that,' said Mona. 'At least, not just that. And how could she blame Creena for her brother's death?'

'People can get strange ideas into their heads.'

'But Creena? Why Creena? You'd think they'd be proud of her, what with her doing so well. It doesn't make sense. Couldn't you have a word with Ida?'

Bessie's heart sank at the prospect.

'I would if it would do any good,' she replied. 'But you know what she's like. No, Mona love, we'll just have to sit it out and let her tell us in her own good time.'

'Mummy, Mummy!'

Little Duggie came racing into the sitting room from the garden and presented his mother with a posy of crimson flowers. Laughing, Mona scooped the toddler up into her arms.

'Oh, Duggie, you shouldn't have taken flowers from your Auntie Bessie's garden. Bessie, I'm sorry.'

'Oh, don't you worry yourself. That fuchsia grows like a weed.' Bessie beamed at the sight of little Duggie's amiable, pink-cheeked face, downy and soft like the skin of a ripe peach. 'He's such a good boy, and he does love his mother. I wonder what Duggie will make of him when he finally comes home!'

I wonder too, thought Mona, her mouth suddenly dry at the prospect.

'*If* he does,' she said. 'Before all that trouble, me and Duggie, well . . . we weren't getting on too well.'

'I know, dear.' Bessie patted her on the shoulder and raised her wrinkled cheek for little Duggie's wet kiss. 'I always suspected that he didn't treat you right. But perhaps the army will make a man of him.'

And perhaps it will simply teach him to beat me harder and more often, thought Mona. She tried to suppress the thought, but the more she did, the more it came: the seductive dream of a buff-coloured envelope, and the telegram inside telling her that Duggie Mylchreest was dead.

It was a warm July evening in Lambeth Marsh, and Jack Doyle was getting distinctly hot under the collar.

He stood at the bar in The Ring and traded jocular insults with the landlord; but his mind was elsewhere, trying to think through conundrums that became increasingly tangled the more he tried to sort them out.

No matter which way you looked at it, the problem remained the same. Things were getting way too hot – not just for Jack Doyle, but for all the other 'gentlemen traders' south of the river. For one thing the Americans were starting to get a grip on all the best rackets, and their tactics were too rough and too ruthless for men like Jack Doyle. And whilst the law was sniffing ever closer to Jack's heels, Sid Clayden's demands were becoming more imperious, more impossible to fulfil. Stealing from the sick, stealing hospital supplies, that just wasn't right.

It was time to cut and run.

But there were things he needed to do first; and in particular, people he needed to see right. He couldn't do a runner without setting up Mo and the kids, making sure they'd have everything they needed. Only a shark like Sid Clayden would let his family down. If there was one thing that Jack had learned from his father, it was that you had to look after your own.

Quite unexpectedly, he thought of Creena Quilliam; the red-haired Manx girl who had been filling his thoughts so frequently of late. He remembered what he had overheard at Mo's, and the memory tightened his chest with a dull ache of rage.

You had to look after your own. Even the ones who didn't realise they *were* your own.

'Howells.'

'Mmm?'

'Get your nose out of that book just for a minute, will you?'

Eleanor Howells lay stretched out on her belly on the bed, her spectacles on the end of her nose and a favourite detective thriller inches from her face.

'What is it, Frankenberg? I'm just getting to a good bit.'

Hester and Creena, framed in the doorway, exchanged glances.

'It's all very well for you, Howells, reading your penny-dreadfuls,' observed Hester with mock indignation, 'but have a heart: some of us are swotting jolly hard for our finals.'

Eleanor treated herself to a faintly malicious grin.

'Ah yes, but I don't remember you being full of the milk of human kindness when I was taking *my* finals, back in June – do you, Quilliam?'

'Well . . .'

'In fact, I distinctly remember Frankenberg keeping me awake half the night, droning on about some dreamy adjutant she'd met at the Café Royal.'

'He *was* fun,' conceded Frankenberg, casting her mind back several dalliances. She shuddered. 'But his parents lived in Scunthorpe.'

'What's wrong with Scunthorpe?' protested Howells. 'I've got a great-aunt in Scunthorpe.'

'What's *right* with Scunthorpe?'

'Have you ever been there?'

'No, and I have no intention of going.'

'Frankenberg, you're such a snob,' muttered Creena.

'Now the day of doom is fast approaching, I suppose you've come to beg for the gift of my superior knowledge,' commented Howells, turning the pages of her paperback novelette.

'No, actually we've come to beg for black uniform stockings,' said Creena.

'Stockings? What happened to yours?'

'I wish I knew,' replied Frankenberg tartly. 'Honestly, I rinsed mine and hung them out to dry in the bathroom, and when I went back to fetch them – they'd disappeared!'

'And Griffiths across the way had two brassières stolen, you know, just the other day,' cut in Creena.

'Well, well,' said Howells. 'This pilfering problem really is getting out of hand. Drugs, food – and now even our underwear.' She giggled. 'If it gets any worse, they'll be stealing the patients!'

'I rather wish they would,' replied Frankenberg.

'Remember your vocation, dear girl,' Howells chided her. 'I thought you'd turned over a new leaf.'

'Yes, well, I have. But there's still one or two I could cheerfully strangle . . .'

Creena paid little attention to Frankenberg's bluster. Over the last six months, Hester had begun to show what she could do – that beneath the snobby, intolerant exterior lurked a good practical nurse; and one who had a real aptitude for the complexities and stresses of the operating theatre. Whether or not she had left it too late to pull her socks up, only next month's finals would tell. That would be the moment of truth for them all.

Howells got up off the bed and walked over to her chest of drawers.

'Only two spare pairs, I'm afraid,' she said, pulling out four of the familiar uniform stockings.

Frankenberg pulled a face.

'I was hoping you wouldn't have any, so Matron would have to let me wear silk.'

'Fat chance!' laughed Creena. The thick black lisle stockings were universally detested by the students, especially as they had to buy them with their own precious clothing coupons. But regulations were regulations.

'Nylon would be bliss,' sighed Howells. 'If only I had a rich American boyfriend like Staff Nurse Kenroy.'

'Personally, I'd settle for having my uniform stockings back,' retorted Frankenberg. 'I wish I knew who's behind all this pilfering. I mean, it's not just the underwear, is it?'

'What this needs,' observed Howells with a wink, 'is the expert touch.'

'But the police haven't managed to catch anyone,' pointed out Creena.

'Ah, but what about a private investigator?'

'What?' snorted Frankenberg.

'You mean like in those detective novels you're always reading?'

Howells pushed her glasses up to the bridge of her nose.

'Precisely – Inspector Howells!'

Hester and Creena burst out laughing, but Eleanor simply gave a defiant toss of her head and went back to reading her whodunnit.

'You'll see!' she said. 'I'll find out what's going on, don't you worry.'

As she walked back along the corridor with Frankenberg, Creena felt just a touch uneasy. She had had her own suspicions over the last few weeks, ever since she had helped Harry pick up his pile of boxes. And what about the time she had seen him hanging around the hospital kitchens, as though he didn't want to be seen?

Could the culprit really be Harry?

On 1 September, 1942, Creena and her set filed into the old hospital ballroom to take their state finals.

This is it, thought Hester Frankenberg, clutching the brand-new gold-nibbed fountain pen which her father and mother had bought her specially for the occasion. I've spent the last three years doing nothing but complain, and now I'm going to fail. And what's more, it'll serve me right. I really did want to be a nurse – why have I gone and messed things up? Why, oh why, didn't I knuckle down and work hard, right from the start?

Marian Clarke-Herbert thought about her sister Lucy, back home now and convalescing after a dreadful farm accident. Lucy had always said her sister was the brains of the family – she'd be extremely miffed if Marian let her down now. So she'd just jolly well have to pass, wouldn't she?

Taking her seat in the quiet vastness of the ballroom, Dillie Bayliss could only marvel that she was here at all. All those years ago, when she had first come to Bishop Street, she could never have dared imagine that her dreams might come true. And would they? Dry-mouthed, she stared into space, willing the ordeal to be over before it had even begun.

For Creena, today was a chance to achieve something – not for anyone else, not any more. Just for herself. She had begun, three years ago, hoping that success would make Mother and Father proud of her; but that scarcely mattered any more. She might as well not exist as far as they were concerned.

But nursing existed; her career existed. And even if her parents never spoke to her again, she would have that. She owed it to herself not to fail. As she picked up her pen to write her name on the fresh white sheet of paper, she understood that the future was now in her own hands.

Chapter 23

Hester Frankenberg adjusted her cap as she got up to leave the nurses' common room.

'It's hardly fair,' she observed. 'In any other hospital we'd be staff nurses by now, not fourth-year probationers.'

Marian raised a cynical eyebrow.

'In any other hospital, Frankenberg, you'd have been chucked out after PTS. I still can't believe you passed your finals. I mean, what about poor Jennie Daventry?'

'I worked hard for those exams,' retorted Frankenberg indignantly.

'Yes – for about a week beforehand,' replied Marian. 'Some of us worked for the whole three years, you know!'

'Fighting again, children?'

Eleanor Howells burst into the room with her usual exuberance. Howells was so full of energy that she didn't simply enter a room – she exploded into it, always ready to jolly her patients back to health and generally set the world to rights. She might be almost twenty-four years old, mused Creena, but she still retained all the qualities that had made her captain of her grammar school's hockey team.

'Oh, don't mind those two,' said Creena, putting down the newspaper and slipping on her coat. 'Clarky thinks it's not fair, Daventry failing and Frankenberg getting through. And Frankenberg's moaning – as usual.'

Howells poured herself a cup of tea, loosened her uniform belt and flopped down into a tatty but comfortable armchair.

'Life's too short,' she said. 'Daventry's bound to pass second time around, and Frankenberg did try hard for her exams.'

'Thank you,' said Hester, with a small but triumphant shake of her perfectly groomed head.

'Even if she did only just pass by the skin of her teeth,' commented Marian.

'Anyhow,' Howells continued, 'we may all have passed, but we're none of us up to Bayliss's standard, are we?'

'Nor likely to be,' added Creena, swinging her bag on to her shoulder. 'She must be up for the gold medal when we do hospital finals next year.'

She recalled how proud Mo Doyle had been when she learned of Dillie's sparkling success, and felt a twinge of resentment as she thought of the letter she had written to her parents, telling them that she, too, had passed. They hadn't even bothered to reply.

'Oh, don't talk about hospital finals,' groaned Frankenberg. 'I've only just got over state finals, and they were two months ago!' She glanced at Creena, buttoning up her coat.

'Off out?'

'I'm not on duty again till six.'

'Got a new chap?' Nothing interested Clarke-Herbert so much as other people's love lives.

'Heavens, no. I just thought I'd pop over to Long Wall Yard for a couple of hours.'

Hester's eyes rolled heavenwards.

'You and your good works! Anyone would think you had a guilty conscience or something.'

Creena's heart stopped for just a split second, and she felt her fingers and toes going very cold as the blood rushed out of them. No one at the Royal Lambeth knew the full story of what had happened; except Dillie. No one knew about the guilt and the bitterness – although Howells had asked once why she never talked about her parents any more. She forced herself to meet Frankenberg's interested gaze.

'If you ask me, Frankenberg, it's you who ought to have the guilty conscience,' she retorted with as much spirit as she could muster.

'What?'

'Bayliss and I spotted you climbing in through the bathroom window on Sunday night. Good job it was Home Sister's evening off.'

'Hope he was worth it,' said Clarke-Herbert. 'But knowing Frankenberg, he probably wasn't.' She drank the rest of her tea and leaned forward conspiratorially. 'Frankenberg's got rotten taste in men.'

Hester did not respond. Surprisingly, she didn't feel very much like being bitchy today. In fact she didn't feel at all well. Perhaps she was getting a cold – or perhaps it was love. He was a very handsome lieutenant-colonel, after all, if a little short.

'Well, I must be off,' said Marian, washing up her cup. 'If I don't get back to my ward, Sister'll think

I've been pilfered, along with all that missing bed linen.'

'And my best silk camiknickers,' said Creena. 'You know, it really is getting out of hand, what with hospital equipment and food being taken as well. They're missing a box of M and Bs from the dispensary, you know. What sort of person robs from sick people?'

'Someone who's even sicker,' replied Frankenberg, smoothing down a stray lock of hair. 'Anyhow, I thought Inspector Howells was supposed to be investigating the case.'

Howells swallowed a mouthful of bread and marge.

'Oh, she is,' she replied. 'It's just a bit more complicated than I'd expected. But I have one or two clues.' She tapped the side of her nose.

'Spill the beans then,' said Marian. 'Tell us who it is.' But Howells shook her head.

'Strictly confidential,' she replied. 'You'll know soon enough.'

As Creena left the sitting room and walked towards the sand-bagged hospital entrance, she wondered if Howells really did have any idea who had been pilfering. Surely her own suspicions had been unfounded – no one who worked in the hospital could possibly bear to steal from it, especially in time of war. And yet . . .

She spotted Harry just as she was crossing the road. He was emerging from the side entrance near the hospital kitchens, and was struggling under the weight of a large lidded pail. What could he be taking away from the hospital? On an irrational impulse, Creena decided to follow him, to see where he would go.

Harry limped along with surprising speed, his club foot proving far less of an impediment than the heavy bucket, which kept swinging against his leg as he walked. From time to time he darted glances around him, as though afraid that he would meet someone he knew and have to provide some sort of explanation.

Not very much further on, he disappeared left into a dingy side- street. For a moment Creena hung back. Perhaps she shouldn't follow him any further. What if he was doing something perfectly honest and above board? Would he ever forgive her for having suspected him? Harry just wasn't the type to be a thief. And yet . . .

In for a penny, in for a pound, thought Creena as she quickened her pace and turned into the side-street – just in time to see Harry disappearing round the back of a bombed-out building.

She followed, watched by a gaggle of children. Even in November they wore nothing but rags – the boys in cut-down trousers and tattered shirts, with perhaps a moth-eaten sleeveless pullover on top; the girls lank-haired and skinny in stained print frocks, topped off with ragged cardigans. On their feet they wore Wellington boots or battered canvas pumps, their hard-pressed mothers too short of money to afford proper shoes.

Three years ago, Creena might have been shocked by them, but now she regarded them with a professional compassion rather than an ineffectual pity. These were children who needed helping in practical ways. She would have to talk about them to Millie Duval. Millie would know what best to do, so as to help them without their feeling patronised.

'One, two, three, O'Leary, my ball's gone down the airey,' sang a thin-faced girl as Creena rounded the corner of the bombed-out house. But the girl's singing was not what Creena was listening to. She could hear another sound – curiously familiar, peculiarly nostalgic. But it couldn't be – could it? Not here on a bomb site, in the middle of Lambeth Marsh.

No, no. She must be mistaken.

'Harry?'

The ward orderly spun round like a safe-cracker caught red-handed.

'Nurse? Nurse *Quilliam*?' Harry's expression was a mixture of astonishment and alarm.

'I'm sorry. I ... er ... Well, I followed you,' confessed Creena lamely.

'Followed me? But why?'

'I saw you coming out of the hospital with that pail, and I thought ... An awful lot of stuff's gone missing lately ...'

'Oh. You did, did you?' Harry's expression became not so much apologetic as belligerently defensive. 'Oh yes, I'm a real hard case, Nurse – a real criminal master-mind. You want to see what's in there?' He indicated the pail.

'I ... er ...' Creena now felt acutely embarrassed – not so much the avenging angel as the fool who had stepped in where angels feared to tread.

'Go ahead. Take a good long look.'

Harry took the lid off the pail and the warm stink of leftover food floated up to Creena's nostrils. She knew that smell – it was the smell of the hot mash her mother had been so adept at making. Two and two fused seamlessly together.

'Could I see them?' Creena asked him.

'See what?'

'The chickens. You're keeping chickens here. I can hear them.'

Harry looked her up and down, quite bemused. He wasn't sure how to take this latest development.

'You want to see the chickens?' he repeated.

'I used to keep hens myself,' said Creena. 'Back home. Twenty-six chickens and a cockerel called Orry. I had a pet hen with a lame leg too,' she added, suddenly thinking that this must sound quite strange.

With a shrug of incomprehension, Harry held out his hand.

'Best take hold then, Nurse. You'll need a hand stepping over all this rubble – proper mess it is round back.'

She gripped his hand and scrambled with difficulty over the pile of shattered bricks, where grass and fireweed had already started to grow. Nature did not waste any time in reclaiming her own, mused Creena. In fact, nature was a far more powerful force than all of Hitler's bombers put together.

'They're through here.' Harry led her through what had once been the kitchen door and out into the remains of the back yard, now fenced off to form a secure enclosure with a battered shed at one end. 'Poor bastards who lived here took a direct hit – pardon my language, Nurse. Five-hundred-pounder took down the house and made a real mess of the yard, but it left the privy with hardly a scratch on it. Bloody daft war, isn't it?'

Creena nodded slowly, but her eyes were fastened on what was inside the wire enclosure. There, scratching about in the dirt, were a dozen russet-coloured hens, their plumage somewhat dulled by plaster dust, but plump and bright-eyed, with yellow-grey legs and bright pink combs.

'You've been taking kitchen scraps to feed your chickens?'

Harry shrugged.

'The odd pail of leftover veg – but only now and then, mind, when there's nothing else going. I figure they won't miss one pail of scraps out of the pig bin.'

'But why?'

'You've seen those kids out there, Nurse. Thinner than mongrel dogs and twice as wild. Their mothers can't feed them – those as have got mothers. Me and my mates have been putting a bit of extra food their way – mainly eggs, but my mates have got a pig over at the ARP post in Southwark, so there's a bit of pork now and then. There's a chicken once in a while, too. Trouble is, none of us can bring ourselves to do the little blighters in.

'The thing is, Nurse, you can't get the corn for the chicken feed. Oh, we get by most of the time, but now and then I get a pail of scraps from the hospital kitchens. I know it's stealing, but . . .'

Creena shook her head and laid her hand on his.

'I'm sorry, Harry. It was stupid of me to suspect you of taking that other stuff.'

'Wish I knew who *was* nicking it,' commented Harry. 'Never mind the chickens – I'd wring *his* bloody neck for him.'

The arrival of the hot mash sent the hens into a frenzy,

clucking and scratching and milling about, with their fat black cockerel marshalling them towards the feeding trough.

'Like a sergeant major he is, Nurse,' observed Harry as he tipped the mash into the trough and it was submerged in a flurry of dusty feathers.

Creena watched the chickens with mixed emotions. Part of her was miles away, in the yard behind Ballakeeill schoolhouse, throwing corn and little pieces of cheese for her mother's hens. She was a schoolgirl again, her tangled red hair escaping from its green ribbon, and a darn in her cardigan where she had torn it whilst out blackberrying with Frankie. She hadn't really minded the scolding, for that day had been perfect, those blackberries so succulent and so sweet as they purpled her fingers and mouth.

Frankie, Robert, Polly the little lame hen who had so loved to be picked up and cuddled: all were gone now, all spirited away. And so was the gangly little girl who had laughed in the autumn sunshine, as Robert chased the escaped cockerel into Ida's spotless kitchen and captured him, covered in flour but crowing for all he was worth.

She and Frankie had sworn that day that they would be best friends for ever; and the promise had seemed such an easy one to keep. The future had seemed as huge and as bright as the great Manx sky, which stretched unblemished from horizon to horizon like a shiny glass dome.

Funny how, in retrospect, her childhood seemed precious, golden, almost perfect. Now, those childhood years might never have existed – for it was plain that Ida and George wished that Creena didn't exist. Perhaps it was better that way. After all, it was obvious that her parents had never loved her the way they loved Robert and Tommy and Amy. Otherwise they would never have done this to her – cutting her off without even giving her a chance to explain.

Yes, it was probably for the best if she simply gave up trying to contact them. That was plainly what they wanted. Perhaps it was what she wanted too.

'Look,' began Harry, 'I'm sorry I spoke a bit sharp.'

'I'm the one who ought to be apologising, Harry.'

Harry hesitated.

'You're not going to tell on me, then?'

'My lips are sealed.'

'You're a pal, Nurse Quilliam. You all right, are you? You looked miles away just then.'

'I'm fine, Harry. Just thinking about something that happened a long, long time ago.'

In the first week of December, Creena found herself outside London for the first time in months and months. Despite the lull in bombing raids, patients were still being routinely transferred from the Royal Lambeth to the EMS hospitals in the country – not only for the patients' safety, but because so much of the London site was out of action.

This was the first time that Creena had escorted patients to Epsom, and she found herself looking forward to it. Twelve weeks on the basement Male Surgical ward had left her drained and longing for a change of scene. It would only mean a single day away from the hospital, but even so it would give her a chance to recharge her batteries, take stock of where she was going.

Once the patients had been made as comfortable as possible in the ambulance, Creena turned to take in a last view of the Royal Lambeth. It was in quite a state. Repeated bombing had brought down two of the ward blocks, and the now abandoned private patients' block was looking decidedly unsteady – shored up all along one side with thick wooden props and *ad hoc* scaffolding. Even in the undamaged blocks the boarded-up windows made the place look derelict.

The poor old Royal. And yet the hospital had kept going night and day, with the casualty department only closing for one night during the whole of the Blitz, when a direct hit had taken out the hospital's electricity and gas supplies, and fractured a water main, flooding half the basement.

Well, the Yanks had finally turned up, Monty's lads had taken El Alamein, and perhaps things wouldn't go all Hitler's way on the Eastern Front either. It wasn't all doom and gloom – not like it had been eighteen months or even a year ago.

The ambulance rattled out of London, taking a circuitous route to avoid potholes and craters, and headed south through the Surrey countryside. It was tolerably pretty; and it was certainly good to see trees and fields again, the grass frost-dusted like icing on a lumpy cake. It wasn't like the island though; where were the hillsides, patched with bracken and heather, and stunted hawthorns gnarled and twisted by the driving wind? Where were the rocky coves and the clear streams? She longed for the glint of the steel-grey, sparkling sea as she stood on Bradda Head, looking south towards Calf Sound.

Before lunchtime they were driving through the gates of the EMS hospital. After so long in London, Creena found its tidiness quite a shock. Standing in rolling green acres, the ward blocks and wooden huts had a neat intactness which jarred after seeing so many buildings in Lambeth Marsh reduced to rubble. Nurses in the crisp uniforms of the Royal Lambeth Hospital bustled in tidy, airy wards, and here and there a window or two stood open, to let the convalescent patients enjoy the benefit of the clean Surrey air. Only the strips of sticky paper crisscrossing the windowpanes reminded the visitor that there was a war on. It was a completely different world.

After settling her patients in their new ward, Creena crossed to the refectory block, where she had been told to report for her lunch before making the return journey. On her way across, she glanced through a window into PTS, which had moved to the Surrey site. Brand-new, well-scrubbed probationers were practising their resuscitation techniques on a dummy, and Creena smiled to herself as she remembered her own ineffectual first efforts. With luck, the war might be over before this batch of first-years returned to the Royal Lambeth – or whatever was left of it by then.

As she was climbing the steps to the refectory block, she almost collided with a brown-haired senior probationer wearing the special badge which Matron had issued to all nurses working away from London, so that they would still feel part of the Royal's tight-knit community.

'Quilliam! Well I never – a friendly face!'

'Daventry! I didn't know they'd sent you down here.'

'Last week it was,' explained Jennie Daventry. 'Principal

Tutor felt it'd be best if I came to Surrey until I do my retake. I came down with Staff Nurse Waverley.'

'Waverley? I didn't realise she was here either.'

'I think Matron felt it'd be best to send her here, after . . . you know . . .'

Creena nodded.

'Terrible business, that.'

'Having lunch?' enquired Daventry. 'I'll join you, if I may. Between you and me, meals are the highlight of the day here – such as they are. It's not exactly gay Paree, but then that's probably why Matron's sent me down here, so that I shan't be distracted from my swotting.'

They collected a tray of luncheon sausage and rice pudding, and sat down by the window.

'I was sorry to hear about your exams,' said Creena cautiously. She knew how awful it was having one's shortcomings raked over.

Daventry shrugged.

'Oh, c'est la vie,' she sighed. 'Between you and me, I just didn't work hard enough. I shall pass next time, you'll see. In fact I daren't fail – Daddy's offered to buy me a super watch if I pass!'

'What's it like here?' enquired Creena. 'It seems very quiet.'

'Quiet? Not really – I mean, the work's enough to keep even Bayliss busy, what with all the injured servicemen. We've started to get quite a few from North Africa now, you know – some dreadful injuries there are, too, and then there's the malaria.' She cut her slice of luncheon sausage up into dainty cubes, as though putting off the moment of having to eat it.

'What do you do in your off-duty? Marian said it was deadly dull when she was down here.'

'There's not much on the go, though Sister Tutor does her best to keep us entertained. Guess what – she starches and gaufres caps for a penny, and uses the money to buy records for us! We have musical evenings once a week. That's about it, though – Frankenberg would go potty.'

Creena chuckled.

'I think she's going potty anyway,' she said. 'She was working on the children's ward and she caught mumps!'

'Really!'

'And of course, none of us can go and see her in case we catch it too, so she's bored to tears. I think she must be driving Sick Bay Sister round the bend.'

'I can imagine. I don't think our Hester would take to the country life, do you?'

'Not unless there were some wealthy farmers for her to set her cap at.'

'Fat chance! Mind you, we Royals are well off compared to the nurses in the mental colony. We share most of the facilities with them, you know. Poor things get paid practically nothing, and they seem to feed them only on bread and jam. Sister Tutor's up in arms about it, trying to get something done.'

'Knowing Sister Tutor, she'll probably succeed.'

Creena finished her first course and moved on to the rice pudding.

'It smells a bit odd,' she commented.

'Oh, that'll be the peppermint,' said Daventry dismissively.

'Peppermint! In rice pudding?'

'Chef seems to think that if he puts peppermint essence into all the puddings, we shan't notice the saccharin.'

Creena took a deep breath, put a spoonful in her mouth and forced it down.

'Hmm. I hate to think what he'll dish up on Christmas Day.'

'Peppermint-flavoured turkey, probably.'

'Ugh! Give me yellow peril every time.'

'How is the dear old Royal?' enquired Daventry. She had only been in Surrey a week, but already the London site was acquiring a certain nostalgic charm.

'Still standing,' replied Creena with a rueful smile, thinking of the barrage-balloon emplacement where the lab block had been, and the private patients' block with its shored-up walls and boarded windows. 'But only just.'

On Christmas Day 1942, the church bells rang out all over the country for the first time in three years. Shaken by the vibrations of traffic and the bells, the private patients' block shed a few more lumps of masonry, but no one paid much heed. Christmas was Christmas, even in wartime, and the bells made the day even more special for everyone at the Royal Lambeth Hospital.

It was as though the whole city was coming out of hiding after a long sleep, called out by the sound of the bells and blinking in the watery, horizontal sunlight. Among them were the woman and five children from Oakley Street who had dragged themselves out of Lambeth North tube station for the first time in almost a year. They had taken to living permanently underground, for fear of the bombing. When at last they were brought in to Casualty on Christmas morning, the children were little better than walking skeletons, their mother half out of her wits after seeing her husband and father killed in the Blitz.

Creena faced the day with mixed feelings. Christmas was a strange time, a time for extreme sorrow and extreme joy, for rejection as well as reconciliation.

Not that there had been any reconciliation – and she hadn't expected that there would be. In the room she shared with Dillie, Creena sat among her Christmas gifts: a cake from Dillie and Mo, a hairbrush from Aunt Bessie, perfume from Cousin Mona and Alexa, and a huge bunch of bananas from Jack Doyle. But nothing from Ida and George. No box of mince pies or a chicken leg meticulously wrapped in greaseproof paper.

Ah well. She leant on the windowsill and watched the world go by. Time to put the past aside and get on with her life. Back on the ward, the medical students would be larking about, the patients waiting for the consultant to carve the turkey, and even Sister would be enjoying a small dry sherry in her office.

Time to emerge from her own dark hiding-place and come to terms with her life as it really was, not as she might once have wished it could be.

By the middle of January, Jack Doyle was also wishing his life could be different – or, at least, that he could be living it somewhere else.

Sid Clayden bit the end off a fresh cigar and spat it out. His piggy eyes narrowed to malevolent slits.

'You've let me down again, Jack Doyle.' He shook his

head in mock sorrow. 'An' that's a damned shame, 'cause I don't take kindly to bein' let down.'

Jack moistened his dry lips with the tip of his tongue.

'I'm sorry, Mr Clayden. Real sorry.'

'Sorry don't pay the bills, Jack. Sorry don't get me back my five 'undred nicker.'

Five hundred quid. The very thought of it made Jack feel queasy. It was more money than he'd ever seen in his life. Which just goes to show what a cheapjack, second-rate spiv I am, he told himself ruefully. Serves me right for thinking I could play with the big boys and not get my fingers burned.

'Look, Mr Clayden. I'll do anything...'

Clayden laughed. It was like hearing a corpse laugh.

'Do what, Jack? Pay me back wiv the profit from your tot stall? Nah. I don't think so, Jack.'

Jack knew it was his fault, that he was up to his neck in it this time. He had organised the card school, used his contacts to bring in the lambs for slaughter. Sid had relied on him to select easy marks, men from all over South London who were addicted to gambling and would sell their souls to get the money to buy themselves into a game.

It had worked all right in the past. But the longer things went on, the wider Jack had to cast his net to find suitable players. And of course, the further outside his Lambeth territory he went, the less he knew, the more he had to rely on his contacts. This time he had fouled up good and proper.

'That was careless, Jack.'

'Yes, Mr Clayden.'

Jack wished that Clayden's latest recruit, 'Gentleman'

447

Johnny Shaw, would stop smirking at him from the corner of the room. He knew Shaw's game all right; the little toerag was just waiting for a chance to muscle in, get him off the scene.

'That cardsharp took me for every penny in the bank, Jack. A cool five hundred. And to think I trusted you.'

'You can trust me, Mr Clayden. It was just a mistake. It won't happen again.'

'No, Jack, you're right. It won't. One more mistake and you're history, Doyle. I'm sure Johnny here would be more than happy to take over your duties – ain't that right, Johnny?'

Johnny pulled on his cigarette and blew a neat smoke ring. Smug bastard, thought Jack.

'Just waitin' for your say-so, Mr Clayden, *sir*.'

'I told you, Mr Clayden, I won't make no more mistakes,' Jack repeated, trying to hide his mingled alarm and exasperation. Yes, he wanted to give up being Sid Clayden's lackey – but not floating face-down in the Thames with a knife in his back. He needed to play this one very carefully indeed – it wasn't just a question of looking out for himself but for Mo and Dillie and the kids too.

'Good,' said Sid. 'I knew you'd come round to my way of thinkin'. But remember this, Jack: Sid Clayden always calls in his debts. And one way or another, you're going to pay back what you owe me.'

'Happy birthday to you; happy birthday to you; happy birthday, dear Albie – happy birthday to you!'

Albie Powell blinked in the light from eighteen birthday candles, carefully saved up over the years by Mona from her children's party cakes. Duggie Mylchreest might have been a blight on her life, but she hadn't let his drunken violence stop the kids from having a normal childhood.

'Go on, Albie – blow them out!'

Sheepish and red-faced, Albie drew an immense breath and blew out all the candles but one – the last one being finished off with relish by his brother Kenny.

'That's cheating!' piped up Mona's elder daughter Voirrey.

'No it isn't, stupid,' retorted Kenny, tweaking her hair.

'Ow – Mummy!'

Little Duggie, meanwhile, was engrossed in the spectacle of his elder sister and distant cousin having a lively set-to on the other side of the table. He watched through the table legs with intense interest as Voirrey stamped energetically on Kenny's foot, and Kenny retaliated by taking a swipe at her – which she dodged with athletic ease.

'Behave!' snapped Alexa, clapping her hands. 'Honestly, Kenny, I'd have thought at your age you'd have known better. It is your brother's birthday party, you know.'

Kenny shuffled his feet. Alexa noticed with a slight softening of the heart that the back of his neck was chafed bright red from scrubbing. When all was said and done he was still just a child. Her child.

'Sorry, Ma.'

'Come on, Albie,' broke in Mona. 'Cut your cake. I'm sorry it isn't very big...'

'Nonsense, you've done wonders,' retorted Bessie. 'You'd never guess it wasn't proper marzipan.' She wondered for a moment what marvel of a cake Ida Quilliam would have conjured up if she had been here – but Ida had found a plausible excuse to be somewhere else. Somewhere where she would not face a barrage of uncomfortable questions about Creena.

'I used ground rice, margarine and almond essence,' explained Mona. 'I got the icing sugar from Giacomo. I don't know where he gets all these things, but I thought it better not to ask!'

Standing in the small circle of guests around the farmhouse table, Alexa watched her elder boy cutting the cake and felt a lump rise in her throat. She wasn't one to cry, but the arrival of Albie's call-up papers had almost broken her heart. One day a boy, the next expected to behave as if he were a full-grown man; it just didn't seem right. It was no time at all since she'd held him in her arms, a tiny, red-faced newborn with blue eyes and a mop of straight black hair. She'd loved him to distraction then, and she still did. And next week he would be leaving for the mainland, to join his army unit. It was downright unthinkable, that was what it was.

'Thanks, Ma. Thanks, Auntie Mona.'

Albie bit into the first slice of birthday cake and wiped the crumbs from his mouth. There was a fine peach-fuzz of hair on his upper lip, but he still ate sloppily – like a boy, not a man.

'Happy birthday, son.' Alexa gave him a swift peck on the cheek then turned away. She didn't want him to see her upset. With a deep breath she turned to Mona and took her by the arm. 'Kitchen,' she said.

'What – why?'

'Now.'

Alexa led Mona out of the parlour and into the kitchen,

shutting the door gently behind them so as to afford a little privacy.

'What's the matter?'

'I'm not blind, Mona.'

Mona returned her gaze quizzically, blonde head on one side, blue eyes wide and innocent.

'I don't understand.'

'It's Giacomo.'

'What about him?'

Alexa sighed. She knew darned well that Mona wasn't nearly as dim as she was making out.

'Do I have to spell it out? Look, Mona, I know what you've been getting up to – you and Giacomo.'

Mona did not respond for a long moment, the silence broken only by the dripping of the kitchen tap.

'Oh,' she said at last.

'Is that all you can say – "oh"?'

'What do you want me to say, Alexa? Do you want me to say I'm sorry? Because I'm not.'

'Oh, Mona.' Alexa's voice was a long, low sigh. She leaned her back against the range, its warmth welcome on this raw February day when the wind roared down the chimneys and rattled the windowpanes. 'You have to get a grip – you have to stop it. Right now.'

'But Alexa . . .'

'Now, Mona.' Alexa's voice softened. How could she make Mona see that she wasn't trying to rob her of the chance for a little happiness, only to stop her getting herself into worse trouble than even Duggie Mylchreest could cause?

She took hold of Mona's hands.

'Look at me.'

Mona's blue eyes flicked up until they were gazing straight into Alexa's.

'It's a dangerous game you're playing, Mona.'

'I'm careful.'

Alexa groaned inwardly.

'But mistakes can happen. They *do* happen. And if they do, Mona, you can't rely on an old drunk like Euan McPherson to get rid of your trouble.'

Chapter 24

'Miss, miss, I done yer a picture.'

Millie Duval accepted the scrawled masterpiece with a smile of genuine appreciation. The stick figure might not win any prizes for artistic merit, but Millie knew that the picture marked a small but significant victory. This was the first time Annie Mason had done anything constructive since she had started coming to the Long Wall Yard shelter group. Mostly she just liked to disrupt whatever the other children were doing.

Millie smoothed out the creases in the picture and scrutinised it. A boldly painted black figure with bright red eyes and enormous round spectacles filled the middle of the picture, accompanied by a small brown blob in the lower right-hand corner.

'Thank you, Annie.'

'That's you, that is, miss,' Annie announced proudly. 'You in your siren suit. Did I get the glasses right?' She scratched one of the sores on her bare arm and the scab broke, leaving a smear of blood on the too-white flesh.

'It's lovely, Annie. But what's this?' Millie indicated the brown blob.

'That's your car, miss, what you drove Cyril to the seaside in.'

Last winter had been too much for Cyril Grimes. The boy had been getting thinner for months, despite Millie's best efforts, and when he started spitting blood she knew that his persistent, hacking cough meant more than yet another bout of bronchitis.

And so Cyril – protesting furiously – had been taken to the Royal Lambeth, where a mild form of tuberculosis had been diagnosed. A week later Millie had volunteered to drive him down to the TB hospital – not simply because Cyril loved cars, but because she feared that if she'd left him to the nurses, he would have legged it back home before they'd so much as got him into the ambulance.

Nine-year-old Abe Collins piped up.

''Ow's Cyril, miss?'

'Cyril's getting better.'

'He ain't goin' to die then?'

'No, he's not going to die. I told you, he's getting better.'

'Cross yer 'eart?'

Millie dutifully drew her finger across her chest.

'Cross my heart.'

'Only, the doc said Mary's ma were gettin' better. 'E just kept on sayin' she were gettin' better, swore she were, but she still pegged out, didn't she?' His facial muscles tensed, and he narrowed his eyes. 'You can't trust no one.'

'You can trust me.'

The boy spat, a small explosion of white phlegm hitting the ground at Millie's feet. She did not flinch. She knew from experience that Abe was only testing her, trying to see if she would lose her temper with him and give him a beating, like his mother's latest boyfriend was always doing.

'That's dirty, Abe Collins. You're a dirty dog,' Annie piped up.

'Dirty dog, dirty dog,' chanted the small circle of children.

'Do you want to do some more painting?' asked Millie quickly, keen to stop this latest disturbance developing into a full-blown riot.

'Dunno, miss. Painting's for kids.'

These children – persistent truants who spent most of their time on the streets from the day they learned to walk – did not take kindly to being asked to sit still. Their concentration span was painfully short. No sooner had you got them sitting down at a table with paints and pencils than half of them would be up and running about, throwing things at each other or trading the most vulgar insults they could come up with.

And at the end of a day or evening session, when the children left the shelter, Millie would always find that something had disappeared – a pot of paint, a sheet of paper, a box of pencils. These children, who had never had anything much of their own, found it difficult to understand that everything Millie provided at the shelter was for them, and them alone. And so, each time something disappeared, she replaced it from her own funds. Sooner or later, she would prove to them that they didn't have to steal things in order to enjoy them.

'Do you want to do some sewing then?'

Annie wrinkled her nose.

'Nah. Summink else.'

The child scratched her head violently. Head lice were quite a problem at Long Wall Yard, but when Creena had suggested washing all the children's hair in quassia lotion, Millie had refused. She didn't want them feeling she was yet another do-gooder, bent on turning them into well-scrubbed, well-behaved, middle-class children. Millie was quite prepared to put up with a few lice if it helped her win the children's trust.

'What then?'

Abe Collins pushed his way forward, an expression of mischief on his face.

'Tell us 'ow you make a baby.'

Millie did not let any trace of emotion show on her face.

'I think you already know that,' she replied.

'Tell us, miss, tell us!' chorused the others. Even the better-behaved girls left off sewing their rag dolls and came over to gather in a circle around Millie's chair.

'Very well then. A man and a woman who like each other very much can make a baby together.'

Abe sneered dismissively.

'That ain't sayin' nothing. I bet she don't even know.'

'Yes, how?' demanded the onlookers. 'Tell us how, we want to 'ear how.'

'Why don't you ask me what you don't know?'

'Do they *do* it?'

'Yes.'

Abe paused for a moment, then pounced.

'So 'ave you done it then, miss?'

Millie suppressed a smile. It still struck her as odd that the children should insist on calling a mother of four 'miss'.

'Yes.'

A frisson of lascivious delight ran around the assembled throng.

'Was you . . . ?'

'Was I what, Annie?'

'Was you *naked*, miss?'

Millie hesitated before replying.

'I don't have to tell you about my private life, Annie.'

'She's fibbin',' sniffed Abe Collins. 'She ain't never done it.'

'Does it hurt?'

'No.'

'But what do you say when you want it to stop?'

Puzzled, Millie shook her head.

'You don't have to. The end comes quite naturally by itself.'

Annie promptly put on a grown-up voice and started shouting the words she had heard night after night, since she was a tiny child:

'I've 'ad enough of it, you filthy beast. Don't you hurt me no more. Let me alone . . .' When she had finished, she turned back to Millie.

'Did you like it, miss?'

'Yes, I did.'

'*Really?*'

'Really.'

Annie shuddered, and a dark shadow of disgust crossed her face.

'I don't want to 'ave a baby, not never.'

'I wish I 'ad a baby,' whispered a girl with lank, mousy hair. 'I wish I 'ad a little baby boy like my sister's. But I ain't got my period yet.'

'Miss,' began Annie.

'Yes?'

'Do boys 'ave a period?'

'No, Annie, they don't.'

Incredulous glances were exchanged around the circle. This, Millie suddenly realised, was the longest time that the children had ever paid attention to anything. Perhaps she ought to ask Creena to give them a proper talk about the facts of life. Ignorance was so dangerous – and many of these girls would be in the family way almost before they had stopped being children themselves.

'Then 'ow . . . ?'

Millie put her hand up for silence. This could go on all night unless she stopped it now.

'Later,' she said.

'Aw, miss.'

'Another day we'll talk about it properly. Now I must go and have a word with Miss Quilliam.'

One of the older boys brought the discussion to a timely halt, pulling his small brother out of his chair.

'I got to take little Jimmy 'ome. He's wet 'isself.'

Millie left the shelter and walked across the yard to another brick-built hut, where Creena was taking some of the smaller children for dressing-up games. The shelter group had inherited a huge box of old theatrical costumes from a bombed-out theatre, and dressing-up had proved surprisingly popular, even with the normally tough and aggressive boys.

She found Creena in the midst of organised chaos, the children screeching with laughter as they chased each other round the shelter, dressed in a glorious mishmash of assorted satin and lace.

'Is everything all right?' Millie asked.

Creena grinned.

'I think they're enjoying themselves.'

'I'd say that's rather an understatement!'

Creena too was enjoying this afternoon, more than she'd expected. She had never been put in charge of a whole group of children before and – although she found it impossible to control them – at least the little ones were friendlier, less mistrustful than their older brothers and sisters. It was just a pity that so few of them came to the shelter group regularly enough for her to get to know them properly.

As Creena and Millie were chatting, the door opened and a small girl ran in, her newly finished rag doll clutched to her chest.

'That's a lovely dolly,' observed Creena.

'Dolly's 'avin' a baby,' announced the small girl.

Creena smiled and patted the girl's head.

'That's nice.'

Millie's expression was one of concern.

'I know, Rosie,' she said to the child, then glanced at Creena and said quietly, 'Dolly's that girl I was telling you about – the thirteen-year-old . . .'

Creena's face fell. Of course, she should have remembered. That poor child – only thirteen years old and pregnant. What must she be going through?

'Dolly's 'avin' a baby,' repeated Rosie, a little louder this time.

'Yes, Rosie, I know she is.'

But the child followed Millie and Creena across the room to the dressing-up box, her voice high-pitched and shrilly insistent.

'She's 'avin' her baby now, miss. I *seen* her.'

Millie froze.

'You saw her? Where – at home?'

'In the girls' lavvies, miss. Dolly's 'avin' a baby.'

'Oh my God,' whispered Millie. 'The poor child's only eight months gone, as well. Cissie – yes, you, Cissie – go and fetch the midwife. It's number ten, Stockwell Street. Quickly!' As they pushed their way through the thronging children and rushed across to the toilet block, she added: 'All I can say is, it's a good job you're here, Creena Quilliam.'

'Was it really awful?'

'Well, it wasn't much fun.'

Creena sat in the probationers' sitting room, a lukewarm cup of tea cradled in her hands.

Dillie leaned forward sympathetically. She, at least, understood what it must have been like for Creena – and why.

'Only thirteen, you say?'

Creena nodded. 'A little kid of thirteen, giving birth on the dirty floor of a toilet block. Can you believe that?'

'I'm afraid I can,' replied Dillie. She had grown up with horror stories of child-mothers, their babies conceived in ignorance or fear.

'By the time we got there, she was in a dreadful state – white as a sheet and too terrified to make a sound! If it hadn't been for Rosie, she'd probably have delivered the infant before we were any the wiser.'

'How are mum and baby?'

'As well as can be expected.' Creena took a small sip of tea. 'Though Dolly's worn out, poor kid. Luckily the midwife came quite quickly and she was marvellous. Whisked the two of them straight off to hospital, and no arguments. The dreadful thing is . . .'

'What?'

'The dreadful thing is that it's her brother's kid, Dillie – her fourteen-year-old brother's!'

'It's not surprising really,' said Dillie. 'Not when you know that these kids sleep four or six to a bed – and sometimes in the same bed as their parents.'

Creena set down her cup.

'I just wish I could do something about it all,' she said reflectively. 'Something that would really make a difference.'

'I think you do quite enough already,' retorted Dillie. 'What with working here and then Long Wall Yard as well. And by the way, if you don't eat that last biscuit, I shall eat it for you!'

As Creena reached out to the plate, the door to the sitting room opened to reveal Eleanor Howells, wearing her best coat and an expression of self-congratulation.

'O ye of little faith,' she grinned, and rummaged in her bulging pockets to produce not one, but three pairs of black uniform stockings, which she tossed into Dillie's lap. 'Yours, I believe!'

Dillie stared at the stockings in blank incomprehension.

'Why are you giving me my own stockings, Howells? Have you gone quite potty? I left them to dry in the bathroom...'

'Indeed you did,' replied Howells. 'And I happened to pass by just as they were being taken *out* of the bathroom by a certain Mrs Stokes.'

'Mrs Stokes – you mean Beryl Stokes the ward maid?' Creena looked from Howells to the stockings and back again. 'You mean she...?'

'Elementary, my dear Quilliam. Mrs Stokes is our phantom laundry-snatcher.'

'But why? It doesn't make sense,' pointed out Creena. 'What would Beryl want with clothes that don't even fit her?'

'It seems the poor woman's been having money problems since her husband went AWOL from the army.'

'So she's been selling what she takes?'

'She'd get a few pennies from the second-hand clothes dealers – and pennies matter when you're hard up.'

'Well!' Dillie sat back in her chair. 'That is a turn-up for the book. What are you going to do now, Howells?'

'Nothing. I don't see what I can do.'

'I suppose you'll have to tell Home Sister,' hazarded Dillie.

'Come off it, Bayliss. If I say anything to Matron or Home Sister, Beryl's sure to lose her job – then she'll be in an even worse pickle than she is already. Besides, I have a feeling she won't be doing it again – not after I caught her red-handed.'

'So it's just the laundry she's been stealing?' said

Creena. 'What about all the other stuff that's been going missing – what about all those supplies from the dispensary?'

'Yes,' agreed Dillie. 'What has Inspector Howells got to say about that?'

Howells threw off her coat and sank into her favourite chair.

'Inspector Howells hasn't a bally clue,' she replied. 'Pass that biscuit, will you? I'm starving.'

It was a moonless April night in Lambeth Marsh, and Jack Doyle moved easily and quickly through familiar streets.

That business with Sid Clayden's five hundred quid hadn't gone away, and Jack was far too sensible to think that it would. But he had plans. You had to have plans, or you'd go crazy, thinking what Sid Clayden could do to you.

Besides, his own freelance trading operations had been picking up a little lately; and that – plus the spring breeze coming in off the river – made him feel his first tinge of optimism in ages. Tonight's deal had left him better off by a full twenty quid, and with four crisp white fivers in your back pocket it was difficult to see nothing but doom and gloom.

Best to keep to the shadows. Didn't want to risk being stopped and asked what Jack Doyle, second-hand clothes dealer, might be doing walking through Lambeth Marsh at three in the morning with a leg of mutton under his overcoat.

He'd accepted the mutton in part-payment for a debt,

but shifting it quickly and discreetly might pose problems, and besides, he had nowhere cool to store it at present. The solution was obvious, of course. He could rely on his guilty conscience to tell him what to do.

He tried the side gate. It was unbolted, as usual, and he slipped through into the yard. Trusting woman, that Mary McConnell. Walking up to the back entrance of the Salvation Army hostel, he left the mutton – carefully wrapped in wet muslin – just inside the back door. She'd be able to make a few gallons of soup out of that, right enough.

Call it an anonymous donation. And it had to be anonymous, because if Captain Mary McConnell knew who the mutton was from she'd probably throw it straight back in his face. She'd had no time for Jack Doyle since she'd figured out his links with the hated Sid Clayden. And what with the things he'd had to do to keep Sid off his back, sometimes Jack didn't have much time for himself.

At any rate, you should always share your good fortune, he'd learned that from his father. Jack was coming to realise that he'd learned a lot from Patrick Doyle, copper or no copper. He was sure Paddy would have understood that sometimes the only way to help people was to use unorthodox methods. If you could turn a profit along the way, well, so much the better. But there was no telling Mo. She was crippled with guilt every time Jack gave her anything. He wished he could make her understand. Her and Dillie . . . and Creena too.

It was getting on for dawn when Jack returned to the house on Bishop Street, stashing his takings under the kitchen lino before going silently up the stairs, two at a time. The sound of Old Bert's snoring seemed to reverberate through the whole house, as though the building itself were alive and breathing.

Jack pushed open the door of his bedroom and Smudge greeted him with a chirrup of recognition before settling his head on his paws and going back to sleep.

He patted the cat on the head. We're all survivors – you, me, and this house – he thought to himself as he lay down on the bed and waited for morning.

'Now you're quite sure you'll be all right on your own, Nurse Morrison?'

'Quite sure, Nurse Quilliam.'

It wasn't that Jocelyn Morrison was an especially bad nurse, but she did lack confidence in her own skills. Creena remembered all too well what that felt like – that first terrifying shift when Staff had gone off the ward and for a whole half-hour she had been in sole charge of fifty-two patients.

Creena still had lingering doubts about leaving Morrison in charge of the ward while she went for her break, but Sister had been quite firm on the matter: 'Nurse Morrison is about to commence her third year of training, Nurse Quilliam. It is about time she learned to accept her responsibilities.'

And about time I learned to delegate mine, Creena told herself sternly. In a few short months, if all her hard work and studying paid off, she would at last become a fully trained staff nurse. She really must stop trying to do everything herself.

'You will send for help *immediately* if there are any problems.'

'Yes, Nurse Quilliam.'

'Mr Kenworthy needs clean pyjamas and another change of sheets. And don't forget to keep a close eye on Mr Honeywell. He's just starting to come round from the anaesthetic and it was a major op, so he'll be feeling pretty groggy.'

'I will, Nurse Quilliam.'

'Good.' Creena took a last glance around the basement ward – *her* ward – and noted with satisfaction that all the bed-castors were in line, all the bed linen crisp and white, the whole ward sparkling with cleanliness. Sister would be pleased. 'I shall be back in fifteen minutes.'

She climbed the steps to the ground floor and made her way towards the dining room, on her way bumping into a damp and particularly grumpy Hester Frankenberg. With her apron drenched and her uniform dress bedraggled, Frankenberg looked less than her usual immaculate self.

'Whatever's happened to you?' exclaimed Creena.

'Don't ask,' replied Frankenberg darkly. 'Truly, Quilliam, I cannot imagine how you could possibly enjoy working with children.'

'Ah,' said Creena. 'Another urchin misbehaving?'

'There I was in Cas, syringing the little brat's ears, and he upped and threw the entire bowl of water all over me.'

'There's gratitude for you,' remarked Creena, unable to conceal her amusement.

'You can stop smirking, Quilliam,' retorted Frankenberg,

stalking off towards the home and a change of uniform. 'You've got a stain on your apron and your cap's come unpinned.'

Blast, thought Creena, looking down at the besmirched white of her starched apron. She would have to change it now, and then there was that extra bed linen she had to beg from Gynae before she went back on the ward. It was five past already, and she had to be back on duty by quarter past. No time after all for that cup of coffee she had been promising herself all morning.

A little later, arms laden with borrowed sheets and pillowcases, Creena hurried along the ground-floor corridor towards the basement staircase. She was a few minutes late, and didn't want to set a bad example to Morrison. Mustn't rush, though, or she'd get one of Sister's lectures. This part of the hospital was rather poorly lit, and she had to feel for the handrail whilst balancing the pile of bed linen between her left arm and her chin. Horrible stairs these were, their stone surface cracked and uneven.

'Nurse – Nurse Quilliam!'

When Creena was about a third of the way down the stairs, Jocelyn Morrison's voice floated up tremulously from the basement. Creena peered over the banister. Morrison was standing at the bottom, her face white with anxiety.

'Morrison – what on earth are you doing off the ward? You know very well you should never . . .'

'Oh, Nurse Quilliam, please hurry . . . it's Mr Honeywell.'

Creena's pulse quickened. Some sixth sense had told her she shouldn't have left the ward.

'Mr Honeywell – what's wrong?'

Morrison's face crumpled.

'He's started bleeding. And I don't know how to stop it...'

Haemorrhage! There was no need to ask any more questions. Creena threw caution to the winds and rushed down the stairs.

'Get Mr Spencer, Morrison. Get him *right now* – do you hear? And find Sister...'

The words dried in Creena's throat as the heel of her shoe caught in a cracked stair tread. It wasn't a big crack, just wide enough to catch her shoe so that her ankle twisted and she lost her balance, her scrabbling fingers slipping from the handrail.

For a split second time seemed to freeze; and then the sheets and pillowcases were scattering, tumbling down the stairs, and she was falling head over heels after them, her body as helpless as little Rosie Palmer's rag doll.

Falling into a world of darkness and silence.

Chapter 25

Swirling lights hovered and swam in the darkness. Eyes still closed, Creena heard a man's voice, reassuring and calm in her confusion:

'It's all right, Creena. Everything's all right.'

She tried to open her eyes but they were heavy-lidded, sluggish. It was the strangest sensation. She was lying on the headland at Grenaugh, the tang of salt spray filling the air, and the crash of surf all around her. The grassy earth felt soft and warm beneath her and she was tired. So, so tired.

Her eyes were screwed up tight against the sun's burning disc. Its light was a steady crimson glow through her closed eyelids. She wanted to open her eyes, but the light was so intense. Her head seemed to throb with a dull, pulsing ache . . .

'Wake up, Creena.'

'Mmm . . . ?'

Creena. Creena. Creena.

The man's voice sounded familiar, reassuring but insistent. She struggled to open her eyes and blinked in brilliant light.

'Mr Honeywell. Nurse Morrison. Have to find Mr Spencer...'

A woman's voice now.

'Mr Honeywell is fine.'

At first Creena could not quite make sense of the faces looking down at her. Everything was fuzzy. She shifted between the starched sheets and tried to focus. There was a nurse's cap and the blue of a staff nurse's uniform dress, the glitter of a fob watch pinned to a crisp white apron. But there was somebody else, too. She turned her head.

'Why am I in bed? Am I ill?'

The man's voice cut in again.

'You had a bump on the head, Creena. You knocked yourself out, but you're fine now. Just a few bumps and bruises.'

The voice made her heart stop for a second, and then she really did believe that she was delirious.

'Frank? Frankie Kinrade?'

'That's right, Creena. It's me, Frankie.'

'No.' Her head reeled. That was impossible. Frankie Kinrade was dead. 'Not Frankie ... can't be Frankie...'

A hand tightened around hers and she blinked, the world coming slowly into focus. Brown eyes twinkled beneath a mop of blue-black, wavy hair. The skin was darker, more deeply tanned than she remembered it, the face a little thinner, but there was no mistaking those eyes, that smile.

'Frankie!'

She struggled to sit up, woozy but suddenly very wide awake. The nurse took her by the shoulders and gently but insistently made her lie down again.

'If you will not rest, Nurse Quilliam, I shall have to ask Mr Kinrade to leave.'

Frank and Creena looked at each other, Creena speechless with astonishment, Frank filled with such a tumult of emotions that he hardly dared speak for fear of embarrassing himself.

'I ... I thought ...' began Creena.

'I know. I'm so sorry, Cree.'

'Why ... what happened?'

Frank hesitated. He hated secrets, but there were some things he could not share.

'I can't tell you, Creena. Not yet.'

'Oh.' Creena looked up at him, still not quite believing that he was there. Her eyelids felt heavy, she wanted to stay awake to ask him more questions, but she couldn't. 'I ... I think I want to go to sleep now. Will you be here when I wake up?'

Frank smiled.

'If you want me to be. I've got a desk job now, Creena. I've been posted to London.'

After a brief convalescence, Creena was deemed fit enough to go back to work, and was posted to the children's ward. The days and weeks passed swiftly, alternating between hard work and off-duty outings with Frank.

As she pushed the trolley back into the treatment room, Creena mused on the events of the last few weeks. She still had difficulty believing that Frank really was fit, well and working here, in London. But it was wonderful to see him again, it really was. It felt as though she had been given a second chance to make their friendship work, and this time she would try her very best to make sure that it did.

All the same, she must keep her feelings in perspective. The awkwardness that had been between them, on that day of parting in 1940, was still lurking just beneath the surface. They weren't carefree children any more, either of them, and you couldn't just pick up the pieces as if nothing had happened. Life wasn't a Hollywood movie; it was gritty, real, often disappointing. She had only to think of her parents to remember that things didn't necessarily work out the way you wanted them to. And she had bitter memories of Oliver Temple to remind her where dreams and romantic notions could lead.

She washed her hands and was just about to go back into the ward when the door opened a couple of inches and a voice hissed:

'Creena!'

She swung round as a familiar figure slid in, closing the door quietly behind him.

'Jack Doyle! What on earth . . . ? If Sister catches you in here . . .'

Jack put his finger to his lips and grinned.

'I got some,' he said. 'Said I would, didn't I?' He fished in the inside pocket of his jacket and took out not one but two Hershey bars. Taking hold of Creena's hand, he laid the chocolate in her palm, curling her fingers over it.

Creena's jaw dropped.

'Jack! Wherever did you get them?'

Jack shook his head and grinned.

'Can't go givin' away all my secrets, or I'll be out of a job, won't I?' He sniffed. 'American, o' course, but it ain't too bad. Reckon the kiddie'll like it?'

Creena's expression faltered between guilt, uncertainty and delight, and finally resolved itself into a smile. That smile made Jack Doyle's hardened heart beat just a little faster.

'You're a good man, Jack Doyle.' She gave him a little peck on the cheek.

'Call it sixpence.' He winked. 'You can owe me.' He leaned back against the door, arms folded, and surveyed the treatment room. 'Don't know 'ow you stick it,' he remarked, nose wrinkling at the smell of disinfectant. ''Orrible pong in 'ere. 'Ow you doin', anyway? I ain't seen you in a while.'

'I'm fine,' Creena replied. And she felt it – felt livelier and more optimistic than she had done in quite some time.

'You're lookin' well,' agreed Jack. 'Bin busy, 'ave you?'

'Didn't Dillie tell you?' Creena slipped the chocolate bars into the pocket of her uniform dress. 'My friend Frank ... the one who was posted missing, you remember?'

'I remember,' said Jack, rather quietly.

'Well, he's come back, isn't that wonderful? We grew up together on the Isle of Man, you know. It's so good to see him again, and to know he's all right. We've been out together a few times on my days off...'

Jack wasn't blind. He could see how much happier Creena was, and he was honestly, sincerely glad for her. Could he help it if he felt jealous too? He decided to take the initiative: nothing ventured, nothing gained.

'Fancy goin' dancin' on Wednesday night?' he suggested.

Creena shook her head.

'That's really sweet of you, Jack,' she said. 'But I'm meeting Frank on Wednesday. We're going out for our tea.'

'Saturday afternoon then? There's a matinée on down the Regal.'

'It's ever so kind of you,' said Creena. 'And I know Dillie's asked you to look after me, but really I'm fine. There's no need to worry about me.' She glanced at the clock. 'Sister'll be back in a mo, you'd best make yourself scarce.'

'Yeah. I suppose I should.'

'Thanks for the chocolate.'

'Any time.'

Getting the brush-off wasn't a new experience for Jack, but it was an unusual one. And what was more unusual still was the way he felt about it, the stubborn, gnawing ache that just wouldn't go away.

Creena would never want him the way he wanted her, that was obvious now. Perhaps it had been obvious all along, only he hadn't wanted to believe it. Well, no matter what, Jack Doyle would always do right by her.

That was the thing about love.

Creena finished making the bed in the side ward and emerged with an armful of dirty laundry, almost bumping into Jennie Daventry who was delivering a set of X-rays to Sister.

'Hello there, Quilliam,' said Daventry brightly.

'You're full of the joys of spring,' observed Creena. 'Couldn't be anything to do with your recent exam results, could it?'

Daventry laughed good-naturedly.

'I'll say. Was I pleased to pass – even if it was second time around! Now I'm looking forward to getting my hospital badge and doing my midder. Pity you and the others will be fully fledged Royals before me.'

'Only if we pass our hospital finals in September,' Creena pointed out. She gave a groan. 'Frankenberg's started swotting, and it's only July.'

Daventry raised a neatly plucked eyebrow.

'She must be keen. That girl never used to do a stroke more than she had to.'

'Bet you're glad to be back up here,' commented Creena. 'Clarke-Herbert's pretty glad she's back from leave, too. By all accounts Norfolk's pretty bleak, and you can't get near the coast for fortifications. Marian reckons country life's vastly overrated.'

'You're telling me! I was getting distinctly tired of all-girl musical soirées. Mind you, we did have the odd diversion. Do you know, one old Lambeth chappie insisted on walking all the way to Epsom because he'd heard Dr Gainsborough had moved to the EMS site and he didn't want to see anyone else!'

After depositing the soiled laundry in the special bin by the ward entrance, Creena washed her hands and patted the dress pocket beneath her apron to ensure the chocolate bars were still there. It wouldn't do to lose them.

Checking that the junior probationers were fully occupied, she slipped back into the side ward, closing the door behind her. The six-year-old boy in the bed looked pasty-faced and thin. He ought really to be down at the Surrey site, but he wasn't at all well, and the doctors didn't want to risk moving him. The news of his father's death in the Sicily landings hadn't helped his recovery, either.

'Hello again, Andrew.'

His face was still turned away, into the pillow, but at least this time he spoke to her. She was making progress.

'Hello, Nurse.'

'I've come to give you something.'

'Is it medicine?'

'No, it's not medicine, not this time.' She noted the look of relief on his face as she sat down on the edge of his bed. Faintly interested, he skewed his head round so that he could look at her. It was strictly against the rules to sit on patients' beds, but Sister wasn't here to see. She leant her face close to the boy's. 'It's your birthday today, isn't it?'

His eyes registered genuine surprise.

'How did you know?'

She tapped the side of her nose knowingly.

'Oh, I know lots of things.'

'Like what?'

'I know that you like chocolate.'

'Chocolate!' He really was interested now.

Creena lifted her apron and put her hand into her uniform pocket. The Hershey bars were quite safe there – a little warm but not too melted in this mid-July heat. She took them out of her pocket, the wrappers bright and inviting. Not for the first time, she had reason to be grateful to Jack Doyle. He might be a rogue, but there was something about him that she couldn't help liking – something fundamentally honest.

Andrew's eyes followed the two chocolate bars anxiously, as though afraid they might disappear at any moment.

'Now you have to promise me something, Andrew,' she teased.

'What?'

'You have to promise that you won't eat all this chocolate at once – if you throw up I shall get into terrible trouble with Sister! Promise?'

'Promise.'

'Happy birthday, Andrew.' She slipped the chocolate bars into the boy's small hand and crept away.

'And then Mrs Hewitt said . . .'

'Go on.'

'She said, "Well, Alf, if you want to stay in bed all day, you'd best go down the 'orspital" – then she broke his nose with the frying pan!'

Frank laughed and she joined in, feeling easier with him now. Not that things hadn't changed between them – there was too much left unspoken for them to have the easy rapport they'd enjoyed as children. But it was good to spend time with him again.

They were taking it slowly, very slowly. There was something dark and serious about Frank since he had returned, and sometimes Creena felt almost as if she were getting to know a stranger. If only there weren't so many secrets, so many secrets on both sides . . .

'I can't think why you like this place so much.' Frank took in the frankly squalid surroundings of Mrs Bates's café in The Cut.

Creena followed his gaze.

'Oh, it's all right as long as you don't eat the meat pies,' she joked, lowering her voice to an inaudible whisper and mouthing, 'Long tails!'

Frank grimaced.

'If it comes to that,' he added, 'I don't really know what you see in London. It's taking quite some getting used to.'

Frank was now working for the Ministry of War as an Italian translator. It wasn't the work he objected to – it was having to live in grimy, airless, urban London. His soul itched for the wide, empty spaces of the island, where a few thousand people might constitute a town and you were never more than a mile or two from the open sea.

'Mind you,' he conceded, 'it's good to be ... you know ... with you again.'

'It is?'

He reached out, gave her hand a reassuring squeeze then thought better of it and withdrew. He'd made that mistake before and he wasn't about to do it again. It was difficult to know what to do, how to avoid taking things too quickly.

'Of course it is, Creena. It's been too long.'

She met his gaze and for a long, silent moment they seemed caught in their own private world, where no one and nothing else existed. The years stripped away, they were two innocent children again, untrammelled by the emotional baggage of their hurts and aspirations.

''Ere – you two. You want another cup of char? I got a fresh pot mashed.'

Snapping back to the present, Creena looked back over her shoulder. Mrs Bates was standing behind her counter, wiping her hands on a towel so grey and greasy that it resembled a mechanic's oily rag.

'No thanks, Mrs B. Perhaps later.'

''Ow about a nice meat pie then?'

Creena and Frank exchanged looks of stifled amusement.

'Er, no thanks, we've already eaten.'

'Please yerself, but it's a lovely pie. No gristle.'

Creena made circles in her cup with her spoon.

'Frank . . .'

'Yes?'

'Why won't you tell me where you've been all this time?'

Frank bit his lip. They'd been through this so many times since he'd returned. How could he explain that there were some things he wasn't allowed to tell her, and others that he simply couldn't bring himself to talk about, not even to Creena? Such terrible things he'd seen; such terrible things he'd done.

'Oh, Creena, I've tried to explain.'

'Tell me again.'

'I've been overseas. I got myself wounded, but now I'm back. As soon as I was well enough and got posted to London I made straight for the Royal Lambeth to see if you were all right – and there I found you, spark out in the sick bay and covered in bruises! Isn't that enough to be going on with?'

Creena looked across the table at him, his shirtsleeves rolled up in the August heat and his collar unbuttoned. He looked quite vulnerable out of uniform; and she wasn't so unobservant that she had overlooked the deep scars on his right arm and throat. She put out her hand and stroked his arm, but felt him flinch, as though afraid of the gentleness of her touch.

'What's the matter, Frank? Can't you tell me about it?'

'I wish I could, I do, Creena. But I just can't.'

She felt vaguely irritated by Frank's inability to talk to her. Hadn't they always told each other everything? And then the hypocrisy of her own thoughts hit her, and she remembered the awful, unspeakable secret which she was hiding from him. How could she expect Frank to confide in her when she was keeping so much hidden in her own heart?

'Anyway,' Frank went on, turning the conversation in a different direction to end the awkward silence, 'seems that's all over for me now, what with getting wounded. They've given me three stripes and a desk, and that's all there is to it.' He swallowed, his mouth uncomfortably bereft of saliva, then took a swig of brick-red tea. 'We could ... er ... get together now and again ... that is, if you wanted to.'

His heart was in his mouth. After all he'd been through, the thing he most feared was Creena's complete rejection – and there was something different about her that he couldn't quite define. Something sad, something secretive. Perhaps the closeness they had once known had gone for ever. But even if he had to settle for just her friendship, that was a million times better than losing her completely.

To his immense relief, Creena nodded.

'I'd like that,' she said. 'I'd like that a lot, Frankie Kinrade.'

* * *

All through the sticky heat of the London summer, Frank worked in an underground complex on the outskirts of London, listening to wireless broadcasts in Italian and translating coded messages from partisans and resistance workers.

The shifts were long, the hours irregular, and as time went on the small army translation and decoding team got to know each other pretty well. On one particularly oppressive night in early September 1943, Frank was sharing a wireless room with Julia Paston, one of the civilian stenographers who transcribed broadcasts and messages from Frank's dictation.

Reaching the end of a long sequence of transmissions, Frank eased off his headphones and rubbed his reddened ears. He leaned back in his chair and raked through his wavy black hair with exhausted fingers.

Julia looked up from her shorthand pad.

'Bushed?'

Frank yawned.

'I'll say. I could murder a pint of Castletown Blue.'

'Castletown Blue – what's that? One of your funny Manx beers?'

Frank clasped his hands behind his head and fantasised.

'Funny? It's wonderful stuff – goes down a treat on a hot summer's day.'

Julia crossed her legs with well-judged precision. These Utility dresses had conveniently short skirts, and if you crossed your thighs just so, you could reveal a tantalising glimpse of smooth, bare knee. Like many young women, Julia had given up trying to find stockings for the summer and had taken to painting her bare legs with gravy browning, so skilfully applied that there was even a fake seam up the back.

At twenty-three years old, Julia Paston was certainly an attractive woman – though a touch too striking to be called simply pretty. Her shoulder-length golden-brown hair was styled into neat rolls which framed a heart-shaped face with dark-brown eyes and a large, sensual mouth. Her nose was pert and slightly upturned. The uncharitable might have criticised her figure as blowsy, but Julia knew exactly how to show off her large, full breasts and hips and tiny waist to full advantage. The plain grey frock she was wearing today clung to her like a second skin – and didn't she just know it.

'You ought to let me take you to some of the pubs I know,' she suggested. 'You know, show you around a bit.'

'Mmm, perhaps,' said Frank a little dreamily, not really listening to what Julia was saying.

If there was one thing that infuriated Julia, it was not being paid sufficient attention. She had gone to immense trouble to make herself look nice for Frank Kinrade, and here he was gazing into space and not giving so much as a glance at her perfectly shaped calves.

She got up from her chair, smoothing the creases out of her dress, and crossed the room to Frank's desk, hitching up her skirt as she perched on the edge. Surely he couldn't ignore her now.

'Someone gave me a couple of tickets for a matinée on Saturday,' she said. 'I don't really have anyone to go with, and it's such a shame to let them go to waste. I don't suppose you . . .

Frank gave an apologetic shake of the head.

'Sorry, Julia. I'm seeing Creena on Saturday, it's her day off before hospital finals. Did I tell you about Creena?'

Julia smiled through clenched teeth.

'Yes, I think you mentioned her,' she said. Only about a million times this week, she added under her breath.

'I must introduce you,' Frank continued. 'You'd like Creena, I'm sure you would.'

Oh, would I? thought Julia as she listened to Frank's enthusiastic monologue. She didn't even know this Creena woman, but already she felt like murdering her.

Chapter 26

'I'm so proud of you, Creena Quilliam!'

'Frank, Frank, you're squashing me – I can hardly breathe,' Creena half laughed, half gasped as he crushed her to him in an immense bear hug of congratulation.

Reluctantly he released her.

'Sorry, Cree – sometimes I don't know my own strength.' He took her by the hand and pulled her down on to the park bench beside him. 'I'm really, really pleased for you, Creena. Can I see your badge?'

Creena opened her handbag and took out the box containing the precious hospital badge which she had at last earned the right to wear. With great care she opened the box, and the badge glinted as it caught the mellow September sunlight.

'May I? Would you mind? I'll be careful with it.'

Frank picked up the badge and inspected it closely. It was a lot bigger than he'd expected – a glorious starburst of polished silver, touched with bright blue enamel on the outer rays of the star. He picked out embossed lettering in the centre: 'Scola RLH'; and turning it over, he saw engraved on the reverse: 'C. Quilliam, September 1943'.

'It's beautiful,' he said, replacing it carefully on its bed of dark-blue velvet.

'I'm terrified of losing it!' smiled Creena. 'We all are. Frankenberg's taken to sleeping with hers under her pillow. If we lose them, they won't be replaced, you know. And Dillie's in such a state about her medal.'

'I'm not surprised,' replied Frank. 'I'd be in a state if someone gave me a solid silver medal and told me not to lose it!'

Dillie Bayliss's silver medal was the talk of Creena's set. And as for Mo, she was beside herself with excitement, telling anyone who would listen that 'my Dillie's done us proud'. Jack had shown his approval in the form of a bottle of *real* champagne.

'It should have been the gold medal, you know,' said Creena. 'Everyone knows that. But the Ass Mat's always had a thing about Dillie not being "the right sort".' She brightened. 'Still, Dillie's as pleased as punch, so that's all that really matters.' She closed the box gently and slipped it back into her handbag. 'I don't think anyone's as pleased as I am, though,' she added.

'Pity about your ma and pa,' observed Frank. 'You haven't patched things up with them, I don't suppose?'

Creena avoided Frank's gaze. Her eyes did not dwell long on the smiling family in the distance either, children and parents sitting together on the grass and sharing a greaseproof-paper packet of sandwiches.

'I don't suppose I will, not now.'

'But why *did* you fall out with them, Creena? You still haven't told me. I know they were always strict with you, but . . .'

'I'd rather not talk about it, Frank. I don't even want to think about it.'

'OK, Creena, I'm sorry. I just thought . . .'

'One day, perhaps. But not now.'

Frank gave himself a mental kick, then made a hasty change of subject.

'Not much of a celebration this, is it? Eating beetroot sandwiches in the park.'

'Oh, I can think of worse. And I like picnics. Do you remember the ones we used to have when we were children?'

'Do I?' Frank's face lit up with the pleasure of recollection. Despite his mother's death, his father's problems, the grinding poverty, there had been far more good times than bad. And so many of those good times had been shared with Creena. 'Hard-boiled eggs, a few bull's-eyes.' He winked. 'And a pocketful of John Duggan's apples.'

Creena burst out laughing.

'Poor Mr Duggan. He was always so sure you'd been in his orchard, but he never did catch you, did he?'

'No, but one of his porkers almost did once – do you remember?'

'Oh yes. He put his pigs in the orchard and the boar took off after you . . .'

'Teeth like razors, it had. Ripped the seat out of my pants an' all – Pa was furious when I got home. I could hardly sit down for days.'

'Perhaps that's when you decided crime didn't pay and it was safer to join the police!'

Frank munched on a sandwich.

'Any idea what you're going to do next?' he hazarded. He had been avoiding asking her, slightly apprehensive of what she might say. What with Creena's friend Marian talking about joining the QAs, perhaps Creena would want to do the same. Perhaps he would lose touch with her all over again.

Creena hesitated.

'Something different,' she replied. 'Something ... I don't know ... something *useful*.'

Frank chuckled.

'Useful! I can't think of anything more useful than nursing.'

Creena shook her head, not sure that she could explain the feeling inside her.

'Oh, I'm a good enough nurse, I suppose...'

'Dillie certainly thinks so. You should hear her singing your praises.'

'... but I'm not a *born* hospital nurse, does that make sense? Dillie is, but I'm not. Whilst I've been helping out at the shelter group, I've begun to realise that there are other things I can do besides working in the wards. Nursing's not just about putting dressings on people's wounds.'

'So what are you going to do?'

'I've been offered a temporary staff nurse's contract at the Royal Lambeth, and I expect I'll accept that for the time being...'

'And then what?'

Creena shook out the last of the sandwich crumbs, then folded up the paper bag and slipped it into her handbag.

'I'm not quite sure yet. Something with children, perhaps.'

'And will you stay in London?' Frank half wished he hadn't asked, but he had to know her answer.

She looked at him, her green eyes lustrous in the autumn sunlight.

'Who knows, Frank?' she replied. 'Who knows what will happen in the future?'

Tommy Quilliam's eighteenth birthday celebrations were a sombre affair – very different from Albie's, reflected Alexa as she passed her empty dinner plate back up the table to Ida.

'Amy, you haven't eaten all your potatoes,' muttered Ida tetchily. She was in a dreadful mood – the slightest thing seemed to spark her off.

'I'm sorry, Mother,' said Amy contritely. She looked so awkward on that straight-backed chair, trying hard to do everything right and mortified by her parents' constant grumbling. Alexa's heart went out to her. 'I wasn't very hungry.'

'Waste not, want not,' growled George. 'Remember the Squander Bug,' but his heart wasn't in it. This damp October weather was making his knee ache, and the tense atmosphere around the tea table was giving him indigestion. He was tired too. Tired of teaching children who would grow up to break their parents' hearts.

'Ah well, I suppose that pig will have to have it,' concluded Ida darkly.

'Yes, Mother,' sighed Amy, watching in mute despair as Ida made great play of conserving the single, half-eaten potato and carting it off to the kitchen with her nose in the air.

'Lovely birthday tea, Mum,' Tommy called to his mother's retreating back; but Ida did not reply.

He knew why she was being so grumpy today – the whole family knew. It wasn't just because he was eighteen now and might get his call-up any day; it was because he had made a point of displaying the birthday card he had received from Creena.

Twice Ida had taken it down off the sideboard and put it in a drawer; twice Tommy had retrieved it, positioning it centre-stage, where everyone would be bound to see it. Mother had never explained why she and Father had forbidden any contact with Creena, and quite frankly Tommy was fed up with it. Wasn't it bad enough to have lost the big brother he idolised, without having to lose his sister as well? 'It's my birthday, Mum,' he had told Ida; and in the end she had given up, and resorted to pretending the card simply wasn't there.

Alexa nudged Mona and they both looked at Bessie, who raised a greying eyebrow. The whole family had long since tired of this mysterious family feud, but no amount of hinting, bullying or cajoling had persuaded Ida or George to reveal its root cause.

To Bessie, George seemed hurt, withdrawn, no longer his usual blustering self. His occasional bouts of violent temper were short-lived but alarming. Ida she found more worrying still: a woman intent on martyrdom, nurturing some dark, festering wound whilst inflicting even more pain on the innocent people around her.

The cake arrived – inevitably a far more splendid

creation than Mona had produced for Albie; but Mona had a feeling that even the most delicious of Ida Quilliam's cakes was doomed to turn to ashes in the mouths of these supremely miserable party guests. It was Tommy she felt really sorry for – poor lad.

'What a wonderful cake, Ida,' said Mona brightly. 'I do wish I had your gift with baking.'

'It is not a gift,' replied Ida. 'It is simply hard work.'

Well, that puts me in my place, thought Mona. And to think how good you were to me when there was all that trouble with Duggie. What on earth has got into you, Ida Quilliam?

Ida set the cake down on the table. From goodness knows where, she had managed to acquire not only icing sugar but cochineal, and proper ground almonds for the marzipan – not to mention several pounds of dried fruit from Mrs Shimmin's 'special reserve'. Normally, Ida would be crowing in triumph over her mouthwatering *tour de force*. But she just looked grim. Bessie noticed how tired she seemed in spite of all that angry, nervous energy; how many more fine lines there were around her eyes.

'Shall we sing "Happy Birthday"?' suggested Bessie, painfully aware of the irony.

She started it off in her reedy high soprano, and the others joined in one by one, but it all sounded hideously out of place in the morgue-like atmosphere of Ida Quilliam's dining room.

Tommy cut the cake and handed slices round. It was delicious, of course, but nobody had much of an appetite. Alexa was glad that she and Mona had left the kids at home

– their natural exuberance would have met with a frosty reception here.

Bessie picked up her glass of home-made ginger cordial and proposed a toast.

'To Tommy,' she said, and they all drank.

'To absent friends,' murmured Tommy, wondering if he would ever see his elder sister again.

As Ida placed the cake stand on the sideboard, among Tommy's birthday cards, her eyes lighted for a few brief seconds on the arrangement of family photographs in their polished silver frames. Look, there was Robert, aged eighteen months, blond and giggling in his smock. Tommy and Amy, the five-year-old boy proudly holding his little sister on his lap.

And Creena. Such a pretty child, a laughing babe of nine months, kicking and squealing on a fur rug. Angelic and innocent. Who would ever have thought . . . ?

How could you? thought Ida, blinking away tears of bitterness and rage. How could you? And she banished all thoughts of the girl who had once been her daughter.

Frank wandered about under the clock at Waterloo station, occasionally glancing up at the time or fiddling with his tie. It was so much easier to look smart in uniform, and he wished he had enough money and coupons to buy himself a decent suit.

He rather regretted asking Creena to meet him here. He felt uncomfortably conspicuous, as though the whole world knew who he was waiting for and was having a jolly good stare at him, maliciously hoping that she would stand him up.

Frank fiddled with the knot on his tie. Another five minutes. She wasn't due for another five minutes. He wandered off to the newspaper kiosk, then thought better of it and turned back for the clock. He couldn't risk her arriving only to find that he wasn't there, now could he? Oh, why was he so darned nervous? He was only meeting a friend.

Julia Paston was also waiting: waiting for the right moment. She stood for quite a long time in the buffet, pretending to drink horrible tea, whilst she watched Frank through the window. Two o'clock, he'd said. At two o'clock he was meeting this Creena woman under the clock at Waterloo.

Over the last few months, Julia had been subjected not only to Frank's reminiscences of the Isle of Man, but also to his treasured photographs of Creena. And quite honestly, she couldn't imagine what he saw in the girl – too tall, much too thin, with a great unmanageable mop of hair and hardly any bust to speak of. What could Creena Quilliam possibly have to interest a man?

At just after five to, Julia emerged from the buffet, glancing in the mirror above the counter to check that her hair was exactly the way she liked it, her lipstick dangerously red and glossy. Her hat was smart but flirty, black with a tiny veil that covered one eye. Slowly, nonchalantly, she pulled on her gloves and walked across the station concourse towards Frank.

Creena hurried along Waterloo Road, thanking her lucky stars for a four-year nursing training which had taught her how to walk almost as quickly as other people could run.

She had got off duty late, and then, on her way to her room in the staff nurses' home, she'd bumped into Harry, who was full of some scheme he'd dreamed up to send the kids from Long Wall Yard on a camping holiday. By the time she'd listened, made her apologies and run to the home to get changed, Creena was distinctly late.

As she hurried down the road, she told herself that there was no need to rush. Frank would wait for her. Surely he would. Her heart fluttered with pleasurable apprehension as she thought of what they would do today. Would they go to the pictures? Or maybe for a walk along the river, or for tea at that little shop Frank had discovered up West? Not that it really mattered. Whatever they did would be fun.

She reached the station a minute before two, and paused for just a second to adjust the seams in her stockings before walking into the concourse.

Frank had his eye on the front entrance, and did not even notice Julia Paston walking towards him from the station buffet.

'Well, well, Frank – fancy seeing you here!'

He wheeled round to see a vision in a dove-grey fitted suit, finished off with a rakish black hat and wedge-heeled shoes.

'You're all dressed up today,' he observed. Even though Julia's vampish attractiveness wasn't really to his taste, he couldn't help noticing that pillarbox-red lipstick, and the way the tailored suit showed off her ample curves.

Julia beamed at this token victory, and gave a little twirl.

'Like it?'

'Mmm? Yes, very nice.' Frank was glancing over Julia's shoulder but he still couldn't see any sign of Creena. He hoped she hadn't changed her mind.

'My sister's a tailoress – she's a real whizz with a needle.' Julia giggled girlishly. 'Not like me, I'm not really the domesticated sort.' Not one bit, she thought to herself. My talents lie in rather different areas.

'That's nice,' said Frank distractedly. 'Off somewhere, are you?'

'Oh – you know,' she replied evasively, fingering the sleeve of Frank's jacket. 'You're not looking so bad yourself. Dressed up for something special?'

'I'm waiting for Creena – didn't I mention it? We're going out for the afternoon.'

Julia's smile did not slip for one second.

'Ah, yes, I think you may have mentioned it.'

Was that her? Chatting casually to Frank, Julia scanned the concourse for a sign of Creena Quilliam. She should be here by now – surely she wasn't going to stand Frank up? That girl didn't deserve a man like Frank Kinrade.

There! A glimpse of red hair, flowing like a banner as Creena walked into the station. Julia stiffened. Well, she supposed the girl was *striking*, but really that was all you could say about her. She glanced up at Frank; he was chattering on about Creena but he hadn't even noticed the girl yet, walking towards him in her cheap green frock.

'Frank?'

Frank stopped talking to take breath.

'What?'

'There's something . . . something I've wanted to do for ages, Frank.'

'Yes? What?'

'Oh, Frank . . .'

Before he realised what was happening, Julia had grabbed hold of him and pulled his face down to hers, pressing her scarlet mouth hard against his lips. He put out his arms, half in astonishment, half to push her away, but only succeeded in letting her press closer to him. After what seemed a long, long time, he finally unfastened her embrace. Gasping, he stared down at her in mingled shock and horror, Julia's red lipstick smeared all over his mouth.

'For God's sake, Julia. What . . . ?'

'Sorry, Frank – I just couldn't resist.' And turning on her heel, Julia sauntered away, her round backside wiggling triumphantly in her tight, knee-length skirt.

Stopped in her tracks, Creena stood and stared, open-mouthed, at the scene before her. Her heart was thumping, and she felt dizzy and sick and angry. Frank – *her* Frank – was kissing a blowsy, common-looking woman, her arms wrapped tightly round his waist. It couldn't be true, it couldn't.

Not you as well, Frank, she thought. Not you.

Gentleman Johnny Shaw took several steps backwards, but Sid Clayden came after him like a rabid bulldog.

'Your idea of a little joke, was it, Johnny?' he snarled. 'Taking those iffy medical supplies out of your cellar and stashing them in my warehouse?'

Shaw shifted uneasily from one foot to the other, his cockiness rapidly evaporating. He just couldn't understand why Sid was so angry with him.

'No, Mr Clayden, sir. Course not.'

'Because if it was, I don't find it very funny. Do you find it funny?'

'No, Mr Clayden. Definitely not, only . . .'

'You done the dirty on me, Johnny Shaw. Set me up wiv the rozzers.'

'No, I ain't, Mr Clayden. I wouldn't do that, you know I wouldn't. I'd never have moved the stuff if I hadn't had that note from you, sayin' it was OK.'

Sid folded his short, pudgy arms over his barrel-like chest. His face was purple with rage, a single vein pulsing threateningly on his temple.

'What note? I ain't written you no note.'

'I got this note – "Put the stuff in my lock-up till the heat dies down," that's what it said. I thought you must've heard about my cellar bein' flooded, and wanted to make sure the drugs an' such was safe.'

Sid snorted his contempt.

'If you're goin' to lie to me, Shaw, you could think up something more original than that.'

'But it's true!'

Sid pushed forward, forcing Shaw against the back wall of his living room.

'Look, Johnny – I don't know if you're winding me up or just plain thick between the ears. But I ain't written you no note, get it?'

Johnny gulped and nodded soundlessly.

'I 'ad a little visit from the coppers last night, Johnny. Very interested they were too – very interested in knowing how all them stolen 'ospital supplies came to be in my warehouse. Tip 'em off, did yer?'

497

'I told you, Mr Clayden, I only done what you told me to . . .'

Clayden grabbed Johnny's shirt by the collar and pulled the younger man towards him, half strangling him as he scrunched up the material in his sausage fingers.

'Listen to me – you think you're so important, don't yer? But you're just a piece of slime, you're nothin'. I made you and I own you. And if I go down because of this, you're coming with me, Johnny Shaw. No matter how far down I go, you're coming too.'

With a pint of ale in front of him and twenty Turkish cigarettes in his monogrammed silver case, Jack Doyle felt considerably better than he had done for months.

Sitting in his favourite cosy corner in The Ring, he took stock of his position. He'd been careful to keep his nose clean, paying off his debt to Sid in regular instalments, keeping him sweet, doing exactly what he was told with no backchat. No doubt about it, things could be a lot worse.

Taking a swig of beer he flicked through the sporting pages, marking off anything that interested him, keeping an eye open for anything that might generate a useful new business opportunity. Reaching the back page, he took to doodling in the margin, switching the pencil from right hand to left and back again, seeing the different effects he could produce.

Suddenly he grinned all over his face. Now wasn't that funny? If he wrote with the pencil in his left hand, the result looked just like Sid Clayden's illiterate scrawl. 'Put the stuff in my lock-up till the heat dies down . . .'

He laughed out loud – so suddenly that the barman

dropped a glass and cursed under his breath as he went to fetch a broom.

Good, bad or just plain stupid, Jack thought to himself, the world was chock-full of gullible people.

Chapter 27

'I suppose I was just being silly,' said Creena, making a lap for Smudge the cat. Smudge jumped up, craning his head to nuzzle the flat of her hand as she ran it down his sleek body from nose to tail. Within seconds he was rumbling contentedly. 'I mean, Frank isn't the sort to do that, is he?'

Dillie ruffled her brown curls with a work-reddened hand.

'Well, a man's a man,' she said. 'But no, I don't think Frank's like that at all. He explained, didn't he?'

Creena nodded.

'He said she just sort of launched herself at him. I must say, she did look the type who might . . .'

'Then I think you ought to let it lie, Creena, really I do. After all, you don't want to lose him again, not after everything that's happened to you both.'

'Well . . . no . . . no, of course I don't.'

'Creena! Surely you've not gone off him?'

Creena shifted a fraction in her seat and Smudge made his feelings on the matter clear by digging his claws into her knees through her best tweed skirt.

'Ouch! Little monster.' She tickled Smudge under the chin as she prised his claws out of her flesh. 'No, of course I haven't. But ... well, quite honestly I'm not quite sure what I want out of all this. If Frank can't trust me with his secrets, and I can't trust him with mine – what sort of future do we have together?'

Dillie scratched her ear thoughtfully.

'Look, Cree, I know you've had a terrible time but you can't always think the worst. I've always found it better just to take each day as it comes.'

'You're right, of course.' Creena rubbed the top of Smudge's head and his mouth opened in an enormous, contented yawn. She pulled a face. 'As usual!'

Although apparently half asleep, Smudge was watching the kitchen door through narrowed eyelids, his large pointed ears swivelling at the distant clanking sound of what just *might* be Auntie Mo scraping boiled fish-heads out of a saucepan.

'Come an' get it, come on, Smudge!'

The sound of Mo's voice galvanised Smudge into instant consciousness, and he sprang lightly off Creena's lap and disappeared into the kitchen.

'Cupboard love,' grinned Creena, getting up and stretching. She glanced at her watch. 'Ah well, I suppose I'd better be leaving. I'm on early tomorrow, and some of us need our beauty sleep!'

'We're off back to the hospital now,' called Dillie, and Mo's head appeared round the kitchen door.

'You take care now, both of you. An' bring Frank next time you come, Creena.'

'I will.' Creena picked up her jacket and put it on.

'Thanks for the advice, Dillie,' she added. 'I reckon Frank and I will just have to wait and see what happens.'

'You do that,' nodded Dillie. 'I know how badly Oliver hurt you, but Frank's different. He'd never do a thing like that.'

Alexa and Mona were chatting as they hung out the washing together, trying to get the sheets out in the drying wind before the threatening grey of the sky turned to squally rain. Autumn was well advanced now, the leaves dropping from the trees in great golden drifts as the harsh November winds blew in over the Irish Sea.

Mona shivered, half wishing she had worn a thicker cardigan. But then again, she did want to look her best for Giacomo, who was mending fences with Enrico and Claudio in the top field. She wondered if they'd have a chance to be alone when he came in for his morning break...

Alexa reached up and pegged a bolster case to the line.

'I don't know how he's going to take to it,' she said.

'Who?'

'Tommy. Ida's Tommy.' She chuckled. 'Fancy Ida's lad being sent down the mines – I don't think it's quite what she and George had in mind.'

Tommy Quilliam – a Bevin boy. Well, there's a turn-up for the book, thought Alexa. Off to some Welsh pit village nobody's ever heard of, to get his hands well and truly dirty; and him with a King William's College education, too, while Alexa's son Albie had got himself into the Royal Signals. It's no wonder Tommy's not very happy, she told herself – his pride's hurt.

'Oh, I expect he'll get used to it,' said Mona, watching out for Giacomo's arrival as she pegged out the last of the washing. 'It's Ida I'm worried about. She seems so angry all the time.'

'I wonder if she knows about Frank and Creena,' mused Alexa as they walked back to the farmhouse together. 'I was so glad to hear he's safe, and they're seeing each other again, you know.'

'I always reckoned those two were made for each other,' replied Mona. 'They were never apart when they were children, getting into scrapes and driving George wild. He never reckoned much to the Kinrades, you know.'

Alexa sniffed.

'Then he's a bigger fool than I thought he was. Don Kinrade may like a drink, but he's a good man. And look what a fine job he's made of bringing up Frank and his sisters. The trouble with the Quilliams is they're snobs. It's a wonder their kids turned out so well, considering.'

Little Duggie was waiting in the kitchen for his mother, a wooden cow clutched proudly in his hand.

'Bessie gave it him for his birthday, to add to his farmyard set,' Mona explained, smiling as she looked down at her four-year-old son. 'He's already saying he wants to be a farmer, you know.'

Despite all the trouble that little Duggie's arrival had caused, Mona never stopped thanking her lucky stars for the child. Like his sisters, Duggie had the sunniest temperament imaginable – with not a trace of the vile temper that had made life with Duggie senior so intolerable. Mona was heartily relieved that he had not one drop of her husband's bad blood in him.

She glanced at the small pile of unopened envelopes behind the clock on the mantelpiece. She'd stopped reading Duggie's letters months ago, and she never wrote back to him, but they still kept coming. Why couldn't he just get out of her life and never come back? Maynrys might be his farm in law, but what interest had he ever taken in it? All he cared about were women and drink. With hindsight, she wondered what she could possibly ever have seen in him.

And then she remembered the long and wonderful love letters he had written to her when she was in Liverpool, the eloquence with which he had expressed his feelings for her. They had been lovely letters, and in a way that made things worse. Duggie Mylchreest had been a different man in the days before he turned to drink, and she had loved the man he used to be.

'How is Bessie?' enquired Alexa, sitting down at the table and hauling little Duggie on to her lap.

'Oh, bearing up.' Mona sat down and poured out two cups of tea. 'Mind you, it's a terrible palaver – now the married camp's been moved to the north end of Port Erin, she can't even get to see her friend Dot without a pass. And if she wants to go to the shops in Castletown...'

'There's precious little to buy if she does,' grunted Alexa. 'I had a devil of a job finding any decent paper to write to Albie. Still, we have to make the best of it, don't we?'

'Bessie certainly has. I think she's decided her bunch of internees aren't so bad after all.'

'Does she still have the same six, then?'

Mona shook her head.

'The two Galician women were released, and they're back in London now. Bessie says she really misses their children – and of course, little Duggie was heartbroken when they weren't there to play with him. I think she's got another couple of Germans now.'

'Hmm,' said Alexa. 'Hope they're not as bad as the first lot. That Hildegard woman was downright poisonous.'

'One of them's quite nice, according to Bessie. She's a teacher – Agathe, I think she said her name was. Apparently she came over here just before the war, as a refugee. She was in the middle of teaching her class the ten-times table when two policemen turned up and carted her off to be interned!'

'Hardly seems fair,' commented Alexa. 'But I suppose the Government has to play safe.'

'There's a lot of things about this war that aren't fair,' sighed Mona, dropping a saccharin tablet into her tea and watching it fizz. And don't I just know it, she thought, as her eyes wandered back to Duggie's letters, lying un-opened on the mantelpiece.

Creena was just thinking of having an early night when there was a knock on her door.

'Come in!'

It was Frankenberg, in an ivory satin dressing gown and matching slippers, her hair freshly washed.

'Phone call for you,' she announced.

'Who is it?'

'How should I know, Quilliam? Some girl with a common accent.'

Puzzled, Creena hurried along the corridor to the telephone and picked up the receiver.

'Hello? Staff Nurse Quilliam speaking.'

The voice at the other end of the line was breathless, excitable, girlish.

'Oh, Creena, darling. Frankie's told me so much about you.'

Frankie? Only Creena called Frank 'Frankie' – or so she'd imagined.

'Excuse me,' she cut in. 'Who am I speaking to?'

The girl at the other end of the line giggled.

'Oh sorry, didn't I say? My name's Alice. I expect Frankie's told you all about me too, hasn't he?' Without waiting for Creena's reply, she carried on, with barely a breath between sentences. 'The thing is, darling, I've been looking for Frankie everywhere and he's not at work, and he's not at his flat, and I need to get a message to him really quickly. And seeing as you're like a sister to him, I thought you might be able to pass the message on...'

Like a sister? Creena's head was spinning. Was that how Frank really saw her? It took considerable effort to get a word in edgeways, but she managed it.

'W-what exactly is this all about?'

'You see, it's like this. I'm doing rather hush-hush work at the moment, so I can't really tell you about it, but I have to work an extra shift this weekend so that means Frankie and I can't go on our little...' she giggled again, 'our little trip...'

'Your...?'

'But I've telephoned the hotel, and they're sure they can

507

find us a double room for next weekend. So if you see Frankie, perhaps you could let him . . . ?'

Creena could feel a darkness creeping over her, a cold iron hand grasping, squeezing at her heart. This woman . . . this woman was going away with Frankie?

The woman's voice was still trilling away brightly, twittering like some silly songbird:

'Frankie's such a darling, isn't he, Creena? He says he's going to buy me the loveliest engagement ring . . .'

Creena hardly heard the rest of the conversation, only dimly aware that she mumbled a few words into the receiver then heard Alice ring off with a cheery 'Bye, darling.'

So much for Frank being 'different'. From now on, Creena Quilliam was going to be nobody's fool.

Julia Paston put down the telephone receiver with a satisfying click. She'd always been a gifted little actress, and 'Alice' was undeniably one of her more successful creations. She'd known people like Creena Quilliam before. The girl was far too gullible and impetuous to have suspected any deception. She'd swallowed it hook, line and sinker.

Once Creena had given Frank his marching orders, the field would be well and truly open for Julia Paston. If she felt the slightest qualm of guilty conscience it was swiftly pushed aside. All was fair in love and war.

Just as Julia was setting down the receiver, the door opened and Frank walked in.

'Phone call?'

'Hmm.'

'Anything important?'

Julia smiled and patted down a curl of golden-brown hair.

'Just a little something that needed sorting out,' she replied. 'But it's all done now.'

'Creena!'

'No, Frank. I've told you, no.' She kept on walking, pigeons scattering for cover at each stride.

'But Creena – why are you so angry with me? I don't understand what's happening.'

'Oh, really?' Creena swung round to confront him. She hadn't expected it to be like this – she felt not so much upset as angry, and angrier with herself than she was with Frank. Her voice was scarcely more than a whisper, steady and controlled. 'Why are you lying to me?'

Frank was utterly aghast. He knew something had gone horribly wrong, but he couldn't for the life of him think what it could be. He'd been so convinced that, slowly but surely, they were growing closer together. When he'd received Creena's message to meet her on the Embankment, he'd never imagined that he would see such pain in those beautiful green eyes.

'Creena, I swear, I haven't the faintest idea what you're talking about.'

'You could have told me you were seeing other women. I wouldn't have minded so much if only you'd been honest with me...'

'You don't mean *Julia*?' He almost laughed with relief. 'If it's that stupid business at Waterloo station, I've explained...'

'Oh, you've explained, all right. I just don't believe you any more, that's all.'

'It's the truth, Creena. She told me – she only did it for a lark.'

'Oh, and what about *Alice*? Is she a lark, too?'

Frank stopped in his tracks, puzzled.

'Alice? Who's Alice?'

'You tell me.'

'I don't know anyone called Alice, I swear I don't.'

'Oh Frank, why don't you just tell me and have done with it?'

Frank gave a gasp of frustration.

'Because there's nothing to tell.'

'I never thought you'd lie to me.'

'Creena, I'm *not* lying to you – I've never lied to you in my life. I *couldn't* lie to you if I tried.'

And that's just the sort of thing Oliver Temple would have said, thought Creena. She'd believed him, too.

'I suppose it's partly my fault,' she said quietly, looking up and watching the barrage balloons dancing slowly and mournfully in the wintry sky. More than partly, she thought to herself. What right had she to expect Frank to be honest with her when she was hiding so much from him?

'What is?'

'We can't turn back the clock. I should have realised things could never be the way they used to be.'

'They can, Creena. Better.'

'No, Frank. I was wrong, I made a big mistake.'

He took her hands and for a moment she let him hold her there, fixing his gaze into hers, willing her to believe what he was telling her.

510

'Please listen to me, Creena.'

She pulled gently but firmly away.

'I don't want to see you any more, Frank. Not ever.'

Frank's light-olive complexion drained to a deadly grey-white.

'You don't mean that.'

'Yes, I do,' she said, and now the words came out simply and calmly. 'This time, Frank, we really are finished. For good.'

'More wine, darling?'

Oliver Temple, smooth and handsome in his dinner jacket and bow tie, reached solicitously across the table and squeezed the hand of his dinner companion. She blushed prettily at his touch, her ivory-white skin taking on a rosy tinge and her long drifts of red hair like burnished copper in the candlelight.

'Oh, Oliver,' she said, ostensibly gazing down at the tablecloth but in reality looking up at him through her long, sweeping lashes. 'I don't really think I should, do you? You'll be getting me tiddly.'

'Nonsense, darling.' He smiled and lifted the wine bottle, gently teasing away her covering hand so that he could top up her glass. She made no further protest. Why should she? Pretty, inexperienced, coquettishly shy, dear little Belinda Burrows trusted him completely.

It was a pity it was such a poor wine – and with the Government setting a fixed price for all restaurants, Oliver hadn't been able to treat Belinda to quite the slap-up meal he'd intended. Still, the girl seemed easily impressed – which was the way Oliver Temple liked his women.

Popsies were all the same really, he told himself; though admittedly he had a positive fetish for pretty redheads. To Oliver, the female sex were silly, gullible creatures you could wrap around your finger. Chase 'em, have some fun and move on, that was his motto.

And he didn't see anything wrong in it, either. Not that he'd always thought like that. When he was a kid he'd dreamed of love, but love couldn't get you the things you wanted in life, could it? Only money could do that – and as the third, unloved and unwanted son of his parents' loveless marriage, he couldn't expect to inherit a penny from his skinflint father. If he wanted money he had to stay married to Lucinda.

Lucinda was a rich bitch, but she loved him, oh yes, she loved him desperately beneath that hard-bitten, callous exterior. She knew that her money was the only reason he stayed with her, but that was an ace she was happy to play if it kept him by her side, her obedient lapdog, her plaything.

Oliver was aware how much it hurt Lucinda to know he was going with other women. Not just one or two, but dozens. Pretty little redheads he could toy with and control, the way Lucinda controlled him. Well, good. She deserved to suffer.

He smiled as he watched Belinda drink. You could tell she couldn't take it. He had high hopes of success tonight.

'It was ever so nice of you to take me out like this,' she said, laying her knife and fork across her empty plate.

'The pleasure's all mine,' he assured her – and with any luck, he wouldn't be lying. 'You're a smashing girl, Belinda, really special.'

512

Belinda giggled, showing off her perfect white teeth and making her small but perfect breasts tremble inside her chaste grey dress.

'Oh Oliver, don't tease! I bet all the girls are after you.'

'Not at all.'

'What about all those nurses at your military hospital then?'

He grimaced.

'Nurses! Ugh. I'd much rather have a pretty AFS girl any day.'

'Oh, Oliver, you don't mean that.'

He took her hand and kissed it gently.

'Oh, but I do, Belinda. I do. I'd much rather have you than any other woman.'

It was laughably easy. He'd done this so many times before that it was almost like reciting a script. He could play these innocent young things like musical instruments.

He dabbed his mouth with his napkin and got up from the table, brushing a stray crumb from his dinner jacket.

'Sorry, darling, but I simply must see a man about a dog.'

He left her with another dazzling smile, and strode off across the restaurant.

Jack Doyle waited a moment longer, until he had seen Oliver disappear through the door of the Gents', then left the bar and crossed to where Belinda was sitting. She looked up in surprise as the man in the loud blue suit arrived at her table.

'Mind if I have a word, miss?'

She looked at him half in puzzlement, half in alarm. Why

should a spiv want to speak with her – and a spiv with an appalling taste in suits at that?

'I ... er ... you're not trying to sell me something, are you?' she hazarded.

Jack made himself comfortable on Oliver's chair.

'I really don't think you ought to do that,' said Belinda, but Jack took no notice.

'Belinda, ain't it? Belinda Burrows?'

She stared at him in astonishment.

'How do you know my name?'

'Never mind that,' he said. 'I just came to give you a bit of advice.'

She giggled. That wine was stronger than she'd thought.

'What sort of advice?'

'About your friend Oliver Temple.' He spoke the name as though Oliver Temple were a smear of dog-dirt on his best two-tone shoes.

'Oliver? What about him? He'll be back in a moment,' she added in case the spiv had any funny ideas.

'He ain't no good, Belinda.'

She looked at him blankly.

'What do you mean?'

'He's the scum of the earth.'

'Is this some sort of joke?'

'I wish it was, lady. Fact is, your precious Oliver Temple's a cheatin' bastard. He's 'ad women all over London.'

'How dare you!' Belinda was scrunching her napkin into a ball. 'How dare you say such terrible things about Oliver...'

As Oliver was returning from the Gents, he noticed a

man sitting at his table – sitting in *his* chair, opposite *his* popsy! The barefaced cheek of it. He quickened his step.

'Is this man bothering you, Belinda?'

'Oh, Oliver – thank goodness you're here!' gasped Belinda, her face pale apart from the rosy circles of her rouged cheeks.

Oliver's grey-green eyes flicked over the ruffian sitting in his chair. There was something vaguely familiar about that sharp-featured face, that unapologetic stare.

'How dare you insult my fiancée!'

Jack's face broke into a cynical half-smile.

'Oh, *fiancée*, is it?' He turned his gaze to Belinda. 'I suppose he forgot to mention his wife?'

'Wife!' The remaining colour drained out of Belinda's face as she threw Oliver a horrified stare.

'He's talking rubbish, darling. I shall have him thrown out immediately. Waiter!'

'Yes, wife,' continued Jack calmly, as though nothing had happened. He took a card out of his pocket, a few spidery lines scrawled across the back. 'Flat Fourteen, Beaumont Court. Go and talk to her yourself if you don't believe me. Lucinda, her name is, ain't it, Oliver?'

There was a moment of horrible, gut-wrenching silence as Belinda fought to come to terms with the bombshell and Oliver glared at Jack. Perfectly at ease, Jack reached into his jacket pocket and took out his monogrammed cigarette case, offering it to the doctor with ironic politeness.

'Fag, mate? You look as if you could do with one.'

'How dare you!' hissed Oliver. 'How dare you make a scene and tell my fiancée these terrible lies?'

'Are they lies, Oliver?' demanded Belinda, suddenly not so sure.

'Of course they are!'

'Then you won't mind me seeing who lives at this address, will you, darling?'

Oliver watched in impotent rage as Belinda gathered up her things and made for the cloakroom, close to tears. He made to follow her but Jack grabbed him by the arm.

'I wouldn't if I were you, mate.'

Oliver shook himself free.

'Get your hands off me. Waiter!' Why didn't that damned waiter come, and why were all the other diners studiously avoiding looking in his direction? Even the barman was engrossed in polishing a glass.

'Why don't you sit down, so's we can 'ave a little chat, *Mister* Temple?'

'Why the hell don't you get out of this restaurant and leave me alone?'

'All in good time, Oliver, all in good time.' He flicked cigarette ash on to the remains of Oliver's dinner. 'Now sit down.'

'Now look here . . .'

'I said sit.' Jack's voice carried a sudden grim authority which even Oliver Temple could not ignore. 'Or do you want me to get up an' tell all these nice people what a bastard you really are?'

With the utmost reluctance Oliver sat. Glancing out of the corner of his eye he noticed a waiter approaching. Thank God for that. At last he'd be able to get this appalling thug out of the restaurant, and maybe he'd even be able to catch up with Belinda before she did anything silly.

'Look, what is it you want – money?'

'I got money, Mr Temple. I got lots of money. Not like you.' Jack sneered with utter contempt as he contemplated Oliver Temple's treacherously handsome face. 'I got to ask you, Oliver, what sort of a man is it that lives off 'is wife's money and 'as 'is way with young girls what don't know no better?' He paused. 'You're just a ponce, Oliver Temple. Nothin' but a stinking rotten ponce.'

The waiter arrived at the table, coolly aloof in his starched shirt and tails. Thank the Lord, thought Oliver, by now distinctly hot under the collar.

'Sir?'

'Have this man removed immediately. Call the police if necessary.'

'I'm afraid I can't do that, sir.'

'What!'

Oliver stared in astonishment at the waiter's impassive face.

'I said, I'm sorry but I can't do that, sir. You see, me and this gentleman, we're old friends.'

It was then that Oliver caught sight of the knife. His heart was pounding like the pistons on a overheated steam engine, every vein in his head throbbing like a fat blue snake.

Oh my God!

The knife was tucked neatly into the waiter's palm, concealing it from the other diners, but Oliver could quite clearly make out the four-inch blade, razor-sharp and glinting with menace.

He tried to swallow, but his mouth was desperately dry.

'If you don't leave me alone, I'll call for help.'

Jack shrugged unconcernedly.

'If you like. Shouldn't bother, though. These good people ain't interested in slime like you. You won't get no 'elp from them. We got an arrangement, see.'

'W-what . . . what do you want?'

'That's better, Oliver.' Jack relaxed in his chair. Nice restaurant this. Supplied the kitchens regular, he did. He'd made a lot of friends here over the years. 'Now we can 'ave that little chat.' He pulled luxuriously on his cigarette, making it last, making Oliver Temple sweat like he'd never sweated before.

Oliver watched him, half in anger, half in terror. He knew he'd seen this man before, but he couldn't quite place him, couldn't remember anything about him except that he was the sort of man you ought to be afraid of.

When Jack spoke again, his tone had changed. He was no longer taunting; he was threatening, the look in his blue eyes steely and unforgiving.

'I know a lot of things, Oliver; and a lot of people. I know everyone in this restaurant for a start – the chef, the barman, the cigarette girl, even the retired lieutenant-commander over there. And believe me, Mr High-and-Mighty, I know all about you. Everything.' He thought of Creena, and the bitter taste of anger filled his mouth. 'I know what you done.'

'What are you trying to say?' Oliver's voice was shaky. The blade was uncomfortably close to his throat, its tip so near to the skin that a light flick would open up the carotid artery. He wasn't angry any more, just plain scared.

Jack stubbed out his cigarette on the lapel of Oliver's jacket.

'I come 'ere to give you a little warning,' he said. 'If you get up to your tricks ever again, Mr Temple, that pretty face of yours ain't goin' to look so pretty no more.'

'You can't threaten me like that!' gasped Oliver, his whole body shaking violently.

'Oh, but I can, pretty boy, I can,' replied Jack with immense satisfaction. 'I got friends everywhere. I know people. No matter where you go I'll know all about you. Step over the line just once, and you get it.' He smiled as he slipped his cigarette case back into his pocket. 'And that ain't a threat; it's a promise.'

It was a damp, murky December evening in Ballakeeill; and behind heavy blackout curtains, Ida and George Quilliam were eating their supper.

Tick. Tick. Tick. The seconds dripped away, time unrolling like a great carpet, upon which no step could ever be retraced.

'Amy will be in Ramsey now,' said Ida. 'It's a bad night — we shouldn't have let her go.'

George speared and ate a piece of carrot, without looking up from his plate.

'She had to go. She'd said she would.'

'But all the same . . .'

'It'll be character-building.'

'I'd still rather she hadn't gone.'

'She won't come to any harm.'

'No. No, I suppose not.'

The Girl Guides had gone up Sulby way to help with a Civil Defence training exercise, and Amy had begged to be allowed to go with them. Ida had felt an irrational fear welling up inside her, but in the end she'd had to let Amy go.

One by one, they had all left her. And before she knew it Amy would go too, and then there would be nothing, no one, no point in anything at all.

George glanced across the table at Ida. She had changed so much that he scarcely recognised her as the girl he had first met and wooed, all those years ago. He remembered that day as if it were yesterday: three laughing schoolgirls on the promenade at Port St Mary: sensible Ida, her scatty sister Bessie and Ida's best friend Jeanie. Jeanie had been the beauty of the trio, but even then Ida had been the dominant one, strong but not shrewish, not eaten away by bitterness like she was now.

Ah, but that had been so many years ago, more years than he cared to count. And the whole world seemed to have turned inside out since then.

'I said the junior children could have their own piglet to look after,' he announced. 'You don't mind, do you? I'm building a second pen.'

Ida sighed.

'Whatever you like.'

'The salvage fund has reached nearly twenty pounds.'

'You don't say.'

'I really must have words with Alfie Gawne's mother. His attendance record is frankly appalling.'

Ida pushed her supper around her plate without any real enthusiasm. She felt angry – angry at George because he could escape the pain by running away into his own little world of pigs and aluminium scrap and naughty children. Angry at Amy because she was young and happy and had all her mistakes still to make. Angry even at Frankie Kinrade, who had had the effrontery to survive when her own first-born son had not.

And most of all, angry with the daughter whose name she could not even bring herself to speak, for fear that she might one day weaken and let in the first, perfidious glimmerings of forgiveness.

Creena gazed for the last time at her room in the staff nurses' home; at the narrow iron bedstead and the table and chair and rug that had constituted her home over these last few months.

Was she really going? She had to look at the bulging suitcase on the bed to remind herself that yes, it was true; after more than four years she was finally leaving the Royal Lambeth Hospital. Her trunk was packed: all locked and labelled ready for the porter to take it to the station, ready for shipping.

Some things were for the best, and right now, leaving London was what was best for Creena.

She glanced at her watch. Just time to say her final goodbyes, and then she must be off or she'd miss the train – assuming there was a train to miss. You really couldn't be sure these days.

Rat-a-tat-tat.

'Yes?'

The door opened to reveal Dillie, wearing her best frock and carrying an armful of brown-paper parcels.

'Thank goodness!' she panted. 'I ran all the way back but I was afraid I might have missed you.'

'Oh, Dillie, you didn't honestly think I'd go without saying goodbye to you?'

Dillie dropped the parcels on the bed.

'This one's from Mo, and this one's from Micky and Kitty, and this one's from Jack but he said not to tell you, and Old Bert says to take care of yourself and always wear proper underwear . . .'

'Slow down, slow down!' Creena pleaded, unable to take it all in.

'Millie Duval gave me this.' Dillie held out a huge home-made card. 'It's from the kids at Long Wall Yard.'

Creena accepted it with a lump in her throat. So this was what all the whispering and giggling had been about on her last visit to the shelter group. She opened up the card. Straggling capitals ran across the inside, underneath a boldly painted picture of a woman with bright scarlet hair: 'MRS KWILLIAM' the caption read. In the distance a lopsided ship was riding on a wavy brown sea, a huge banner of purple smoke emerging from its funnel.

'A perfect likeness, eh?' chuckled Dillie.

All around the inside of the card ran the shaky signatures of thirty or more children – some obviously written with care, others little more than squiggles. But they meant the world to Creena. This was just about the first thing that the kids from Long Wall Yard had ever worked on together, as a team.

'And this,' Dillie produced a small package from her dress pocket, 'this is for you from me.'

Creena unwrapped it carefully and found a small brooch inside: a little silver cat decorated with black enamel.

'It isn't quite a Manx cat,' Dillie conceded, 'but it looks a bit like Smudge – I thought it might remind you of me and Mo.' She looked at Creena, suddenly very sad. 'You won't forget us, will you?'

'Oh, Dillie!' Creena embraced her friend with violent enthusiasm, trying hard not to cry. 'I couldn't, not ever! I shall come and see you, and you and Mo and the kids must come and see me. We can go swimming at Grenaugh.'

'I can't swim,' said Dillie, not sure whether to laugh or cry.

'I'll teach you.'

They hugged for ages, neither wanting to let go just yet. In the end it was Dillie who drew gently away.

'You are all right, aren't you?' Her brown eyes searched Creena's face anxiously. Creena nodded.

'I'm fine,' she said. 'Just angry. With myself, mostly. I guess I didn't know Frank as well as I thought I did.'

'I'm so sorry,' said Dillie with a shake of the head. 'Frank didn't seem the sort to . . . well, you know.'

'They never do, do they?' pointed out Creena.

Dillie paused.

'It's not too late to change your mind, you know. You don't have to go back to the island. You could still stay. Matron's crying out for a staff nurse on Female Surgical.'

Creena's long-suppressed tears turned to laughter.

'What – put up with Sister Meredith all over again? No thanks!' She took Dillie's hands and held them very tightly. 'No, Dillie, it's time to move on.'

'You're absolutely sure?'

'Positive. The married camp at Port Erin needs a welfare nurse to look after the mothers and children, and it's a chance for me to make a fresh start. I'm looking forward to it.'

'What about the trouble with your parents though? Won't it be awkward, with them only a few miles away?' Dillie looked concerned, but Creena just shrugged.

'They've made it clear they don't want to know me. Why should I let them stop me doing what I want to do, or being where I want to be?'

Creena was determined to escape from the blackness now. She had had enough of guilt and self-loathing. If her parents couldn't forgive her, the least she could do was try and learn to forgive herself.

And so she was going home to the island. Not to Ballakeeill; but to rented rooms in Castletown, where Uncle John had once lived. Perhaps there she would find her new beginning; perhaps not. But either way, she was going to try.

Chapter 28

Micky hopped from one foot to the other in the chilly December air, trying to keep himself warm as he watched the stallholders hawking their wares along The Cut. Fear was welling up inside him like a black tide.

'Apples, lady. Lovely rosy apples.'

'Bag o' specks please, Joe.'

'Carrots, get yer carrots. Make yer see in the dark they do.'

A woman with a red nose and dark, greasy hair handed over her money.

'I'll 'ave two pound. Maybe I'll be able to see what me old man's gettin' up to in the blackout!'

Peals of raucous laughter rang out around the stall and Micky used the diversion to edge a little nearer. He was glad he hadn't let Kitty come with him. She'd probably give the game away. Kitty was still just a kid, whilst he – at twelve years old – would soon be old enough to leave school.

Not that he spent any more time there than he had to. This war had changed the way he looked at things. Now he knew there were more important things than sitting in a stuffy classroom, whatever Auntie Mo might say. He had acquired responsibilities. With Dad a prisoner of war and Jack about to do a flit, he would soon be the head of the household. He had to get money from somewhere to help Auntie Mo.

You ain't as clever as you think you are, Micky my boy, mused Jack as he watched from the shadows. Hands thrust deep in his trouser pockets, he followed at a discreet distance as Micky sauntered with apparent casualness along the double row of stalls. It wasn't difficult to guess what he was doing. Anyone with half an eye could see the kid was on the nick.

But it was a busy morning in the market, and shoppers were not as vigilant as they might have been. At the very moment when the middle-aged woman in a cut-down man's overcoat was leaning over a barrow, prodding the apples and proclaiming their inferior quality, young Micky was slipping his hand into her shopping basket, extracting her purse with shaking fingers.

Bloody hell, thought Jack, moving in fast. Nicking apples, that's one thing; but I never took you for a dip, Micky Bates. And you're not even a good one.

He seized Micky by the shoulder and spun him round. With luck he might be able to salvage the situation, The purse was still in the boy's hand, and the look on Micky's face almost – but not quite – made Jack laugh. At least the little sod had the decency to look guilty.

'Uncle Jack! I . . .'

Before Micky had a chance to say another word, Jack had prised the purse from his grasp and was tapping its owner on the shoulder. She turned round with an irritated expression.

'What you want?'

Jack held out the purse. It was bulky with coppers. Meagre pickings for a sneak thief, but a fortune to some. That handful of pennies was probably all she had to keep her family on for the rest of the week.

'I think you dropped this,' he said.

The woman snatched it off him with a look of intense suspicion, opened it up and quickly surveyed the contents.

'I 'ope it's all here.'

'It is.' Jack threw Micky a look that nailed him to the spot.

'It better be. And you ain't gettin' no reward. I know your sort, Jack Doyle.'

Jack shrugged.

'I ain't after no reward.'

The woman seemed mollified, her tense facial muscles relaxing slightly.

'Oh. Well, that's all right then. Ta very much, I'm sure.' She turned away, leaving Jack and Micky looking at each other uncomfortably.

'I want a word with you,' said Jack grimly.

'Uncle Jack . . .' Micky squirmed.

'Shut up or I'll hand you over to that copper.' Jack nodded in the direction of an ominous dark-blue helmet, bobbing above the milling heads of the crowd. He stooped and his face loomed large in Micky's terrified gaze. 'And I mean that.'

With Jack's vice-like grip on his arm, Micky shuffled

miserably through the crowds and into the relative privacy of a small alleyway which led off the market.

'I can explain,' he said in a small voice, all his pretended bravado slipping away with every passing second.

'I doubt it,' said Jack.

'I were only . . .'

'Only what, Micky? Only thievin'? Why the 'ell did you go an' do a thing like that? You was always a good boy – honest, kept yer nose clean.'

Micky stopped kicking the cobblestones and lifted his head.

'I were doin' it fer Kitty an' Auntie Mo. So's they'd 'ave money when you've gone.'

Jack let out a long sigh of exasperation.

'For Gawd's sake, Micky, do you think I'd let Ma and you starve?' He patted the breast pocket of his jacket, where he kept the wallet with his daily takings. 'I made provisions, understand? *Provisions*.'

Micky's young face went through a series of expressions: relief, embarrassment, anger, sulky resentment.

'I were only doin' same as you do,' he said.

Jack exploded into instant fury, taking Micky by the shoulders and shaking him so violently that the boy let out a cry of alarm. Realising what he was doing, Jack let him go.

'Don't you ever say that again. I ain't never taken from them as couldn't afford it. *Never*. You don't steal from your own, understand?'

Micky nodded silently, reluctantly. He knew he'd been stupid but he wasn't going to admit it without a struggle.

Jack's voice softened. In his heart he understood only

528

too well what Micky had tried to do. He hadn't exactly been a good role model for the boy in the past, and now – when his family seemed threatened – it was hardly surprising that even honest, open Micky might turn to crime for a quick solution.

'What you were doin', Micky, that ain't the answer.' Jack pulled out his cigarette case and lit up nervously. He'd never been any good at this Dutch-uncle stuff. 'There's other ways – like stoppin' at school an' doin' what you're told an' gettin' a decent job.'

'You never done none of that,' Micky pointed out, as Jack had feared he might.

'Yeah, well, maybe I should've.'

Micky felt confused. He'd always hero-worshipped Uncle Jack, despite Auntie Mo's warnings about him. Now Jack was forcing him to look at him in a new way, and he didn't like it. Micky made himself voice the question he'd been too afraid to ask.

'Is that why you're joinin' the army, Uncle Jack?'

Jack slipped the silver cigarette case back into his inside pocket.

'Sort of.'

'But you don't 'ave to, do you? Dr Cohen says you ain't fit. You could stay 'ome with us.'

Jack restrained him with a hand on his shoulder.

'Dr Cohen says whatever you want if you pay him enough,' he said. 'And now he says I'm A1. So there ain't no stoppin' me joinin' up, is there?'

'I still don't understand,' protested Micky.

'You will one day,' sighed Jack. 'I ain't no hero, and that's a fact. But sometimes there's things you 'ave to do, even if you don't want to.' And some you do want to, he thought, casting his mind back to that git Oliver Temple. He fingered the brim of his fedora. Gawd but it would be tough exchanging it for a forage cap. 'The thing is, Micky, when I'm away you'll be the man of the house.'

'I know, Uncle Jack, that's why . . .'

'Shut up and listen. You'll be the man of the house and you're goin' to have to act like it, not like some stupid kid. Get yourself nicked by the cops and you ain't no good to no one. Got that?'

Micky nodded dumbly.

'You got to promise me, Micky – no more thievin', and you'll stay at school long as you can. An' you'll look after your Auntie Mo and your sister. Promise?'

Micky hesitated for a split second, but you couldn't argue with Jack Doyle.

'Yeah, all right.'

'An' there's another thing you can promise me; that you'll never, ever 'ave anything to do with a man called Sid Clayden. You got that?'

Micky looked puzzled, but nodded.

'OK. I promise.'

'Good. Well, now that's done you can go 'ome an' tell your Auntie Mo I'm bringin' a nice piece of beef for dinner.'

'Are you goin' to tell her . . . about . . . ?' Micky's face was ashen with dread. If there was one thing worse than being found out by Jack, it was being found out by Auntie Mo.

Jack shrugged.

'Let's just say it's between you an' me for now, shall we?

But if you do it again, Micky Bates, I'll get to 'ear about it.
And then there'll be hell to pay, you mark my words.'

'You mean you won't tell 'er?'

'Shove off, will yer, Micky, before I change my mind.'

He watched Micky running off between the stalls,
describing a zigzag path around old dears and their
scrawny dogs. He was just a kid, just a stupid little kid
who'd meant well – uncomfortably like himself at the
same age, thought Jack with a twinge of remorse. If
Micky went off the rails, he couldn't help thinking it
would be his fault.

But Micky wouldn't. He wasn't a bad lad, it was just that
he didn't think. Micky was fundamentally honest, clever
too, and he'd just had the fright of his life. When this god-
awful war was over, there'd be new opportunities for bright
boys like Micky. No one would have to end up in the
trouble Jack Doyle had got himself into.

Slowly he strolled through the market, taking in all the
familiar landmarks of his own childhood as though he were
seeing them for the very first time. In a week, maybe ten
days, he'd be gone, packed off to join his army unit, and
then what? It was quite possible he might never see
Lambeth Marsh again.

'Afternoon, Jack.'

'Afternoon, Harry.'

Harry Greenberg, of Greenberg's High-Class Tailors,
darted out of the doorway of his shop with a swatch of
chalk-striped worsted over his arm.

'How about a new suit, Jack? I got some lovely stuff.
Here, feel the quality.'

Jack smiled as he waved the suiting away. Harry was

right, it *was* lovely stuff. It'd make up into a beautiful double-breasted two-piece, and Harry was always happy to ignore the Government regulations about narrow lapels and no turn-ups.

'Sorry, mate,' he said. 'But I ain't goin' to need no new suits for a while. I'm goin' away, see.'

'OK, OK.' Harry looked disappointed but resigned. 'But any time you want to do a little business, you contact me, right?'

'Right,' said Jack, and walked on past the ironmonger's shop and the fish stall, laid out with salt cod and great big lumps of whale meat and snoek, eyeless on a dirty marble slab.

That business with Sid Clayden had really opened his eyes, made him see himself for what he was, what he had become. He'd realised to his surprise that he'd rather be dead than a boot-licking lackey to a man like Clayden, and he'd never imagined he'd feel like that.

The thing was, you couldn't define everything in shades of grey. Sometimes things really were black and white, like Mo Doyle always said they were. Black and white; right and wrong: he had conveniently blurred such concepts for far too long. He didn't want to go, but even Jack Doyle had to do his bit.

It wasn't as if there was anything stopping him. He'd made ample provision for Mo and the kids, and any lingering hopes he might have had about Creena had disappeared now that she had gone back to the Isle of Man. Not that he had ever been in with more than the ghost of a chance, if he was honest with himself he knew that. But he couldn't help wishing that, just once, she had been able to see past the cocky façade into his heart and understand that Jack Doyle thought the world of her.

Tonight, at 12 Bishop Street, there would be a good thick piece of beef, traded from Simms the butcher in return for Jack's favourite blue cashmere suit. No point in hanging on to it any longer – where he was going he wouldn't need it, and besides, it'd be out of fashion by the time he got demobbed.

When he arrived home, Mo would greet him at the door with tears in her eyes, full of sadness and joy and pride. Old Bert would shake his hand and Edna Tilley would wipe her eyes on her beetroot-stained apron. And Smudge the cat would lick his lips in pleasure; because, like Jack, he understood the futility of wondering what might happen in the future.

The best you could do was take care of today.

George Quilliam leant over the wall of the pigsty and scratched Maisie's bristly hide with the back of his garden rake. She grunted and snuffled her appreciation, squealing in protest every time he dared pause for a rest.

Soon it would be time to go back in, but he felt no inclination to do so. Although it was 20 December, there were few signs of Christmas spirit at Ballakeeill school. The annual nativity play had left George with little taste for celebration, and he hardly even had the energy to sustain the ongoing feud with that oaf John Duggan.

The news – via Mona – that Creena was back on the island had come as a shock. George wasn't blind. He knew that Amy had been silently delighted, afraid to show her pleasure in the presence of her grim-faced parents, who had never once explained to her why it was that they would have nothing to do with their elder daughter. Secretly, George felt they owed Amy an explanation. But how could they offer her one? How could you tell an innocent sixteen-year-old girl what a shameful thing her sister had done?

Ida had taken the news with apparent indifference, as though being told about the actions of a stranger.

'Is that so?' she had said, and then gone back to her mending. But George had seen her hand trembling as she drew the wool tight over the domed head of the darning mushroom. Whether she admitted it or not, it was plain to see that Ida Quilliam couldn't get Creena out of her mind.

According to Mona, Creena was working in the married camp at Port Erin, and living in Castletown. She had rooms in Arbory Street, just across the parade from Queen Street, where first his grandfather and then his brother John had lived. George's thoughts kept returning to the days of their childhood, when he and John had made regular trips to Castletown to visit their grandfather.

Winter or summer, they had always played on the shingle shore behind Grandfather's house, the salt spray stinging their bare legs and faces as they ran about the rock pools, slipping and sliding on flat grey stones that slid across each other like tea plates. Later on, it had seemed natural that John would come to live in that same tiny, narrow, sea-lashed house in Castletown.

John. A dart of anger pierced George's nostalgia. What a good-for-nothing he had turned out to be, roaming the world on a series of second-rate cargo ships until at last his luck had run out. A fine uncle he had been to Creena, filling her head with fantasies, undoing all the strict moral education which George had instilled into her at Ballakeeill School.

'George! George!'

Ida's voice boomed across the empty schoolyard and George reluctantly turned away from the pigsty.

'Coming, dear.'

He wanted the strength of his anger to remain constant, as a mark of loyalty to Ida. But he could not prevent the doubts creeping in from time to time, the pain from stabbing at his heart as he thought of how his family was scattering, fragmenting, leaving him with nothing. What Creena had done was very wicked, there was no denying that. But how many times had John done wrong – and no matter how often he had condemned his brother, George had never stopped loving him.

If he tried hard enough, could he stop loving Creena?

'Thank you, Mona – and Happy New Year!'

Creena stood for a little while in the gathering dusk, waving as the old farm van coughed and spluttered into the distance and disappeared; then turned and walked towards the centre of Castletown.

It was good of Mona to invite her to the farm for New Year's Day – her first day off since she'd started work at the internment camp. It had been better still to feel part of a family again. And there had even been presents – small, unexpected Christmas gifts from Tom and Amy, smuggled to the farm by Mona as though they were contraband – which in a way they were. It was good to know that her brother and sister at least still wanted to know her.

'Happy New Year, gel. And how're you doin?' An extremely old man was shuffling his way very slowly down the street, almost bent double by his arthritic spine.

'Happy New Year, Mr Gelling. I'm very well, thank you. And yourself?'

'Ach, middlin' bad, middlin' bad,' replied old Joshua Gelling, ninety if he was a day. 'Still, the good Lord's seen fit to spare me another year, so I mustn't be after complainin'.' He twisted his tortoise neck upwards so that he was looking at her. 'Been to see your folks over Ballakeeill?'

'Er, no. My cousin Mona at Kewaigue.'

'Ah.'

Never had a single syllable carried so much meaning. That was the trouble with the island, mused Creena; sooner or later everyone knew everyone else's business. It took some getting used to again, even after the naturally inquisitive inhabitants of Lambeth Marsh. London – and a nurse's uniform – at least offered a little anonymity.

'She still got them Eyetie internees workin' for her, then?'

'Yes, she has. They do all the heavy work on the farm.' Old man Gelling shook his head.

''Tis well I remember the first war, gel. We was livin' over Peel way then, an' my Annie did live in mortal fear of them internees at Knockaloe. Thought they was goin' to kill us in our beds, she did. But they was harmless, the most of 'em. If you ask me, all men's pretty much the same underneath.' He pulled his coat more tightly around his shoulders and leaned on his stick. ''Tis a raw wind brewin' up,' he observed. 'I'm glad my days on the herrin' boats is over.'

They walked on very slowly, past the long row of painted cottages which Creena knew so well. Even in the dusk it was easy to make out the peeling, cream-coloured façade of Curlew Cottage, where her Uncle John had lived. But that had been long ago, when she was just a child. She was a grown woman now, a grown woman sorting out her problems for herself.

Bidding old Mr Gelling a polite good evening, she turned into the square. Once the capital, Castletown retained an old-world grandeur seen nowhere else on the island. Elegant houses with wrought-iron balconies ran along one side of the parade, one of them once the residence of Nelson's helmsman at Trafalgar, one of Creena's distant ancestors, Captain Quilliam. In the centre stood the Smelt monument, a truncated pillar in yellow stone; and towering above the whole rose the reassuringly solid battlements of Castle Rushen.

Creena felt comfortable here. She knew Castletown almost as well as she knew Ballakeeill, having spent so many summer days at her uncle's cottage, listening to his tales of life on the high seas.

It was chilly tonight, old man Gelling was right. She thrust her gloved hands into her pockets, her breath misting the air in front of her face and her auburn hair frizzy with static electricity inside its snood. She wondered what it was like in London, whether there was snow in Lambeth Marsh, and whether Dillie and Mo were missing her as much as she was missing them.

As she headed home to her rooms above the bakery in

Arbory Street, she thought of how her life had changed since war broke out, almost four and a half years ago.

Creena knew she ought to make one last effort to make contact with her parents. But they would refuse to see her if she turned up at Ballakeeill, and writing letters was a waste of time. The best chance of success was to find an intermediary. And the obvious choice was Aunt Bessie.

She'd been avoiding Bessie ever since she arrived back on the island. Her aunt had always been good to her, and yet ... when all was said and done, Bessie was Ida Quilliam's sister.

Well, she couldn't put it off forever. One of these days she'd have to pluck up the courage to go and see Aunt Bessie.

Staff Nurse Dillie Bayliss. *Senior* Staff Nurse Dillie Bayliss. It had a ring to it.

Dillie couldn't keep the smile from her face as she gave her hair a final tidy and made sure that her cap was straight. Its starched bow didn't half cut into the soft flesh under her chin, but what did a little discomfort matter? Yes, she was working under crabby old Sister Meredith, instead of doing her midder as she'd planned, but that didn't seem to matter either. Once the war was over there would be plenty of time for plans. Matron had promoted her to senior staff nurse. And that was more than Dillie had ever dreamed she could achieve.

As she strode down the corridor towards Female Surgical, Dillie thought of Arnold. Some men would have resented her success, but not him. How pleased he'd been for her. She still had the bunch of flowers he'd given her, arranged in a milk jug in her room. Where on earth had he managed to find such lovely flowers in the middle of winter?

'Morning, Nurse Bayliss!'

'Morning, Harry.' She lowered her voice and grinned. 'How are the chickens? Quilliam especially wanted me to ask about the chickens.'

'Oh, right as rain. She all right, is she, Nurse Quilliam?'

'I had a letter from her the other day. She says the internee women are keeping her on her toes. Oh, and I heard from Clarke-Herbert. She's having a whale of a time in the QAs.' Dillie sighed, momentarily saddened. 'Funny, really – I'm happy for them, but I do miss them all, especially Creena. Sometimes I just wish it could be the way it used to be, when we were all probationers together.'

'She gave me a real ear-bashing about those chickens, your friend Quilliam,' remarked Harry philosophically, leaning on his trolley. 'But she's got spirit, that girl. Give her my best when you write, Nurse.'

This war seemed to be all about being separated from people, thought Dillie as she walked into the ward. Separated from friends, separated from family. Now even Jack had left Lambeth – and who could ever have guessed that Jack Doyle would let himself be conscripted for active service? These days she never seemed to stop worrying – about Jack; about Creena; about Kitty and Micky, growing up in a world that had almost forgotten what peace was like; about Marian, dodging the bullets at some front-line field hospital.

And she worried about Mo, too. Good, stoical Mo, who had always been strong for everyone else, never giving a thought to herself or her own needs. How would she fare without Jack to scold and bully; Jack who had quietly taken care of her despite her pride and her protests?

You can't take all the cares of the world on your shoulders, Dillie Bayliss, she told herself as she swept into Sister's office to hear the morning report. Just do what Paddy Doyle would have told you to do: get your head down and work, and take care of your own.

'Frank. Frank, you haven't drunk your tea.'

Frank did not even bother looking up.

'I'm not thirsty.'

Julia Paston nudged the cup and saucer a little closer.

'Oh, go on, just try. You've had nothing since we came on duty last night.'

This time Frank's gaze met hers briefly, then wandered back down to the desktop.

'I told you, Julia,' his voice was firmer this time, 'I don't want it. You have it.'

Julia drew up her chair and sat on the other side of his desk, searching for things to say. This hadn't gone at all as she had planned.

After she had made the telephone call, she had simply sat back and waited for something to happen, telling herself that if that hadn't put Creena off Frank, she would just think up something else. Julia Paston was a very persistent woman when there was something she wanted. And she wanted Frank Kinrade.

She'd known it was over between Frank and the Quilliam girl the minute he stepped into the office, that Friday morning, with a face as long as a wet weekend. It had worked like a charm! It was obvious that the silly girl had believed every word, and given Frank his marching orders. Now the field was open for someone who really deserved his affections.

Only it hadn't worked out that way – at least, not yet. She had tried every trick in her sensual armoury, but still Frank was resisting her ample charms.

'Why don't you tell me what's the matter, Frank?' she pouted, hoping her soft voice would make him look at her, see the ruby lipstick she had put on just for him.

'Nothing's the matter. I'm just tired.'

'Is it,' she lowered her voice, 'is it woman trouble?'

Frank pushed the cup away from him and looked up.

'If it was,' he replied, 'I'd hardly tell you about it. Look at all the trouble you got me into.'

'Me?' She looked back at him with perfectly feigned innocence.

'Yes, you. Or have you forgotten that time at Waterloo station?'

Julia giggled at the memory.

'Oh, Frank,' she said. 'I just got carried away, I said I was sorry. Didn't I say I was sorry?'

Frank sighed. Julia *had* apologised to him very prettily after the Waterloo incident. In fact, she'd been perfectly nice to him ever since. Whatever it was that had made Creena so angry with him, whatever it was that had made her so determined never to see him again, it seemed unlikely that it had anything to do with Julia Paston.

'Yes, you did,' he conceded. Julia was being nice to him, sure enough, but that didn't make him feel any better. Creena had told him it was all over between them and it was obvious that she meant it. His one letter to her had been returned unopened, with a scrawled message on the envelope: 'Not known at this address.' Yes, she meant it all right – and somehow he was going to have to accept it.

'Look,' said Julia, leaning her folded arms on the desk and resting her chin on them, 'why don't you let me take you out of yourself a bit? I know this club . . .'

'No.' Frank shook his head. 'Not that.'

'How about the pictures then? Or a theatre. If you like, we could just go for a walk in the park . . .'

'No.' Frank's voice was almost a whisper. 'It's very kind of you, but no.'

He glanced at the clock and saw that it was almost eight forty, ten minutes after he should have left for home. He shuffled his papers and handed one to Julia as he got up.

'If you could just get this typed.'

'Yes, of course I will.' For once, Julia was at a loss to know what to say. Frank Kinrade was proving a very tough nut to crack. But it was worth it, she knew it would be worth it in the end.

'Thanks.' Frank put on his coat and took his hat off the stand.

'I . . . I meant to ask you if you fancied coming to meet my Aunt Ethel next month,' Julia cut in. 'She's the one who lives on the farm in Essex. I thought it might make you feel at home . . .'

'It's very kind of you,' replied Frank, 'but I probably won't be here next month.'

Julia's heart missed a beat.

'You're going on leave?'

Frank shook his head.

'I've asked the army for a transfer.'

'No!'

'I've had enough of London. In fact, I've had enough of pretty much everything.'

'But Frank. Frank...'

'You know how it is. I'll see you tomorrow.'

He pushed open the door and it swung back behind him, wafting cold draughts of air into the already chilly room. Suddenly Julia felt more alone than she had ever done in her whole life. She had lost. For the first time she really understood that she had lost. Frank would never be hers. His heart still belonged to that silly red-haired creature in the cheap green frock.

It's your loss, Julia told herself. Yes, it's your loss, Frank Kinrade. And she let out her grief in great hacking sobs, there in the half-light of the underground room where no one could hear her.

Chapter 29

No, no, no, no, no.

Why did this have to happen now? Why did it have to happen at all?

Mona Mylchreest sat in the farmhouse kitchen and re-read the telegram with unseeing eyes. Not that she needed to read it again; she already knew it off by heart. The Manx Regiment were returning from the Far East to a heroes' welcome, and Duggie had telegraphed her from Southampton to tell her the news she had been dreading for the last four and a half years.

Duggie Mylchreest was coming home.

Alexa had gone out and taken Kenny with her, seeing Mona's anger and upset, and sensing that she wanted to be alone to come to terms with what was happening. It wasn't as if it was unexpected. Yet Duggie's telegram filled her with rage. COMING HOME, that was all it had said. COMING HOME SEE YOU SOON STOP D. Coming home, indeed – as if nothing had ever happened and he'd never taken a fist to her in his life. Coming home, as if he had any right to call this place his home.

A shadow moved across the kitchen window and she

jumped half out of her skin, but it wasn't Duggie. It was only Antonio, beaming all over his fat little face, his black hair plastered to his head with sweat, even in this inclement February weather. He knocked respectfully at the door and entered, wiping his boots on the mat.

'Good morning, signora.'

'Good morning, Antonio.'

'The sick cow, she much better today, signora.'

Mona smiled. Antonio really did have a way with the stock – a curious attribute for a young man who had previously worked as a waiter in an Italian restaurant. In point of fact, Antonio had come to enjoy life on the farm so much that when – as a low-risk Category B internee – he had been offered the chance of release from internment, he had actually turned it down.

'I go help Giacomo with sheepses, yes?'

'That's right, Antonio.' She handed him a flask from the draining board. 'Here's some tea. I'll bring sandwiches out to the barn about eleven thirty.'

'Si, signora. Thank you, signora.'

He touched his cap respectfully and was gone. Why, oh why, did Duggie have to come back like this, destroying the happy, secure world which she had created for herself and the children? She thought of Giacomo and her anger turned to pain. She didn't love Giacomo, of course – but then, why should she love him? Had Duggie thought of love when he'd bedded half the women in the south of the island? What did she care about love any more? Love had only got her into endless trouble and she'd had enough of it. What was it Antonio would say? Finito.

* * *

'It's a long time since we did this,' observed Máire as she and Creena walked back towards Castletown from Scarlett Point.

'And last time the sun was shining,' added Creena, turning her face into the wind so that it blew her auburn mane out behind her, flicking the stray tendrils from her face.

It was a wild day; a typical February day, in fact, with huge white breakers rising up out of a storm-grey sea to lash the rocky shoreline all the way from Scarlett to the lighthouse at Langness Point. Sea birds fought the intermittent gusts which sent them swooping and fluttering down through the thunderous sky, in search of elusive food.

Creena and Máire struggled to stay upright in the powerful wind, its full force buffeting them as they walked along the exposed shoreline to the outskirts of the town. Creena almost had to shout to make herself heard.

'I'm glad you came back. I was afraid you might stay there.'

'In Ireland?'

Creena nodded. She had been worried when she heard that Máire had gone back to her home village in County Cork. But Máire shook her head.

'There's nothing left for me there. I only went back for a few days, to get things straight with my dad.'

'And you did?'

Máire nodded.

'It's all over, finished. The island is my home now and I'm staying here. It's silly to try and turn back the clock.'

Coats wrapped tight against the biting cold, they hurried

into the shelter of a row of cottages. Máire looked at Creena, wondering how best to broach the subject.

'You and your parents. I don't suppose you've . . . ?'

Creena shook her head.

'Hardly. They know I'm on the island, but they haven't been in touch and neither have I.' She paused. 'I suppose I ought to try, but, well . . .'

'But after all this time you're not even sure you want to?'

'It really hurt me at first, when they cut me off like that. But now it makes me angry.'

'There's still time for them to see sense,' suggested Máire.

'Perhaps. But do you know what really bothers me, Máire?'

'What?'

'Not knowing how they found out about . . . you know. My getting pregnant and losing the baby.'

Máire took Creena's hands in hers.

'You know I would never tell . . .'

'Never. I know.'

'You've been a good friend to me, Creena. The best. I'd never do anything to hurt you.'

Arm in arm they walked on into the shelter of the town square.

'How are you liking your work at the camp?' enquired Máire, thinking that now was a good time to change the subject.

'Well – it's certainly different from nursing at the Royal Lambeth!'

'What are the women like – are they friendly?'

Creena shrugged.

'Some are, some aren't. Some of them try to make your life difficult, but it's hard to blame them. How would we feel if we'd been cooped up for years on end and kept getting turned down by the Release Board?'

Crossing the square, they took the left-hand fork and headed down Arbory Street, a narrow thoroughfare lined with small shops – Cubbon's the butcher's, Corlett's 'the modern grocer', James Cooper's joinery workshop, Eaton's cycle shop, and of course the dairy.

Mr and Mrs Baker's Town Dairy had been a particular favourite with Creena and Robert when they were children, its black and white striped awning shading a window crammed brimful of the most mouthwatering delicacies: bull's-eyes and Manx Knobs, butter toffees and liquorice torpedoes. And then there had been the wonderful home-made ice cream, oozing with eggs and butter and cream.

'Robert and I used to come here in the summer,' explained Creena, pausing to gaze into the window, now sadly denuded of its treasure-trove of goodies. A faded cardboard cutout depicted a smiling mannequin popping a chocolate cream into her mouth. 'Whenever we had pocket money from Uncle John we'd come and spend it here.' She closed her eyes in glorious recollection. 'It was heaven.'

'And what *did* you spend it on?'

'Oh – toffees and bull's-eyes and liquorice twist and ices ... all the things that kids love.' She laughed. 'Mother and Father would have been furious if they'd known how we gorged ourselves. Father tried to make us save all our pennies in our piggy banks. But he never did find out.'

A little further on, on the opposite side of the road, stood the baker's shop.

'Here we are,' Creena announced, taking a key from her pocket and unlocking a small side door. The warm, yeasty aroma of baking bread rushed out. 'My room's on the second floor – it's hardly Government House, but it's home.'

Dusk was approaching on a gloomy afternoon in early February. Soon all the light would be gone, and already the Italians had left the farm for the night. Little Duggie had had his tea and was playing quietly in the parlour. Alexa had taken Kenny and the girls for a 'duty' visit to Ballakeeill, and Mona was alone with her thoughts.

As she dried the dishes and put them away, she glanced nervously at the kitchen clock. She wished with all her heart that she could make time stand still, so that she wouldn't have to go through with this, this ordeal that she had dreaded more than any other.

Wiping her hands she took off her apron and studied herself in the mirror by the coat rack. Why had she gone to all this trouble just for the benefit of that thug Duggie Mylchreest? Her fair, naturally curly hair was neatly arranged about her face. Only the finest of tiny lines showed at the corners of her blue eyes and her new dress showed off the girlish figure which had attracted so many men when she was a carefree sixteen-year-old.

She was cold but she didn't want to put on a cardigan. That would spoil the glamorous effect she'd spent ages creating. She intended Duggie to suffer before she ordered him out.

A knock on the door threw her into confusion. So soon? She hadn't expected him for another half-hour at least, she wasn't ready . . . Quickly she fiddled a stray curl into place and took two, three, four long breaths to steady her nerves. Closing the kitchen door behind her, she switched off the hall light. It wouldn't do to be caught infringing blackout regulations, even here in the middle of nowhere.

Rat-a-tat-tat. A second knock, more impatient this time.

'All right, I'm coming.' Her voice sounded high-pitched and quavery. Damn this woman's body that made her such a poor match for her husband's brute strength.

Lifting the latch, she opened the door. He was there on the doorstep, a bulky black silhouette against the deepening royal blue of the evening sky.

'Mona.'

There was a long pause. She felt hot and cold, shaky and afraid. She wanted to slam the door in his face, but forced herself to speak.

'I suppose you'd better come in.'

She closed the door and switched the light back on. As she returned to the kitchen Duggie followed, shuffling under the weight of his kitbag and a massive battered suitcase, held shut with a couple of old belts knotted together.

They stood for a long time in silence, on either side of the big oak table, as though watching each other for signs of weakness. He was a lot thinner, thought Mona to herself. There was noticeably less flesh stretched over the bones of that all-too-familiar face, and there were dark purple shadows beneath those eyes. You could pity a man like that – if it wasn't Duggie Mylchreest.

'You'll be wanting a cup of tea.' Mona picked up the kettle and filled it. It rattled as her shaking hand set it down on the hob.

'Mona . . .'

'I don't suppose you've eaten either.'

'It's been a long time since I saw you, Mona.'

Silence.

'You weren't at the homecoming parade in Douglas. I thought you'd be there.'

She gave a dry, cynical laugh.

'Oh yes, bit of a hero again, aren't you? But then I always did think killing people was just the job for you.'

'It wasn't like that. If you'd seen what I saw . . .'

Coming out from behind the table, he placed his hand on her arm and she snapped round to face him, her eyes full of fury. Her voice was cold and hard, all the nervousness gone out of it now.

'Don't you dare touch me, Duggie Mylchreest. Don't you dare touch me ever again.'

He stepped back, clearly astonished by Mona's reaction.

'You've changed,' he said, not so much accusing as puzzled.

'Yes, Duggie, I've changed. I've grown up over these last few years, and do you know what? I don't need you any more. I don't need some womanising brute of a husband coming home when he feels like it, and beating me black and blue.'

Duggie's jaw dropped, his hands tensing as they gripped the tabletop behind him. Mona waited for the inevitable blow. Would it be the flat of his hand stinging into the side of her face, or a vicious punch to the belly, so the bruises wouldn't show? She stared back at him as she steeled herself for the pain. There was neither fear nor fatalism in her eyes; only defiance.

'Go on,' she taunted him. 'Why don't you hit me? That's the answer to everything for you, isn't it? Army teach you some new ways to hurt people, did it? Go on . . .'

'I don't want to hit you.'

Duggie's words could not have been more of a surprise to Mona if he had said he was going to fly to the moon.

'Really.'

'Really, Mona.' He sank down on to one of the kitchen chairs and as she looked down at him she saw the first flecks of grey in his cropped brown hair. 'I've changed too.'

'You would say that, wouldn't you?' Mona tapped her fingers on the draining board as she prayed for the kettle to reach the boil. 'You just think you can walk back in here and take over, as if nothing had happened. Well it's not going to be like that, let's get that straight right from the start.'

For a moment she saw a spark of anger return to his eyes.

'It's my farm, Mona. You can't throw me off my own farm.'

'Oh, can't I?' Mona wondered if she was really saying these things, or if the whole thing was just a wild dream. 'I don't care whose farm this is on paper, Duggie, but I'm the one who's spent nearly five long years looking after it, making it pay. You never gave a damn about me or this farm. All you cared about was women and whisky. If it hadn't been for the Italians . . .'

'Italians? You've not had those bastards working on this farm? How could you?'

'How could I? I could because if I didn't we'd have lost the farm, understand? Gone for ever, Duggie. Gone because of your own bloody stupidity.'

He stared at her. He had never heard his wife talk like this before, never really imagined she was capable of standing up to him. In the past he had always relied on her fear to maintain his ascendancy over her. Now he saw with chilling realisation that all the fear had gone. She was more than a match for him, and he knew it.

The tragedy was, he really had changed. In North Africa, he'd seen and done things that could turn a man's wits; things that had so sickened him he'd wept like a baby. That cold, star-filled night in the desert, when the big gun had taken a direct hit. Kneeling on the sand with the fire-blackened corpse of his best friend cradled in his arms . . .

How could he make her understand?

'If it wasn't for Antonio and Giacomo,' Mona continued, 'there wouldn't be a farm for you to come back to.' She turned her face away a little as she added, 'Antonio's being released soon and he wants to stay on. I told him he could.'

'You what . . . ?'

'I told him he could.' Her eyes met Duggie's and this time there was no contest.

'You never wrote to me,' said Duggie.

'Why would I want to write to you? What have you ever done but hurt me?'

'You're my wife. You're mine . . .'

'I don't belong to anyone. And if you want any sort of place in my life you're going to have to earn it.'

Duggie stared at his feet, impossibly huge in his army boots. They seemed to swim in and out of focus.

'I . . . I'm sorry.'

'That's nice,' said Mona, warming the teapot.

'I really am.'

'Sorry for what?'

'For . . . everything. For what I've done.'

'You'll have to do better than that, Duggie. A lot better than that.'

Duggie took a deep breath. This did not come easy. In the old days he would have knocked seven bells out of her for daring to talk to him like this. But not now. Not any more. Things had changed.

'I'm sorry I hurt you. I'm sorry I lost my temper and got drunk and ran around with other women.'

Mona was silent for a few endless seconds.

'I suppose it's a start,' she said.

She turned and walked out of the kitchen, leaving Duggie behind her like a deflated balloon – no longer the conquering hero, no longer the swaggering brute who had stormed out of Mona's life in 1939.

She returned a few moments later, a small boy holding her hand. He was a pretty child of four or five, blond and fair-skinned like his mother, and his eyes were a bright cobalt blue beneath sleepy lids.

As soon as he saw Duggie the boy brightened and his round face was lit up by a beaming smile.

'Hello. Are you my daddy?'

Mona let go of the boy and pushed him gently forward, her eyes never leaving Duggie's face for a second.

'Well?' she said.

Duggie senior's eyes travelled from the boy to Mona and back again. He seemed dumbstruck by the child, unable to speak or move. And then he reached out his hands and pulled little Duggie to him.

'Hello, son,' he said, and, his eyes filling with tears, he embraced the child as his own.

Life down the pit was not like Tommy had imagined it. It was much, much worse.

Coal dust had ingrained itself into his skin so deeply that not even hours of scrubbing could remove it. His hands were calloused, his back ached and his eyes were sore from dust and grit.

He'd wanted to be in the RAF, like his brother; still, war was war and you couldn't have everything you wanted. But frankly he'd rather have been doing almost anything than hewing at a coalface at the bottom of an immense hole in the ground.

'Get a move on there, bach! It's not bloody Butlins, you know.'

A gruff Welsh laugh echoed down the gloomy gallery and others joined in the derision.

'Ruddy nancy-boys,' said Idris Jones. 'Can't 'ardly lift a knife and fork, let alone a pick and shovel.'

'Send 'im home to his mother,' said another voice nearby. 'He wants 'is nappy changing.'

Tommy did his best to close his ears, driving his pick harder into the coalface as if to make a point. He was accustomed to the taunts, and it wasn't as if he was the only one taking the stick – it was the same for all the Bevin boys. Mind you, he was his own worst enemy. It certainly hadn't helped his popularity much when he'd spoken out against going on strike. 'It's all right for you, boyo, your folks aren't starving,' they'd said. And they had a point.

Really, you couldn't win. It was dangerous and unpleasant work, but you never got any respect for it. The Welshmen looked down on you because you weren't Welsh, and because you'd had an education. When you went home on leave, your friends and family looked down on you because you didn't carry a gun. And as for chatting up girls! Most of them wouldn't look twice at an adolescent coal miner, still wet behind the ears.

But that was war for you, thought Tommy to himself. Nobody had ever said it would be fair.

A faraway, muted rumbling caused him no great concern. The pit was full of peculiar noises – the rumble and clatter of the coal trucks, the rattle and whine of the metal lift cage, descending the shaft.

But this. This was new and different. And it was getting louder.

'Mind yourself, boyo – she's going!'

Rough hands wrenched him to one side and he opened his mouth to protest, but suddenly the whole world seemed to be shaking itself to pieces. Great lumps of rock were falling from the roof, pit props snapping like toothpicks. And in the feeble light from his Davey lamp he saw Idris Jones and his two companions disappearing under a mound of pitch-black rubble.

Seconds later, there was silence. Dust filled Tommy's eyes and lungs. He coughed it free, tears scoring white lines down his blackened face as his eyes watered uncontrollably.

He had to get those men out. He had to do something. Desperate to be of use, he joined the small group of stunned miners digging away with their bare hands at the rubble. The gallery was completely blocked – goodness knows how they were going to get out, even if they did manage to free their comrades – but Tommy could only think about the men lying buried under the heaped-up rocks.

An arm. He could feel an arm. He cursed the lack of light; but there could be no question of lighting any naked flame in this deathtrap of a place, where a spark could turn into an inferno in seconds. He scrabbled away. The arm twitched, alive, moving. Got to get him out.

And then it happened again. The rumbling, the shaking, the end-of-the world blackness that felt as if it might never end.

'There's nothing wrong with your little boy, Frau Kessler.'

The German woman eyed Creena contemptuously.

'It is the food. You do not feed us properly. My child needs good food, not your English slops.'

'Nutritionally, the food is quite adequate,' Creena assured her. 'If you have a complaint, ask your house representative to go and see the commandant. But I can promise you there is nothing wrong with your son.'

'I know my own boy,' she said. 'My poor little Hans is so thin. He is ill, I tell you.'

Creena kept smiling, though in her mind's eye she was strangling Frau Kessler.

'Dr Jefferson says he is quite well, just a little pale because he doesn't get enough fresh air and exercise. It's a lovely spring day out there. Why won't you let him play games on the beach with the other children?'

Frau Kessler drew the boy back into her own protective embrace.

'Mutti knows best. My little Hans knows that.'

Creena thought he looked bored and frustrated by his mother's attitude, but she didn't dare say so. You had to be so careful not to tread on anyone's toes. Most of the time an uneasy calm reigned among the internee families, but only yesterday there had been an ugly fight in the dining room between two of the Austrian women. No one had been able to find out precisely what had caused it; and in all probability nothing much had. The smallest thing could provoke fits of temper among people who had too long been denied liberty.

It didn't help that so many women internees in low-risk categories had already been released, leaving a discontented nucleus – some genuinely a threat to British security, many simply unlucky, some even the victims of grudges and malicious lies.

'Look, Frau Kessler,' said Creena. 'Fräulein Mannheim takes singing and games, and painting and drawing classes for the children. Don't you think those would give Hans a new interest? I'm sure he'd feel better if he had something to occupy his mind.'

At this suggestion, Frau Kessler bristled with indignation.

'Let *her* take care of my little Hans? Let him be taught with Jewish children? I would rather kill him with my own hands.'

Pushing Creena aside, Frau Kessler left Creena's office in drifts of fox-fur and French perfume. Everyone knew that Hildegard Kessler was the wife of a senior Nazi official, and that she was highly unlikely to be released until the end of the war; but even so, her attitude to Agathe Mannheim puzzled Creena. There seemed such unfounded prejudice there. But then the camps were full of prejudice. And with the terrible stories that had started coming out of Germany, life was becoming increasingly uncomfortable for the German internees.

Creena was glad that Agathe had been brought from the adjacent single women's camp to teach the children. The pay might be a pittance, but having a job was an important source of self-esteem for any internee, an antidote to boredom and depression. She liked the girl . . . and besides, as Agathe had been one of Bessie's internees, it was as though there was already a link between them.

She settled down to complete some paperwork – the least favourite part of her job. The family camp had been moved from Port St Mary to Spaldrick – the northern end of Port Erin – back in August 1942. Creena divided her time between welfare work at the camp and giving nursing care and advice at the camp medical centre. Any seriously ill internees were sent under guard to Noble's Hospital, in Douglas.

It was a varied life, and – despite the frequent minor crises – Creena was settling into a routine. The changes in her own attitudes surprised her. Whereas she had once wondered how she could ever care for an enemy without anger and resentment, she now found that impartiality was almost automatic. You could not spend six months in a place like this without realising that the war was being conducted by ordinary human beings – on both sides.

A timid knock made her look up. A young woman with black bobbed hair and pale skin was standing in the open doorway to her office.

'May I have a word, please?'

Her English was excellent but heavily accented, each word chosen with precision.

'Yes, of course, Agathe. What is it?'

Agathe Mannheim came in and closed the door behind her.

'It is probably nothing.'

'Tell me anyway.'

'Two of the children in my singing class – they have spots, lots of pink spots. I thought I had better tell you.'

Oh no, thought Creena, not another outbreak of chickenpox. With so many children in close contact with each other, it was small wonder they were always catching things.

'I'll telephone Dr Jefferson right away,' Creena promised. 'And in the meantime, try and keep them away from the other children – we don't want them all catching it.'

One thing was for sure, she thought to herself as she picked up the telephone and rang the doctor. Whatever was causing this outbreak of spots, you could be certain that Frau Kessler would blame it on the food.

Creena smoothed down the skirt of her coat, adjusted her hat so that it sat more snugly on her tumbling auburn locks and wondered if perhaps she ought to have brought a present.

She felt exactly the way she had done when she was a little girl, remembering the school holidays when her mother had packed her off to stay at her aunt's because she kept getting under Ida's feet.

It had taken a long time to pluck up courage to come and visit Aunt Bessie. What was she going to say now that she was here? How was she going to explain why she had been avoiding Bessie ever since she got back to the island? What if Bessie felt the same way as her sister . . . ?

Creena showed her pass to the guard and walked into the single women's camp at Port Erin. Dispassionate eyes glanced at her and glanced away as she walked along the seafront and turned left. It was just another Sunday afternoon and no one was the least bit interested in her, or why she was here. Yet Creena felt as though everyone was watching her, waiting for Aunt Bessie to slam the door in her face.

There, near the top of the road, stood the Ben-my-Chree guest house, its gardens as neat and tidy as ever and a row of yellow flowers dancing merrily in the breeze. The house seemed very quiet – what if Bessie wasn't at home? She should have let her know that she was coming. But what if she'd refused to see her? Oh, it was no use agonising. Best to get it over with.

Creena's legs felt like lead as she got closer, and those last few steps up to the front gate were sheer agony. She opened the gate and it squeaked and grated as she closed it behind her. It was too late to turn tail now.

She rang the bell and waited at the bottom of the steps, nervously twisting her white gloves about her fingers.

After an eternity she heard footsteps in the hallway and the door opened a fraction of an inch.

'Ja?'

The sense of anticlimax hit Creena like a punch in the stomach.

'Miss Teare – is Miss Teare at home?'

'Jawohl. One moment please.' The woman turned on her heel and closed the door in Creena's face. She could hear her retracing her footsteps down the hall and shouting up the stairwell: 'Be-ssie, Be-ssie.'

A few moments later Creena saw a familiar shadow through the obscured glass, the silhouette of an elderly lady with long grey hair pinned into a bun. Her stomach twisted itself into a multitude of knots. Please, please, please, she prayed to herself as the door opened for the second time.

Bessie Teare and Creena Quilliam looked at each other in silence for a few seconds. Was this all it would amount to, wondered Creena – a silent moment of rejection on a doorstep?

'Aunt Bessie,' she whispered, no longer a grown woman but a guilty child.

'Oh, Creena, my dear,' smiled Bessie, and putting her arm around Creena's shoulders she drew her inside.

Chapter 30

About a week after her conversation with Aunt Bessie, Creena was coming downstairs from her attic rooms when she noticed an ordinary brown envelope lying on the doormat.

Funny, that. The postman never called this early in the morning. Besides, there didn't seem to be any address on the envelope – only a single word inked in block capitals: CREENA.

Intrigued, she picked up the envelope and tore it open. Inside was a single sheet of paper, folded twice. She unfolded it and, although the note was unsigned, she recognised the handwriting instantly. However hard he might try to disguise it, George Quilliam's educated copperplate hand was as distinctive as the shape of his nose. She read the note quickly:

'Your brother is in hospital in Bangor, North Wales. He was in a mining accident on 8 May and has injuries to his arm and chest but he is expected to make a full recovery.'

Creena stared at the message, deeply shocked. The words seemed to swim before her eyes. Tommy – in hospital? She had been pleased to hear he had gone down the mines, so sure that now he would be protected from harm. Poor, innocent Tommy, who had never done any harm to anybody. She must get in touch straight away, send him a long letter, anything to help him get better. She shivered as she thought how perilously close she had come to losing him.

A sudden thought struck her. The eighth of May? But that was almost three weeks ago. Why would her father decide to tell her about Tommy now, if he had thought fit to conceal the news from her for so long?

She recalled her long, comforting chat with Bessie. In a way it had been frustrating, for Ida and George had not given Bessie any explanation as to why they had cut their daughter off. She clearly hadn't known about Tommy's accident either, yet she and Ida had always been so close.

Could Bessie have worked some small act of magic upon her father? Creena held the note tightly in her hand and tried not to hope too much.

'Mother.'

'What is it now, Amy?' Ida Quilliam glanced up irritably from her knitting. She was making a new pair of socks for George from two old unravelled pairs, and had just reached a tricky point in her calculations.

Amy sat on the edge of her chair, almost bursting with excitement.

'You know that Lady Baden-Powell is coming to the island next week?'

'What about it?'

'She's opening the new scout and guide centre, and Miss

Snell has picked me to represent guides in the south of the island at the evening celebration.'

'Has she indeed?' George Quilliam took his nose out of his book for a moment. 'And what would you have to do?'

'Present a bouquet to Lady Baden-Powell, and give a little speech of welcome.'

'Hmm, good.' George allowed himself to bask in the reflected glory of his daughter's achievements. Amy might lack Tommy's academic cleverness, but cleverness was not to be encouraged in a girl. Her compliant and sensible nature had never given him a moment's worry.

'You can't possibly go.' Ida did not even bother looking up from her knitting.

'But Mother!'

Amy looked glum and George raised a greying eyebrow to contemplate his wife in bewilderment.

'I see no reason why not, Ida.'

Ida went on knitting furiously, the steel needles clack-clacking against each other like castanets.

'I will not have any daughter of mine gallivanting about the island at night,' she said.

'But Mother, you let me go on the Civil Defence exercise!'

'I'm sure Miss Snell would chaperon her,' cut in George, alarmed by his wife's increasingly irrational behaviour – which he was sure would be all the more extreme were she to discover that he had sent that note to Creena.

'I won't have it. I'm sorry, that is my final word on the matter.'

'Oh Mother, please!' Amy's brown eyes were unnaturally bright as she fought back the tears. 'It's not fair . . .'

'A great many things in this life are unfair.'

Amy's naturally placid nature flared into unaccustomed passion.

'I want to go, Mother! I *will* go!'

Ida glanced up at her, then looked away.

'You will learn to control your temper, young lady, or you will go to your room.'

George caught Amy's pleading gaze, and suddenly the short rein of his temper snapped clean in two.

'For pity's sake, woman, what on earth has got into you!' he bellowed. 'Can you not see how unreasonable you are being?'

Ida rounded on him with bitter fury.

'Unreasonable, am I? And this from a man who gives more attention to his pigs than he gives to his wife!'

'Is that any wonder?' snapped George. 'You drove Creena away, you drove Alexa away, and if you are not very careful you will drive Tommy and Amy away too. Is that what you want? Is it?'

Ida returned his fiery gaze with a stony stare.

'How dare you,' she said coldly. 'How dare you mention that girl's name in my house.'

'She is your daughter,' replied George quietly.

'No daughter of mine would do what she did.'

And, picking up her knitting, she swept out of the sitting room, leaving George and Amy staring at her empty chair.

It was early June 1944, and Mo Doyle was enjoying the quietness. She was no fool. She knew it was the calm before the storm, sensed that Hitler hadn't done with Lambeth yet.

As hazy June sunlight filtered into Mo's spotless parlour, she picked up the framed photograph which had pride of place on the mantel shelf above the fireplace. It showed Paddy in his constable's uniform: young, strong Paddy, black-haired and handsome as Jack was now, brave and incorruptible and precious as pure gold.

Of course, she'd thought he would be with her for ever. Well, you didn't think about death when you were little more than a kid, did you? Even if three of your brothers and sisters had died from diphtheria, and your mother had gone giving birth to the last of twelve. There was something about being young, something that stopped you thinking about the bad things and only allowed you to look forward, to the good things that were bound to be just around the corner.

She set the photograph back on the mantel shelf. There she was in the picture beside him, her thin white arm hooked through his strong, serge-clad one, relying upon him for support as she posed for the camera in the white dress that had been hers just for one day. They'd started from nothing, and her in the family way, but they hadn't had a bad time together, had they? Saved up a little nest egg and never spent money they didn't have. Not like some she could mention.

'Oh, Paddy,' she said softly to herself. 'Why did you have to go an' leave me like that?'

Now Jack had left home, too. She was proud of him for what he'd done. He hadn't had to go, she knew that. And he'd seen her right – left her enough to get by on for a long time to come, and always sent her something with his letters too.

She missed him, though. Good or bad, he was her only son and there were times when only he would do. Times when she longed to turn round and see him coming in up the back yard, hat tilted rakishly on his brilliantined hair and a little something for tea secreted in his overcoat pocket.

She looked out of the window into Bishop Street. They hadn't done anything with what was left of number 3, just put a wooden fence round it and a sign telling the kids to keep off. It was like a red rag to a bull, that sign. Soon as they saw it, the kids were swarming all over the bomb site like flies round a jam-jar, and that Billy Wiggins was the worst of 'em.

But not Micky. He was a good boy, Micky, getting down to his schooling now; and Kitty was growing up clever, just like Dillie. They'd do all right for themselves, those two. And they'd both grown so much that their pa would hardly recognise them when the war was over and he finally came home.

The war *was* almost over; you could feel the expectation in the air. Oh, there would be more bad times to come for Bishop Street, Mo knew that. A man like that Hitler wouldn't give up without a struggle, he was bound to have something up his sleeve. But whatever it was, it wouldn't work. London had taken all he could give in the Blitz, and if need be it could take some more.

It was almost over now. Almost all over.

She felt so tired today. A little rest, that was what she needed. Mo took a look at the sturdy wooden clock on the mantelpiece – Paddy's clock, the one he'd been given by his colleagues as a wedding present. Two whole hours till Old

Bert would be back, clamouring for his tea, and the kids were both at school. Plenty of time for forty winks.

Mo settled herself comfortably in Paddy's old chair and let her heavy eyelids close. Tired. So tired. She wasn't as young as she used to be, she needed to rest.

Images flitted through her mind. Wasn't that Dillie, that frightened, skinny little kid? How she'd changed since the day she'd been dumped on Mo's doorstep with nothing but a grubby old teddy bear and a spare pair of knickers. And look – there was Jack as a boy, presenting her with an armful of daffodils he'd nicked from the park.

And Paddy. Look, look, there was Paddy. Paddy as a young man, his dark hair slicked back with pomade and his black boots polished to a high gloss.

He had a lopsided grin on his face, the way he always used to when they were courting, and her old heart felt as light as it had done all those thirty-five years ago.

She'd worked hard, looking after her Paddy, keeping him smart. There couldn't be any harm in having a little rest. After all, it was almost over now.

It was on the day of the camp social that Creena heard the news about Mo Doyle.

She was called to the commandant's office to receive a sad, crackly telephone call from Dillie.

'I had to tell you straight away, Creena.'

'What's happened, Dillie? Are you all right?'

'I'm fine. It's Mo . . . She passed away in her sleep.'

No, no, it couldn't be true. Mo Doyle had died in her sleep, with no hint that she had even been ill. It felt like the end of the world. There would be no more visits to Bishop

Street for tea and sympathy and common sense. One moment she'd been there, the next she was gone.

'Oh, Dillie . . . I'm so, so sorry.'

'I loved her so much, Cree. I never really knew my mother. Mo *was* my mother.'

'I loved her too, Dillie.' Creena's voice cracked with emotion as she tried to hold back the tears. Mo Doyle hadn't only been a mother to Dillie and Jack and the kids.

'I know you did.'

And sensible, calm, composed Dillie broke down, her whole body shaken with convulsive sobbing, her grief all the more heart-rending to Creena because she was hundreds of miles away, at the end of a very bad phone line. They wept together, unable to say anything that would comfort either of them.

All morning, Creena had felt curiously numb. The worst thing was that she couldn't even get leave to attend the funeral, to pay her last respects. Mo had seemed so permanent, somehow, her love a huge downy blanket that spread out over anyone who needed it. She'd picked Creena up when she was at her lowest ebb, dusted her down and sent her out fighting. It was going to take a long, long time to accept that she was gone. And how would poor Jack take it? He was devoted to his mother. And the kids, Micky and Kitty, who would take care of them now?

Creena's head was in a whirl. She was glad that today was so busy. The monthly camp socials had started out as a rather sad affair, in the early days before the mixed camp had been set up, when husbands and wives might be interned at opposite ends of the island. Now that there was a family camp, these painful separations were less common, though not unheard-of. The socials were looked forward to now as an opportunity to have a dance, have fun, meet up with relatives and sweethearts from other camps.

The morning was taken up with arranging the ballroom, putting out the chairs and setting out refreshments. Anticipation showed on formerly apathetic faces, moods became sunnier to match the beautiful June day. Even women who were barely on speaking terms seemed to be getting along, suspending hostilities for a day.

In due course, the men trooped in and the camp band squeaked and scraped into life on the *ad hoc* stage. Assorted couples moved slowly around the floor, others preferring to sit out the dancing and simply gaze into each other's eyes.

Creena hung around on the fringe of things. There was no need for her to be here really; it was like being an intruder at someone else's party. No one would miss her for a few minutes. Silently she slipped out of the ballroom, through the foyer and out on to the front steps.

It was less stuffy and oppressive out here in the fresh air. She sat down, feeling the heat from the sun-baked stones through her thin summer skirt. Drawing up her knees she hugged them, allowing herself for a few precious moments to drift away from reality.

'Creena?'

Creena twisted her head round to see who was calling her name. It was Agathe Mannheim, carrying a little silver tray rattling with clean cups.

'Oh. Hello, Agathe.'

'I'm not disturbing you?'

'No,' Creena lied.

'Could I have a word?'

'Yes, of course.'

Agathe set down the tray and sat down on the steps next to Creena.

'I just wondered . . . would it be possible to invite a guest teacher to take my drawing class out for the day?'

'I suppose it might – do you have someone special in mind?'

Agathe coloured slightly.

'I . . . yes, I do. He is a friend, a good friend.'

'A professional artist?'

'No, not exactly. But he is much more talented at drawing than I am. Actually, he is here today . . .'

'He's an internee?'

Agathe shook her head.

'A prisoner of war, in Douglas. He was a pilot, but he was injured – his back, he cannot walk very well.'

'A prisoner of war! Oh, Agathe, I don't know about that.'

'He is an architect, Creena, and he draws so beautifully. We would learn so much from him . . .'

Her eyes pleaded with Creena to understand, to read between the lines of the unspoken message. Already he meant so much to her, and because they were not married or related it was so very difficult for them to meet, to find acceptable excuses for being together.

'It isn't really anything to do with me. You'd have to make an application to the commandant. It could be very complicated.'

'But it might be possible?'

'I suppose so. You would have to have an escort, of course. And it would depend on what this friend of yours is like, whether he's trustworthy . . .'

A deeper voice cut in, and Creena swivelled round to see a man silhouetted against the glass doors. The sounds of music and laughter floated out from the room behind him.

'Do *you* think I am trustworthy, Nurse Quilliam?' Tired sea-green eyes twinkled in a face prematurely lined by pain, a face a little scarred on one side by the marks of burning. He was leaning heavily on a stick. 'I think perhaps you did not care for me very much when last we met, nicht wahr?'

Creena stared at the man, her mouth agape with astonishment.

'Herr Menz? No, it can't be.'

He gave a polite nod of the head. As he descended the steps Creena noticed how slowly and stiffly he walked, his spine imperfectly mended from the day when his Messerschmitt had plunged, nose-first, into the Thames mud. He certainly didn't look much like a threat to national security.

'Lothar Menz, Nurse Quilliam. My apologies if I startled you.'

It's a small world, thought Creena. Smaller than I ever imagined – and I certainly didn't imagine I'd ever see *you* again. Strange how you never quite leave the past behind.

'I . . . er . . . Agathe tells me you draw and paint,' Creena began, startled by Menz's sudden reappearance in her life. She could still recall how much she had hated him for not being the monster she thought he ought to be. Now all that hatred had evaporated. He just looked like a sick, middle-aged architect who ought to be in a sanatorium.

Agathe was by Lothar's side now. They were looking into each other's eyes, smiling. Creena recognised that look and for a second, no more, she felt jealousy tighten its cold fingers around her heart. That was the look of love, new born and fresh and exhilarating.

'I draw a little,' he conceded.

'Lothar!' protested Agathe. 'He's so talented, Creena.'

'Not as talented as Agathe is at music,' Lothar countered, directing his words at Creena. 'Did she tell you that she studied at the Berlin Conservatoire before she became a schoolteacher?'

'Only for a year. And they threw me out!'

The mock argument ended in a flurry of German insults, and Lothar laughed. Happiness seemed to wipe years off his careworn face.

'I am sorry, Nurse Quilliam. We are disturbing you when you wanted a little peace and quiet.'

'It's all right.' Creena was gazing into the middle distance, trying so hard not to let her emotions win that her voice was an expressionless monotone. 'I ought to go back in anyway.'

Agathe slid back on to the step beside her.

'Is there something wrong?'

'Wrong? What makes you think that?'

'You seem . . . as if there is something on your mind.'

Creena stared fixedly at her toes.

'I had a telephone call.'

'Bad news?'

'About a friend. A very, very dear friend has died.' She felt a lump rising in her throat and swallowed it down ruthlessly.

'I'm sorry.' Agathe wanted to comfort Creena, but it was so hard to find the words. She liked this Manxwoman, but when all was said and done they scarcely knew each other.

'She was like a mother to me, and I never even thanked her for all she did. Do you think she knew how grateful I was?'

'I'm sure she did.'

'There is much loss in this war, much pain,' said Lothar. He'd changed a good deal since that mad day in 1939 when he'd decided to join the Luftwaffe because they'd offered to take care of his children. Now he didn't know if he'd ever see them again. If it came to that, he didn't even know if they were still alive.

'I just wish,' said Creena softly, to no one in particular, 'I just wish there'd been time to say goodbye.'

'Who'd 'ave thought it, eh? Who'd 'ave thought it of Old Bert?'

Tommy Jones, head barman at The Ring, poured himself a glass of beer and toasted Mo Doyle's memory. It was the best wake the inhabitants of Bishop Street had seen in a long, long time.

Thanks to Old Bert, Mo had had a grand send-off – nice hearse, solid wood coffin, chief mourner in a shiny black top hat and everything. No one had ever guessed in their wildest dreams how much money the old codger had stashed away in that trunk under his bed. Not useless paper stuff, either – a big bag of gold sovereigns. His offer to foot the bill ''cause she were a toff, she were' had set Bishop Street reeling.

'Gawd knows where he got all that money,' reflected a regular.

'If I were you I wouldn't ask,' interjected a fat man with a wart on his nose. 'Just enjoy the free beer while it lasts. We could all get bleedin' blown up tomorrer.'

We could an' all, thought the landlord as he flicked a dead fly off the top of his beer. Them flying bombs Hitler was sending over had really knocked London for six. Hadn't been expecting 'em, see. Thought Jerry'd had his chips good an' proper, what with the Allied lads landing in Normandy.

The first Bishop Street had known of the V1s was when a great silvery-blue thing twenty-five feet long went sailing over Lambeth Marsh and blew half of Price Street away. It had only just missed the shelter group at Long Wall Yard.

Dillie sat in a corner of the public bar with Old Bert, a small milk stout untouched on the table in front of her. Jack was somewhere in Europe, Creena stuck in the Isle of Man with no chance of getting compassionate leave at such short notice. Dillie had had to keep busy up until the funeral, but now it was over she felt drained.

'Drink up, gel,' said Old Bert encouragingly. 'You need your strength.'

'Later,' said Dillie.

'Now,' said Old Bert firmly. 'What d'you reckon Mo would've said if she knew you weren't lookin' after yerself proper? An' your Arnold don't want some pasty-faced rasher of wind, neither.'

Reluctantly Dillie drank down a little of the milk stout.

Bert was right. She was going to need all her strength, what with keeping on her nursing job at the hospital *and* moving into the house on Bishop Street to look after Micky and Kitty.

'I'm very grateful, Bert,' she said, setting her glass down on the table.

'She were a good woman, Mo Doyle,' observed Old Bert, peering into the bottom of his empty glass. 'Never took a penny more rent than she 'ad to, an' she always put a good dinner on the table.' It was a fitting epitaph.

Even Ena Marshall had good things to say about Mo – now that she was gone.

'Not that we always saw eye to eye,' she conceded, putting her glass on the bar for a top-up. 'But she were straight, I'll give 'er that. Straight as a die.'

Dillie was half listening to the chatter around her, half keeping an eye on the kids. That Billy Wiggins was a bad lot, you had to have eyes in the back of your head or the tinned ham and pineapple chunks would go for a walk.

A tap on the shoulder made her jump.

'Not now, Micky – oh, it's you, Eric.'

Jack's old sparring partner Eric Coates looked not so much smart as shifty in his black suit, and was clearly sweltering in the June heat.

'Could I have a quiet word, Dillie?'

'Yes, of course.'

Eric's eyes swivelled round and fixed on Old Bert, still contemplating the empty beer glass in front of him as though it would magically refill itself without his having to get up and go to the bar.

'A *quiet* word.'

Old Bert's selective deafness served him well.

'Wot?'

'You 'eard, Bert. Sling yer 'ook, will yer?'

'All right, all right, I know when I'm not wanted.' Bert heaved himself to his feet and shuffled off to the bar, muttering, 'Ain't got no respect, that's 'is trouble.'

Eric slid into Old Bert's vacant chair, glancing around him.

'What's all this about?' demanded Dillie. 'If it's anything dodgy, I don't want to know.'

'No, no, nothin' like that.'

'What then?'

'I got summink for you from Jack.'

Eric reached into his inside pocket and pulled out a bulky brown envelope.

'He left it with me for Mo. Now she's gone, he wants you to 'ave it.'

'What is it?'

He nudged it across the table with a pudgy finger.

'You know, a little summink. A nest egg. Enough to keep you an' the kids going.'

Dillie stared at the envelope for a few seconds, then shook her head.

'I can't take it.'

Eric stared back at her in disbelief.

'But it's money.'

'I know it's money.'

'Jack wants yer to 'ave it.'

'Well I don't want it.'

Eric's breath escaped in an explosion of frustration. He scratched his head.

'Honest to God, Dillie, yer gettin' more like Mo Doyle every day.'

'Good,' said Dillie. 'Mo had pride. I'll manage.'

'Pride's one thing, Dillie, but you're just bein' stubborn. I'm only tryin' to help you out. What about them kids, eh? You want them to suffer?'

It was precisely the wrong thing to say. Dillie's back stiffened, her neck arched, her eyes narrowed.

'Don't you tell me how to bring up those kids, Eric Coates,' she said haughtily. 'I'll bring them up right, and I'll do it without any help from you – or Jack.'

Damn, thought Eric Coates as he watched Dillie stalk off to the other side of the bar. But his lips curled in a half-smile of admiration.

Mo Doyle might be dead and gone, but whilst Dillie Bayliss was around her spirit would live on.

'Another G and T, pussycat?'

'Just a tiny one then, tiger.'

Julia Paston was in clover, relaxing on an elegant *chaise-longue* in Gerald Trenchard's drawing room. At last, at long, long last, she had found a man who exceeded all her hopes and expectations. So he was a few years older than she was – twenty-five years older, to be precise – but what did that matter? She'd always liked older men, and Gerald was so kind and attentive. And rich.

She loved him, really she did. That was the funny thing about it. Who'd have thought that her ideal man, the love of her life, would turn out to be a paunchy fifty-year-old brigadier?

He'd asked her to marry him and of course she'd accepted. War or no war, the wedding would be huge, with a vast champagne celebration afterwards at Gerry's country seat. They would both be ridiculously happy, and Julia would never have to take shorthand dictation again.

When Gerald went off to phone his farm manager, Julia set to thinking again. There was only one fly in the ointment: her own guilty conscience. Why oh why had she made that spiteful, childish, idiotic telephone call to Frankie's girl?

All right, so the Quilliam girl had asked for it, but it hadn't made any sense in the end, had it? She hadn't got Frank Kinrade. And the more she thought about it, the more she came to the conclusion that she hadn't really wanted him in the first place. Not *really*. He'd just been a challenge.

She sat at Gerald's Davenport writing desk, doodling on a piece of blotting paper.

Maybe. Oh no, she couldn't. But then again, perhaps she could. Perhaps she should. Wipe the slate clean and then get on with her own life. They did say confession was good for the soul, and with all the bad things Julia had done in her time, well, she had to start somewhere.

That Quilliam girl. Christina, was it? No, Carina ... Creena, that was the name. Even now Julia found the thought of her irritating, but there was no accounting for tastes and Frank had evidently idolised her. It was Frank she felt guilty about really, not Creena. She hadn't wanted to ruin his life.

Now, where had the girl worked? The Royal Lambeth

Hospital, wasn't it? A letter sent there ought to reach her. She picked up the pen, hesitated for a moment, then began writing.

Chapter 31

Máire was listening to the wireless when she heard a loud knocking at her front door.

Outside in the October downpour stood Creena, her red hair hanging in sodden tendrils and her raincoat almost soaked through.

'Can I come in?'

'Saints preserve us, Creena! You've picked a fine day to go for a swim.'

She took Creena by the arm and led her into the kitchen, where she stood dripping on the stone-flagged floor. Máire took her raincoat and handed her a towel.

'I'll make us some tea, shall I? Then you can take your shoes off and dry them in front of the fire.'

'Máire – I've done a terrible thing.'

Kettle poised over the sink, Máire gave Creena a quizzical look.

'Terrible? What sort of terrible?'

Creena sank damply on to a kitchen chair, pushing her bedraggled hair off her face. Her fingers were white and clumsy with cold.

'I got this letter this morning. Here – you'd better read it.'

She opened her handbag and took out an envelope, redirected by Home Sister from the Royal Lambeth Hospital to the baker's shop in Arbory Street.

Máire put down the kettle and took the letter.

'Are you sure? I mean, it looks personal.'

'I don't have any secrets from you,' Creena reminded Máire. 'Not you, of all people.'

'Well – all right then.' Máire sat down at the table and unfolded the letter.

Dear Creena,

We only saw each other the once, at Waterloo station, but you most probably remember me. Your friend Frank Kinrade and I worked together at the Ministry and got pretty close.

The thing is, I did something I shouldn't have and I reckon I should put the record straight. Do you remember getting a telephone call from a girl called Alice, who said she was your Frank's fiancée and they were going away together? Well, none of it was true. It was me, you see, and I made it all up. I called you and pretended to be Frank's girl – I only did it to make you jealous. He used to go on about you all the time and I wanted to steal him from you. I thought I was in love with him, I suppose, but that was a mistake.

Anyhow, I've got the perfect man now and it isn't Frank Kinrade. And if I've got my Mr Right, it seems only fair that you should have yours.

Frank never was unfaithful to you. He isn't the

type. You should have trusted him more, shouldn't you?

Yours,
Julia Paston.

Máire put down the letter very slowly, her face a mask of shock and anger.

'You think . . . this is true?'

'I'm certain it is. Believe me, a bitch like that wouldn't miss a chance to have the last word.'

'Oh, Creena. I don't know what to say.'

Creena's elbows were on the table, her face propped on her hands.

'I've really gone and done it this time, haven't I? How could I have let myself be taken in so easily?'

'From what you said, it was a pretty convincing act she put on.'

'Oh, it was! The details she gave, the things she said about her and Frank. I was so sure it was all true. She's a very accomplished actress, is our Julia. And I'm sure she's had plenty of real-life experience to draw upon,' she added bitterly, her green eyes flashing fire.

'There's no return address,' remarked Máire.

'Are you surprised?' retorted Creena. 'She's afraid if I knew where she was I'd go straight down there and slap her smug little face for her.'

'Would you do that?' said Máire, surprised.

'Yes, I jolly well would.'

They sat in gloomy silence for a while, alone with their own private thoughts.

'So what *are* you going to do?' asked Máire at last.

'What can I do? If I could only set things straight...'

Máire fiddled with the cross and chain she always wore, the one she had been given for her first communion.

'Would you talk to Frank if you had the chance? Only, you've always said you never wanted to see him again.'

Creena wiped a trickle of rainwater off her face, pushing her sodden hair back off her forehead.

'Yes, but this changes things, doesn't it? It changes everything.'

Máire looked up.

'And if you could talk to him...?'

'There isn't much chance of that, is there? I don't even know where he is. And I wouldn't dare ask Don Kinrade, not after the way I've treated Frank.'

'But *if* you had the chance?'

'Yes, I would. At least, I'd give it a try.'

Máire took a deep breath.

'You know you said we didn't have any secrets from each other?'

'Well, we don't.'

'Actually, we do. Have secrets, I mean. Well, one secret.'

Creena looked baffled.

'You've lost me.'

'Creena ... I know where Frank is.'

Creena's jaw dropped, and her hands fell to the table, gripping the edge.

'Where – how?'

'I saw him a couple of weeks ago, quite by accident. At

first I wasn't sure it was him, and then when I was sure . . . well, I thought if I told you it would only make you angry or upset. You did say you never wanted to hear from him ever again . . .'

'You *saw* him? Where is he?'

Máire swallowed hard, the irony of the situation almost turning her words into a nervous laugh.

'He's on guard duty at Onchan internment camp.'

Frank liked to go to a pub in Onchan on the evenings when he was off duty. There wasn't much else to do if you didn't have a girl to take out, and Frank had lost interest in girls.

'Pint of Red Label please.'

'Pint of Red Label it is.'

'Filthy evening out there,' observed Frank, shaking the raindrops off his collar.

'It is that,' agreed the barman. 'Mannanan's cloak is thick out there an' no mistake.'

As the day had progressed, a dense greyish-white mist had descended over the eastern coast of the island, turning day into dusk and dusk into a swirling, impenetrable blanket which was said to be the cloak of the wizard Mannanan, thrown about the island to repel unwanted visitors. Blackout or dim-out, it made little difference when the island was in the grip of one of Mannanan's famous moods – either way you couldn't see your hand in front of your face.

Perhaps, pondered Frank, Mannanan objected to the prisoners of war being brought over to replace the internees who were due for release from Onchan in November.

'How's things at the camp then?' enquired the barman. Murdagh Faragher liked nothing better than a good gossip. It was just as well Frank knew how to keep his mouth shut.

'Middling,' replied Frank.

'No troubles, then? No escape tunnels like they found over at Peveril camp?'

'Now why would a man want to escape when he's being transferred in a month's time?' pointed out Frank.

'Ah, but you want to watch out for them Jerry POWs when they come. They'll be off like greyhounds if you let 'em, yessir.'

'I'll do that,' Frank assured him. Tired of Murdagh's endless banter, he went to sit down.

No one had been more surprised than Frank to find himself back on the island. His first posting after the Ministry of War had been organising a resettlement camp for Italians newly released from the internment camps, helping them to pick up the threads of their new lives, find ways of coming to terms with their lost years. And now, that job done, he found himself in Onchan, waiting with mixed feelings for the German POWs who would shortly take the Italians' place.

He had good reason to have mixed feelings about the Germans – and the Italians. Good reason, too, not to want to be back on the island. It wasn't easy, being here where everything reminded him of her. And the island felt different – or was it that the island had remained the same but he had changed beyond recognition?

The war would be finished soon, that much was obvious. Well, he'd make sure his dad got the girls through school, help find them decent jobs, then he'd not stick around. There'd be a whole world to lose himself in out there, and he'd never have to remember . . .

'Frank.'

Memory was so strong. Just when you thought you'd conquered it, up it would pop with another cruel mirage. Get out of my head, get out of my head and let me alone, he pleaded. That's all over now.

'Frank . . . please.'

He looked up as she spoke his name again. She was standing there, pale, bedraggled, soaked to the skin; but it was her. It was her all right.

It was Creena.

Don Kinrade beamed all over his red face as he ladled Manx broth into a chipped white soup plate. In the middle of the large pan floated a muslin-wrapped jam roly poly, boiled in the broth in the traditional Manx way.

'It's Gwennie's own recipe,' he said. And Frank's fifteen-year-old sister smiled and nodded as she handed round the plates.

'I made the bread,' chimed in her fourteen-year-old sister, Ailish.

'Which is why it's gone down in the middle,' retorted Gwen drily.

'It did not! And you didn't put enough salt in the broth.'

'Hush, hush,' their father chided them. 'Creena'll think she's walked into the henhouse, hearin' you two go on like that.'

Creena sat at the Kinrade family table for the first time in over five years. She'd been a child then, she saw that now. As much a child as Ailish, with her pigtails and her defiance.

'Ailish is singing in the Cruinnaght on Tuesday night,' Frank told Creena, passing her the little dish of salt.

'Ach, she's good with the Gaelic an' no mistake,' said Don proudly. 'An' she's a lovely soprano on her.'

'Perhaps we could come and hear you sing,' suggested Frank. He was looking meaningfully at Creena. 'I used to come and see you sing in the Guild, didn't I, Creena? Until that time you spotted me in the audience and forgot your words!'

Creena felt awkward. She wanted to go, of course she did, but . . .

'I don't know,' she said. 'Perhaps Ailish wouldn't want me there.'

Don Kinrade gave vent to such an explosion of laughter that the whole cottage seemed to shake, and Creena was sure the coloured plates would come crashing down off Elena Kinrade's prized Manx dresser.

'Not want you there! You're practically family, Creena-gel.'

'You heard,' grinned Frank. 'You'll have to let me take you now.'

'What's London like?' asked Gwen, taking off her apron and sitting down at the table. 'Is it as big as it looks in the pictures?'

'Bigger,' replied Creena.

'And is it very grand?'

Creena wrinkled her nose.

'Sort of,' she said. 'In parts. But lots of it is just dirty and run-down. And other bits are cosy and friendly,' she added, thinking of Mo and Dillie and Bishop Street.

'Were you ever in an air raid?'

'Yes. Lots of times.'

'What was it like?'

'Horrible.'

'You must have been scared.'

'Of course I was!'

Gwen dipped a hunk of bread in her broth.

'It sounds terrible,' she said.

'It is,' said Frank.

'Do you miss London then?' demanded Ailish, looking Creena straight in the eye.

The question stopped Creena in her tracks, her spoon halfway to her mouth. Do I miss it? she asked herself. Do I? Oh, I miss Dillie, I miss Mo, I even miss Frankenberg sometimes, but London?

'No,' she said, surprising herself. 'No, I don't. Not one bit.'

Ailish, never one for tact and diplomacy, wanted to know more. She grinned knowingly.

'Did you miss Frank?'

Creena looked at Frank. He hardly dared look back at her for fear of what she might say.

'Yes,' she said, her eyes searching out Frank's. 'I missed him a lot.'

'That's quite enough of that, young lady,' said Don Kinrade firmly to his younger daughter. 'Creena hasn't come here to answer your silly questions. Eat up, an' mind your manners.'

After the meal, Creena insisted on washing the dishes and Frank offered to dry. Don retired to a discreet distance with a pint of ale, taking Gwennie and Ailish with him.

'I'm glad I came,' said Creena, pouring boiling water on to baking soda for the greasy pans. 'I wasn't sure if I should, but I'm glad now.'

'Surely you knew Dad and the girls would be pleased to see you,' protested Frank.

'There's no reason why they should be. Not after the way I treated you.'

'You had reason enough. Julia Paston made sure of that,' he added with a touch of bitterness.

'And then there's Mother and Father,' Creena continued. 'They're only a mile or two up the road. I did think I might walk into Mother and she'd cut me dead.'

Frank threw his tea towel on to his shoulder and came up behind Creena, sliding his hands round her waist.

'I don't understand what all this is about, you and your parents,' he said, 'but whatever it is, I'm sure it's not of your making.'

'You don't know that . . .'

'Yes I do, Creena. I know *you*.' He tightened his embrace just a fraction. 'I've been a bloody fool,' he said.

She turned round in surprise.

'You! Why you?'

'I should have realised Julia was behind what happened, done something to find out why you were so upset, instead of just . . .'

'I told you I never wanted to see you again,' Creena said. 'What could you have done?'

'Well, you're back now,' said Frank, and he darted the tiniest of kisses on to the back of Creena's neck. She shivered.

'Cold?'

She shook her head.

'No, not that. It's nice.'

'Then I'll do it again.'

He kissed her again, more insistently this time, and suddenly she wanted to answer his kisses, hold him close and never, never let him go. But something was holding her back; a memory, the shadow of a guilt that would not free her from its clutches. A dark secret she might never have the courage to disclose.

He felt her tense in his arms, not understanding the shadow that had crossed her mind, the pain that had clutched at her racing heart.

Could she ever find the strength to tell Frank about Oliver? And if she did, could he find it in his heart to forgive her?

Bessie Teare was out visiting. She liked to call on Agathe Mannheim whenever she could get a pass for the married camp, and a little bird had told her that on Mondays Agathe's gentleman friend Lothar would be at the camp, giving drawing lessons and – most important – deepening his acquaintance with Agathe.

Bessie liked romance. She liked to see people happy together, and from the little she had seen of Lothar she fancied he might make a good match for Agathe. Both were rather studious and artistic, both quiet-tempered, both had a hatred of this dreadful war which had torn so many families apart.

And few more comprehensively than the Quilliams, she mused grimly, thinking of Ida's increasingly irascible behaviour and its effects on young Amy. The trouble was, Ida had virtually cut herself off from the rest of the family. Alexa she barely tolerated, Mona and Duggie were too busy re-establishing their own demarcation lines to care much about Ballakeeill, and Bessie – Ida's own sister – could scarcely get two words out of her.

Sooner or later, some hard talking was going to have to be done.

It was a chilly November day, and Bessie walked along with brisk strides, a basket of home-made cakes over her arm. There were many worse places to site a prison than on this beautiful seaside promenade, but a prison was what it still was.

Agathe greeted her in the foyer of the hotel where she had been billeted.

'You're looking well, my dear,' Bessie observed at the sight of Agathe's rosy cheeks. 'Is it love?'

'Oh, Bessie, don't say that, please!' Agathe squirmed in embarrassment but Bessie was relentless.

'You must tell me how you and your gentleman friend are getting on,' she insisted. 'If you don't, I shan't have anything to gossip about and you know how I love to gossip.'

'He's very nice,' Agathe admitted. 'I like him very much.'

'Good,' declared Bessie. 'You must invite me to the

wedding. Now, are you going to tell me what's been happening here since I last saw you?'

They sat down together under the watchful eye of a Home Office official. Bessie knew her visits were regarded with some suspicion – and friendships between locals and internees were generally discouraged. But she didn't give a damn what anyone thought. She liked Agathe.

'Something dreadful happened last week,' Agathe told Bessie. 'One of the little girls in my class came running up to tell me she couldn't wake her mummy. Oh, it was terrible.'

'And what had happened?'

Agathe leaned closer.

'It's better if you don't tell.'

'I shan't say a word.'

'The poor girl had tried to do away with herself, isn't that the most awful thing?'

'Awful,' Bessie agreed. And it wasn't the first suicide attempt in the camp, either. There had been that dreadful business with the Nazi woman whose body was washed up on the rocks; and the elderly internee who'd had to be taken to Ballamona mental hospital.

'Poor Hannah,' sighed Agathe. 'She has her children here with her, but her husband ... she does not even know if he is alive or dead. And some of the other women are very unkind to her.'

'Women can be very cruel sometimes,' Bessie remarked – but the full meaning of her words was lost on Agathe. Agathe had never met Ida Quilliam.

'It is easier for the children,' Agathe explained. 'They

adapt quickly, make friends, learn to accept things as they are. It is not so easy for their mothers.'

'No,' agreed Bessie sadly. 'It's never easy for mothers.' But she couldn't help thinking that some of the internee women at Port Erin and Port St Mary put Ida to shame. 'How are Lothar's drawing classes, my dear? Are they going well?'

'Very well. He is such an inspiration to the pupils.' Agathe's face lit up at the thought of Lothar. Not just an inspiration to his pupils, thought Bessie with a certain glow of satisfaction.

'You want to hang on to him, Agathe,' she said. 'He's a good man, and there aren't so many of them that you can afford to let them get away. I never married, you know. The Great War took my young man from me.'

'There would be many difficulties for us, Bessie. His children . . .'

Bessie dismissed Agathe's doubts with a wave of the hand.

'There are always difficulties. If you love each other you'll hardly notice them.' She leaned forward, touching Agathe on the arm. 'Now, you must tell me how my niece is getting on. Does she seem happier?'

'Well . . . yes, I think so.' Agathe felt embarrassed at talking about Creena behind her back.

'Is she still seeing her young man?'

'She talks about Frank a lot. So I suppose she must be.'

Bessie heaved a sigh of relief. At last something seemed to be going right for Creena.

'Thank goodness for that,' she said. 'I was beginning to

think those two would never see sense. Now, shall I pour us another cup of tea?'

It was the week before Christmas, and breath made little white clouds on the crisp December air.

Creena and Frank were walking over Mull Hill towards Cregneash, as they had often done when they were children; with the wild green sea below them and an ice-blue sky arching overhead.

They trudged through the frosty grass together, lost for a moment in their own thoughts. Frank was wondering if he had overstepped the mark, kissing Creena that night at his father's cottage. She had said she wanted him to, but why had she tensed up at his touch? Was it stupid of him to hope that she could love him?

Creena was afraid to let herself be too happy, unable to banish the guilty secret that burned like a low flame inside her, threatening to flare up and engulf them both.

'Do you remember?' began Frank. 'We came up here with Máire and Padraig once, when it was pouring with rain.'

'I remember. You'd sworn it would stay dry all day . . .'

'Anyone can make a mistake,' Frank grimaced.

'. . . and poor Máire's shoes let the water in. Padraig gave her his jacket to cover her head, so he got soaked as well! We looked like drowned rats by the time we got back to Port Erin. And it was all your fault, Frankie Kinrade!'

She gave him an affectionate jab in the ribs and he retaliated by snatching off her beret and holding it behind his back.

'Give!' she demanded.

'Shan't.' He dodged out of the way of her grasping hand.

'Please!' she pleaded.

'Not until you promise.'

'Promise what?'

'That you'll never say goodbye again.'

Creena looked into his dark-brown eyes and saw that he was deadly serious. The laughter faded from her heart and she turned away, unable to meet his gaze.

'Oh, Frankie,' she whispered.

Frank cursed himself for the clumsy oaf that he was. He handed her back her beret and she stuffed it into her coat pocket.

'I'm sorry,' he said. 'I shouldn't have said that.'

'It's just . . .'

'You don't have to explain.' But I wish you would, thought Frank as they walked on together. I so wish you would.

They walked a little further, the old Manx village of Cregneash spread out beneath them with its thatched roofs and whitewashed walls. Somewhere in the distance a cockerel crowed.

'I'd never have thought it of Padraig,' mused Frank.

'Thought what?'

'That he'd do what he did. He was always such a pacifist, always so sure he'd never get involved in anyone's war, let alone one that wasn't his.'

Creena shrugged.

'He did what he felt he had to do. The war's changed a lot of people. Look how it's changed Mona's Duggie.'

Duggie Mylchreest was an interesting case in point,

thought Frank. When he'd left the island he'd been a drunken thug, with no more respect for himself than he had for his wife. But since he'd got back...

'That's supposing he really has changed,' Frank commented.

'Mona says he hasn't had a drink since he got back. And he's really taken with little Duggie. He always wanted a son, you know.'

'Well, I hope it lasts,' replied Frank. 'Mona deserves more than Duggie's ever given her, especially after everything she's done with the farm. I hope he really has changed for the better.'

'You've changed, Frank.'

Frank stopped in his tracks, turned to look at Creena.

'The war's changed you,' she repeated. 'You're different, somehow. I don't know ... sort of darker, more serious...'

Frank passed the back of his hand over his brow. It was perishing cold up here, but he was sweating. Unwelcome memories were crowding into his mind.

'I'm sorry,' he said. 'The things I've done – they can't help but change a man.'

'Tell me.' She took hold of both his hands and held them fast.

He shook his head, as though trying to shake out the memories.

'I can't.'

'Please, Frank. I want to know, I need to know. Where were you, all that time? What were you doing when you got wounded?'

Frank let out a long, painful sigh. He hadn't told a living

soul what he'd been through. Maybe it was time he did. Maybe Creena was right, and she did need to know, if they were ever to stand a chance of things working out between them.

'I told you I was abroad. Well, I was in Sicily,' he said.

'Sicily!'

'With my mother being Italian and me knowing the lingo, well, I had to volunteer. Didn't have much choice really.' He shivered, not with cold but with the horror of what he had seen.

'What on earth did you do there? The Allies didn't land in Sicily until ages after . . .'

'I was a saboteur.'

Creena stared at him, uncomprehending.

'You . . . ?'

'I lived and worked with the partisans. It wasn't so difficult to blend in, I can pass for an Italian.'

'And what did you do?'

'I blew things up, I made things difficult, I . . . I killed people. A lot of people.' His eyes closed in pain at the remembrance of what he had done, of what he had had to do. The lives he had taken to save other lives. Was that right? Would Creena reject him if she could see into his head and understand the depths of savagery to which he had been driven? He no longer felt capable of moral reasoning.

Creena tightened her grip on his hands.

'You had to kill, Frank. You did what you had to do, just like Padraig did.'

But Padraig never killed people with his bare hands, thought Frank. Padraig never had his hands wet with the blood of a seventeen-year-old Fascist cadet in a uniform two sizes too big for him. Unable to find the words to explain it all to Creena, he had to fight to stop the tears pouring down his face.

'What happened to you, Frankie?' Creena's gentle fingers touched his throat. He flinched as her fingertips met the top of the deep scar which ran from collarbone to belly. 'How did you come to be so badly hurt?'

'They captured me,' he replied, unable to look her straight in the eye. 'The Germans. They handed me over to the SS . . .'

'You were tortured?'

He nodded, unable to speak for the shuddering terror that was once again awash in his guts. Yes, he had been tortured. Even now he could recall the searing pain, the mocking faces of his tormentors. But nothing they had done to him could compare with what had happened to his friends, to those who had sacrificed themselves to help him escape. He thought of them, and wondered if the guilt would ever go away.

'Oh, Frankie.'

She drew him towards her, putting her arms about his shaking body. She had never seen him so vulnerable and so frightened before, and for the first time she understood the great strength that must be within him to have withstood all that he had gone through.

'I'm not going to say I understand,' she said. 'Because I don't. How could I? I wasn't there. But I understand more than you think . . .'

She was thinking of the soldiers who had passed through the Royal Lambeth on their way to the EMS hospital.

Victims of the Italian campaign, many of them amputees who had had to undergo their amputations with nothing but ice to deaden the pain. The Italians had done their best for them, but in war the best was often little better than nothing at all. How much worse it must have been for Frank . . .

Suddenly Frank drew back. His eyes seemed clearer now, less clouded, as though it had been a relief to open his heart to her. But Creena saw that, for the moment at least, he would not tell her any more. He could not.

'You were right,' he said huskily. 'War changes people. It's changed me. It's changed you too.'

She looked down at her feet, the honesty of his gaze suddenly uncomfortable to her. Could he see the guilt in her eyes?

'There's something, isn't there, Creena? Something you want to tell me . . .'

'No, no, nothing,' she lied. How could she begin here, now, to open up the catalogue of her shame? 'Nothing that can't wait.'

They descended the hill towards Cregneash and the Calf, the only sounds the crashing of the waves and the irregular beat of their footsteps on the hard surface of the roadway.

Frank was right. They had changed, both of them. They weren't the same people they had been in the days before their innocence was stripped away. And their feelings for each other had changed too; the dynamics of the relationship between them shifting, reforming into a new pattern. Any love that might grow between them now would have to be new too; a completely new beginning.

'A lot of things have changed,' observed Frank, taking hold of Creena's hand and warming it in his. But whatever else may change, he thought to himself, I'll always love you.

Chapter 32

Christmas 1944 came and went in a whirl for Dillie Bayliss. Between working as a senior staff nurse at the Royal Lambeth and keeping a watchful eye on Micky and Kitty, she scarcely had time to stop and think.

It was a drizzly day in January 1945, and Old Bert was in his usual warm spot in the kitchen. On the kitchen table stood Kitty, a wriggling nuisance in stockinged feet, her brand-new dress a mass of pins.

'It ain't straight, you know, it's all crooked,' Bert observed, sucking on the stem of his ancient pipe.

'I know it's crooked,' replied Dillie with as much patience as she could muster. 'She won't stand still.'

'Owl' said Kitty, jerking away as the sharp point of a dressmaking pin jabbed into her knee.

'That's what happens when you wriggle about,' said Dillie unsympathetically.

'It 'urts,' whinged Kitty, rubbing a tiny pink mark on her knee.

Dillie put down the packet of pins and folded her arms belligerently. She looked just like Mo when she did that, thought Old Bert. Not a bad girl, that Dillie Bayliss, she had spirit.

'Now just you listen here, Kitty, if you don't stand still on that table I won't be able to pin up the hem properly and I'll have to sew it up crooked. And your dad won't think much of that, will he?'

'S'pose.'

As if by a miracle, the wriggling ceased – long enough for Dillie to jab another half-dozen pins into the generous hem. There was no point in skimping – the material had been difficult to find and expensive to buy, and with rationing the way it was and Jack away in the back of beyond, she couldn't be sure when she'd be able to get any more.

'You look lovely,' said Dillie brightly.

'It's too big,' complained Kitty.

'You'll grow into it.'

'Is Dad really coming 'ome?'

'I told you.'

'Tell me again.'

Kitty never tired of hearing about the telegram that had told them Eddie was coming home at last.

'Your dad's been in a prisoner-of-war camp, but now he's been liberated and he's coming home.'

'When?'

'Soon.'

'When?'

'I told you, soon. Now stand still and stop waving your arms about. I want to see if it's straight.'

'It ain't,' said Old Bert promptly. 'It's all up on one side.'

Wearily Dillie began unpinning the right side of the hem. Skilled though she was with a needle, sewing for Micky and

Kitty was not one of her favourite pursuits. The fittings were always a battle of wills. Not that she begrudged the time and trouble she'd spent on the two of them. They were good kids – Micky's last school report was the best he'd ever had. She'd miss them if their dad took them away from Bishop Street.

'Where's Micky?' asked Kitty. 'I want him to see me in my new dress.'

''E's gone out lookin' for that darned cat,' grunted Old Bert. 'Don't know why 'e's botherin'.'

'Smudge has run off for good, ain't he, Auntie Dillie?'

Dillie could see that Kitty wanted reassuring, but she didn't like lying to the kids. 'I don't know, Kitty.'

'Why's he gone?'

'Maybe he's found a new home,' hazarded Dillie.

'Typical bloomin' cat,' grumbled Old Bert. 'Give me a Jack Russell any day.' Hypocrite, thought Dillie. You were more upset than anyone when Smudge went out one night and never came back.

And I know the real reason why Smudge has gone, she told herself silently. He always was Jack's cat, a bit of a rogue like him. He's gone to look for Jack.

'Auntie Dillie . . .'

'What is it now, Kitty?' Dillie had a mouthful of pins.

'Are you and Uncle Arnold goin' to get married? Billy Wiggins says you are.'

'Well, Billy Wiggins should mind his own business,' replied Dillie with a vehemence which covered up her embarrassment. Really, the very idea! Not that the thought hadn't crossed her mind . . .

'Are you, then?'

'Mind your own business!'

'That's not fair.'

'Shush!' Dillie spun Kitty round to check the back of the hem. At last it seemed straight. 'All right, you can get down now.'

'When you get married, will Auntie Creena come an' see us?'

'Do give over, Kitty!'

'Can I be a bridesmaid?'

'How can you be a bridesmaid if there isn't going to be a wedding?'

This at least shut Kitty up for a few moments. But it wasn't long before she was chattering on again as she eased out of the dress, wriggling carefully out of the way of the pins.

'Auntie Dillie . . .'

'Oh, Kitty, what now?'

'When Dad comes home . . .'

'Mmm?'

'Will Uncle Jack be coming home, too?'

'More tea, anyone?'

'Thanks, Mona,' nodded Frank. 'Lovely cake.'

'Yes, lovely,' agreed Creena, holding out her cup to be refilled. 'Where's Duggie this afternoon?'

Mona giggled, looking quite girlish again in her pretty blue frock and with her blonde hair newly washed and curled.

'Believe it or not, he's in the lambing shed with Antonio. He worked all night with the ewes, then

610

had a couple of hours' sleep and went straight out again.'

'But I thought he said he'd never work with an Italian,' said Frank.

'Oh, he did – but he changed his tune quick enough when he saw what a good worker Antonio is.'

'Giacomo and the others have gone now, then?'

'Y-yes.' Mona looked just a touch flustered for a moment, then recovered her composure. 'After all, Italy's fighting with the Allies now – it stands to reason the Italian internees would be allowed to go home. I'm glad Antonio's staying on, though. He's *such* a nice boy.'

Creena thought she caught just a twinkle of mischief in the corner of Mona's eye, then it was gone and she was the respectable farmer's wife again.

'Duggie's thinking of expanding the farm when the war's over,' she announced with a certain pride. 'You know, buy or rent a few more fields, get in some extra livestock.' Frank and Creena exchanged surprised glances.

'He's taking a real interest in the farm now, then?'

'Oh, he talks of little else. The thing is,' Mona sipped tea daintily, 'the thing is, he wants to build it up so that he has something really worthwhile to pass on to little Duggie.'

A welcoming voice made Frank and Creena turn round.

'Hello, you two! Mona, you never said they were coming to tea.'

'That's our fault, Alexa,' smiled Creena. 'We just sort of called in on the off-chance.'

'Well, we're really pleased to see you,' beamed Alexa.

She pushed a gangly youth through the door in front of her. 'Aren't we, Kenny?'

'Yes, Ma,' replied the youth. 'Cake – t'riffic! Can I have a piece?'

Alexa regarded Kenny disdainfully.

'No manners,' she sighed. 'Four years with nice respectable people, and he's still got no manners.' She took a seat by the fire and helped herself to a cup of tea.

'I hear you're leaving the island,' remarked Frank.

Alexa nodded. She was half happy, half sad to be going home.

'We're off back to Liverpool next week – it seems safe enough now, and I've been offered a good job. Albie's coming home on leave too, so it should be a good homecoming. Anyhow, we can't impose on Mona forever.'

'Oh, Alexa...' protested Mona.

'No, Mona, we can't stay forever, especially not now your Duggie's back home.' She looked at Mona over her cup of tea. 'You just make sure he behaves himself this time,' she added.

'Oh, he will,' Mona assured her. 'I think he's had his fill of unpleasantness.'

'And what about you two?' Alexa directed her attentions at Creena and Frank. 'Have you named the day yet?'

Creena felt like an embarrassed teenager being interrogated by her parents.

'Alexa, please ... we ...'

'We haven't quite got to that stage just yet,' cut in Frank. 'It's been a long time ... we're just getting to know each other again.'

Mona threw Alexa a withering glance.

'Who's put her foot in it again, then?' she teased.

'Oh, don't mind me,' smiled Alexa. 'I'm always saying the wrong thing, famous for it. It's just nice to see you together again, that's all.'

'Oh, by the way,' said Mona, relishing the moment, 'did I tell you my news?'

All eyes were on her. She winked at Alexa and announced:

'Didn't I tell you? I'm expecting again.'

Jack Doyle took off his forage cap and wiped his brow. Well, here he was in a bombed-out house in Belgium, doing his bit for King and Country, and it was tough going – tougher than he'd expected.

It was supply and demand, see. Working in stores was one thing, keeping the army running smoothly, but supplying those extra special orders was rather more problematic. The Canadians wanted peaches, the Free French had a thing about silk, the British wanted nylons to send back to their girls – and the Yanks; the Yanks were a pain in the backside, because who could get pastrami and ice cream in the middle of war-torn Belgium? If anybody could, Jack Doyle could.

It was quite a challenge, this lark. And the biggest challenge of all was not getting caught.

He was heaving tins of corned beef down the steps into the cellar – nice big cellar, lovely and dark – when a voice at the top of the steps made the hairs stand up on the back of his neck.

'Doyle?'

Oh Gawd. Maybe he'd been too cocky. He nudged the

last tin of corned beef a little deeper into the shadows and climbed back up the steps.

'Lance-Corporal Doyle? *Jack* Doyle?'

At the top of the steps a squat, rather bulky soldier was standing, three stripes on his battledress. Jack sort of recognised the man, but couldn't quite place him. He was sure he knew that voice from somewhere, that soft, rich, Yorkshire brogue. He jammed his forage cap back on his head.

'Sergeant?'

'Remember me?'

'I . . . er . . . I'm not sure.'

'John Hebden's the name. We met a few years back – Black Saturday it were.'

John Hebden! Jack remembered him now. How could he have forgotten that terrible afternoon down Lambeth tube, when his guilty conscience had been so effectively jolted into life?

'I remember, Sarge.' He tried to stand up straight and look as soldierly as possible. It wasn't easy. His pockets were full of chocolate bars.

'Thought you 'ad asthma and flat feet, Jack,' observed Hebden with a touch of humour.

'They . . . er . . . got better, Sarge.'

'That's good.' Hebden peered into the gloom at the bottom of the cellar steps. 'Business booming, is it?'

'I . . . er . . .'

'I remember summat you said that day, Jack. You said if I was ever in need of help to come to you. That were right, weren't it?'

'Er . . . yes, Sarge.'

'I'm glad to 'ear it, Jack. 'Cause now you're here, you can do summat for me.'

'Anythin', Sarge.'

'I hear you can get stuff, Jack. Difficult stuff, like.'

A slow smile of understanding spread across Jack's face.

'Think I'm with you, Sarge. What is it – nylons for the wife?'

Hebden shook his head.

'You seen the kids round here – the little Belgian kids?'

'Poor little bleeders,' said Jack. 'Half starved to death, some of 'em, an' their mothers sellin' themselves for a loaf of bread.'

'Exactly. I'm glad you and me see eye to eye, Jack. We're goin' to help them little kids, you and me.'

'Yes, Sarge, but . . . ?'

'You'll supply the stuff for a little party, won't you? Couple of hundred kids, I should think. Plenty of fruit – they need fruit, oranges if you can get 'em, and from what I hear, you can – bread, chocolate, sweets, meat, vegetables . . .'

''Ang on a mo, Sarge,' cut in Jack. 'Who's payin?'

'Paying?' Sergeant Hebden scratched his head in apparent puzzlement. 'Nobody's paying, Jack. You're doing it out of the goodness of your heart, that's right, i'n't it?'

Jack felt slightly faint. He thought of Micky and Kitty and managed a weak smile.

'That's right, Sarge. I'm doin' it out of the goodness of me 'eart.'

'Creena, there's something I want to talk about, something I want to ask you.'

'Not now, Frank. Please . . .'

She walked a little faster along Castletown harbourside, small boats bobbing on the high March tide. She was afraid of what she knew he wanted to ask her, afraid that she would weaken and say yes, and have to hide the secret deeper than ever inside her heart.

Frank caught up with her and made her stop and look at him.

'Every time I want to talk, you turn away. Is it me? Is there something wrong with me?'

'No, no, Frank, nothing like that, I promise.'

'Then what?' Frank kept pace with her as she walked along, refusing to let her get away from him this time.

She reached a bench overlooking the sea and sat down.

'Something inside myself. Something I'm ashamed of.'

'You've got nothing to be ashamed of, Creena.'

'I've told you before, Frank, you don't know that. You don't know me as well as you think you do.'

'I know you well enough to want you for my wife.'

Creena was sure Frank must be able to hear her heart pounding in her chest.

'Please, Frank, don't ask me that.'

'Why not, Creena? Don't you love me?'

'I do love you,' she whispered, the words filling her not with joy but with sadness. 'You know I love you.'

'Then why?'

Frank took her hand. She did not resist, but it hung limply in his, refusing to respond to the urgent passion of his touch.

'If you won't marry me, Creena, the least you can do is tell me what it is that's keeping you away from me,' he said.

She looked at him, surprised at the bitterness in his voice. 'Stop doing this to me, Creena.'

'I don't want to hurt you . . .'

'Then don't torture me! My heart's been yours since . . . longer than I can remember, don't you realise that? I've never stopped loving you for a moment, not one moment.'

'No, Frank, please.'

'If you won't marry me, Creena, set me free. Tell me you don't love me.'

A single tear escaped and rolled down her cheek, where it was almost instantly dried by the blustery March wind.

'I can't.'

'Then trust me.' He thought of that day on Mull Hill, and all that he had told her. 'I trusted you.'

'If I tell you, you won't want me any more.'

'Nothing is that terrible.'

Her green eyes searched his face, almost willing him to punish her.

'Not even going to bed with a married man?'

He gazed out to sea, hiding the tears of relief that were welling up in his eyes.

'Is that all?' he said, very quietly.

She stared at him in astonishment.

'Didn't you hear me, Frank? I said . . .'

'Yes, yes, I heard. But it doesn't change a thing, Creena. Surely you don't think I can stop loving you just because . . .'

'I was carrying his child, Frank. I lost it.' A second tear escaped from her brimming eyes, and then a third; the memory of her grief returning as she relived that terrible night at Máire's cottage. 'I didn't know he was married, Frank, truly I didn't. I was so stupid I didn't even know I was pregnant...'

He took her in his arms and held her close as though she were a child herself, letting her weep and rejoicing when she did not push him away. For a long time he did not speak, only kissing and stroking her long red hair as she let the pent-up grief come coursing out of her.

'Is this why your parents won't speak to you?'

She nodded, her voice coming in halting sobs.

'I think so. They won't say, but it must be.'

'Then they should be ashamed of themselves.' He pulled slightly away from her to look into her beloved, beautiful face. 'And I'm going to ask you again, Creena, and I'm going to keep on asking you until you say yes.

'Will you marry me?'

She gazed up into his face, understanding at last the feelings that had been pent-up inside her for so long, refusing to die. For the first time she felt the full force of her love for him, acknowledged it and let it fly free.

'You're sure, Frankie? Really sure?'

'Couldn't be surer.' He kissed her again, and this time she responded with real passion, her whole body trembling with joyful need. 'Will you marry me, Creena Quilliam?'

'Yes, Frankie.' She felt his strong arms enfolding her and then the tears came again, tears of happiness and release. 'Oh yes!' She stroked the hair from his forehead and kissed away the last of the darkness and the fear. There was wonderment in her voice as she whispered:

'If you only knew how much I love you, Frankie Kinrade...'

* * *

'I'm sick and tired of all this nonsense, Ida. It's about time we had a serious talk.'

'I've got nothing to say to you, Bessie. You're wasting your time coming here.'

Ida picked up the empty laundry basket and carried it back indoors, Bessie trailing exasperatedly in her wake. Shielded from the too bright April sunshine, Ida's kitchen seemed gloomy and depressing. George was teaching, Amy working in a dress shop in Douglas; Ida had plenty of time on her hands to brood in this empty house.

'How's Tommy?'

At this unexpected tack, Ida stopped scrubbing carrots and unbent a little.

'Much recovered. He has a surface job at a mine in Ebbw Vale now.'

'You must miss him.'

'Of course I do.'

'And I don't suppose Amy is at home as much as she used to be.'

Ida's lips pursed. Why did her sister have to seek out all her weakest spots?

'She has quite a busy life, now she's working in the shop,' she replied.

'So it must be very quiet here for you, day after day, all on your own. I can't imagine George is much company . . .'

Ida wheeled round, her face set into that stubborn, aggressive expression Bessie had come to know so well.

'And what business is it of yours, Bessie Teare?'

'I'm your sister. I care about you. *All* of you.'

'Oh yes, and what is that supposed to mean?'

Bessie drew up a chair to the kitchen table.

'Sit down, Ida.'

'I don't want to sit down.'

'For pity's sake, Ida, will you do as I say!'

Surprised by the firmness of Bessie's tone, Ida reluctantly sat.

'That's better,' said Bessie. 'Now we can have that chat. I suppose you've heard that Creena and Frank are getting married?'

'It is of no interest to me,' replied Ida coldly. But Bessie could see the pain in her eyes.

'You won't be going to the wedding?'

'No. And neither will George.'

'She's your daughter, Ida.'

'I have one daughter. Amy.'

'Creena's your daughter and you can't turn your back on her – not at a time like this.'

'She turned her back on me when she . . . when she did what she did.'

Bessie took a deep breath. She wanted to shake Ida until her teeth rattled, but losing her temper would only make matters worse.

'Very well, Ida. What *did* she do? Never once have you explained that to me. What thing did Creena do that was so terrible you can't even bring yourself to speak to her?'

The colour drained from Ida's face.

'Since you're so friendly with the girl, I expect she's told you herself,' she said bitterly.

'I want to hear it from you.'

'She got herself in trouble.'

Bessie gave a disbelieving snort.

'Girls all over the world get themselves into trouble, Ida. Our own cousin Florence was a good three months gone when she got married, or have you forgotten that?'

Ida was staring fixedly ahead as though confronted by a horrible spectre that refused to go away.

'Oh, I could have lived with that, Bessie. A tiny child, I could have welcomed a tiny, innocent child.'

'Then why are you so angry?'

'She did something far, far worse than get herself in the family way. Creena...'

'Creena what?'

'She got rid of it.'

Bessie stared at Ida. Ida stared at the wall. The silence was broken only by the sound of a dripping tap.

'Got rid of the baby? What ever gave you that idea, Ida?'

'Oh, she made out that she'd come home for her brother's funeral, her poor brother's funeral. But really she'd just come home to get rid of the baby. How could she do that, Bessie? How could she kill her own unborn child?'

'But Ida, she didn't! You don't understand...'

'Oh, I understand all right.' Ida's voice was icy with bitterness. 'I understand very well. The first chance she got, she went off to stay with that O'Keefe girl. And that night they called out McPherson – Jane Kermeen saw him coming out of the O'Keefe cottage...'

'But Ida...'

'Euan McPherson, Bessie. Everyone knows how that man makes his living. If he'd been a real doctor they'd have struck him off for what he did to my friend Jeanie – or have you forgotten that? Her and her unborn babe, both dead because of him. Oh, he took away her trouble, right

621

enough.' She gave a dry sob. 'And my own daughter paid him to kill her baby.'

'And that's what you really think? That Creena paid McPherson to give her an abortion?'

'I'm no fool, Bessie.'

Oh but you are, thought Bessie. We all are, the whole damn lot of us, for letting this break us apart.

'Ida.' Bessie got slowly to her feet and walked round to the other side of the table. 'Ida, listen to me. For once in your life you *have* to listen to me, do you hear? And I'm not leaving this house until I've made you understand the truth.'

Chapter 33

'It's a beautiful May morning, Creena.' Dillie stooped to peer through the little low window, tucked under the eaves. She breathed in the pure Manx air. 'And you're a beautiful bride. Frank's a lucky man.'

Creena contemplated her reflection in the dressing-table mirror. She hardly recognised herself in the chic dove-grey suit Dillie had made for her. It really was a wonderful creation – the single-breasted jacket had padded shoulders and a snugly fitted waist, and Dillie had made her exactly the right white silk blouse to wear underneath. Creena was sure it must be parachute silk . . .

'Well, your Arnold's going to be even luckier when you make an honest man of him,' she replied.

'If I ever do,' laughed Dillie, putting the final touches to Creena's hair.

'You'd better. I want to be your matron of honour.'

'Well, I think you're ready now.' Dillie put the last of the precious hairpins in place and stood back to let Creena get up. 'Let's see the full effect.'

Creena got to her feet, a trifle unsteadily; putting on the

white gloves which, according to tradition, a Manx groom should present to his bride.

'I'll never walk gracefully in this skirt,' she giggled. 'It's so tight I can hardly breathe!'

'It shows off your figure a treat,' Dillie assured her. 'I wish I was lovely and slim like you.'

'Where ever did you get the material?' Creena smoothed her hands over the tightly fitting woollen serge. It felt like a dream.

Dillie tapped the side of her nose knowingly.

'Let's just say it was a little wedding present from our Jack.' She glanced round what had once been Don and Elena Kinrade's bedroom. 'You and Frank have done rather well for wedding presents all round – it's almost worth getting married!'

There was a vast assortment of boxes and parcels at the Kinrade cottage, some still unopened. Everyone in Ballakeeill seemed to have sent something – except Ida and George Quilliam. There was a boot-scraper from Billy Callister, table napkins from Alexa and a hideous china ornament from the Duggans; and Amy and Tom had clubbed together to buy a lovely tea-set. There were one or two unexpected presents, too. Lothar Menz had sent one of his watercolours, and Hester Frankenberg had turned up trumps with a pair of silver sugar tongs. A set of saucepans might have been more practical, but that was Hester for you.

'Happy?' Dillie asked her.

'Happy as anything. Except I wish . . .'

'I know. Your ma and pa.'

'I don't want to seem ungrateful, and it's so good of Don,

letting us have the wedding from his cottage. It's just that I wish things could have been different.'

'It's rotten of your ma and pa not to bury the hatchet. But you mustn't let it spoil your day.'

'Don't worry, I shan't.' Nothing was going to spoil this day, not even her parents' antipathy. For the first time in her life Creena knew exactly what she was doing, where she was going. From now on, her home would be with Frank; and they would make a new life, a new family, a new future, together.

The war in Europe was over at last; and in a matter of months, maybe a year at most, Frank would be demobbed. But there would still be work to do – work for them both. Already they had talked about bringing some of Millie Duval's shelter group over to the island for a holiday; sharing with them the childhood joy that they had rediscovered, and which they would never risk losing again.

Sunlight poured in through the cottage window, turning the rich red of Creena's hair to a dazzling flame. The wild flowers in her bouquet gave off a heady scent.

'It'll soon be time,' said Dillie, checking her watch. 'Don's decorated the pony and trap beautifully. You mustn't be more than ten minutes late, mind, or Frank will think you've jilted him! Now – have you got something old?'

Creena fingered Frankie's good-luck charm and nodded.

'Something new?'

'My suit.'

'And I know you've got something blue, because I sewed the ribbon into your petticoat myself!' She opened her handbag and took out a tiny silver cross. 'Here you are – something borrowed,' she said. 'Mo gave it to me, she told me it was her mother's before her.'

Creena's fingers closed over it tightly.

'I'll take good care of it, Dillie.'

'I know you will. And Frank will take good care of you. Now – are you ready?'

A man's voice floated up the narrow stairwell from the hallway.

'Creena. You ready yet, gel?'

'I'll be down in a moment, Don.'

She picked up her bouquet and adjusted her hat.

'Do I look all right?'

Dillie smiled.

'I'm hardly the person to ask, Creena! I made the suit.'

'Yes, but . . .'

'You look grand. Now hurry up or the Reverend Cullen will have gone off home. I'll join you when I've powdered my nose.'

Creena took the stairs as fast as she could in her borrowed high-heeled shoes, clinging on to the wobbly banister for dear life. Don was waiting for her in the hallway, his beaming face scrubbed red and a plaster on his neck where he had cut himself shaving.

'You're a sight for sore eyes, Creena Quilliam.'

'And you're a terrible flatterer, Don Kinrade!'

'There's someone waitin' for you in the kitchen,' he said. Creena thought he looked faintly uncomfortable, but then Don Kinrade never did look comfortable when he'd had to force his rebellious body into a suit.

'Who . . . ?'

'I'll be outside with the cart when you're ready. Micky an' Kitty are goin' over in John Duggan's car.'

With that, he was gone, leaving Creena standing alone in the hallway. Hesitating for just a moment, she pushed open the kitchen door.

'Creena.'

Creena froze in her tracks, clutched at the door frame, suddenly dizzy. This couldn't be happening, it couldn't. Please, not more unpleasantness, not on her and Frankie's special day.

'I . . .' With an effort she composed herself. 'I didn't think you'd want to come.'

George Quilliam got slowly to his feet, his tall frame stiffer than ever in his best grey suit, turning his hat round and round in his hands as though it helped him to think of something to say.

'I trust we are not unwelcome here.' The words were formal, unbending, but the look in his eyes was softer, almost pleading. Creena returned his gaze, her emotions in turmoil, her body trembling with shock, unable to take it all in.

Seeing Creena's confusion Amy stepped forward, terribly grown-up in her plain pink frock with the crocheted collar.

'Tom and I . . . he couldn't be here, but we bought you a present.' She held out a small wrapped package and Creena took it, automatically, hardly seeing it. Amy gave Creena a peck on the cheek. 'You look so beautiful.'

'Thank you. Thank you, I . . .'

But Creena's eyes had already strayed from Amy and George to the other side of the room; to Ida Quilliam, standing alone by the kitchen range. Creena could not get over how she had aged since she last saw her, her face lined and her hair more white than grey, with just a few flecks of the dark, glossy chestnut colour that had been her pride and joy.

Ida took a step forward. She seemed uncertain, unsure of what to do or say.

'We came to wish you well,' she said quietly. 'You *and* Frankie.' Her voice cracked, and Creena was astonished to see the brightness of tears in her eyes. 'I wanted so much to come. It isn't every day that my daughter gets married.'

Creena stood rooted to the spot, unable to move, unable to speak, afraid that this was all a dream.

'M-mother . . . ?' she whispered, and held out her hand.

And then they were embracing, mother and daughter, Ida weeping in her daughter's arms, repeating over and over again:

'I'm so sorry, Creena, forgive me. I was so wrong. Please forgive me . . .'

All at once, Creena saw how the strength that had been Ida's was now hers; that the child she had been was gone for ever, and in her place stood an independent young woman who no longer needed forgiveness, but to forgive.

'Everything's all right,' she whispered, and suddenly she knew that it was.

There weren't any bomb sites in Ballakeeill, but it was a lot better than Wiltshire. For a start they were about to set off for Auntie Creena's wedding, and weddings meant wedding breakfasts, with mountains of interesting food to be devoured. Micky munched thoughtfully on a piece of pilfered sponge cake as he and his sister peered through the kitchen window of Don Kinrade's cottage.

'Who's that with Creena?' whispered Kitty. 'That old man and that old lady?'

'That's her ma an' pa,' Micky replied authoritatively.

'Why's her ma crying and kissin' her an' stuff?'

Micky shrugged dismissively.

'Dunno. People do that stuff at weddings.' He scratched his neck, longing to take off the stiff collar Dillie had made him wear. She was a bit of a dragon, was Auntie Dillie, but he quite liked that. He loved his dad, of course he did, but he'd miss Auntie Dillie if she went and married Arnold. 'You have to do a lot of kissin' when you get married.'

'Oh,' said Kitty. 'Got any of that cake left?'

He dodged away.

'Get yer own!'

'I can't – not with them people in the kitchen.'

'Well you ain't havin' none of mine!'

'Yes I am.'

'No yer not.'

'Yes I am . . .'

She made a grab for the piece of cake and it flew out of Micky's hand, landing smack in the middle of Don Kinrade's vegetable plot.

'Now look what you've done!'

'It would never have 'appened if you hadn't been so greedy!'

Dillie put her head out of an upstairs window and shouted down to them:

'Micky, Kitty – stop arguing and get a move on, or the car'll go without you.'

'Suits me,' muttered Micky as he loped off in the direction of the cottage. 'I'd rather stay 'ere an' finish off them ham sandwiches.'

The herring gull wheeled lightly and gracefully in the warm air over Ballakeeill. A wedding procession was heading off in the direction of the kirk, but the sea birds had no more interest in weddings than Micky and Kitty had.

Swooping down over the little croft, the gull caught sight of the discarded piece of cake lying on the ground and devoured it in a single swift movement. Then, lifted by the power of its great grey wings, it soared towards the flawless blue dome of the sky, riding high above the glassy blue of a sunlit sea.